PRAISE
LAURUS

'Interweaving an impressive array of images, stories, parables and superstitions, Vodolazkin builds a convincing portrait of 15th-century Europe... *Laurus* cannot be faulted for its ambition or for its poignant humanity. It is a profound, sometimes challenging, meditation on faith, love and life's mysteries.'   *Financial Times*

'In *Laurus*, Vodolazkin aims directly at the heart of the Russian religious experience and perhaps even at that maddeningly elusive concept that is cherished to the point of cliché: the Russian soul.'   *The New Yorker*

'At once stylistically ornate and compulsively readable... enchanting.'
                                                                                Times Literary Supplement

'A masterpiece by any standards... the novel flows in the spirit of the invincible Russian literary tradition of pathos and Dostoevskian depth; and at yet other times, it is a pure philological triumph... Vodolazkin's archaic seasoning is complemented by his sublime sense of humour... As Zachar Prilepin said before me, I am simply filled with an unending sense of happiness that such a novel exists. You open it and close it, something has happened to your soul.'   *Huffington Post*

'*Laurus* is no seamless dream of Russia's past, but a very clever, self-aware contemporary novel that nevertheless holds that dream deep in its heart... Under the spell of *Laurus*, we imagine what it would be like to measure life in seasons and harvests rather than clocks and clicks, to walk in hallowed paths and receive ancient wisdom, to suffer and cleanse the soul.'
                                                                            Los Angeles Review of Books

'The best book I read all year was *Laurus*, a remarkable novel by Russian writer Eugene (Evgeny) Vodolazkin, a professional philologist of the Middle Ages. Reminiscent of the work of Umberto Eco and Gabriel García Márquez, *Laurus* tells the story of an unlikely Orthodox Christian holy man in 15th-century Russia and his adventures, hardships, and triumphs in a time of plague and war. A mysterious sense of sanctity illuminates every page of this novel, but filled with a sense of earthy sensuality, *Laurus* is far from a neat, pious tale. Depicting goodness in an authentic way is one of the most difficult things for a novelist to do, but Vodolazkin, miraculously, succeeds. It's a terrific tale, and you emerge from this book with a sense of the world's re-enchantment and a renewed belief in the holy, in the reality of a transcendent order, in a world grown indifferent to its presence. *Laurus* gave me hope.'

'Best Books of 2015', *The American Conservative*

'Vodolazkin is a beautiful storyteller… an epic journey novel in all the best traditions. There are countless colorful characters, exciting twists of fate and profound truths in the protagonist's words and deeds… *The Idiot* meets *The Canterbury Tales* meets *The Odyssey*.'   *Russian Life*

'Vodolazkin, an expert in medieval folklore, transforms the dreadful past into a familiar stage on which to explore love, loss, and fervent perseverance… In a stroke of brilliant storytelling, Vodolazkin forgoes historical accuracy and instead conjures a cyclical, eternal time by combining biblical quotes, Soviet bureaucratese, and linguistic conventions of the Middle Ages (in this translation, rendered into Old English). The result is a uniquely lavish, multilayered work that blends an invented hagiography with the rapturous energy of Dostoevsky's spiritual obsessions.'   *Booklist*

'A remarkable novel… Russia's answer to *The Name of the Rose*.'

Atticus Lish, author of *Preparation for the Next Life*

'Bold, rich and complex, *Laurus* deals with large issues: the concept of time, love and death, love and guilt.'   *Historical Novel Society Review*

'*Laurus* is in one breath, a timeless epic, trekking the well-trodden fields of faith, love and the infinite depth of loss and search for meaning. In another, it is pointed, touching, and at times humorous, unpredictably straying from the path and leading readers along a wild chase through time, language and medieval Europe… Vodolazkin has found a subtle balance and uses it to impressive effect.'   *Asymptote*

'A gripping, weirdly fascinating read.'   *Complete Review*

'A novel about the life of a 15th-century Russian monk might sound an unlikely bestseller, but Eugene Vodolazkin's extraordinary tale *Laurus* became a literary sensation, won Russia's Big Book award in 2013, and was shortlisted for numerous other prizes. This fall it's published in English. So what's the appeal? Vodolazkin's spiritual odyssey transcends history, fusing archaism and slang to convey the idea that "time is a sort of misunderstanding"... Vodolazkin explores multifaceted questions of "Russianness" and concludes, like the 19th century poet Fyodor Tyutchev that Russia cannot be rationally understood. This is what leads him, with a gradual, but unstoppable momentum, to place faith and the transcendent human spirit at the center of his powerful worldview.'   *Washington Post*

'Winner of Russia's National Big Book Prize, this saga of 15th-century Russia captures both its harshness and its radiant faith in a narrative touched by the miraculous.'   *Library Journal*

'Love, faith and a quest for atonement are the driving themes of [this] epic, prize-winning Russian novel that, while set in the medieval era, takes a contemporary look at the meaning of time... With flavours of Umberto Eco and *The Canterbury Tales*, this affecting, idiosyncratic novel... is an impressive achievement.'   *Kirkus*

'*Laurus* is without a doubt one of the most moving and mysterious books you will read in this or any other year. The world of its characters is spiritually spellbinding, and the reader should not be surprised to find that it evokes within himself a desire to pray, and thereby take what feeble steps he can to walk alongside the humble healer Arseny on his life's pilgrimage.'
                    The American Conservative

'A fine balance between the ancient and archaic... the ironic and the tragic.'
                    Time Out

ABOUT THE AUTHOR

EUGENE VODOLAZKIN was born in Kiev and has worked in the department of Old Russian Literature at Pushkin House, St. Petersburg, since 1990. An expert in medieval Russian history and folklore, he has numerous academic books and articles to his name. His debut novel *Solovyov and Larionov* (Oneworld, 2016) was shortlisted for the Andrei Bely Prize and Russia's National Big Book Award. *Laurus*, his second novel, won the National Big Book Award and the Yasnaya Polyana Award and was shortlisted for the National Bestseller Prize and the Russian Booker Prize. He lives with his family in St Petersburg, Russia.

ABOUT THE TRANSLATOR

LISA C. HAYDEN is a literary translator whose translations from the Russian include Vladislav Otroshenko's *Addendum to a Photo Album* and Marina Stepnova's *The Women of Lazarus*. Her website, Lizok's Bookshelf, focuses on contemporary Russian fiction. She received her MA in Russian literature at the University of Pennsylvania and lived in Moscow during 1992-1998. She lives in Scarborough, Maine.

Eugene Vodolazkin

Translated from the Russian by
Lisa C. Hayden

ONEWORLD

A Oneworld Book

First published in North America, Great Britain and Australia
by Oneworld Publications, 2015
This paperback edition published 2016
Reprinted, 2016, 2017

Originally published in Russian as *Лавр* by AST, 2012

This publication was effected under the auspices of the Mikhail Prokhorov Foundation
TRANSCRIPT Programme to Support Translations of Russian Literature

A CIP record for this title is available from the British Library

ISBN 978-1-78074-871-9
eBook ISBN 978-1-78074-756-9

Typeset by Tetragon, London
Printed and bound in Great Britain by Clays Ltd, St Ives plc

Oneworld Publications
10 Bloomsbury Street
London WC1B 3SR
England

To Tatyana

CONTENTS

TRANSLATOR'S INTRODUCTION

When I read *Laurus* in early 2013, I had no idea I'd ever translate the novel. I simply read the book, enjoying Eugene Vodolazkin's medieval Russian setting and following the emotional and physical journeys of his main character, a man who seems to live four lives in one.

The more I read, the more *Laurus* bewitched me, keeping me up at night with accounts of pestilence, apocalyptic thoughts, medieval winters, and pilgrimage. It wasn't just the plot that fascinated me, though. Vodolazkin's language—which blends archaic words, comic remarks, quotes from the Bible, bureaucratese, chunks of medieval texts, and much more—reflects the novel's action. Like the story itself, which sometimes jumbles what we think of as the natural order of time, the novel's language spans many centuries, creating a kaleidoscopic effect that Vodolazkin develops in such a way that it feels utterly natural. Anachronisms and archaic vocabulary have a way of popping up in the book like forgotten items you find when the snow melts in the spring.

When I was in Moscow in the fall of 2014, several Russian readers told me they thought *Laurus* must be impossible to translate because of the archaic language. That aspect of the translation wasn't as hard as I expected it to be: despite never having taken courses in Old Church Slavonic, I was often able to figure out meanings through intuition or familiar roots. An old dictionary lent by a friend and websites with Middle English translations of the Bible helped me develop English versions of the archaic passages in Vodolazkin's texts. Colleagues later checked my translation. Some of my versions blend multiple

English translations: wherever possible, I've attempted to use words that are unusual yet familiar to readers. This isn't too different from Vodolazkin's approach to archaic vocabulary: he, too, often adapts old texts so they're comprehensible to contemporary readers. And don't be surprised to find one-word bursts of odd spelling in *Laurus*, or places where words like "helpe" or "synned" live side-by-side with "rip-off" or "in the loop."

I like to think of *Laurus* as containing layers of language that are a bit like the cultural strata—strata found during an archaeological dig that witness aspects of human life, history, and culture at various times—that Vodolazkin mentions in the novel. The thickest, dominant layer of language in *Laurus* appears to be fairly neutral in tone but it's slightly stylized and it's certainly embellished by thin strata of elements I mentioned above, such as bureaucratese, as well as ecclesiastical terminology, contemporary idioms, and references to Russian classical literature.

Laurus presents the translator with numerous other challenges, and I've found in email correspondence with some of the book's translators into other languages that many of us had difficulty determining translations for names of certain medicinal plants. I found the Internet and some herbal medicine books lent by a local Russian doctor helpful, and a book about the history of herbals was fun reading; some of my colleagues even checked names with botanists. It turns out (of course!) that not all the herbs mentioned in *Laurus* can be found in nature or traditional herbals. Some of these mystical plants have odd names that I've played with a little. I should offer my own version of Vodolazkin's advice about the herbal treatments mentioned: please don't try these at home.

Perhaps the most difficult element of *Laurus* for the translator comprises only a few dozen words: proper names, particularly personal names. Some of the personal names in the book are shared or echoed by individuals of various nationalities, resulting in varying spellings, too. The book's title, *Lavr*, presented the biggest challenge: in Russian, "Lavr" is a personal name and "*lavr*" is a plant, the laurel, but "*lavr*" most likely means nothing to the English-language reader and "Laurel" is a feminine name. Beyond that, I generally have a preference for not anglicizing character names: Mikhail, for instance, remains Mikhail rather than becoming Michael. In the end, after discussions with Vodolazkin and Oneworld editorial director and publisher Juliet Mabey, we decided to use "Laurus" as Lavr's name in the English translation. Beyond the fact that that's the only way to preserve the connection of the title to the character and the metaphorical importance of the plant, it also preserves a momentum that Vodolazkin, very rightfully, thought was important to keep.

What I find most interesting about using "Laurus" is that the name has come to feel organic to me: by the time it arises, Vodolazkin has already established so many connections between various centuries, people (often with diverging name-spellings), and places that the name "Laurus" would fit right in place even if it felt completely out-of-place. I don't want to spoil any of the book's specifics so will just say that one of my favorite aspects of *Laurus* is that many actions and utterances seem to occur outside their expected times and locations, or almost recur, in a way that begins to feel natural and almost comforting, rather than contradictory or peculiar.

I mentioned above some of the colleagues who helped me in various ways with the translation. Liza Prudovskaya read an entire draft, checking it against the original, making detailed commentaries, and answering questions. Olga Bukhina signed on as a checker of archaic words but looked at far more than that, making suggestions and egging me on to amp-up my slang. Book-lenders include Katherine Young for the old dictionary, Solomon Yusim for the herbal medicine books, and my beloved Scarborough Public Library for stacks of books about the Middle Ages. Thank you to Banke, Goumen & Smirnova Literary Agency for inviting me to translate excerpts of *Laurus*. I am grateful to Juliet Mabey of Oneworld for her strong interest in contemporary Russian fiction and for hiring me to translate *Laurus*. Her edits, observations, humor, and commitment to the book have been invaluable. Copy-editor Will Atkins's patient questions, suggestions, and musings went a long, long way in making my translation more readable. Finally, Eugene Vodolazkin was patient, thorough, and warm whenever I asked questions about the book, and I thank him for reading my translation and offering comments. Of course I thank him even more—both as a reader and a translator—for writing the novel in the first place. Becoming an author's English-language voice is an honor, particularly for a book you love. I hope Lavr will speak to you as Laurus.

LISA C. HAYDEN, APRIL 2015

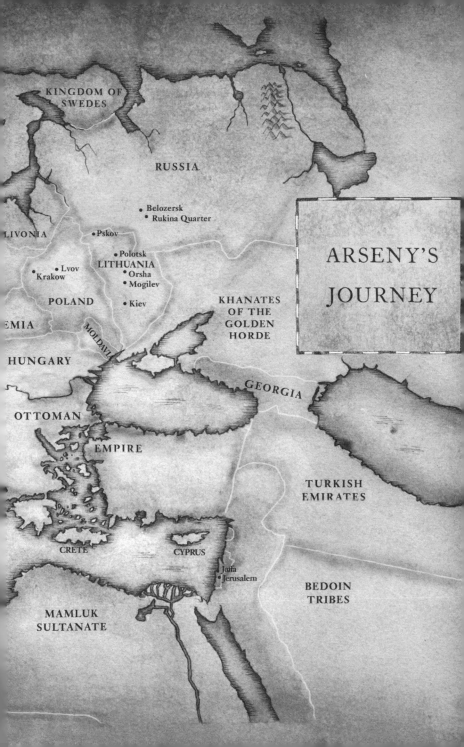

PROLEGOMENON

He had four names at various times. A person's life is heterogeneous, so this could be seen as an advantage. Life's parts sometimes have little in common, so little that it might appear various people lived them. When this happens, it is difficult not to feel surprised that all these people carry the same name.

He also had two nicknames. One of them—Rukinets—referred to Rukina Quarter, where he came into the world. But this person was known to most people by the nickname Doctor, because he was, more than anything, a doctor to his contemporaries. He was, one should think, something more than a doctor, because what he achieved went beyond the limits of a doctor's possibilities.

It is thought that the word *vrach*, for medical doctor, comes from the word *vrati*, which means *to say an incantation*. This similarity supposes that words—words as such, no matter what they meant—played an essential role in the medical treatment process. The role of words was more significant during the Middle Ages than it is now because of the limited selection of medications. So speaking a lot was a necessity.

Doctors spoke. They knew certain methods for treating ailments, but they did not pass up opportunities to address disease directly. Uttering rhythmic phrases that outwardly lacked meaning, they *said an incantation* over the illness, smoothly convincing it to abandon the patient's body. The line between doctor and medicine man was relative during this period.

Patients spoke. In the absence of diagnostic technology, patients needed to describe, in detail, everything occurring within their ailing bodies. Sometimes they thought the illness left them, bit by bit, along with their unhurried, pain-steeped words. They could speak only with

3

their doctors about all the details of their illnesses, and this made them feel better.

The patients' relatives spoke. They clarified their loved ones' statements or even amended them, because not all illnesses permitted the sufferers to give reliable reports of what they had gone through. Relatives could openly express concerns that the illness was untreatable and complain (the Middle Ages was not a sentimental time) that it is difficult to deal with an ill person. This made them feel better, too.

The defining trait of the person under discussion is that he spoke very little. He remembered the words of Arsenius the Great: I have often regretted the things I have said, but I have never regretted my silence. Most often he looked wordlessly at the patient. He might say only, your body will still serve you. Or, your body has become unsuitable, prepare to leave it; know that this shell is imperfect.

His renown was great. It spread throughout the entire inhabited world; he could not avoid notice anywhere. His appearances drew together many people. He would cast an attentive gaze upon those present, his wordlessness transferring itself to those who had gathered. The crowd froze in place. Only small clouds of steam—instead of words—left hundreds of open mouths, and he would watch how they melted in the frosty air. And the crunch of January snow under his feet was audible. Or the rustle of September foliage. Everyone awaited a miracle and the sweat of expectation rolled down the faces of those in attendance. Salty drops fell, resonating on the earth. The crowd parted, letting him through to the person he had come to see.

He would place his hand on the patient's forehead. Or touch wounds. Many believed that the touch of his hand could heal. And thus the nickname Rukinets, given to him because of his place of birth but rooted in the word *ruka*, for *hand*, acquired additional meaning. His doctoring skills were honed over the years, reaching, at the zenith of his life, heights that seemed unattainable for a human being.

It was said that he possessed the elixir of immortality. It is even said from time to time that this giving healer could not die as all other people do. The basis for this opinion is that his body had no traces of decay after death, maintaining its former appearance after lying under an open sky for many days. And then it disappeared, as if its possessor had grown tired of lying there: he stood up and left. Those who think this, however, forget that only two people have left the earth in flesh and blood since the Creation of the world. Enoch was taken by the Lord at the revealment of the Antichrist and Elijah was raised to the heavens in a chariot of fire. Holy tradition does not mention a Russian doctor.

Judging from his infrequent statements, he did not intend to reside in a body forever, if only because he had worked with bodies his entire life. Most likely he didn't have the elixir of immortality, either. Somehow, things of this sort don't fit with what we know about him. In other words, one can say with certainty that he is not with us at present. It is worth adding, however, that he himself did not always understand what time ought to be considered the present.

THE BOOK
OF COGNITION

He came into the world in the Rukina Quarter, by the Kirillo-Belozersky Monastery. This occurred on May 8 of the 6,948th year since the Creation of the world, the 1,440th since the Birth of Our Savior Jesus Christ, on the feast day of Arsenius the Great. Seven days later he was baptized with the name Arseny. To prepare the newborn for his first Communion, his mother did not eat meat for those seven days. In expectation of the cleansing of her flesh, she did not go to church until the fortieth day after his birth. After her flesh had been cleansed, she went to an early service. She prostrated herself in the church vestibule and lay there for several hours, requesting but one thing for her baby: life. Arseny was her third child. Those born previously had not lived out their first year.

Arseny survived. On May 8 of the year 1441, the family held a service of thanksgiving at the Kirillov Monastery. After respectfully kissing the relics of the Venerable Kirill, Arseny and his parents set off for home and Christofer, his grandfather, remained at the monastery. The seventh decade of his years would end the next day and he had decided to ask Nikandr, the elder, what to do next.

In principle, replied the elder, I have nothing to tell you. Just this: live, O friend, close to the cemetery. You are so gangly that it would be difficult to carry you there. And there's this, too: live alone.

That is what elder monk Nikandr said.

B̃

And so Christofer moved close to one of the nearby cemeteries. He found an empty log house some distance from Rukina Quarter, right next to the cemetery fence. The house's masters had not survived the last pestilence. These were years when there were more houses than people. Nobody could bring themselves to settle in this sturdy and spacious but heirless house. Particularly next to a cemetery filled with the plague dead. But Christofer brought himself to do so.

It was said that even then he pictured the further fate of that place quite distinctly, that, even at that remote time, he allegedly knew that in 1495 a cemetery church would be constructed on the site of his log house. The church was built in gratitude for the favorable conclusion of the year 1492, the seven thousandth year since the Creation of the world. The anticipated end of the world did not come to pass that year, but Christofer's namesake did discover America (though nobody paid any attention to this at the time), unexpectedly for himself and others.

The church is destroyed by the Poles in 1609. The cemetery falls into neglect and a pine forest grows in its place. Apparitions chat up mushroom pickers from time to time. In 1817, the merchant Kozlov acquires the forest to produce lumber. Two years later, a charity hospital is built on the cleared site. Exactly one hundred years later, the district secret police move into the hospital building. In keeping with the property's initial purpose, that institution organizes mass burials there. In 1942, the German pilot Heinrich von Einsiedel wipes the building off the face of the earth with a well-aimed hit. In 1947, the plot of land is retooled as a military proving ground and transferred to the Seventh Tank Brigade of the Order of the Red Banner, named for Kliment Voroshilov. The land has belonged to the "White Nights" gardening association since 1991. The group's members unearth large quantities of bones and missile shells along with potatoes, but they are in no rush to complain to the local authorities. They know nobody would grant them other land anyway.

It fell to us to live on land like this, they say.

This detailed vision indicated to Christofer that the land would stay untouched in his lifetime and his chosen home would remain intact for fifty-four years. Christofer understood that fifty-four years was considerable for a country with a turbulent history.

It was a five-wall house: in addition to the four outer walls, its log framework had a fifth, interior, wall. Partitioning the framework formed two rooms, one warm (with a stove), the other cold.

When he took up residence in the house, Christofer checked for cracks between the logs and replaced the bull's-bladder that was stretched over the windows. He took oily beans and juniper berries and mixed them with juniper chips and frankincense. He added oak leaves and leaves of rue, ground it finely, placed it upon coals, and worked to fill the house with smoke all day long.

Christofer did not consider this precaution excessive, despite knowing the pestilence left houses on its own, over time. He was afraid for the relatives who might visit him. He was also afraid for those he treated, because they were constantly in his house. Christofer was a herbalist and all sorts of people came to see him.

People came with torturous coughs. He gave them ground wheat with barley flour that he mixed with honey. Sometimes some boiled farro, too, because farro draws moisture from the lungs. Depending on the type of cough, he might give pea soup or water from boiled turnips. Christofer differentiated coughs by sound. If the cough was indistinct and didn't lend itself to definition, Christofer pressed his ear to the patient's chest and listened to his breathing for a long time.

People came for wart removal. Christofer ordered them to apply ground onion with salt to the warts. Or rub them with sparrow droppings mashed with saliva. He thought ground cornflower seeds, which were to be sprinkled on the warts, was the best method for treatment, though. The cornflower seeds drew the root from the warts so they would never grow on that place again.

Christofer also helped with bedroom matters. He immediately identified visitors with these concerns based on how they entered and hesitated at the door. Their tragic and guilty gaze amused Christofer but he did not let that show. Without ceremony, he called upon them to remove their pants, and the guests silently complied. Sometimes he sent them to wash in the next room, recommending they pay particular attention to the foreskin. He was convinced the rules of personal hygiene should be upheld, even in the Middle Ages. He listened, irritated, to the unsteady flow of water from the dipper into the wooden tub.

What wilt thou saye of this, then, he wrote on a piece of birch bark in a fit of temper. And how can it be that women let men like this near them? What a nightmare!

If the secretive member had no obvious damage, Christofer inquired about the problem in detail. They knew he was discrete so were not afraid to tell him. If there was no erection, Christofer suggested supplementing meals with expensive anise and almond or an inexpensive mint syrup; all increase the seed and promote bedroom thoughts. The same effect was attributed to the plant with the unusual name of *livelong*, as well as to simple wheat. Finally, there was also *hare's ear*, which had two roots, white and black. An erection would arise from using white but vanish with black. The drawback to this method was that the white root had to be held in the mouth at the crucial moment. Not everyone was willing to do that.

If all that did not increase the seed and promote bedroom thoughts, the herbalist moved from the plant world to the animal world. Those who had lost their potency were advised to eat cockerel kidneys or duck. In critical situations, Christofer gave orders to obtain fox balls, grind them in a mortar, and drink them with wine. For those not up to that task, he proposed eating ordinary hen's eggs while alternately taking bites of onion and turnip.

Christofer did not exactly believe in herbs; more likely he believed God's help would come, through any herb, for a specific matter. Just as that help comes through people. Both are but instruments. He did not ponder why each of the herbs he knew was associated with strictly defined qualities; he considered that question frivolous. Christofer understood Who had established that association, and that was all he needed to know.

Christofer's help to his fellow man was not limited to medicine. He was convinced the mysterious effects of herbs spread through all aspects of human life. It was known to Christofer that the plant *sow thistle*, its roots as light as wax, brought success. He gave it to commercial traders so they would be received with honor and rise to great glory wherever they might go.

Only be not proude beyond means, Christofer warned them. For pryde is the root of all sinne.

He gave sow thistle only to those of whom he was absolutely certain.

More than anything, Christofer loved a red plant, known as *the tsar's eyes* or *round-leaved sundew*, that was about the height of a needle. He always had it with him. He knew it was good to have some on his person when beginning any matter. Bring it to court, for example, so as not to be convicted. Or sit at a banquet with it and fear not the heretic lying in wait for anyone who lets his guard down.

Christofer did not like heretics. He recognized them using *Adam's head*, also known as *mandrake*. When gathering this plant near marshes, he blessed himself with the sign of the cross and the words: have mercye upon me, O God. After that, Christofer gave the plant to a priest for sanctification, asking that it be laid on the altar and kept there for forty days. When he carried it after the forty days had elapsed, he was able to guess, unfailingly, who was a heretic or a demon, even in a crowd.

For jealous spouses, Christofer recommended *duckweed*, though not the duckweed that covers marshes but the dark blue plant that spreads on land. It should be placed at the head of the bed by the wife: when she falls asleep, she will tell everything about herself on her own. The good and the bad. There was another method, too, for compelling her to start talking: owl heart. It was supposed to be applied to a sleeping woman's heart. Few people took that step, though: it was frightening.

Christofer himself had no need for these remedies because his wife had died thirty years before. They had been caught in a thunderstorm while gathering plants and she was killed by lightning at the edge of the forest. Christofer had stood, unable to believe his wife was dead: she had just been alive. He shook her by the shoulders and her wet hair streamed along his hands. He rubbed her cheeks. Her lips stirred silently under his fingers. Her wide-open eyes looked at the tops of the pine trees. He urged his wife to stand and come back home. She was silent. And nothing could force her to speak.

On the day he moved to his new place, Christofer took a medium-sized piece of birch bark and wrote: After all, they are already adults. After all, their child is already one year old. I am of the opinion they will be better off without me. After thinking a bit, Christofer added: most important, this is what the elder advised.

They began taking Arseny to see Christofer after he turned two. Sometimes they would leave with the child after a meal. More often, though, they would let Arseny stay for a few days. He liked being at his grandfather's. Those visits turned out to be Arseny's first memories. They were also destined to be the last thing he forgot.

Arseny loved the smell in his grandfather's house. The smell was composed of the aromas of the multitude of herbs drying under the ceiling, and that smell did not exist anywhere else. Arseny also loved the peacock feathers a pilgrim had brought to Christofer. They were fanned out on the wall, and the design on the feathers was surprisingly similar to an eye. When the boy was at Christofer's, he felt he was somehow under observation.

He also liked the icon of the martyr Saint Christopher, which hung under the Savior's image. It looked unusual amongst the stern Russian icons: Saint Christopher had the head of a dog. The child examined the icon for hours and his grandfather's features, little by little, began showing through the touching figure of the *cynocephalus*. Shaggy brows. Wrinkles extending from the nose. A beard that began at the eyes. His grandfather dissolved into nature even more readily because he spent most of his time in the forest. He began resembling dogs and bears. And plants and stumps. He spoke in a creaky, wooden voice.

Sometimes Christofer took the icon from the wall and gave it to Arseny to kiss. The child thoughtfully kissed Saint Christopher on his shaggy head and touched the dulled paints with the pads of his fingers. His grandfather observed the icon's mysterious current flow into Arseny's hands. One time he made the following note: the child has a special awareness. His future presents itself to me as outstanding but I have difficulty foreseeing it.

Christofer began teaching the boy about herbal treatments at the age of four. They wandered the forests from morning till night gathering various plants. They searched for the *pheasant's eye* plant near ravines. Christofer showed Arseny its sharp little leaves. Pheasant's eye helped with hernia and fever. When this plant was given for fever, along with cloves, sweat would begin streaming off the patient. If the sweat was thick and gave off a strong and nasty odor, it was necessary (Christofer stopped short, looking at Arseny) to prepare for death. The boy's unchildish gaze made Christopher feel ill at ease.

What is death? asked Arseny.

Death is when people are silent and do not move.

Like this? Arseny sprawled on the moss and looked at Christofer, not blinking.

As he lifted the boy, Christofer said inside, my wife, his grandmother, was lying exactly like that, and that is why I was very frightened just now.

There is no reason to be afraid, shouted the boy, because I am alive again.

On one of their walks, Arseny asked Christofer where his grandmother now dwelled.

In heaven, answered Christofer.

That same day, Arseny decided to fly to the heavens. The heavens had long appealed to him and the attraction became irresistible after this announcement that his grandmother, whom he had never seen, dwelled there. Only the peacock feathers, from a bird most certainly of paradise, could help him with this.

Upon returning home, Arseny got a rope from the entry room, took the peacock feathers from the wall, and used a ladder to climb onto the roof. He divided the feathers into two equal bunches and firmly tied them to his arms. Arseny was planning a short trip to the heavens this first time. He wanted only to inhale its azure air and, if things worked out, finally see his grandmother. He could also say hello to her from Christofer while he was at it. As Arseny imagined things, he could easily return in time for supper, which Christofer just happened to be preparing. Arseny went up to the roof ridge, flapped his wings, and took a step forward.

His flight was rapid but brief. Arseny felt sharp pain in his right foot, the first to touch the ground. He could not stand and so lay silently, stretching his leg under his wings. Christofer noticed the broken peacock wings beating at the earth when he went outside to call the boy to supper. Christofer felt Arseny's foot and knew it was fractured. He applied a plaster with ground peas to the injured place so the bone would knit together quickly. He bound a small strip of wood to the leg so it could have some rest. He took Arseny to the monastery so his spirit would strengthen along with his flesh.

I know you are planning to go to heaven, said Elder Nikandr, as soon as he saw Arseny. Forgive me, but I think your course of action is outlandish. When the time comes, I will tell you how it is done.

They began gathering plants again as soon as Arseny was able to put weight on the foot. At first they walked only in the nearby forest, then they would go further and further each day, testing Arseny's strength. Along the banks of rivers and streams they gathered *nymphaea*—reddish-yellowish flowers with white leaves—to treat poisoning. Near those same rivers, they found the *enchanted river plant*. Christofer trained Arseny to recognize it by its yellow flower, round leaves, and white root. Horses and cows were treated with this herb. At the forest's edge they gathered *windflower*, which grew only in spring. It should be pulled up on the ninth, twenty-second, and twenty-third of April. Windflower should be placed under the first log when building a log house. They also went looking for the mysterious *sava*. Christofer displayed caution here because encountering this plant carried the threat of muddling the mind. But (Christofer crouched down in front of the child) if this plant is placed on a thief's tracks, the thieved item will return. He put the sava in his basket and covered it with burdock. Along the way home, they always gathered pods from the herb known as *river crossing*, which repelled snakes.

Put a seed in your mouth and water will part, Christofer once said.

It will part? asked Arseny, serious.

With prayer it will part. Christofer began to feel awkward. Everything is about prayer, after all.

Well, then why do you need that seed? The boy lifted his head and saw Christofer was smiling.

That is the legend. It is up to me to tell you this.

Once they saw a wolf while they were gathering plants. The wolf was standing a few steps from them, looking them in the eyes. His tongue dangled from his jaw and trembled from panting. The wolf was hot.

We will not move, said Christofer, and he will leave. O great martyr Georgy, do helpe.

He will not leave, Arseny objected. He came so he could be with us.

The boy walked up to the wolf and took him by the scruff. The wolf sat. The end of his tail stuck out from under his hind paws. Christofer leaned against a pine tree and attentively watched Arseny. When they headed for home, the wolf set off after them, his tongue still hanging like a little red flag. The wolf stopped at the border of the village.

After that, they often ran across the wolf in the forest. The wolf sat beside them when they ate lunch. Christofer tossed him pieces of bread and the wolf would catch them in the air, his teeth clattering. He stretched out on the grass and pensively stared straight ahead. When the grandfather and grandson returned home, the wolf escorted them right to the house. Sometimes he spent the night in the yard and the three of them would set out together in the morning to look for plants.

When Arseny grew tired, Christofer would sit him in a canvas bag on his back. An instant later he would feel Arseny's cheek on his neck and understand the boy was sleeping. Christofer stepped, gently, on the warm summer moss. With the hand not carrying his basket, he straightened the straps on his shoulders and shooed flies away from the sleeping boy.

At home Christofer pulled burrs from Arseny's long hair and sometimes washed his hair with lye. He made the solution from maple leaves and the white herb called *Enoch*, which they gathered together in the low hills. The solution made Arseny's golden hair as soft as silk. It gleamed in the sun. Christofer wove leaves of *garden angelica* into his hair, so people would love him. While he did so, he recognized that people loved Arseny anyway.

An appearance from the child cheered people up. All the residents of Rukina Quarter felt it. When they took Arseny by the hand, they did not want to let it go. When they kissed his hair, they felt as if they had drunk from a deep, fresh spring. There was something in Arseny that eased lives that were anything but simple. And people were grateful to him.

Before bed, Christofer told the child about Solomon and the Centaur. They both knew this story by heart but always appreciated it as if they were hearing it for the first time.

When the Centaur was brought to Solomon, he saw a person buying himself boots. The Centaur began laughing when the person wanted to know if the boots would last for seven years. As he walked further, the Centaur saw a wedding and began weeping. Solomon asked the Centaur why he was laughing.

I sawe on that person, said the Centaur, that live he will not until the seventh day.

And Solomon asked the Centaur why he was weeping.

How sad am I, said the Centaur, that live this groom will not until the thirtieth day.

The boy once said:

I do not understand why the Centaur laughed. Because he knew the person would be resurrected?

I do not know. I am not sure.

Christofer himself also felt it would have been better if the Centaur had not laughed.

Christofer placed *purple loosestrife* under Arseny's pillow so he would fall asleep easily. Which is why Arseny fell asleep easily. And his dreams were placid.

At the start of the second septenary of years in Arseny's life, his father brought the boy to Christofer.

Rukina Quarter is restless, said the father, people await the plague scourge. Let the boy stay here, far from everyone.

You may stay, too, Christofer offered, and your wife.

I have, O father, grain to reap. Where will we find foode in winter? Arseny's father just shrugged his shoulders.

Christofer crushed some hot sulfur and gave it to him so they could drink it later at home, with egg yolk, washed down with rosehip juice. He ordered them not to open the windows and to lay a fire with oak logs in the yard every morning and evening. When the coals begin smoldering, toss wormwood, juniper, and rue on them. That is all. That is all that can be done. Christofer sighed. Guard thyself against this sorrow, O son.

Arseny began crying as he watched his father walk to his cart. How short he was, walking with a springing gait. After half-sitting on the side of the cart, he tosses his feet onto the hay. Takes the reins and makes a kissing sound to the horse. The horse snorts, jerks its head, and gently sets off. The hooves make a muffled sound on the tamped earth. His father rocks a bit. Turns back and waves. Diminishes in size and merges with the cart. Turns into a dot. Disappears.

Why wepest thou? Christofer asked the boy.

I perceave on him the sign of death, answered the boy.

He cried for seven days and seven nights. Christofer was silent because he knew Arseny was right. He had also seen the sign. And knew, too, that his herbs and words were powerless here.

At noon on the eighth day, Christofer took the boy by the hand and they set off for Rukina Quarter. It was a clear day. They walked, not trampling any grass and not raising any dust. As if they were on tiptoes, as if entering a room where someone was deceased. On the approach to Rukina Quarter, Christofer took a root of garden angelica soaked in wine vinegar and broke it into two pieces. He took half for himself, giving half to Arseny.

Here, hold this in your mouth. God's power is with us.

The settlement greeted them with the howling of dogs and the lowing of cows. Christofer knew those sounds well, they could not be confused with anything. This was the music of the plague. Grandfather and grandson slowly walked along the street but only dogs rushed to see them, pulling at their chains. There were no people. As they neared Arseny's house, Christofer said:

Walk no further. There is death in the air here.

The boy nodded because he saw death's wings. They hovered over the house. They quivered over the ridge of the roof like warm air.

Christofer crossed himself and entered the yard. Sheaves of unthreshed wheat lay near the fence. The door into the house was open, its gaping rectangle looking sinister under the August sun. Of all the colors that day, it had absorbed into itself only blackness. All possible blackness and cold. What could remain among the living after ending up in there? Christofer hesitated and took a step toward the door.

Stop, a voice rang out from the darkness.

This voice reminded him of his son's voice. But only reminded him. As if someone, not his son, was using that voice. Not trusting the voice, Christofer took another step toward the door.

Stop or I will kill you.

A crash rang out in the darkness and a hammer knocked against the door jamb as if it had tumbled out of someone's hand.

Let me examine you, Christofer rasped.

He felt a lump in his throat.

We already died, the voice said. And we have nothing to do with the living. That Arseny may live, do not enter.

Christofer stopped. He felt a vein pulsating on his temple and understood his son spoke the truth.

Something to drink, Arseny's mother moaned from the darkness.

Mama, Arseny shouted and dashed into the house.

He ladled water from a wooden bucket and gave it to his mother, who had fallen from a bench. He kissed her jelly-like face but it was as if she were sleeping and could not open her eyes. His palms could feel the inflamed nodes in her armpits when he tried to pick her up off the floor.

My son, I can no longer wake up...

Arseny's father's hand seized him and flung him toward the threshold. It was Christofer who dragged Arseny away. Arseny shouted as he had never before shouted, but nobody in the quarter heard him. When silence came, he saw his father's dead body on the threshold.

~ε

Arseny moved in with Christofer after that. The boy is unquestionably gifted, Christofer once wrote. He grasps everything right away. I have taught him about herbal healing and it will provide for him during his life. I will impart to him much other knowledge to broaden his horizons. May he learn how the world was created.

One starry October night, Christofer took the boy to a meadow and showed him where the earthly firmament and the heavenly firmament meet.

In the begynnynge God created heaven and the earth. He created them in order that people not thinke heaven and earth were without begynnynge. Then God devyded the lyghte from the darcknesse. And called the lyghte daye and the darcknesse nyghte.

Grass affectionately rubbed against their feet and meteorites flew above their heads. Arseny felt the warmth of Christofer's hand on the back of his head.

And God created the sun to lyghte the daye and the moon and the stars to lyghte the nyghte.

Are the orbs large? asked the boy.

Yes, well, you know… Christofer wrinkled his brow. The moon's circumference totals 120,000 stadia, and the circumference of the sun is, roughly of course, three million stadia. They only seem small: their real sizes are difficult to even imagine. Go upon the hill so high, and gaze down on the field below. Do not the grazing flocks seem as ants unto thine eyes? Thus are the orbs.

They spoke for the next several days about orbs and omens. Christofer told the boy about the double sun he had seen more than once in his life: its appearance to the east or to the west signifies great rain or wind. Sometimes the sun looks bloody to people, but this happens due to hazy vapors and indicates high humidity. Sometimes sunbeams look like hair, too (Christofer was stroking Arseny's hair), and it is as if the clouds are burning, but that indicates wind and cold. And if the rays bend toward the sun and the clouds blacken at sunset, that indicates foul weather. When the sun is clear at sunset, that indicates calm, bright weather. A three-day moon that is clear and thin also indicates clear weather. If the moon is thin but also seems fiery, this indicates strong wind, and then when both the moon's horns are even and the northern horn is clear, that indicates easing westerly winds. In the event of a full moon darkening, expect rain, and in the event of the moon tapering from both sides, expect wind, but if there is a ring around the moon, this is a sign of foul weather, and if the ring darkens, that is very foul weather.

Since this obviously interests the boy, why not tell him about it? Christofer asked himself.

One time they came to the shores of the lake and Christofer said:

The Lord ordered the waters to produce fishes to swim in its depths and birds to soar in the heavenly firmament. All of them were created to navigate their appropriate elements. The Lord also ordered the earth to produce a live soul, for four-legged animals. Animals were docile toward Adam and Eve until the Fall. One could say they loved people. But now that is only in rare cases; somehow everything went wrong.

Christofer ruffled the scruff of the wolf, who was trotting behind them.

And when it comes right down to it, the birds, fishes, and animals are similar to people in many ways. That, you see, is where our overall connection is. We teach each other. The lion cub, Arseny, is always born to the lioness dead, but the male lion comes and breathes life into it on the third day. This reminds us that human children come to life only at christening—if death occurs before that day, it lasts for all eternity, there is no heaven. And then there is the fish with many legs. No matter what color stone it swims up to, it takes on that color: if it is white, it turns white, if it is green, it turns green. Some people, child, are the same: they are Christians with Christians and infidels with infidels. There is also the phoenix bird who has neither mate nor children. It eats nothing, but flies among the Lebanese cedars, filling its wings with their aroma. When it grows old, it flies up into the sky and ignites from heavenly fire. When it descends, it sets fire to its nest and burns up itself, reappearing later in the ashes of its nest as a worm, from which a phoenix bird develops over time. And thus, O Arseny, those who take on suffering for Christ are reborn in all their glory for the Kingdom of Heaven. Finally, there is the caladrius bird, which is completely white. Yf one falls into illness, he can learne from the caladrius yf he will live or die. And yf he will die, the caladrius will turn his face away but yf he will live, the caladrius will merrily fly up into the air against the sun—and everyone will understand the caladrius took the sick person's sore and scattered it in the air. And that is how Our Lord Jesus Christ ascended the tree of the cross and imparted to us His purest blood to heal sin.

So where can we get that bird? the boy asked.

You shall be that bird yourself, O Arseny. After all, you can fly a little.

The boy nodded pensively and his seriousness made Christofer feel ill at ease.

The last leaves were blowing from the shore onto the lake's black waters. The leaves tumbled in disarray along the brownish grass, then quivered on the lake's ripples. And sailed further and further off. Fishermen's deep boot-tracks were visible at the very edge of the water. The tracks were filled with water and looked age-old: left behind, for ever and ever. Leaves floated in them, too. A fishing boat swayed not far from the shore. The fishermen pulled a net with hands reddened from cold. Their foreheads and beards were wet with sweat. The sleeves of their clothing were heavy with water. A medium-sized fish thrashed in the net. Glistening in the dim autumn sun, the fish whipped up a froth around the boat. The fishermen were satisfied with their catch and loudly shouted something to each other. Arseny could not make out their words. He could not have

24

repeated a single word the fishermen said, though he heard them distinctly. Unhurried, the words turned into sounds and dissolved into the expanse, after shedding the shells of their meaning. The sky was colorless because it had given all its hues to summer. There was a smell of woodsmoke.

Arseny felt joy because they would also build a fire in the stove and enjoy a special autumn coziness when they came home. Like everyone else around them, they lit black fires. Once the fire got going, the house's walls warmed, their thick logs holding the warmth for a long time. A clay stove held it even longer. The stones placed at the stove's far wall got red hot. Smoke rose under the high ceiling and pensively went out through an open vent over the door. The smoke seemed like a living being to Arseny. Its leisureliness calmed him. The smoke lived in the upper part of the log house, which was black from soot; the lower part was tidy and bright. The upper and lower parts of the log house's walls were divided by *polavochniks*, wide boards onto which the soot sprinkled. If a fire was properly stoked, the smoke did not sink below the *polavochniks*.

It was Arseny's responsibility to build fires in the stove. He brought in birch logs from the woodshed and laid them in the stove like a little house. He pushed sticks of kindling between the logs. He got the fire going with smoldering coals taken from the *ocheloks*, special niches within the stove, where layers of ash preserved coals to use for lighting. He buried the coals in dry leaves and blew with all his might. The leaves would slowly change color. Burning now from their underside, they still appeared to be shrinking indifferently, but that grew more complicated for them with each instant: the fire seized them abruptly, from all sides at once. The fire spread from the leaves to the kindling wood, and from the kindling wood to the logs. The sides of the logs began to burn. If they were damp, they crackled, shooting out sheaves of sparks. The child saw a phoenix bird in the fiery blizzard and pointed it out to the wolf sitting next to him. The wolf squinted every now and then but it was unclear if he actually saw the bird or not. Arseny looked doubtfully at the wolf and announced to Christofer:

He's sitting unnaturally, I would even say tensely. I think he simply fears for his skin.

The boy was right. The sheaves of sparks that flew out of the stove brought a distinct disquiet to the wolf. Only when the fire had settled into an even, complete burning did the wolf sprawl out on the floor and lay his head on his paws like a dog.

For what you have tamed, you become responsible forever, Christofer said, stroking the wolf.

At times, Arseny saw his own face when he looked inside the stove. It was framed by gray hair that was gathered on the back of his neck. His face was covered with wrinkles. Despite the dissimilarity, the boy understood it was a reflection of himself. Only many years later. And under different circumstances. It was the reflection of someone who is sitting by a fire and sees the face of a light-haired boy and does not want the person who has entered to disturb him.

The person entering the room shifts from foot to foot at the threshold and, placing a finger to his lips, whispers to someone over his shoulder that the Doctor of All Rus' is busy now. He is observing the flame.

Let her in, Melety, says the old man, not turning. What do you want, O woman?

I want to lyve, O Doctor. Helpe me.

And you do not want to die?

There are those who want to die, explains Melety.

I have a son. Take pity on him.

Is he like that one? The old man points at the mouth of the stove, where the image of a boy is discernible in the contours of the flame.

There is no reason for you to kneel, my lady (Melety is agitated and gnawing his nails). He does not like that.

The old man tears his gaze away from the flame. He approaches the kneeling princess and sinks to his knees alongside her. Melety walks out, backwards. The old man takes the princess by the chin and looks into her eyes. He wipes her tears with the back of his hand.

You, O woman, have a tumor in your head. That is why your vision is worsening. And your hearing is dulling.

He embraces her head and presses it to his chest. The princess hears the beating of his heart. The labored, elderly breathing. Through his shirt, she feels the coolness of the cross he wears around his neck. The rigidity of his ribs. She herself is surprised she notices all this. Behind the closed doors, Melety is cutting splinters from logs so they may be burned as lamps. There is no expression on his face.

Believe in the Lord and His Most Blessed Mother and ask their helpe. The old man's dry lips touch her forehead. And your tumor will shrink. Go in peace and grieve no more.

Why do you weep, O Arseny?

I weep from joy.

Arseny wordlessly turns to the wolf. The wolf licks away his tears.

~5

Man was created from dust. And will turn to dust. But the body that is given to him for the duration of his life is splendid. You must know the body as well as possible, O Arseny.

That is what Christofer said as he embalmed Andron Novgorodets before sending the deceased off to his homeland. Christofer was rubbing cedar resin mixed with honey and salt into Andron's skin at one of the bathhouses in Rukina Quarter. Andron's whole body shuddered every now and then from Christofer's touch and seemed alive. Reinforcing that impression was the deceased's large member, which did not seem to correspond to Andron, who was short of height though firmly built. Arseny thought Andron would stand up at any minute, thank Christofer for his troubles, and go outside for fresh air. But Andron did not stand. After a nighttime fight, he lay with a fractured skull and the first corpse-spots on his back. The out-of-towner Andron had taken an interest in the girls of Rukina Quarter (that was just yesterday). That caused the fight. Today Andron was preparing for his final journey to Novgorod.

God's boundless wisdom is reflected in the small human body (said Christofer) like the sun in a drop of water. Each organ is thought out down to the smallest detail. The heart, for example, nourishes the whole body with blood and they say our feelings are concentrated in the heart, which is why it is securely protected by the ribs. The teeth are of hard bone because they chew, the tongue recognizes taste and that is why it is as soft and porous as a sponge, and the ear was created in the form of a shell to catch flying sounds. And protruding ears, by the way (Christofer ran a finger along Andron's ear), are a sign of empty talk. But there is also an inner ear that is not visible. It leads sounds from the outer ear to the brain, and the brain turns the sounds into speech. Vessels from the eye go to the brain, too, and so the brain also turns letters into words. The brain is the body's tsar and it is at the very top because—of all earthly beasts—only man is a rational being and walks upright. His incorporeal thinking, located within the body, ascends to the heavens and comprehends the perfection of this world. The mind is the soul's eyes. When those eyes are damaged, the soul becomes blind.

What is a soul? Arseny asked.

It is what the Lord breathes into a body, what distinguishes us from rocks and plants. The soul makes us living beings, O Arseny. I compare the soul to a flame that originates in an earthly candle but has no earthly nature as it strives skyward, toward its kindred elements.

If a soul makes something alive, does that mean animals have them? Arseny pointed at the wolf, who stood alongside them.

Yes, animals have souls but the soul is kindred to their bodies and contained within their blood. And, mind you: people did not eat animals until the flood, they spared their souls, for an animal's soul dies with its body. A human's soul, though, is of a completely different nature from the body and does not die with the body, for the human soul cometh from nothing else but the Creator Himself and was inspirited by His grace.

What fate is judged for human bodyes?

Our body disintegrates into dust. But the Lord, who created the body from the dust, can make our disintegrated bodye come together. And as you know, it only seems to us that the body decomposes without a trace, that it mixes with other elements, becoming soil, a river, grass. Our body, O Arseny, is like quicksilver that lies broken into tiny beads on the earth but does not mix with the earth. It lies there by its lonesome until some skilled craftsman comes and collects it all, putting it back into a vessel. And that is how the Almighty will collect our decomposed bodies again for the universal resurrection.

Thanks to Christofer's labors, the decomposition of Andron's body was halting. The body had a dull gleam and gave off the scent of cedar. It was improbably white. The exceptions were the face and the arms up to the elbows, which preserved traces of a recent tan. After he finished rubbing in the embalming ointment, Christofer began winding Andron in linen strips. He ripped them with a loud tear from a piece of fabric he had been brought with him, moistening them in the ointment and tightly pressing them to the body of the deceased. Andron did not resist. His eyelids, loosely closed, lent him a sarcastic and even somewhat reckless look. It seemed Andron was chuckling at the perspiring Christofer's efforts. It was as if he was letting it be known with all his person that he would certainly make it to Novgorod under any circumstances.

Christofer did not look at Andron's face. He wrapped his body, strip by strip, tightly knotting the ends.

Since the conversation had already turned to the body, Christofer said, I'll tell you how children are conceived. After all, you are no longer a child anymore, and it is time for you to know that ever since the time of the Fall of Adam and Eve, people are no longer created by the Lord but give birth to their children themselves. Later they die because they acquired the gift of death along with the gift of birth. A child is conceived from male seed and female blood. Male seed gives the firmness of bones and sinews, and it is female blood that gives flesh its softness. Blood, as you know, is red and flows through the blood vessels but male seed is located here (Christofer points out Andron's large balls as he wraps them up against Andron's thigh) and it is white.

Arseny did not tell Christofer he knew the color of seed. He had spoken about this to Elder Nikandr in Confession.

Keep your hands above the bedspread, Elder Nikandr had advised.

This was not at home but at the cemetery, Arseny said.

Well now, that is quite something, elder Nikandr said with a whistle. At the cemetery and everything. It is live people who lie there, after all.

I saw only the dead.

For God, all are living.

Arseny turned away:

But I have begun to fear death.

The elder ran his hand along Arseny's hair. He said:

Each of us repeats Adam's journey and acknowledges, with the loss of innocence, that he is mortal. Weep and pray, O Arseny. And do not fear death, for death is not just the bitterness of parting. It is also the joy of liberation.

3

Arseny learned to read at an early age. Within a few days he had learned the letters Christofer had showed him and could soon combine them into words without difficulty. At first it bothered him that the words in most books were not separated from one another, but rather flowed in a continuous series. One day, Arseny asked why the words were not written separately.

But are they really pronounced separately? said Christofer, answering the question with a question. I will also tell you this. At times it is not crucial how a word is spoken and by whom. All that is important is that it has been spoken. Or, at the very least, thought.

Christofer's notes written on birch bark became Arseny's first—and much-loved—reading. There were several reasons for this. The birch-bark manuscripts were written in large, distinct penmanship. They were not large in size. They were Arseny's most accessible reading because they were lying all around the house. Finally, Arseny saw how they were made.

Christofer worked on preparing birch bark in spring, during the time a tree's sap is in motion. He peeled it from the trunks in neat, wide bands that he then boiled in brine for several hours. The bark grew soft and lost its brittleness. Christofer cut the bark into even sheets after processing it. It was now ready for use, a perfect substitute for expensive paper.

Christofer did not dedicate any particular time to writing. He could write in the morning, afternoon, and evening. Sometimes, if an important thought came into his head during the night, he would get up and write it down. Christofer wrote down what he had read in books: And King Solomon had seven hundreth wives and thre hundreth concubynes, and eighte thousande books. He wrote down his own observations: on the tenth day of the month of September, Arseny's tooth hadst fallen out. He wrote down his doctorly prayers, contents of medicines, descriptions of herbs, information about natural anomalies, weather omens, and brief edifying statements: guard thyself from the silence of a loathsome man as if he were a loathsome dog who doth steale in secret. He used a bone stylus to scratch out letters on the inside of the birch bark.

Christofer did not write because he feared forgetting something. He never forgot anything, even when he reached old age. For Christofer, the written word seemed to regulate the world. Stop its fluctuations.

Prevent notions from eroding. This is why Christofer's sphere of interest was so broad. According to the writer's thinking, that sphere should correspond to the world's breadth.

Christofer usually left his writings in the places where he had made them: on the bench, on the stove, on the woodpile. He did not pick them up when they fell to the floor: he vaguely anticipated their discovery, much later, in a cultural stratum. Christofer understood that the written word would always remain that way. No matter what happened later, once it had been written, the word had already occurred.

By watching and following Christofer's movements, Arseny already knew where to search for his notes. Sometimes, the place where one manuscript turned up would be the location for another one, or even more, that very same day. At times, Arseny's grandfather seemed like a hen carrying golden eggs that needed only be gathered in good time. The boy even learned to guess the nature of what was written, based on Christofer's facial expression. Knitted brows led him to surmise that the current manuscript denounced heretics. An expression of quiet joy accompanied predominantly edifying statements. According to Arseny's observations, Christofer pensively scratched his nose when specifying heights, volumes, and distances.

The child read the birch-bark manuscripts out loud. Basically, during the Middle Ages people read predominantly out loud, at the very least simply moving their lips. Arseny piled the notes he particularly liked in a special basket. Yf someone choketh on a bone, appeal for help from the Saint Vlasy. Vasily the Great sayeth Adam was in Paradise forty dayes. Have not a friendship with a woman, and do not burne in fyre. The variety of information staggered the child's imagination.

But the scope of Arseny's reading was not limited to birch-bark manuscripts. The *Alexander Romance*, the ancient story of Alexander the Great, lay under one of the icons in the holy corner. This book had been copied at one time by Feodosy, Christofer's grandfather. It is I, Feodosy, a sinner, who made a copie of this book in memory of brave people, that their deeds not go unremembered. That is how Feodosy addressed his descendants on the first page. He found in Arseny his most grateful reader.

Arseny carefully moved the icon aside and took the book from the holder with both hands. He blew the dust from the binding and ran his hand along its darkened leather. There was no dust on the binding but Arseny had seen Christofer act in this manner. Then the boy began on the clasps, unlatching them with a quiet brass sound. It is I, Feodosy... Under that note was a portrait of Alexander made by his great-great-grandfather. Its hero sat in an uncomfortable pose with a royal crown on his head.

Arseny read the *Alexander Romance* constantly. He read it sitting on the bench and lying on the stove, squeezing his arms between his knees and his head resting on his palms, in the mornings and in the evenings. Sometimes at night, by the light of a burning splinter lamp. Christofer did not object: he liked that the boy read a lot. The wolf would approach Arseny at the first words of the *Alexander Romance*. He settled at the boy's feet and listened to the unusual narration. He carefully followed the events in the life of the Macedonian king, right along with Arseny.

And so it emerged that Alexander discovered savage people when he arrived in the East. Their height was two *sazhens* and their heads (Arseny's hand was on the wolf's head) were shaggy. After six days in the middle of the desert, Alexander's troops encountered astonishing people with six arms and six legs each. Alexander killed many of them and took many alive. He wanted to bring them to the inhabited world but nobody knew what these people ate, so they all died. The ants in that same land were of such size that one of them dragged a horse off into its lair after capturing it. And then Alexander ordered straw be brought to the lair and set afire, and the ants burned to death. Later on, after walking another six days, Alexander saw a mountain to which a man was bound with iron chains. That man was a thousand *sazhens* in height and two hundred *sazhens* in width. Alexander was surprised when he saw him but dared not approach. And that man wept and they heard his voice for another four days. From there, Alexander arrived in a forested area and saw other strange people: they were people above the waist but horses below the waist. When he attempted to bring them to the inhabited world, a cold wind blew upon them and they all died. And Alexander walked from that place for one hundred days, feeling desolation when he neared the boundaries of the universe.

Arseny closed the book, which he had been reading at the cemetery in the rays of the setting sun. It was not yet cold. Stones that had warmed during the day radiated heat. When the boy stretched out on a gravestone, he felt the warmth with his entire body. The stone bore no name.

Why are there no names on the graves? Arseny once asked.

Because they are already known to the Lord, responded Christofer. And their descendants have no need of the names. In one hundred years nobody will remember who they belonged to. Sometimes that even happens after fifty. Or maybe even after thirty.

Do people remember like that in the whole world or only in Rukina Quarter?

The whole world, I suppose. But especially in Rukina Quarter. We do not build marble crypts and we do not carve out names, for our cemeteries are granted the right to turn into forests and fields. Which is gratifying.

Does that mean our people have a short memory?

One might say that. It is just that memory should not be too long. That, you know, is not for the best. After all, some things should be forgotten. As it happens, I remember (Christofer indicated a gray stone) that Yeleazar Windblower lies here. He was a prosperous person and could afford a stone like this. But I would have remembered him without the stone. This person had a slight limp and spoke with a sharp, guttural voice. He spoke in spurts, going silent from time to time, so his speech limped, too. He suffered from excess gases. He farted loudly and I gave him a chamomile infusion. I gave him dill water and other antiflatulence treatments. And forbade him to drink freshly drawn milk before bed. But since he had a cow, Yeleazar loved milk beyond measure and drank his fill in the evening hours. Which led to winds in the belly. Yeleazar also loved carving wood. And nobody in Rukina

Quarter carved better than he, especially where window frames were concerned. He sniffled when he worked. He would keep saying something in low tones, as if to himself. He ran his palm along his lips, as if he were stopping his speech. As if he were afraid of what had been said. When it came right down to it, though, there was nothing dangerous in what he said. So he would hold forth about the qualities of wood, about what all of us in the quarter already knew: that oak is hard and pine is soft. And can you believe it, O Arseny, his window frames are still up, but people no longer remember Yeleazar? One might ask a young person, who is this Yeleazar? And he would not answer. And even the old men only vaguely remember him because they remember indifferently, without love. But the Lord remembers with love and does not let any small detail slip his memory, thus He does not need his name.

Arseny is lying on the warm stone. He is lying with his belly down, the closed *Alexander Romance* alongside him. The heads of yellow buttercups touch his face. It is ticklish and he smiles. The wolf wags his tail the slightest bit.

Yeleazar, fart, the boy quietly requests. Even if it is just once. Let that be your signal from there.

Offended, Yeleazar remains silent.

The elder Nektary was killed during the stifling days of July. The elder lived in a forest cell not far from the monastery. Birds sat on his shoulders in the mornings and he gave them bread he had obtained from the monastery. Elder Nektary had been tortured before his death, with the expectation of money being found, but he had no money. He had only a few books. They were taken and the elder's tortured body was left in the glade in front of his cell. The monastery's novices found the body the next morning and thought he was dead. His spirit, however, continued to keep watch in the body, but only two words remained: I forgive. The scoundrels, though, continued roaming the region, languishing as they awaited Judgment Day. They attacked solitary travelers and distant hamlets, and nobody knew what they looked like because, as yet, nobody had come away alive.

One day they killed a man who was walking with a dog. They took the man's clothing and threw the body to lie in the road, but the dog stayed to keep watch over its master. And a merciful man who owned a roadside hostelry found him. He recited the prayer for the eternal rest of God's servant, only God knows his name, and committed his naked body to the earth. After seeing this act of mercy, the dog followed him and even stayed at his hostelry.

And then one day a certain drunkard attempted to enter the hostelry and the dog began barking horribly, preventing him from entering. When this happened several more times, the people of the hostelry remembered the dog's history and suspected something was amiss.

The man was caught and subjected to dunking. He was bound and thrown into the lake, where he began sinking. This made everyone begin to think the man was innocent, just as he had maintained, but then an instant later he appeared over the lake's ripples, swimming as if nothing at all had happened. He shouted that alcohol was holding him on the surface because it was lighter than water, but everyone understood it was evil forces holding him there.

After his guilt became apparent to everyone, he was subjected to torture with red-hot iron, another test he did not pass, since the character of the burns made it obvious he was lying. After he had been burned good and proper, he told them they ought to search for the other scoundrels, who numbered three, in an abandoned hamlet five versts away. They galloped those five versts so fast it might have been one, and surrounded the hamlet so no one could leave. They found two of the men in the very first house, along with the books taken from the elder. They did not notice that they had killed them as they were tying them up. And when they returned, they learned the man caught earlier was deade after the torture. Being humanitarians, they breathed a sigh of relief, because they had given the deceased men hope for Judgment Day: if not for acquittal (the dead men had, after all, killed a holy man), then at last for leniency, so that after suffering the ordeal *here*, their ordeal would be lessened *there*.

But the fourth scoundrel remained at large. They made additional attempts to capture him but that was challenging because both his appearance and even his identity were unknown.

Who is he? Arseny asked, woeful.

A Russian man, who else, Christofer answered. There does not seem to be an abundance of others here.

And then one day, as dusk was settling in, they noticed motion in the cemetery. More likely they sensed it. Disquiet had been breathed onto them from the wordless country graveyard. Arseny seemed to see in a flickering shadow the shadowy shape of someone deceased, but Christofer appealed to his grandson to maintain his presence of spirit. It was clear to the old man that it was the living who should be feared. All the unpleasantries that had occurred in his life hitherto had certainly originated with them. Without explaining anything to Arseny, he ordered him to leave the house unnoticed and go to the village to get people.

Let us go together, Grandfather. There is no need to stay here.

No, said Christofer, lighting a splinter lamp. I need to stay so as not to arouse his suspicions. Go, O Arseny.

Arseny went outside.

He appeared in the doorway again a minute later. He flew through the door, as if he were carried by some external power. That power quickly made itself known to Christofer, too. The old man immediately recognized the figure standing behind Arseny. It was death. Death gave off the smell of an unwashed body and the inhuman gravity that causes horror to arise in the soul. The gravity that everything alive could feel.

That made the trees outside the window lose their leaves before their time. And birds fall from the sky in horror. The wolf crawled under the bench, his tail between his legs.

This little bird was planning to fly a long way but he did not get far.

He said this in a hoarse, unlubricated voice. Scratching a tangled beard. After hesitating, he pushed the bar on the door. He approached Christofer, who sensed his fetid breath.

What, are you frightened, landsman?

Believe thou in Christ? Christofer asked him firmly.

We live in the woods and pray for the goods. That is our belief. And we are in need of money, too, landsman. Have a look, will you?

And how is it I am your landsman?

The intruder winked. You are a landsman because you can consider yourself as already belonging to the land. (He reached into his boot top for a knife.) I am going to send you there.

I will give you money, and you may go with God. We will not tell anyone about you.

No, you definitely will not tell anyone. (He smiled toothlessly. He turned around and struck Arseny with the knife handle. Arseny fell.) Hurry up, landsman: I will hit with the blade from now on.

He exaggeratedly brandished the knife.

The wolf jumped.

The wolf jumped and hung on the intruder's arm. He had clamped his jaws above the elbow and was hanging there, his paws pressed into the man's side. This was the arm without the knife. The arm with the knife plunged into the wolf's fur several times but the wolf continued to hang there. He had clenched his jaw for the ages. And then the knife fell. The right arm reached with a lifeless, mechanical motion to help the left. It grabbed the wolf by the scruff and began tearing him away from the afflicted flesh. The wolf's muzzle stretched as if it were a mask being pulled off. His eyes turned into two white spheres. They looked off at the ceiling and reflected the flaring splinter lamp.

Christofer picked up the knife but the visitor was not thinking about the knife. Agonized, he finally succeeded in tearing the wolf from himself. What remained in the wolf's jaws? A piece of shirt? Of flesh? Bones? The wolf himself did not know what it was. He was lying on the floor and snarling, not unclenching his teeth. He did not have the arm, though, because the visitor seemed to be leaving with his arm. Something seemed to be hanging from his shoulder but it was now impossible to know exactly what. It hung like a whip, limp and flimsy, and Arseny thought it could even fall off. The visitor beat at the door but just could not get out. Christofer held him by his intact arm and unbolted the door. The man hit his head on the lintel as he left. He banged himself again in the entryway. His small steps rustled through the autumn leaves. He went quiet. Disappeared. Dissolved.

Glory be to You, O God Almighty, for you did not desert us. Christofer sank to his knees and made the sign of the cross over himself. He bent over Arseny. The boy was still lying on the floor; his cheek and hair were smeared with blood. Even by the light of the splinter lamp, the blood looked especially bright on Arseny's light-colored hair.

Only his brow was cut but it was nothing terrible. Christofer helped Arseny stand. We will paste it up with plantain.

Wait a minute, Arseny stopped him. Check to see how the wolf is.

The wolf was lying in a pool of blood. He was not moving. Christofer forced open his jaw and pulled out something frightening. He carried it outside the house, not showing Arseny. The wolf's tail quivered when Christofer returned.

He's alive. Arseny was happy.

Alive? Christofer snuffled as he looked over the wolf. I do not see any stable life in him. Only short-term signs.

The wolf quivered slightly; his head rested on his paws.

Save him, Grandfather.

Christofer took a knife and sheared off the fur around the wounds. He warmed a mixture of medicinal oils and carefully applied it to the cut flesh. The wolf trembled but did not lift his head. Christofer sprinkled ground oak leaves on the shaved parts of the wolf's body. He covered them with pieces of ham that he warmed after taking them from the ice pit, then began binding them with linen. Arseny lifted the wolf and Christofer slipped the fabric under him. The wolf did not resist. Never before had his body been so pliant. There was no more spring in his muscles. His eyes were open but they reflected nothing beyond agony.

Arseny lit the stove and Christofer brought some straw from the shed. They neatly piled the straw by the stove and carried the wolf there. The wolf looked at the fire without blinking. Fire no longer disquieted him.

Arseny sensed the wolf had no more strength left. He sat, pressing hard into the bench with his hands. The last thing he remembered was Christofer's soothing touch when he laid a pillow under his head.

The wolf was not in the house when they awoke in the morning. A bloody trail stretched from the stove to the door and from there into the yard. The trail left off in the slippery, decaying leaves on the road.

We will find him, he cannot have gone far. Arseny looked at Christofer. Why are you quiet?

He went off to die, said Christofer. That is a characteristic of animals.

At Arseny's insistence, they set off in search of the wolf. They did not know where to search and so went where they had first seen him. But the wolf was not there. They went to other places the wolf knew but did not find him. The short autumn afternoon was verging on sunset.

It was already twilight when they sighted the intruder from the previous evening. He was smiling at them with a jowl that was falling off, and his arms were opened wide as if for a welcoming embrace. There was nothing natural about those embraces. The vestiges of his death-throes had hardened in his wide-open arms. And in his hopeless striving to stand, too. Arseny tried not to look at the dreadful mess where his left arm had been, but his glance returned, relentlessly, to the very place below the shoulder where white bone flashed. The arm injured by the wolf had already been eaten at. There was no need to doubt that their arrival had interrupted someone's supper. Arseny vomited when Christofer approached the dead man up close.

You will feel better now, said Christofer.

They did not speak until they had almost reached home. When they were already near the cemetery, Arseny said:

I do not know how the wolf left in that linen. That would, after all, be difficult.

It would be difficult, Christofer acknowledged.

Arseny nestled his head into Christofer's chest and began sobbing. His words came out with his sobs. They moved jerkily and loudly, like jolts. Disturbing the voicelessness of the cemetery.

Why did he go off to die? Why did he not die with us, the ones who loved him?

Christofer wiped Arseny's tears with his scratchy touch. He kissed his forehead.

It was his way of warning us that everyone remains alone with God at the final moment.

Christofer decided to take Communion for the Feast of the Protection of the Mother of God at the Kirillov monastery. He arranged for the travel with some men from the quarter who were among his visitors. A cart came to get Christofer and Arseny the night before the feast day. Four other people on their way to the monastery for the holiday were already sitting in the cart. Four plumes of vapor flowed from their lips when they greeted the new passengers. They did not utter another sound for the rest of the journey, preserving their words for the impending Confession. Hooves rang out on the frozen earth, echoing their silence. The thin crust of ice covering the snow crunched under the rims of the wheels. A frost had hit the night before and the mud had frozen into furrows and clods, turning the road into a washboard. Arseny heard his own teeth chattering. He tried clenching his jaw as firmly as he could to keep from biting his tongue. He did not even notice himself falling asleep.

He awoke when the cart stopped. The moon illuminated the torn edges of the clouds. Crosses raced through the clouds, cleaving them into pieces. As Arseny looked at the dark, massive cupolas, he thought he had never seen such a tall building. They looked more significant and mysterious in the night darkness than during the day. This was a House of God. It glowed inside with the light of hundreds of candles.

The new arrivals began by bowing to Saint Kirill: a total of twenty-eight years had passed since the day of his death. And eight years since the day of his Glorification. After placing candles at the venerable man's reliquary, Christofer and Arseny stepped back into the semidarkness. From there, they listened to the end of the all-night vigil. From there they saw Elder Nikandr come into the center of the church and begin preparing those who had arrived for Confession.

After the elder had pronounced the prayer, he took a small—only an octavo—notebook titled *Sins of Medium Gravity Characteristic of Laypersons and Clericals*. Minor sins were not included in the notebook because they were not considered worthy of being pronounced aloud. (Repent of them on your own, he taught his flock, don't pester me with them. Nonsense like this could mean you don't make it to what's important!) To avoid immortalizing serious sins, the elder did not write them down. He asked that they be conveyed directly into his ear, and he then entombed them in that ear for the ages.

The list of sins of medium gravity included tardiness in arriving at a church service, or its opposite, leaving the service prematurely. Or—during the aforementioned service—wandering around the church, and having extraneous thoughts. Improper observation of a fast, laughing to the point of tears, coarse language, idle talk, winking, dancing with devilish minstrels, using false measurements and false weights with a customer, stealing hay, spitting in someone's face, striking with a

42

scabbard, starting rumors, condemning a monk, gluttony, drunkenness, and spying on bathers. Elder Nikandr's list was only beginning when Arseny sensed his eyes closing again.

When, toward morning, they moved on to personal Confession, Arseny and Christofer had almost nothing to add. It turned out that there were surprisingly few life situations Elder Nikandr had not foreseen. Christofer hesitated as he was confessing, and looked the elder in the eye.

What do you want to read in my eyes? asked the elder.

You knowest that yourself, O father.

I will tell you only that the reckoning does not go on for years. And not even for months. Accept that information calmly, without sniveling, as befits a true Christian.

Christofer nodded. He saw the weary Arseny crouched by a pillar at the other end of the church. The wind tore in through doors that continually opened and closed, and a chandelier swayed over the boy's head. The candles' flames flickered and stretched but did not go out. From the dampness in the wind, Christofer understood that the weather had warmed toward the end of the night. He heard the calls of distant roosters but beyond the church walls it was darkness that still gaped, cut into tidy rhombuses by the grated window.

Christofer inspected the house carefully after they returned from the monastery. Two days later, the logs and boards he had ordered were brought from the quarter. Christofer and Arseny propped up the roof frame with a beam then changed the upper courses of logs, which had rotted from rain and warm condensation. Christofer tested the joints between the logs' framework and plugged the many cracks with flax and moss. He then replaced holey floorboards with new ones. An aroma of freshly planed wood spread through the house along with the smell of herbs. Arseny sensed haste in Christofer's work but he helped his grandfather without asking anything.

When dusk settled in, Christofer would test Arseny's knowledge on the subject of herbs. He corrected or supplemented Arseny's answers as necessary, but he rarely needed to: Arseny remembered superbly everything Christofer had ever told him.

On other evenings, Christofer looked through his books and manuscripts. He glanced through some quickly, stopping at certain pages and reading them, as if in thought. He moved his lips. Sometimes he would tear himself away from a page and look at the splinter lamp for a long time. This behavior surprised Arseny because in their home everything was usually read out loud.

What readest thou, O Christofer?

Books of Abraham not from the Holy Scriptures.

Go on, reade it out loud, I shall listen.

And so Christofer read. He moved the manuscript away from his eyes like an old man and read about how the Lord sent Archangel Michael to Abraham.

The Lord sayde:

Say unto Abraham that the time has come for him to go forth from this life.

Archangel Michael set off to see Abraham and returned again:

It is not so simple, he said, to announce a death to Abraham, a friend of God.

And then everything was revealed in a dream to Isaac, son of Abraham. And Isaac arose during the night and began to knock at his father's room, saying:

Open the door for me, father, because I want to see that you are still here.

When Abraham opened the door, Isaac threw himself upon his neck, weeping and osculating him. And Archangel Michael, who was spending the night in Abraham's home, saw them weeping and wept with them, and his tears were as stones. And Christofer wept, too. Arseny wept seeing how the ink on the sheet grew vivid from Christofer's teardrops.

And the Lord ordered Archangel Michael to adorn Death—who was coming to Abraham—with great beauty. And Abraham saw that Death was approaching him and he was very afrayde and said to Death:

I implore thee, tell me, who may this be? And I ask you to get away from me, for my soul became confused when first I saw you. I cannot abide your glory and I see your beauty is not of this world.

While the boy slept during the nights, Christofer wrote on birch bark about those properties of herbs that he had not previously revealed in full to his grandson because of his youthfulness. He wrote about herbs that bestowed oblivion and about herbs that promoted bedroom thoughts. About *dill*, with which to sprinkle hemorrhoids, about the herb *chernobyl*, known as *wormwood* and used against wizardry, about *ground onion* to treat a cat bite. About the plant *scarem* that grows in low lands (do carry it on your person ther, wher thou wish to ask for some money or bread; yf you ask a man, place it on the right side under your shirt, on the left yf you ask a woman; yf there are minstrels playing, toss that herb under their feet and they will fight). To fend off temptation and wanton daydreaming, drink a tisane of *lavender*. To verify virginity, drink water in which an agate has lain for three days: after drinking the agate water, a woman who has lost virginity will not be able to hold the water within. Carrying turquoise on one's person protects from murder because that stone has never been seen on a murdered person. A stone from a rooster's stomach returns states taken by an enemy. He who wears a magnet is pleasing to women. Golde rubbed and taken internally cures those who speake unto themselves and ask questions of themselves and answere themselves and become downhearted. Dry, grind, and dissolve wild-boar lung in water. He who drinks this water will not become drunk at a feast. That is all.

One December morning in 1455, contrary to his usual habit, Christofer did not leave his bed. He raised himself up and sat on the bed but had no strength to move further. Christofer told those who came to him for certain matters:

Speake not to me of the earthly, for I have no more in common with the living. My weakening members give no doubt of anything excepte quick death and the Savior's Judgment Day in a future tyme.

And the visitors left.

Toward midday, Arseny helped Christofer go out to the facilities. Only then did he grasp that the old man was already almost unable to walk. Arseny cast Christofer's arm across his shoulder and dragged him across the yard. Christofer's legs trailed behind him, powerless. They kept moving, taking turns, as if by old habit, and scraping at the freshly fallen snow. After returning to the house, Arseny asked:

What shall I get you, Grandfather?

Let me catch my breath, child. Christofer was sitting, hunched, on the edge of the bed. Perspiration had formed on his forehead. Let me catch my breath.

Lie down, Grandfather.

Yf I lie down, I will die at that very hour.

Do not die, Grandfather, for I will be left alone on this earth.

And therfore, child, mortal fear took hold upon me. My heart is breaking and I am crushed to leave you, but I cast my sorrow on the Lord, as the prophet says. From this time on, He will be your grand-father. Beholde, therefore I shall leave this world, O Arseny. Heal people with herbs, for you, too, shall make a living from this. But better yet, enter the monastery, you will be ther a lampe unto the Lord. Will you do as I say?

Do not die, Grandfather. Do not die… Arseny breathed in and choked.

But what am I supposed to do, Christofer shouted, with the last of his strength, if I shall die as soon as I lie down?

I will prop you up, Grandfather.

For three days and two nights, Christofer sat on the bed, one foot lowered to the floor, the other stretched along the bench. Arseny helped him maintain his sitting position. He propped up his grandfather's back with his own back and he regulated his grandfather's heartbeat with his own heart. And restored his quickening breathing to normal. The boy only absented himself a few times, to have a quick drink of water and use the facilities. On the third day, Elder Nikandr came from the monastery and ordered Arseny to go outside for a while. He sat with Christofer for a fairly long time. As he left, he saw how Arseny propped Christofer up. He said:

Let him go, O Arseny. It is because of you that he lacks the courage to leave.

But Arseny only leaned his back even harder into his grandfather's back.

Keep vigil with him until midnight, said the elder, and then let him go.

At around midnight, Arseny thought Christofer was feeling better and that his breathing was not so labored. Arseny saw his grandfather's smile, surprised he could see it with his back. He felt relief as he watched his grandfather walk around the room and touch the bunch of immortelle hanging in the corner. This made all the herbs hanging under the ceiling sway. The ceiling itself swayed, too. As he stroked the sleeping boy's cheek, Christofer told the Lord:

Into Thy hands, I comende my spirite; have mercy on me and grant me eternal life. Amen.

He crossed himself, laid down beside his grandson, and closed his eyes.

Arseny awoke early in the morning. He looked at Christofer, lying beside him. He inhaled all the available air in the house and shouted. When Elder Nikandr heard this shout at the monastery, he told Arseny:

There is no need to shout so loudly, for his passing was peaceful.

When people in the quarter heard Arseny's shout, they set aside their day-to-day cares and headed toward Christofer's house. Their healed bodies preserved memories of Christofer's good deeds.

And so began the first day without Christofer, and Arseny wept away the first half of that day. He looked at the arriving residents of the quarter but his tears washed away their faces. Worn by grief, Arseny went to sleep during the second half of the day.

By the time he awoke, it was already night. He began weeping again when he remembered that Christofer was now gone. Christofer was lying on the bench, where a candle stood at his head. Another candle illuminated the Eternal Book, which had formerly lain on a shelf. Elder Nikandr held the candle. He stood with his back to Christofer and Arseny, and read the Book to the icons in a muffled voice.

Here, read for a while, said the elder without turning, and I'll sleep a bit. And be a pal, enough with that howling.

Arseny took the candle from the elder's hands and stood before the Book. He saw out of the corner of his eye how the elder settled in on the bench alongside Christofer after moving him slightly. Lines from the Psalms kept floating before his eyes and his voice did not obey him. Arseny cleared his throat and began to read. Thou shalt treade upon the Basilisk and Adder, the yonge Lyon and the Dragon shalt thou trample under thy fete. Arseny read and thought about how Christofer might need to undertake the same actions. Arseny turned to Elder Nikandr.

Who is this Basilisk?

But the elder was sleeping. He was lying shoulder to shoulder with Christofer and both had their arms folded on their chests. Their noses dimly gleamed in the candlelight. Both were identically motionless, and both seemed dead. Arseny, however, knew Christofer was the only one of them who was dead. Nikandr's temporary necrosis was a display of solidarity. In order to support Christofer, he had decided to take the first steps into death with him. Because the first steps are the most difficult.

a͞ı

Christofer's funeral took place the next day. When they had filled the grave with earth, Elder Nikandr said:

After spending the days of his life in the house by the cemetery, he will spend the days of his death in the cemetery by the house. I am convinced that the deceased will only welcome this type of symmetry.

The cemetery was quiet. It had been visited rarely since the time of the last plague because those who had gone there before now dwelled in other places. Christofer's repose had become all-embracing after his move to the cemetery.

After the funeral, grateful residents from the quarter invited Arseny to move in with them, but Arseny refused.

Christofer's memory, he said, should be preserved in his last place of residence, which he had fixed up to the best of his abilities. Here, said Arseny, each wall preserves the warmth of his gaze and the scratchiness of his touch. How, one might ask, could I leave this place?

They did not dissuade him. To some extent, it was easier for them that he stay in Christofer's house. This way, the physician's familiar and customary abode remained intact. By continuing to give out needed remedies from Christofer's home, Arseny himself quietly became Christofer in people's eyes. And even the journey the villagers had to take to receive the medicine was worthwhile because of the firm realization that everything was remaining in its proper place.

That realization immediately simplified the relationships between the doctor and his patients. Men and the women all disrobed in front of Arseny with the same ease they had formerly disrobed in front of Christofer. Sometimes it seemed to Arseny that the women did so even more easily than the men; he would then experience uneasiness. In the beginning, he touched their flesh with the tips of his finger, but soon after—this was about ill flesh, after all—he would place his entire palm on their flesh without agitation, even squeezing and kneading, if necessary.

The ability to lay hands, to ease pain with the laying-on of his hands, was part of what determined Arseny's first nickname: Rukinets, rooted in *ruka*, for hand. That nickname was actually typical for his part of the world. It was what people from other places called residents of Rukina Quarter. People visiting from far away had also named Christofer "Rukinets."

This nickname had no meaning for residents of the quarter because they were also Rukinets. Things worked out differently for Arseny. Even within the quarter itself, people began identifying him as Rukinets. This was generally perceived as a sort of issuing of honorary citizenship, like calling his beloved Alexander by the name "Alexander the Macedonian." When the renown of Arseny's remarkable hands reached lands where nobody had heard of Rukina Quarter (and that was the majority of places), the nickname lost its meaning again. And then they began calling Arseny "Doctor."

The adolescent Arseny's pudgy, childish hands took on noble contours. His fingers stretched longer, the knuckles became more prominent, and previously invisible tendons tensed under his skin. The movements of his hands grew smooth, his gestures expressive. These were the hands of a musician who had inherited the most astonishing of instruments as a gift: the human body.

Arseny's hands lost their materiality when they touched a patient's body; it was as if they flowed. There was something in them that was cool, like fresh water from a spring. Those who came to Arseny in his early years found it difficult to say if his touch was curative, but they were already convinced that it was pleasant. Accustomed to the pain that usually accompanied treatment, these people may have experienced, deep down in their souls, doubt about the benefit of pleasant medical actions. This, however, did not stop them. In the first place,

Arseny treated them with the very same methods Christofer had treated them with, and Arseny did not have any more blatant failures than Christofer. In the second place (and this was probably the most important thing), the villagers simply had no real choice. Under the circumstances, pleasant treatment could be preferred over unpleasant in good conscience.

As far as Arseny was concerned, it was just as important for him to be around people. Beyond paltry money, people brought him bread, honey, milk, cheese, peas, dried meat, and much more, allowing him not to have to think about food. But the value of these visits was not so much that they provided Arseny sustenance. The point was, first of all, the interaction, which made Arseny feel better.

Patients did not leave after receiving the help they needed. They told Arseny about weddings, funerals, construction, fires, payments to landowners, and harvest prospects. About those who had arrived in the quarter and about the quarter residents' journeys. About Moscow and Novgorod. About princes in Belozersk. About Chinese silk. They found themselves realizing they did not want to cut short their conversations with Arseny.

With Christofer's death, it suddenly turned out that, essentially, Arseny had had no other interaction. Christofer had been his only relative, conversation partner, and friend. Christofer had dominated his whole life over many years. Christofer's death had turned Arseny's life into something empty. Life seemed to remain, but it no longer had anything inside. After becoming hollow, his life lost so much of its weight that Arseny would not have been surprised if a gust of wind had carried it off into high, high places beyond the clouds and, perhaps, simultaneously brought him closer to Christofer. Sometimes Arseny thought that was exactly what he wanted.

The visitors were the only link connecting Arseny to life. Arseny was, undoubtedly, glad of their arrival. But it was not the visits themselves or the opportunity to speak that gladdened him. Arseny knew the patients still saw Christofer in him, making each visit like a continuation his grandfather's life. In closing the resulting emptiness, Arseny himself began to feel a little as if he were Christofer, and that identity was tacitly confirmed by the visitors.

Arseny was terse with his callers, despite valuing their interaction. Perhaps things worked out this way because Arseny was expending all his words in discussions with Christofer. These discussions occupied the greater part of the day and took place in various ways.

Arseny went to the cemetery right after getting out of bed in the morning. It is obvious that the word *went* bears a bit of exaggeration here: he had only to go beyond the fence outside the house to be in the cemetery. The house and the cemetery shared a fence, and there had been a gate in it from time immemorial. Christofer was buried alongside the gate. He did not wish to be taken far from his home in death so had selected his resting place while still alive; he showed no remorse now. Not only did he know about everything that took place in the house, he was almost in it. "Almost" because, remembering the relativity of death, Christofer was also aware that there were separate residences intended for the living and the dead.

A village carpenter slapped together a bench by the mound formed from frozen clumps of earth. Arseny sat on the bench and talked each morning with Christofer, who was lying under the hill. He told him about his visitors and about their illnesses. About the words they had said to him, the herbs he had infused, the roots he had ground, the movement of clouds, and the direction of the wind—about everything, in short, that it was now difficult for Christofer to get a sense of on his own.

Evening was the most difficult time for Arseny. He simply could not get used to Christofer's absence by the stove. The flickering of the fire on his thick-browed and wrinkly face had somehow seemed as primordial and ancient as fire itself. That flickering was a property of fire, an integral characteristic of the stove, something that, essentially, had no right to disappear.

What had happened with Christofer was not the absence of someone who had departed for the unknown. It was the absence of someone who was, nevertheless, lying nearby. When the weather was frosty, Arseny threw a sheepskin on the mound. He certainly knew that Christofer was not sensitive to the cold in his current condition, but life in the heated house became unbearable when he thought of his grandfather lying there without heat. The only thing that saved Arseny in the evenings was reading Christofer's manuscripts.

Solomon sayde: better to dwell in emptie earth than to dwell with a chydynge and an angrye woman; Philo said the just man is not he who will not offend but he who could offend but does not wish to; Socrates saw his friend, who was rushing to artists to order his image be carved upon rock, and he said to him, you are rushing for a stone to become like yourself, why not take care that you do not become like a stone; Philip II of Macedon assigned a certain person to serve amongst other judges when he learned the judge was coloring his hair and beard, and he barred him from judging, saying: yf you are not true to your hayrie lockes, how can you be a true judge unto people; Solomon sayde: There be thre thinges too wonderfull for me, and as for the fourth, it passeth my knowledge: The waye of an aegle in the ayre, the waye of a serpent over the stone, the waye of a shippe in the see, and the waye of a man wyth a yonge woman. Solomon did not understand this. Christofer did not understand this. Life would prove that Arseny did not understand this, either.

It began to smell like spring at the end of February. The snow had not yet melted but the approach of a northern spring was obvious. Bird calls had become raucous, as in spring, and the air had filled with an unwinterly mildness. It was suffused with a light that had not been seen in these parts since the end of autumn.

When you died, Arseny told Christofer, nature was already dark. But now it is bright again and I weep that you do not see this. If I am to speak of the most important thing, then the skies seem to have heightened and turned light blue. Certain other changes are taking place, too, and I will report about them as they develop. In essence, I can already describe certain things.

Arseny wanted to continue but something stopped him. It was a gaze. He sensed it without even seeing it. The gaze was not severe, more likely hungry. To a greater degree: unfortunate. It flickered from behind distant gravestones. Following it, Arseny saw a kerchief and red locks of hair.

Who are you? asked Arseny.

I am Ustina. She stood from a crouch and silently looked at Arseny for about a minute. I want to eat.

A whiff of ill-being came from Ustina. Her clothing was dirty.

Come in. Arseny showed her the house.

I cannot, answered Ustina. I am from the places where there is pestilence. Bring something out for me to eat and leave it. I will take it when you go.

Come in, said Arseny. Otherwise you will freeze.

Several large teardrops rolled down Ustina's cheeks. They were visible from a distance, and Arseny was surprised at their size.

Yesterday they did not allow me into the quarter. They said I carry the pestilence with me. Can it be that you do not fear the pestilence?

Arseny shrugged his shoulders.

My grandfather died and now I fear little. All is God's will.

Ustina entered, not raising her eyes. When she took off her torn sheepskin coat, it was obvious she was doing so for the first time in many days. The smell of an unwashed body spread through the house. Of a young female's body. The smell's lack of freshness only strengthened its youthfulness and femaleness—it contained within it the utmost concentration of both things. Arseny felt agitated.

Ustina's face and hands were covered with abrasions. Arseny knew sores could also occur on the body, from not changing clothing. Cleanliness must be returned to the body. He placed a large clay pot of water in the stove. In that long-ago time, nothing was boiled *on* a fire, it was cooked *beside* a fire. That is how the stove was designed.

Ustina sat in the corner, her hands clasped on her knees. She was looking at the floor, on which there lay straw sprinkled with soot. Her clothing seemed like an extension of that straw: black and matted. And it was not even clothing, but rather something not intended for a person.

When small bubbles began gathering on the surface of the water, Arseny took the largest grasper and carefully (the tip of his tongue was on his lip) dragged the pot out of the fire. He poured some cold water into a small wooden tub he had placed in the center of the room. Then he poured hot water from the pot. Added an alkaline solution of the herb Enoch, mixed with maple leaf. He placed a pitcher of cool water alongside for rinsing.

Bathe thyself, yf thou wylt.

He went into the next room, where it was unheated, and closed the door behind him. Ustina rustled her ragged clothes. Arseny heard her carefully step into the wooden tub and touch its sides with the dipper. He heard the sound of water. The sound in his own head. He leaned his back against the rimy wall and felt relief. He let out a prolonged breath and observed the steam slowly dissolving in the air.

What cloothes am I to put on? Ustina asked from behind the door.

Arseny thought. He and Christofer had nothing feminine in the house. Arseny's mother had worn Christofer's dead wife's clothes, but everything had to be burned after the pestilence. Looking away from Ustina, Arseny went into the room and opened a chest. On the chest's open lid he placed some of the clothing that had been lying on top. He found what he sought. He held out his red shirt to Ustina, still not looking at her. He blushed anyway. He blushed easily, like all light-haired people.

Ustina slid her arms into the sleeves and the linen fell softly on her shoulders. Clothing Arseny had previously worn now embraced such

55

a different body. This is what their peculiar union consisted of. Arseny did not know if they both felt that to the same degree.

The shirt proved too long for Ustina so she rolled up the sleeves. She saw a piece of linen fabric in the clothes chest.

May I?

Of course.

She wrapped the fabric around her waist and hips, over the shirt. It ended up looking like a grown woman's skirt, tied round with a cord also found in the chest. She looked at Arseny. He nodded and felt the surging tenderness that was reflected in his glance. He lowered his eyes and turned red again. A lump had formed in Arseny's throat from compassion for the thin, red-headed girl who had donned his shirt. He thought he had never before pitied anyone so passionately.

Yes, I forgot, do show me if you have any sores on your body.

Ustina pulled aside the collar of the shirt and showed him a sore on her neck. After hesitating, she undid a button and showed him one sore on her underarm. Arseny inhaled the scent of her skin. The wounds were small but moist. Arseny knew they needed to be dried. He went to the shelf that held many little pots tied in rags, and thought for a moment. He found a small pot with burnt willow bark. He sprinkled a little on a clean scrap of fabric and moistened it with vinegar. He applied it to the sores, one by one. Ustina bit her lip.

Be patient, please. Have you any other sores?

I have but I cannot show them.

Arseny held out the scrap of fabric to her.

Here, dab at them yourself, I will not look. He turned toward the stove.

Ustina's rags were lying by the stove, and their proximity to the fire decided things. Arseny tossed them in the stove without saying a word. It was a natural motion, and he made it. But there was in that motion a sign of irreversibility. This is how it was in some tale he had heard from Christofer. Watching as the flame enveloped the shabby clothes, Arseny thought that Ustina would now wear his shirt constantly. He also thought she was, essentially, his age.

He gave Ustina some bread and kvass, and felt the touch of her lips on his hand.

That is all there is for now, said Arseny, pulling away his hand.

He wanted to add something else but sensed his voice was not obeying him.

There was no hot food in the house because Arseny never cooked anything. In his day, Christofer had taught him to prepare simple dishes, but after his grandfather's departure there was no more point in that—or so Arseny had thought. Ustina tried to eat unhurriedly but did not succeed very well. She broke small pieces from the heel of the bread and slowly placed them in her mouth. She swallowed them almost without chewing. Arseny observed Ustina and felt her kiss on his hand.

He poured some whole oat grain, husks removed, from a sack. He covered it with water and placed it in the oven to cook. He had decided to treat Ustina to porridge for supper.

Everyone died in our village, said Ustina, only I was left. And I dread my final hour. Do you dread it?

Arseny did not reply.

Ustina suddenly began singing in an unexpectedly strong, high voice:

The soul and white body say goodbyes,
forgive me, my white body *(she inhaled some air)*,
you, my body, will go into the damp earth,
to the damp earth I do commit you *(a vein on her throat swelled)*,
for them to eat, the worms so cruel.

Ustina went silent and calmly looked at him. As if she had not even sung. She did not avert her eyes. Her drying hair, not yet braided, shone, fluffy, around her head. Thy hayrie lockes are like a flocke of goates upon the mount of Galaad. In these forgotten times hair was more exciting than now because it was usually covered. Hair was almost an intimate detail.

Arseny did not lower his eyes as he gazed at Ustina. He was surprised that they did not find it difficult to withstand each other's gaze, that the thread stretching between them was more important than the feeling of unease. He delighted in her red glow. And how the linen thread holding her cross rose and fell on her collarbone in time with her breathing. This was the only thing remaining on Ustina that was her own.

In the evening they ate the porridge, to which Arseny added flax oil. They sat by the hearth, holding clay dishes on their knees. The last time he had sat like this was with Christofer. Arseny inconspicuously watched the play of light on her hair, so akin to flame. It was braided now and looked completely different. Ustina stretched her lips amusingly as she brought the wooden spoon (carved by Christofer) to her mouth. It was like a kiss. A kiss for Christofer. Arseny remembered how those spoons had been carved: also in winter and also by the stove. When he looked at Ustina yet again, she was sleeping.

He carefully took the dish and spoon from her hands. Ustina did not awaken. She continued to sit, composed and restlessly, as if she were surmounting, in her sleep, some difficult journey known only to her. Arseny put Ustina to bed on the bench. He gently lifted her from the chair, trying not to awaken her, and was amazed at her lightness. Her head rested, thrown back, on Arseny's arm: he held out his elbow to support it. He saw the veins on Ustina's temples through her translucent skin. And sensed the scent of her lips. Thy lippes are like a rose-colored rybende. He pressed his cheek to her forehead. He gently laid her on the bench and covered her with a sheepskin.

Arseny sat at the headboard and looked at Ustina. At first he sat, arms folded on his chest, then with his palm pressed against his chin. Sometimes a light tremor crossed Ustina's face. Sometimes she cried out. Arseny ran his palm across her face and she calmed.

Sleep, sleep, Ustina, Arseny whispered.

And Ustina slept. The linen under her gathered in folds. Her cheek touched the bench's wood. Arseny carefully lifted her head to smooth the folds. Without waking up, Ustina took Arseny's palm and laid it under her cheek. He had to bend and support his right hand with his left. A few minutes later, Arseny began feeling pain in his back and in his hands, but this was pleasing for him. It seemed to him that he was removing part of Ustina's burden through his slight suffering. He did not even notice himself dozing off.

He awoke from the ticklish motion of eyelashes along his palm. Ustina was lying with her eyes open. A flicker from the coals in the stove reflected in her eyes. Arseny's palm was wet from her tears. He touched Ustina's eyelids with his lips and sensed their saltiness. Ustina moved over as if she were freeing up a space for him:

I got frightened in the darkness.

He sat alongside her on the edge of the bench and she laid her head on his knees.

Stay with me, O Arseny, until I sleep.

Through his clothing he felt the warm breath that came with her words.

I will stay with you until you sleep.

I have nobody but you. I want to firmly embrace you and not let you go.

I also want to embrace you because I am afraid alone.

Then lie down with me.

He lay down. They embraced and lay that way for a long time. He lost track of time. He trembled with fine trembling, though he was all sweaty. And his sweat mixed with her sweat. And then his flesh entered her flesh. In the morning, they saw the linen had become crimson.

A new life had started for Arseny, a life filled with love and fear. With love for Ustina and with the fear she would disappear just as suddenly as she had arrived. He did not know exactly what he feared: a hurricane maybe, lightning, fire, or an unkind glance. Perhaps all of them together. Ustina was not separate from his love for her. Ustina was love and love was Ustina. He carried it as if it were a candle in a dark forest. He feared that thousands of greedy night-creatures would fly toward that flame all at once and extinguish it with their wings.

He could delight in Ustina for hours on end. He would take her hand and, slowly lifting a sleeve, feel the barely perceptible golden hairs with his lips. He laid her head on his knees and drew a fingertip along the spectral line between her neck and chin. Tasted her eyelashes with his tongue. Carefully took the kerchief from her hair and let her hair down; braided it. Unbraided it again and slowly ran a comb through it. Imagined her hair was a lake and the comb was a boat. He saw himself in that comb, gliding along the golden lake. Felt he was drowning and feared being saved more than anything.

He never showed Ustina to anyone. When he heard a knock at the door, he would throw Christofer's sheepskin on her and send her to the next room. Casting a glance at the benches, he would search for anything that could betray Ustina. But there were no such things. There was really nothing feminine in Christofer and Arseny's housekeeping. He would open the front door once he was convinced the door to the neighboring room was firmly closed behind Ustina.

Ustina sat there soundlessly and Arseny examined his patients. His appointments had become briefer, something his visitors noted.

Arseny no longer kept up his end of conversations. He examined and palpated diseased flesh without uttering superfluous words. Listened to grievances with concentration and gave instructions. Accepted commensurate payment. After all the medical words had been said, he looked at the guest, marking time. Patients associated that with the doctor's increasing busyness and treated him with even more respect.

Nobody knew about Ustina. She hardly ever showed herself in the yard and nothing was visible from outside through the small windows stretched with bull's-bladder. Strictly speaking, nothing was visible when looking through them from inside, either. So even if someone took it upon himself to peer through Arseny's window, he would not learn much. But of course nobody peered in.

Once, during an appointment with a sufferer of male impotence, Ustina sneezed on the other side of the wall. Not loudly but she sneezed; the room was, after all, cold. The patient looked questioningly at Arseny and asked what the noise was. Arseny responded with an uncomprehending glance. He suggested the visitor not distract him from the problem, otherwise he would never figure it out.

Never, Arseny emphasized, and then recommended eating more carrots.

As he was seeing his guest out, Arseny trod deliberately loudly but Ustina did not sneeze again. When she finally came in, Arseny asked that in future she sneeze into the inner part of the sheepskin because fur muffles sounds.

That is what I usually do, Ustina said. But this time it happened so suddenly that I simply did not have time to cover myself with the coat.

Arseny's interactions with visitors took on a certain absentmindedness. It became ever more noticeable that Arseny's thoughts were in other places. If his visitors had known of Ustina, they would have placed his thoughts in the next room. But they would not have been completely correct.

Arseny did not simply think about Ustina. He was submerging, little by little, into a distinct, complete world consisting of himself and Ustina. In that world, he was Ustina's father and her son. He was her friend and brother, but most of all, her husband. Ustina's orphanhood left all those responsibilities open. And he took them on. His own orphanhood offered the exact same responsibilities for Ustina. The circle was closing: they were becoming everything for one another. The perfection of that circle made anyone else's presence impossible. They were two halves of a whole and any addition seemed not only redundant to Arseny but also inadmissible. Even for only a minute and without obligations.

Arseny saw the perfection of their union in the fact that their seclusion did not burden Ustina. He felt she saw the reason and purpose of this sort of life with the same sharpness as he. And even if she did not see it, well, she had, quite simply, grown infinitely weary from roaming, and so accepted his constant presence as undeserved good fortune.

In the evenings they read. They used an oil lamp so as not to keep having to stand up and change the splinter lamps. The lamp burned dully but evenly. Arseny read because Ustina was not literate.

Thanks to Arseny, she heard for the first time of Antiphon's prophesies for Alexander. The ruler of the whole world, Antiphon said, will die on the iron earth under a sky of ivory. And Alexander was seized by fear in the land of copper. That fear glimmered from the duskiness of Ustina's eyes. And Alexander ordered his warriors to study the earth's composition. After studying the earth's composition, they found inside it only copper, without iron. Alexander, who had a soul stronger than iron, commanded that they continue their forward movement. And so they moved along the copper earth and the clopping of horse hooves on copper sounded to them like thunder...

Ustina tenderly touched Arseny's shoulder.

Understodest thou what thou redest or dost thou but turn the pages?

Ustina clasped her arms around her knees, pressing more firmly into Arseny. She asked him to read without hurrying. He nodded but began hurrying again without noticing. The five pages they had allocated for the evening were read faster and faster each time and Ustina asked Arseny again and again what made him hurry so. He pressed his cheek to her cheek instead of answering. A jealous thought was arising, that in the evening time Alexander interested her more than Arseny.

Sometimes they read of the Centaur. The Centaur carried his wife in his ear so as to hide her from others. Arseny wanted to carry Ustina in his ear, too, but had no such capacity.

At the end of March, Ustina said:

A babe is in my wombe, for the custom of women is come upon me.

As she said this, she pressed her palms into the wood of the bench, slouching a little, and looking beyond Arseny. Arseny was throwing logs into the stove at that moment. He took a step toward Ustina and knelt before her. His hand was still squeezing a log. It fell and resonantly rolled along the floor. Arseny burrowed his face into Ustina's red shirt. He felt her hand—loving and weak of will—on the back of his neck. With a soft motion, he laid Ustina on the bench and slowly, fold by fold, began lifting her shirt. After baring her belly, he pressed his lips to it. Ustina's belly was as flat as a valley and her skin was firm. An anxious line of ribs bounded her stomach. And nothing foretold of changes. Nothing indicated who was inside and preparing to break those lines. As he glided his lips along her belly, Arseny grasped that only Ustina's pregnancy could express his immeasurable love, that it was he growing throughout Ustina. He felt happiness that he now existed, constantly, within Ustina. He was an integral part of her.

Arseny grasped that Ustina's new condition would make her even more dependent on him. That may be why the fear of losing her lessened slightly while, on the other hand, the tenderness he felt toward her took on an unprecedented keenness. Arseny experienced tenderness when he saw the eagerness with which Ustina had begun to eat. Her appetite seemed funny even to her. She snorted and breadcrumbs flew all over. Arseny experienced tenderness when Ustina's face grew gray and she felt nauseous. He got nutmeg oil and fed it to Ustina from a spoon. He slowly pulled the spoon toward himself, his eyes following as Ustina's lips glided over it. And he also tirelessly delighted in her eyes, which had become completely different in pregnancy. Something damp and vulnerable had appeared in them. Something reminding Arseny of a calf's eyes.

Sometimes sadness shone through those eyes. The isolated existence with Arseny was, undoubtedly, her happiness. But it was something else, too, that was becoming more noticeable with each passing day. Arseny, who seemed like the whole world to her, still could not replace the whole world. The feeling of isolation from life with others begot anxiety in Ustina. And Arseny saw that.

One day, Ustina asked if they could purchase some women's clothing for her. She had been wearing the same clothes as Arseny for the whole time she had been living with him.

Is it unpleasant to wear my clothes? Arseny asked.

It is pleasant, sweetheart, very pleasant, it is just that I would like to wear something of my own. I am a woman after all...

Arseny promised to think. He truly did think but his deliberations came to nothing. He could not buy a woman's dress without revealing the secret of Ustina. There was nobody he could trust with the task. And there could be no discussion of sending Ustina to the quarter alone. In the first place, it would take no effort whatsoever for the villagers to find out where she had come from and, in the second place, well, Arseny loudly sighed and felt a lump rolling in his throat. He could not imagine Ustina leaving him for even half a day.

After some time had passed, she reminded Arseny of her request, but did not receive an answer. A few weeks later, it was already too late to think about buying anything: Ustina's enlarged belly would have made it impossible to go and find suitable clothing. So then she began altering Arseny's things for herself.

Not going to Communion worried him far more than clothing. Arseny was afraid to go to church because the road to the Eucharist ran through Confession. And Confession meant telling about Ustina. He did not know what response he would receive. To marry? He would have been happy to marry. But what if they said to leave her? Or live in different places for a time? He did not know what they might say, because nothing like this had ever happened to him before. In his fear of disobeying, Arseny did not go to church and did not confess. Nor did Ustina go.

One day she asked:

Will you take me as your wife?

You are my wife, who I love more than life itself.

I want to be yours, O Arseny, before God and man.

Be patient, my love. He kissed her in the dimple over her clavicle. You will be my wife before God and man. Just be patient for a while, my love.

They went into the forest almost every day. In the beginning that was not at all simple because there was still deep snow in the forest. They walked, stumbling in snow up to their knees, but they walked nevertheless. Arseny knew Ustina needed fresh air. Furthermore, even a difficult outing like this was better for her than sitting at home. Shod in Christofer's boots, Ustina often got blisters on the soles of her feet. Winding her feet with scraps of fabric did not help the situation. The size actually did matter, even though boots were sewn from soft leather in those days, albeit without considering the difference between the left and right feet. Ustina's feet were very different from Christofer's.

Ustina followed, right in Arseny's tracks. They walked along the exact same path each morning, and each morning they trampled a new path as if for the first time, because it had been covered with fresh snow during the course of a day. Drifted snow smoothed over their trampled path even if there had been no fresh snowfall. A strong wind always blew in the open space between the cemetery and the forest.

The wind subsided after they entered the forest. Sometimes they could find their tracks there. Those tracks were also snow-sprinkled, and other tracks—a wild animal's or bird's—sometimes intersected them, but they existed. They did not vanish without a trace, or so it seemed to Arseny.

It was not as cold in the forest as it was on the way to the forest. Perhaps it was even warm. A shroud of snow on branches, accumulated over the days, looked like fur to Ustina. She loved to shake it from the branches and delight in how it settled on their shoulders.

Will you buy me a fur coat like this? Ustina asked.

Of course, answered Arseny. I will certainly buy one.

He very much wanted to buy her a fur coat like that.

The snow began melting in the middle of April and immediately looked old and shabby. And porous from the rains that had begun. Ustina no longer wanted a fur coat like that. She stepped from one melting hummock to another, cautiously watching her feet. All the forest's grime had emerged from under the snow: last year's foliage, pieces of rags that had lost their color, and yellowed plastic bottles. Grass was already breaking through in glades that the sun reached, but the snow was still deep in denser places. And it was cold there. Even that snow finally melted, but the puddles it made remained until the middle of summer.

In May, Ustina traded her boots for shoes Arseny had woven from bast. Ustina liked the bast shoes because they were woven for her feet and—this was the main thing—woven by Arseny. He carefully wound the shoes' ties around each leg, not allowing her to bend, and she liked that, too. The shoes were light but they leaked. Sometimes Ustina came home with wet feet, but she did not want to return to wearing boots, no matter what.

I will just be more cautious when I walk, she would tell Arseny.

Their outings became much longer. Now they did not just walk in the near forest but also in places far from any homes, places Christofer had once showed Arseny. Arseny felt calmer in those places. Sometimes they saw people in the near forest and hurried to hide after noticing them from a distance. Now that they were going far away, though, they did not meet anyone.

You are not afraid to get lost, Ustina asked Arseny.

I am not afraid for I have knowen these valleys since the very cradle.

On these outings, Arseny brought a bag with food and drink. There was also a sheepskin for them to sit on during lengthy rests: Arseny took care that Ustina did not strain herself. As they strolled, they gathered herbs that nature had sprouted as it revived. Arseny described for Ustina the properties of the herbs, and the breadth of his knowledge astounded her. He also told her about how the human body is built and the habits of animals, about the movements of the planets, historical events, and the symbolism of numerals. He felt like a father to her in those moments. Or, if he was thinking of the source of this knowledge, a grandfather. To Arseny, the red-haired girl seemed like clay in his hands, clay from which he molded himself a Wife.

By now it would be an exaggeration to say nobody knew of Ustina's existence. People had seen them both in the forest, more than once, if only from a distance. Of course they were not acquainted with Ustina, but they could recognize Arseny without difficulty, even from a distance. And when they visited Arseny in his home they heard Ustina on the other side of the wall, because a person cannot be noiseless forever. Many guessed someone was living at Arseny's, but since he was hiding it, nobody asked him anything. Arseny was their doctor and people were always afraid to annoy the doctor. For his part, Arseny apparently guessed about those hunches, too. He did not attempt to either confirm or deny them. It suited him that nobody asked him anything, no matter what their reason. It was enough for Arseny that nobody came in contact with his world, the world where only he and Ustina existed.

At the beginning of summer, when Ustina began to find long walks tiring, they sat outside the house ever more often. A few logs and boards were left over from repairing the house, and Arseny decided to construct a shelter in the yard. As he was fitting one board against the next, he remembered, pained, that Christofer had been managing a similar repair project less than a year ago. Using his grandfather's voice, Arseny asked Ustina to give him this or that tool, but it didn't sound as good as when Christofer spoke. And the boards didn't fit together as well. What would Christofer have said about his project? And what would he have said about Ustina?

The shelter abutted the back of the house and was not visible from the road. Arseny hung up some strings and several weeks later they were overgrown with dense bindweed. The roof was covered with thatch and did not leak. Now they could get fresh air in any weather. They most loved sitting under the shelter in the evenings.

On one long July evening, Ustina asked Arseny to teach her to read and write. That request initially surprised him. He could read everything they needed to read and that was a part of their complementariness. Arseny broke a flower off the bindweed and cautiously placed it on the tip of Ustina's nose. Why do you need to know? Arseny wanted to ask her, but he did not ask. He went into the house and came back out with the Psalter. Arseny sat alongside Ustina and opened the book. He touched the very first cinnabar initial with his index finger. The letter glowed, reddish, in the rays of the setting sun.

This is the letter B. The word "Blessed" begins with it here.

Blessed is the man that doth not walke in the counsell of the ungodly, Ustina recited, unhurried. Nor standeth in the waye of sinners, nor sitteth in the seate of the scornefull.

Arseny silently watched Ustina. She laid her head on his shoulder.

I know many psalms by heart. From hearing them.

That proved very useful for her in learning to read and write. After reading a few letters, Ustina would remember an entire phrase, which helped her instantly recognize the letters that followed. Arseny had never expected her learning to go so quickly.

More than anything, Ustina liked that letters had names that carried meaning. She pronounced them to herself, her lips constantly moving, as she went through the old Russian alphabet. *Az. Buki. Vedi. I. Know. Letters.* She would break off a branch and write the names of the letters on the tamped earth in the yard and on forest paths. *Glagol' Dobro. Say good things.* The names gave the letters independent lives. The names gave them an unexpected meaning that bewitched Ustina. *Kako Liudie Myslete? Rtsy Slovo Tverdo. How think you, people? Speak a firm word.*

To top it all off, the letters had numerical meanings. The letter *az* under a *titlo* meant the numeral one, *vedi* was a two, and *glagol'* was a three.

Why does *v* come after *a*, asked Ustina, surprised. Where, one must wonder, is *b*?

The designation of the numerals follows the Greek alphabet, and it has no such letter.

Do you know Greek?

No (Arseny placed his palms on Ustina's cheeks and rubbed her nose with his), that is what Christofer said. He did not know Greek, either, but he felt many things intuitively.

Ustina's astonishment at the properties of the letters was reinforced further by their numerical properties, which were no less surprising. Arseny showed her how the numerals added and subtracted, multiplied and divided. They denoted the acme of human history: the year ҂е҃ф (5500) since the Creation, when Christ was born. They also signified the end of history, which miraculously appeared in the ghastly numeral of the Antichrist: х҃ѯѕ (666). And letters expressed all that.

Numerals had their own harmony, which reflected the overall harmony of the world and all that exists within it. Ustina found numerous pieces of information of that sort by reading Christofer's manuscripts, which Arseny brought to her by the armful. A week hath seven dayes and serves as a prototype for human lyfe: the first day is a childe's birth, the second day is for a yonge man, on the third day he is a growne man, the fourth day is for the middle of the lyfe, fifth is the day of graying, the sixth day is for old age, and the seventh day is for the ende.

The symbolism of numerals was not Christofer's only pastime. Ustina also found records of distances among his manuscripts. From Moscow to Kiev was a thousande and a half versts, from Moscow to the Volga was 240 versts, from Beloozero to Uglich was 240 versts. Why did he write all this down? Ustina wondered as she read. Arseny responded to her in thought, saying Christofer had not, of course, been to either Moscow or Kiev or the Volga. It was possible that 240 versts, which appears twice, caught his attention in those data. The deceased attributed particular significance to coincidences like this (Arseny replied), though he did not fully grasp their meaning. What is important is that you and I already understand each other without words.

$$\overline{\text{SĪ}}$$

Ustina's pregnancy was not progressing without difficulty. She complained from time to time about headaches and dizziness. In those situations, Arseny rubbed her temples with dill oil or a wild-strawberry tisane. Because of her shyness, Ustina kept quiet about certain indispositions that arose. Constipation, for example. Arseny shamed her when he noticed it, saying they were now one whole, and she must not be shy with him. He gave her a tincture of young elderberry leaves for her constipation. Together they had gathered those leaves in the spring and together they had boiled them in honey.

Ustina's sleep was not restful. Arseny could guess when she had woken up in the middle of the night because he would not hear her breathing. Ustina breathed though her nose, loudly and evenly, when she slept. To restore her sleep, Arseny gave her an infusion of tree moss before bed.

Ustina's body was testing the endurance of her spirit in an obvious way. Heartburn tormented her constantly. She experienced heaviness and pain in her womb, the place the baby was located. Her growing belly itched mercilessly from the touch of Arseny's linen shirt. Ustina's feet swelled from the burden she carried. Her facial features looked puffy. Her eyes had become sleepy. An unfamiliar absentmindedness had come into Ustina's gaze. Those changes were noticeable to Arseny and they worried him. He saw in Ustina's lackluster eyes the beginning of weariness from pregnancy.

The newness of her condition helped her overcome the indispositions in the first months. As time passed, her condition was no longer new. It was habitual and onerous. And then autumn came and the days grew short, as they do in the north. The gloominess cloaking the Land of the White Lakes brought out despondence in Ustina. She saw nature dying and could do nothing about it. As she watched leaves fall from the trees, Ustina also shed tears.

She was now observing the changes in her body as if from afar. It was ever harder to see her former self—flexible, quick, and strong— in this bloated, unwieldy creature. Someone had lodged that self in another's body.

But it was not just any someone, it was Arseny. When that thought hit her, it was as if she had touched bottom, pushed off, and swum to the surface again. And here she opened herself up to all the joys that surrounded her. Ustina's joys were more vivid than her sufferings.

She rejoiced when her appetite awoke within her, because she knew she was not eating alone but with the child. She rejoiced at the colostrum that kept appearing on her nipples. She indulged herself in impetuous fantasies about the future child and shared them with Arseny:

If a girl is born, she will grow up the prettiest in Rukina Quarter and marry a prince.

But Rukina Quarter has no princes.

Well, you know, in that case he will come here. If a boy is born, which would really be preferable, he will be light-haired and wise, like you, O Arseny.

Why do we need two who are light-haired and wise?

That is what I want, sweetheart, what is wrong with it? I see nothing wrong with it.

One day Arseny slowly ran his palm along Ustina's belly and said:

It is a boy.

Glory to God, I am so glad. Glad about everything. Especially the boy.

Ustina usually stroked her belly while sitting on the bench. At times she could feel movements of the one sitting inside. After what Arseny said, she had no doubt it was a boy. Sometimes Arseny placed his ear against her belly.

What is he saying? asked Ustina.

He is asking you to be patient just a little longer. Until the beginning of December.

Okay, fine, since he is asking. I think even he is tired of sitting around there.

You cannot even imagine how tired he is of it.

Ustina sang to amuse the little boy:

O Mother, O Mother, Mother of God,
Mary the Blessed (*Ustina made the sign of the cross over herself and her belly*),
Where, O Mother, did you spend the nights?
I spent the night in the city of Salem,
In God's church behind the throne
I slept but a little but much did I see,
As if I had given birth to the Christ Child,
I swaddled him in swaddling,
Wound him in silken sashes.

Arseny said nothing, though he thought about how her piercing voice could be heard from the road. Let her sing, he thought; after all, it will be more fun for the baby.

She sewed clothing.

It is bad luck, she said, to sew clothing for an unborn child.

But she sewed anyway. She took the material from Christofer's things.

Sewing from the property of the dead, she said, is also not encouraged.

As she made stitch after stitch, she would sigh deeply, making her whole huge belly begin moving. Her hands created swaddling clothes and doll-sized trousers and little shirts.

She made dolls, too. She made them from rags and drew on them in various ways. Wove them from straw. The straw dolls were all identical and all resembled Ustina. She burst into tears when Arseny told her that.

Thank you (she nodded) for the compliment. Thank you very much.

Arseny embraced her:

I said it out of love, you silly fool, nobody loves you or will love you as I do, our love is a special case.

He pressed his cheek to her hair. She warily freed herself and said:

Arseny, I want to take Communion before I give birth, I am afraid to give birth without Communion.

He placed his palm to her lips:

You'll take Communion after you've given birth, my love. How would you go to church now, in this condition? And after giving birth, you know, we'll open up to everyone and show our son and take Communion and it will get easier because nothing will need to be explained to anyone when the child is here, the child will justify everything, it will be like starting life with a clean slate, do you understand?

I understand, answered Ustina. O Arseny, I am afraid.

She wept often. She tried to make it so Arseny did not see but he saw, because they were inseparable for all those months and it was difficult for her to weep in secret.

It was ever more difficult to read to Ustina. Her attention was scattered. It was hard for her to sit and hard to lie. She had to lie on her side, not on her back. She asked Arseny to read to her ever more frequently now, and of course he did.

And then it happened that Alexander the Great came to the swampy places. And Alexander became ill but there was not even a place in those swamps for him to lie down. Snow fell from heavens unknown to him. And Alexander took off his armor and ordered his warriors to place all their armor together. Thus they assembled a bed for him in a boggy place. He laid on it, exhausted, and they covered him with shields to keep the snow from him. And Alexander suddenly realized he was lying on the iron earth under a sky of ivory...

Stop. Ustina turned heavily onto her other side and was now lying with her back to Arseny. Snow fell here today, too. Why are you reading all this to me...?

I'll find something else for you, my love.

Ustina turned toward him again.

Find me a midwife. That is what I will need soon.

Why do you need some ignorant midwife? Arseny was surprised. You have me, after all.

Have you really ever delivered a baby?

No, but Christofer told me about it in detail. And he wrote everything down, too. Arseny rummaged around in the basket and took out a manuscript. Here.

Is it possible to deliver a baby by what is written? Ustina asked. And beyond all that, you know, I do not want you to see me that way. I do not want it, O Arseny.

But are we not one whole?

Of course we are one. But I still do not want it.

Arseny did not argue. But he did not look for anyone.

31

Ustina's water broke during the twilight hour on November 27. She did not realize this immediately, only when her bed had become soaked. Arseny remade the bed with some linen while she sat over the chamber pot. He began shaking. When Ustina laid down again, he lit their two oil lamps and one splinter lamp. Ustina took him by the hand and sat him down alongside herself. Do not worry, sweetheart, everything will be fine. Arseny pressed his lips against her forehead and began crying. He felt a fear the likes of which he had never felt in his whole life. Ustina stroked the back of his head. Her contractions began an hour later. Her face glistened frightfully in the duskiness and he did not recognize that face, with its beads of sweat the size of peas. Other facial features were now showing through the usual ones. They were unsightly, puffy, and tragic. And the former Ustina was no longer there. It was if she had gone and another had come. Or not even come: this was the former Ustina, and she was continuing to leave. She was losing her perfection, drop by drop, becoming less and less perfect. As if she were becoming more embryonic. The thought that she might leave forever took Arseny's breath away. He had never considered that. The gravity of that thought turned out to be great. It dragged him down and he slipped from the bench onto the floor. It was as if he heard the faraway knock of a head on wood. He saw how awkwardly Ustina was rising from the bench and bending toward him. He saw everything. He was conscious but could not move. If he had known the gravity of that same thought before, his fear of speaking about Ustina in the quarter would have seemed laughable to him. Arseny slowly sat: I will run to the quarter for a midwife, in the blink of an eye. It is already too late (Ustina

75

was still stroking him), I cannot be left alone now, we will somehow figure this out, the only thing that disturbs me… I did not want to say, said Ustina, I was not sure… Arseny sat Ustina down on the bench. He covered her hand in kisses and her speech was still all separated into diffuse words that would not join up in his head. He knew that this horror had not seized him for no reason. Ustina touched her belly: I have not heard him since yesterday… The boy. I do not think he is moving. Arseny extended his palm toward her belly and cautiously ran it from top to bottom. His palm froze at the bottom of her belly. Arseny looked at Ustina, unblinking. He no longer felt life in her womb. The heart he had heard there all those months was no longer beating. The child was dead. Arseny helped her lie on her side and said, the boy is moving, calmly give birth. He sat on the edge of the bench and held Ustina by the hand. He changed the splinter lamp time after time. Poured more oil into the lamps. Ustina sat up in the middle of the night: the boy died, so why are you silent, you have been silent for several hours already. I am not silent, Arseny said (did he not?), from somewhere in the distance. How can I be silent? He darted to Christofer's shelves, knocking over the chamber pot. He turned and saw the pot slowly rolling under the bench. How could I be silent? But I also cannot speak. Arseny got a tisane of the herb chernobyl, or wormwood. Drink some of this. What is it? Drink it. He raised her head and placed a mug to her lips. He heard loud—for the whole room to hear—swallows. This is the herb wormwood. It expels… What does it expel? Ustina choked and the tisane ran from her nose. The herb wormwood expels a dead fetus. Ustina began soundlessly weeping. Arseny took a small box down from the shelf and sprinkled the contents on the coals. A sharp, unpleasant smell spread through the room. What is that? Ustina asked. Sulfur. Its smell speeds up labor. A minute later, Ustina vomited. She had not eaten anything in a long time and vomited the tisane she had drunk. Ustina laid down again. And Arseny stroked her again. She felt the contractions start up again. Pain overcame her. What she felt was first a pain in her belly, then it spread to her entire body. It felt to her as if the pain from all the surrounding hamlets had gathered in one spot and entered her body. Because her—Ustina's—sins had exceeded the sins of the entire area and eventually that had to be answered for. And Ustina began shrieking. And that shriek was a snarl. It frightened Arseny, and Arseny grabbed onto her wrist. He frightened even Ustina, but she could no longer not shriek. She shifted her leg, even as she continued lying on her side, and Arseny began holding her leg down. That leg bent and straightened: it was like an independent, vicious being that wanted to have nothing to do with the motionless Ustina. Arseny held her leg with both hands but still could not restrain it. Ustina turned abruptly and he saw, in a streak of falling light, feces glistening on her inner thigh. Ustina continued shrieking. Arseny could not understand if the baby was moving or not. He remembered other touching as he felt the hair around her female place under his hand, and he prayed to God to transfer Ustina's pain to him, even to transfer only half the pain. In her moments of lucidity, Ustina thanked God that she had been granted to suffer for herself and for Arseny, so great was her love for him. Arseny most likely felt rather than saw when the baby's head appeared in Ustina's female place. By touch, the head was huge, and the despairing Arseny thought it would not be able to come out. The head was not coming out. The crown of the head appeared, again and again, for a short while, but then disappeared again. Arseny tried to work his fingers under it but his fingers could not get through. He even thought he had pushed the head in deeper as he tried to pull it out. He broke into a fever. The fever was unbearable and he stood up straight, throwing his shirt off in one tug. As before, the baby's head was not visible. Ustina's shrieks grew quieter but they were more frightening, since they had not lost their strength because she felt better. Ustina was falling into unconsciousness. Arseny saw she was leaving and began shrieking at her, to hold her back. He slapped her on her cheeks but Ustina's head flopped lifelessly from side to side. Arseny threw her leg onto his shoulder and tried to enter her female place with his right hand. His hand did not really seem to be getting through, but his fingers sensed the baby. Top of the head. Neck. Shoulders. His fingers closed up at the place where the neck becomes the head. They moved toward the exit. There was a cracking sound. Arseny was no longer thinking about the baby. That the baby might be alive after all. He was thinking only of Ustina. He continued pulling the child by the head as he fought his rising nausea. He saw the lips of Ustina's female place had ruptured and he heard her ghastly shriek. The baby was in Arseny's hands. He did not begin crying when he came into the world. Arseny cut the umbilical cord with the knife he had readied. He slapped the baby. He heard that was what midwives do to induce the first breath. He slapped again. The baby was silent, as before. Arseny carefully laid him on a swaddling cloth and bent over Ustina. The contractions were continuing. Arseny knew this was the afterbirth coming out. He cleaned off the bloody mucus that came from Ustina, putting it into the chamber pot. An entire piece of linen was drenched in blood and he thought there was more blood than there should be at birth. He did not know how much there should be. He only saw that the bleeding had not stopped. He was frightened because the blood was flowing from the womb and he could not stanch it. He took some finely grated cinnabar in his fingers and went as deeply into Ustina's female place as he could. He had heard from Christofer that grated cinnabar stops bleeding from wounds. But he did not see the wound and did not know the exact place from which the blood flowed. And the bleeding did not stop. More and more was soaking the bedding. Ustina lay, her eyes closed, and Arseny felt life abandoning her. Ustina, do not leave, Arseny shouted with such might that Elder Nikandr heard him at the monastery. The elder was standing in his cell, in prayer. I am afraid it is already useless to shout, said the elder (he was watching as the first snowflakes of the year floated in through the open door and, just as a draft blew out the candle, the moon broke out from behind ragged clouds and illuminated the doorway), which is why I will pray for your life to be preserved, O Arseny. I will pray for nothing else in the coming days, said the elder, latching the door. Utter silence settled into the house for a minute and Ustina opened her eyes in the midst of that silence: it is a shame, O Arseny, that I am leaving in this gloom and stench. And the wind once again began whistling outside the window. Ustina, do not go, Arseny shouted, my life ceases with your life. But Ustina could no longer hear him because her life had ceased. She was lying on her back and the leg that was bent at the knee was turned to the side. Her arm dangled from the bench. It was squeezing a corner of the linen. Her face was turned in Arseny's direction and her open eyes looked at nothing. Arseny was lying on the floor alongside Ustina's bench. His life was continuing, though that was not obvious. Arseny lay there for the rest of the night and the next day. Sometimes he would open his eyes, and he had strange dreams. Ustina and Christofer were leading him, as a little boy, by the hands through the forest. He thought he was flying when they lifted him over the hillocks. Ustina and Christofer laughed, for his sensations were not mysterious to them. Christofer kept bending for plants and placing them in a canvas bag. Ustina was not gathering anything, she simply slowed her pace and observed Christofer's actions. Ustina was wearing a red men's shirt that she was planning to give to Arseny at the appropriate time. And that is what she said: This shirt will be yours, you need only change your name. Since you have no objective possibility of being Ustina, name yourself Ustin. Is that a deal? Arseny looked up at Ustina. It's a deal. He thought Ustina's seriousness was ludicrous, but he did not show it. Of course it's a deal. Christofer's bag was already full. He still continued gathering plants, though, and they fell from his bag onto the path in time with his steps. The entire path, as far as the eye could see, was strewn with Christofer's plants. But he kept gathering more. There was, in that activity, which looked pointless at first glance, a unique beauty and expansiveness. And a generosity that was indifferent to whether it was necessary or not: it came about only through the favor of the giver. When morning came, Arseny noticed the light but he did all he could not to wake. Even in his sleep, he was afraid to discover Ustina had died. A special morning horror seized him: the coming of a new day, without Ustina, was intolerable for him. He once again nourished himself with sleep until he was unconscious. Sleep streamed through Arseny's veins and beat in his heart. With each minute, his sleep became deeper, because he feared waking up. Arseny's sleep was so deep that his soul abandoned his body at times and floated under the ceiling. From that moderate height, it contemplated Arseny and Ustina, both of them lying there, and was surprised that Ustina's soul, so beloved, was absent from the house. Upon seeing Death, Arseny's soul said: I cannot abide your glory and I see your beauty is not of this world. Right then, Arseny's soul noticed Ustina's soul. Ustina's soul was almost translucent and thus inconspicuous. Can it be that I also look like that? thought Arseny's soul, wanting to touch Ustina's soul. But a gesture of warning from Death stopped Arseny's soul. Death already held Ustina's soul by the hand and intended to lead her away. Leave her here, wept Arseny's soul, she and I have become entwined. Get used to separation, said Death, it is painful, even if it is only temporary. Will we recognize each other in eternity? asked Arseny's soul. That depends in large part on you, said Death: souls often harden during the course of life, and then they barely recognize anyone after death. If your love, O Arseny, is not false and does not fade with the passage of time, one might ask, why would you not recognize each other there, where there be not illness, nor sorrow, nor groaning, but where there shall be everlasting life? Death patted Ustina's soul on the cheek. Ustina's soul was small, almost childlike. Her response to the affectionate gesture was more likely fear than gratitude. This is how children respond to those who take them from their kin for an indefinite period: life (death) for them will, perhaps, not be bad, but it will be completely different from what they are used to, lacking the former structure, familiar events, and turns of speech. As they leave, they keep looking back and seeing their frightened reflections in the teary eyes of their kin.

҃НІ

Arseny woke up after darkness had fallen. His arm knocked against Ustina's dangling arm. Her arm was cold. It would not bend. The coals in the stove had long gone cold but something still gleamed ever so slightly in the small oil lamp under the icon of the Savior. Arseny brought a candle to the lamp. He held it cautiously so as not to extinguish the last fire remaining in the house. The candle flared (not immediately) and lit the room. Arseny looked around. He gazed attentively, noticing every little thing. Scattered items. Broken little pots of remedies. He did not miss a single detail, because it all allowed him to continue not looking at Ustina. And then he looked at her.

Ustina was lying in the same position as yesterday but she was completely different. Her nose had sharpened and the whites of her open eyes were sunken. Ustina's face was alabaster but the tips of her ears were a minium red. Arseny stood over Ustina and feared touching her. He was not experiencing disgust; his fear was of a different nature. There was nothing of Ustina in the body sprawled out in front of him. He extended his palm to her half-bent leg and cautiously touched it. He drew his finger along her skin: it turned out to be cold and rough. It had never been like this during Ustina's life. He tried to straighten her leg but was unable, just as he was unable to close her eyes. He was afraid to apply pressure. Whatever he touched was, perhaps, very fragile. He covered Ustina with a bedspread, everything but her face.

Arseny began reading the prayer service for the departed. He asked God to deliver Ustina fro the snare of the hunter and fro the noisome pestilence, that she not be afraid of any terrour by night, nor for the arrowe that flieth by daye. From time to time he turned and looked at her face. He heard his own voice from afar. At times, it contained the sound of tears. The voice dully announced that God was commanding the angels to keep Ustina safe in all her journeys. Arseny remembered how Ustina had gone, holding Death by the hand, how her shape had diminished until it turned into a dot. It was Death with her then, not angels. Arseny tore his eyes from the sheet.

You should be in the arms of the angels now, he meekly addressed Ustina. They shall beare thee in their handes, that thou hurt not thy foot against a stone.

He turned again and it seemed Ustina's face had flinched. He could not believe his eyes. He raised the candle slightly and stepped closer. The shadow of Ustina's nose was shifting around her face. And more than the shadow was moving: Ustina's face was changing along with the shadow. This change did not look natural. It did not correspond to Ustina's living facial expressions, but there was also something in it that was not characteristic of a dead person. Even if Ustina was not completely alive, she was not exactly fully dead, either.

Arseny was afraid he might let the small shoots of life he had noticed in Ustina expire. He might let them freeze, for example. Only now did he sense that the house had cooled down over the last day. He rushed to the stove and lit a fire. Arseny's hands shook from agitation. It suddenly occurred to him that everything depended on how quickly he could now manage to get a fire started. The wood was already crackling a few minutes later. Arseny still did not look at Ustina, giving her time to pull herself together. But Ustina did not get up.

So as not to scare off the shoots of life within Ustina, Arseny decided to pretend he had not noticed them. He continued reading the prayer service for the departed. After that, he began reading the Psalms. He read them unhurriedly, distinctly pronouncing each word. He came to the end of the Psalter and pondered. He decided to read it again. He finished toward morning. To his own surprise, he felt hungry and ate a chunk of bread.

It was as if the food had opened his nostrils; he drew in air. The smell of rotting flesh was apparent. Arseny thought the smell was coming from the baby. And there truly were signs of decomposition on the small body. At dawn, Arseny moved it closer to the window.

You never saw sunbeams, he told the baby, and it would be unjust to deprive you of light, even in such small quantities.

Of course Arseny secretly hoped Ustina would intervene in his conversation with their son. But she did not intervene. And even the position she was lying in remained, outwardly, the same.

He decided to read the Psalter over Ustina a third time. At the tenth Kathisma, he perceived movement on the bench. He continued to observe by keeping his peripheral vision on the bench, but the movement did not recur. Arseny felt bewildered when he finished reading the Psalter. He did not know what else he could read over Ustina, in the shaky position between life and death where, by all appearances, she now resided. He remembered that in life she had loved hearing the *Alexander Romance* and so he began reading the *Alexander Romance*. Her reactions to the book about Alexander had always been lively, so now, in Arseny's opinion, it could play its own positive role.

He read the *Alexander Romance* over Ustina until the next morning. After a bit of thought, he read *The Apocalypse of Abraham, Legend of the Indian Kingdom*, and stories about Solomon and the Centaur. Arseny purposely chose things that were interesting and likely to stimulate life. As night fell, he took to reading those of Christofer's manuscripts that did not contain day-to-day instructions and recipes. Arseny read the last manuscript at dawn: a desecrated robe mayn't be washed with anything but water and only tears may washe away and cleanse desecration and spiritual feces.

He had wept out all his tears over the previous days and they never came again. He had no more voice: he read the final manuscripts in almost a whisper. He had no strength. He sat on the floor, leaning against the kindled stove. He did not notice when he dozed off. A rustling by the window woke him. A rat was sitting alongside the baby. Arseny motioned with his hand and it ran away. He realized that if he wanted to preserve his son's body, he should not sleep. He looked at Ustina. Her facial features had swollen.

Arseny stood up, with difficulty, and went over to Ustina. A ripe smell hit his nose when he lifted the bedspread a bit. Ustina's belly was huge. Much larger than in the days of her pregnancy.

If you truly did die, Arseny said to Ustina, I should preserve your body. I had expected you would need it in the short run but since things have not turned out that way, I will make every effort to preserve it for the impending universal resurrection. First and foremost, of course, we'll stop stoking the stove, which promotes tissue decomposition. Besides, flies are already circling now and, honestly, their appearance surprises me because this is not typical for November. Our son particularly concerns me: he looks very bad. Essentially, our task is not as complicated as it might appear at first glance. According to my grandfather, Christofer, it is fully possible the end of the world will come in the seven thousandth year since the Creation of the world. If we consider that 6964 is coming right up, our bodies still need to hold out for thirty-six years. You have to agree that is not so long compared to the amount of time that has elapsed since the Creation of the universe. Cold spells are on the way and we will all be lightly frozen. Of course then summer will come thirty-six more times (summer can be hot, even in these parts) but we will manage to settle into our new situation before the warm season, for the first months are not only difficult, they are also decisive.

From that day on, Arseny stopped lighting the stove. He also stopped eating, because he no longer felt like eating. He occasionally drank water from the wooden bucket. The bucket stood by the door and he would notice thin films of ice covering the water in the morning. One time, he thought Ustina was moving when he was drinking water. He turned and saw that her raised leg, the one he had moved aside, was now lying on the bench. He walked over to Ustina. Looks were not deceiving him. Ustina's leg truly had descended. Arseny took hold of the leg and discovered it would bend again. He took Ustina's dangling arm and gently placed it on the bench. Arseny knew rigor mortis of the flesh had already gone by, but he forbade his heart to beat faster. A glance at Ustina's belly killed all hope. It had distended even more and expelled everything that had not managed to come out of her female place on the day of her departure.

Arseny no longer read anything. He saw from Ustina's condition that she was no longer up for reading. He spoke with her ever less because for now he could not tell her anything reassuring.

I am frightened for our boy, he said one day, because today I saw white worms in his nostrils.

He said that and then regretted it, for what could Ustina do here; she was not in such an easy position herself. Her nose and lips had bloated and her eyelids were swollen. Ustina's white skin had become an oily brown and was bursting and oozing pus in places. Her veins were unnaturally and distinctly green under her skin. Only her hair, all stuck together, continued to retain its reddish color.

Arseny sat by the stove, hugging his knees and staring incessantly at Ustina. He no longer even got up for water. Sometimes he heard knocking at the door and experienced quiet joy that he had managed to latch the door before his transition into motionlessness. He did not answer the shouts or pay attention to footsteps in the yard. When they stopped, Arseny again submerged himself into tranquility. A feeling of repose seized him ever more intensely and fully. And from somewhere at the very depths of that repose there sprouted, like a meek flower growing out from under the snow, the hope of seeing Ustina soon.

One day he noticed movement by the window. The bull's-bladder that was stretched across the frame tore with a pop and then a hand with a knife came into view. Behind it was a face. But the hand covered the nose right away and the face itself disappeared. Arseny sensed movement of air and heard screams. They were addressed at him. He turned to Ustina again and stopped looking at the window. A short time later there came the sound of banging on the door. Arseny saw the door shake. He regretted that he had not managed to die before that knock.

The top of the door gave way and crashed over the high threshold. Those who had broken it down did not rush in. They were obviously terrified and were really in no hurry to come in. Arseny recognized the two in front. They were Nikola Weaver and Demid Hay, people from the quarter who had come to him for treatment more than once. They stood on the fallen door and spoke quietly amongst themselves. They covered their mouths and noses with the collars of their heavy, rough woolen coats.

When Demid headed toward Ustina, Arseny said:

Do not touch.

Arseny gathered his strength and stood. He wanted to impede Demid from approaching Ustina but Demid lightly pushed him in the chest with the palm of his hand. Arseny fell and did not move. Nikola poured some water from the wooden bucket on him. Arseny opened his eyes.

He is alive, said Nikola.

He took Arseny under the arms, lifted him a bit, and propped him against the stove. Arseny's head slipped onto his shoulder but his eyes remained open. Demid said the bodies they had found needed to be brought to the potter's field. Nikola said they should get a wagon from the quarter for that. They sent some third person, who had not uttered a word, for the cart.

The potter's field was a mournful place. Somehow, even the cemetery whose fence Arseny and Christofer lived beside seemed more comforting. The potter's field was located on a hill two versts from Christofer's house. There lay the plague dead, pilgrims, the strangled, unchristened babies, and suicides. Those drowned by waters, and taken by battle, and kylled by kyllers, and stricken by fyre. Suddenly surprised, those who had fallen from lightning, were deade from frost and every sort of wounde. The lives of these unfortunates were varied and it was not life that united them: their resemblance to one another consisted of death. It was death without Confession.

Those who died such deaths were given no funeral service and were not buried in ordinary cemeteries. They were brought to the potter's field. There the bodies were lowered to the bottom of a deep pit and heaped with pine branches. These deceased thus became the "heaped." They lay in a common pit, languishing from their own restlessness and having no place in this world. Every now and again their gray faces, sprinkled with sand, peered out from under the branches. It was an especially sad sight in the spring when the melting snow moved the branches out of place. Then the heaped deceased—deprived of eyes and noses—appeared in their least attractive condition, their arms and legs slipping onto neighboring bodies as if they were embracing one another.

Even their lot, though, was not hopeless, thanks to the boundless mercy of our Lord and Savior Jesus Christ. A priest came from the Kirillo-Belozersky monastery on the Thursday of the seventh week after Easter and gave a service for the heaped deceased. This day was known as Semik. They filled the pit and dug a new one. And the new pit remained open until the next Semik.

Difficulties did not always end for the heaped deceased even after the service, though. They were remembered in days of poor harvests. It is no secret for those who honor tradition that more often than not it was the heaped deceased who became the reason for calamities. There was a superstition that those whose lives were cut short did not die immediately. Damp Mother Earth did not accept them and pushed them out, forcing them to find some use for themselves on the surface.

It was as if these dead people lived out, in their other existence, the time taken away from them, but they did so while inflicting losses on those around them. They destroyed harvests and created summer droughts in their search for ways to expend their unspent strength. People well versed in such matters explained the dryness, saying the deceased (particularly those who died from boozing) were experiencing an inhuman thirst and were sucking moisture from the earth.

In difficult times those heaped deceased who had already been buried were sometimes exhumed and dragged away to thickets and swamps, despite protests from the clergy. Of course sometimes they were left in place but only after having been exhumed and turned face down. Needless to say, this might seem like a half-measure to some, but even this was considered a lesser evil than blatant inaction.

When it came right down to it, the position of the living was not so simple, either. When they buried those who had not made their Confessions, they aroused the wrath of Damp Mother Earth and she answered with spring frosts. When they did not bury them, they aroused the wrath of the deceased themselves, who ruthlessly destroyed the harvest in the summertime. In a complex situation such as this, Semik was, essentially, a judgment worthy of Solomon. If they did not commit the dead to the earth before the end of spring, those who cultivated the earth got through the period of light frosts without losses. By concluding the burial service and funeral during the seventh week after Easter, they could hope the vindictive deceased would not destroy their mature harvest.

Now Ustina had to end up among these deceased. They intended to toss her—Arseny's eternally beloved Ustina—into the potter's field. Along with a son who had not even received a name. Demid and Nikola wound their hands in rags, carried Ustina out of the house, and placed her on the cart that had driven up. A minute later, Nikola carried out the half-decomposed baby in his outstretched hands. Residents of the quarter slowly came behind the cart and gathered. They did not enter the house but stood, silent, in the road.

Arseny, who had been sitting vacantly on the floor until then, stood and took a knife off the stove and went outside. He was moving slowly but steadily, as if he had not spent all those hours in a daze. The sound of bare feet slapping at the earth became audible in the quiet. His eyes were dry. The crowd standing by the cart recoiled, for they sensed that his power was far above any human power.

He laid his hands on the cart:

Do not touch.

He shouted:

Do not touch!

The horse snorted.

He shouted:

Leave them with me and go back to where you came from. They are my wife and my son, and your families are in the quarter, so go on back to your families.

The visitors did not dare come closer. They saw his marble-like fingers on the knife handle. They saw the wind blow at the fluff on his cheeks. They were afraid of Arseny himself, not the knife. They did not recognize him.

That is a sharp object, give it to me, please.

Elder Nikandr appeared from the very depths of the crowd. He walked, holding his hand out to Arseny and dragging his foot. The crowd parted before him as the waves of the sea parted before Moses. The monk accompanying him followed.

Trust me, I am not in the best shape right now, but I decided I had to show up here and take the knife away from you.

They want to take Ustina and the child away to the potter's field, said Arseny. And they do not understand at all that the dead can be resurrected in no time at all.

The knife fell from his hand into the elder's extended hand.

Give them these bodies since this has nothing to do with the bodies, said the elder. If you place them in a normal grave, then they—and he pointed Arseny's knife at the crowd—will dig them up during the very next dry spell. You will dig them up, am I right, you heathens? he asked those standing round, and they cast their eyes down. They will dig them up, you can count on it. As far as resurrection and the saving of the souls of God's deceased servantes, well, I'll present that information to you, as they say, tête-à-tête.

The elder signaled to the monk to wait outside a bit. He took Arseny by the arm and Arseny immediately slackened. As they walked up the stairs to the front door, the elder's foot slipped several times on the steps. Those who were standing saw that and began weeping. It had been revealed to them that the elder's resolute spirit was in irreconcilable contradiction with the decrepitude of his body. They knew how things like this ended. The cart noiselessly began moving. Elder Nikandr and Arseny disappeared inside the doorway.

First I will speak about death, said the elder, and then, if things work out, about life.

He sat on the bench and indicated the place next to him. After Arseny had sat down, the elder pressed his hands against the bench and lowered his head. He spoke without looking at Arseny.

I know you are dreaming about death. You are thinking death now possesses everything you held dear. But you are wrong. Death does not possess Ustina. Death is only carrying her to Him Who will administer justice over her. And thus, even if you decide now to give yourself to Death, you will not be united with Ustina. Now, about life. You think life has nothing of consequence left for you and you see no purpose in it. But it is precisely at this time in your life that the greatest purpose has revealed itself.

The elder turned to Arseny. Arseny stared straight ahead, unblinking. His palms were lying on his knees. A fly crawled along his cheek. The elder shooed away the fly, took Arseny by the chin, and turned his face toward him.

I will not pity you: you are to blame for her bodily death. You are also to blame that her soul may perish. I should have said that beyond the grave it is already too late to save her life, but you know what, I will not say that. Because there is no *already* where she is now. And there is no *still*. And there is no time, though there is God's eternal mercy, we trust in His mercy. But mercy should be a reward for effort. (The elder had a coughing spell. He covered his mouth with his hand and the cough puffed out his cheeks as it tried to escape.) The whole point is that the soul is helpless after leaving the body. It can only act in a bodily way. We are only saved, after all, in earthly life.

Arseny's eyes were dry, as before:

But I took away her earthly life.

The elder looked calmly at Arseny:

So then give her your own.

But is it really possible for me to live instead of her?

If approached from the proper perspective, yes. Love made you and Ustina a united whole, which means a part of Ustina is still here. It is you.

The other monk knocked, entered, and gave the elder a saucer with burning coals. The elder sprinkled them in the stove. He tossed some twigs on top and laid several logs on them. An instant later, fire was licking at the logs. The elder's pale face turned pink.

Christofer advised you to enter the monastery. I am asking myself why you did not obey him and I cannot find an answer... (He approached Arseny.) Well, goodbye, or something, because this is our last meeting. As circumstances would have it, my life will cease very soon. If I am not confusing things, it will occur on December 27. At midday or so.

The elder embraced Arseny and headed toward the door. He turned on the threshold.

You have a difficult journey, for the story of your love is only beginning. Everything, O Arseny, will now depend on the strength of your love. And, of course, on the strength of your prayers, too.

Winter that year turned out to be unlike any other winter. It was neither frosty nor snowy. It was foggy and misty, not even like winter but like late autumn. If snow fell, it mixed with rain. It was clear to the population that this sort of snow could not live in this world. It melted before reaching the ground and brought joy to nobody. People wearied of winter as soon as it had a chance to begin. They saw a sinister portent in what was happening with the weather. And it proved true.

The day after Christmas, Elder Nikandr slepte. At the end of Christmas vespers he announced to the brethren that he intended to celebrate his birthday, on the twenty-seventh day of the month of Decembre. The elder monk had never celebrated his birthdays and the intrigued brethren gathered at his cell at the set time.

This is a birthday for eternity, he explained from a wooden sleeping bench in the corner. His arms were crossed on his chest.

The brothers began sobbing when they grasped what was happening.

I saye unto you: sob not for me, for thys day I wyll loke upon the face of my Lord. I saye unto you, too, O Lord, I commit my spirite to Thy hands, have mercy upon me and give me lyfe eternall. Amen.

Amen, repeated those who had gathered, as they watched Elder Nikandr's soul leave his body.

Their eyes dried and their faces lit up. The monastery filled with people from the surrounding area who expected miracles, for a newly departed holy man contains a special power. And they received according to their faith.

Meanwhile, winter still had not really begun. The roads were totally soggy and the rivers had not frozen over.

Getting from point A to point B, they wailed in the quarter, either seems impossible or is overly complicated. We are practically deprived of roads, they said, something we did not have before now, either, in the true sense of the word.

But even the absence of roads did not prevent the spread of the primary misfortune of the time: the pestilence. The disease was first discovered in Belozersk, the princedom's primary city. From there it slowly moved to the southeast. It captured village after village like a hostile army, behaving ruthlessly in the occupied territory.

Everyone remained in place because there was nowhere to escape the disease. Even overcoming the washed-out roads did not necessarily lead to salvation. According to rumors that reached the residents of Belozersk, the weather was raw in all Rus', which meant outbreaks of the pestilence could flare up anywhere. After getting started in autumn, as often happens, the disease could not be killed by frost during the winter because winter never set in.

The residents of Rukina Quarter were already worried about the pestilence, though it had not yet reached the quarter. Foreseeing the arrival of the pestilence, they decided to get advice from Arseny. The changes in Arseny had frightened residents of the quarter and at first they did not want to go to him. In light of the impending danger, however, they were left with no choice. They found Christofer's house empty when they arrived.

The door was not closed and they made their way in unimpeded. Despite complete order, it was obvious nobody lived in the house any longer. More accurately, it was an unlived-in order. The villagers touched the stove, which turned out to be completely cold. There was not even the memory of warmth inside, something that is unmistakable in stoves that have been recently stoked. The villagers searched to see if Arseny had left a note anywhere. But there was no note, either. Dreading the very worst, they peered under the benches, looked around the outbuildings, and even took a walk though the cemetery that abutted the house. The villagers found no traces whatsoever of Arseny, dead or alive. It could happen that he had melted away, for wax melteth before the fire, they thought. More accurately, they simply did not know what to think.

THE BOOK
OF RENUNCIATION

ã

But Arseny had not melted away. On the day they were searching for him at Christofer's home, he was already a dozen versts away. Two days earlier, he had tossed a canvas bag on his back and left the hamlet.

He had placed a scant number of remedies and medical instruments in the bag. Christofer's manuscripts took up the rest of the space. This was an insignificant part of the deceased's writings—his written legacy was so extensive it would not even have fit into a large bag. And Arseny's bag was not large. He felt regret, forced as he was to leave behind many wonderful manuscripts.

Arseny walked out of the house and headed for Koshcheevo. From Koshcheevo to Pavlovo and from Pavlovo to Pankovo. His feet slid along wet clay, he fell into deep puddles, and his boots quickly took on water. Arseny's route was not direct, for he had no clearly defined geographical goal. And it was unhurried. When entering yet another village, Arseny would ask if there was pestilence. There was no pestilence in the first villages he saw. They still knew Arseny there and so let him into their houses and even fed him.

In light of the early darkness, Arseny had to spend the night in Pankovo. When he set out again in the morning and came to Nikolskoe, he was not allowed in. They were not letting anyone into Nikolskoe, in order that no one carry the pestilence scourge into the village. Arseny was also not let into Kuznetsovoe, which lay one verst from Nikolskoe. Arseny headed for Maloe Zakoze but it turned out that logs blocked the entry into Maloe Zakoze. He went in the direction of Bolshoe Zakoze but the very same sort of logs lay there, too.

Velikoe Selo was next on Arseny's route. The entry was open but it was immediately obvious to Arseny that an air of ill-being hovered over the place.

It smells of trouble here, Arseny told Ustina. Our help is needed in this village.

This was the first time he had addressed Ustina since her death, and he felt trepidation. Arseny did not ask her forgiveness because he did not consider himself eligible to be forgiven. He simply asked for her participation in an important matter and hoped she would not refuse. But Ustina remained silent. He sensed doubt in her silence.

Believe me, my love, I do not seek death, said Arseny. To the contrary, actually: my life is our mutual hope. Could I really seek death now?

They did not open the first house to him. They said the pestilence had come to the village. Arseny asked where, exactly, there were sick people, and they indicated Yegor Blacksmith's house. Arseny knocked at that house. There was no answer. Arseny took a linen rag from his bag, covered his mouth with it, and tied the ends on the back of his head. He crossed himself and entered.

Yegor Blacksmith was lying on a bench. His huge arm was hanging down. His hand clenched into a fist from time to time, showing that he was still alive. Arseny took Yegor by the wrist so he could check how strongly his blood was moving. Hardly any movement was apparent, though. Yegor unexpectedly opened his eyes at Arseny's touch.

Drink.

There was no water in the house. An overturned dipper lay on the floor, right by Yegor's hand; under it glistened the last drops of moisture. It was obvious Yegor had knocked over the dipper but lacked the strength to fetch more water from the well.

Arseny went outside and headed toward the well sweep. The crane-like sweep had a dead appearance. Its wooden neck, which had been secured to the log that formed its torso with a clamp, creakily danced in the wind. Arseny lowered a wooden bucket into the well. The underground water stood high, unbound by ice. Arseny saw his reflection in the water and did not recognize it. His face had become different.

My face has become different, he told Ustina. These differences are difficult to define but they are obvious, my love.

He went back inside and gave water to Yegor Blacksmith. Arseny supported Yegor's head with his hand and Yegor drank, seeing nothing. He choked as he swallowed. The water flowed along his beard and streamed under his shirt. He could not get enough to drink. He held onto Arseny's hand with his own hand, and Arseny could barely hold its weight. This person had been very strong, thought Arseny, and, oh, he is so weak now. Just several days of illness had transformed him into a powerless heap of meat. Which would begin to decompose in several days. He sensed there was already no life in that body.

Yegor unexpectedly opened his eyes.

Art thou my angel of death?

I am not, said Arseny, denying it.

Do tell, O angel, how I shall be judged.

Arseny watched as Yegor's eyelids slowly shut.

Thou shall soon die, Arseny quietly said, but Yegor could no longer hear him.

He breathed heavily and drops of sweat rolled from his forehead, disappearing in his thick hair. Sitting alongside him, Arseny remembered how he had sometimes looked at the sleeping Ustina. Her chest had moved, barely noticeably, under the bedspread. Sometimes Ustina would loudly inhale air through her nostrils and turn onto her other side. Rub her cheek. Move her lips. Arseny moved his lips, too. He was reciting the prayer for the dying. His glance gradually took on sharpness and he saw Yegor behind Ustina's features. Yegor was dead.

Arseny went to the neighboring houses. There lay the living and the dead. He dragged the dead outside and covered them with pieces of canvas and brushwood. Arseny felt signs of life in one of the bodies as he was dragging it outside. He noticed there was still a soul clinging to the body. It was a young woman's body.

Something is telling me, he told Ustina, that this is not a hopeless case.

He carried the woman back into the house. It was warm there because the owners had still been on their feet that morning and stoked the stove. Arseny laid the sick woman on her stomach and examined her neck. Swollen glands—buboes—had spread along her neck like huge, minium-red beads. Arseny blew on the embers in the stove and threw in more wood. He took his instruments from his bag and laid them out on the bench. He thought for a bit. He chose a small lance and brought it to the fire. When the lance had been cleansed in the flame, he went over to the patient. He felt the buboes with his free hand. After choosing the largest and softest bubo, he stuck the point into it and squeezed it with two fingers. A thick, cloudy fluid with an unpleasant smell flowed from the bubo. Arseny felt its viscous flow with his fingers but he did not find it repulsive. For him, the pus running along the woman's neck was the disease's visible departure from the body. Arseny experienced joy. Feeling node after node with the pads of his fingers, he squeezed the plague from the patient.

After the neck, Arseny moved to the underarms, and then from the underarms to the groin. He sensed other smells there, too, besides the smell of the pus, and that agitated him. So much of me is brutish, thought Arseny. So much. After finishing the treatment, he let her blood in the places with the most buboes. The blood was foul there and had to be drained. The woman came to and began moaning when Arseny pierced the first blood vessel.

Be patient, O woman, Arseny whispered to her, and she again fell into unconsciousness.

He pierced blood vessels in various parts of her body and she moaned each time but no longer opened her eyes. Arseny covered her with a blanket when he finished.

And now: sleep a long sleep and gather your strength. And awaken not for death but for life. Your prognosis is favorable.

With those words, Arseny left the house. By the end of the day, he had been in several other houses, had dealings with the dead and the living, and seen the living transform into the dead. In one of the houses, he discovered the rag had fallen from his face. There was no time to search for a new one and so he prayed to his Guardian Angel, who was on his right shoulder, warding off the scourge of pestilence with his wings. Arseny felt an angelic waft of air from time to time and that calmed him. Now he could fully concentrate on treating the ill.

Arseny held the wrists of the ill and took heed of the movement of their blood. Sometimes he drew his hand along their chests or along the top of the head. This revealed to him the most likely journey preordained for the ill person. If recovery awaited the patient, Arseny smiled and kissed the person's forehead. If death was predestined for him, Arseny noiselessly wept. Sometimes no preordination was presented and then Arseny fervidly prayed for the the ailing person's recovery. He would transfer vitalizing strength to the patient as he held the lying patient's hand. He would let go the hand only when he sensed that the struggle between life and death was resolving itself in favor of life.

This sapped much of his strength that day because never had so many people required his help all at once. In the last of the homes he visited, Arseny fell asleep alongside the patient. He slept and dreamt of his Guardian Angel, who was warding off the scourge of pestilence for him. He did not furl his wings, even at night. Arseny was surprised at the Angel's indefatigability and asked how he did not tire.

Angels do not tire, said the Angel, because they do not scrimp on their strength. If you are not thinking about the finiteness of your strength, you will not tire, either. Know, O Arseny, that only he who does not fear drowning is capable of walking on water.

In the morning, Arseny and the patient awoke at the exact same time. And the patient knew that he was well.

В̃

Arseny stayed in Velikoe Selo for two weeks. He treated and washed the sick. He gave them food and drink, first and foremost drink. And he taught those who recovered how to care for the sick.

You are not under the power of the pestilence now, Arseny told those who had recovered. It can no longer touch those who have broken free of its clutches.

Not everyone believed him. Some, fearing the ailment would return, quietly left the village, going where there was no pestilence. They soon realized this was a mistake. Their bodies, weakened by illness, could not ward off the adversities of the journey, so the slush and cold fog of the road completed what the plague had lacked the power to accomplish. Those who stayed (they were the majority) believed in Arseny as they believed in themselves. He was their savior and his healing confirmed in their eyes the rightness of his words. They entered the plague houses together with Arseny but no harm came to any of them.

When Arseny had enough helpers to care for the living, he devoted himself to the dead: they could not wait, either. Even the dead who had been brought outside were decomposing, unrestrained. The embarrassed grimaces of the deceased clearly showed they were not to blame; they required immediate help. A cart was found and loaded with bodies. They were taken off to the nearest potter's field, three versts away, and there they stayed, to await Semik. Those who took care of the deceased did not cry. In those days nobody really cried, for tears cannot soften the grief of so much death. Beyond that, there were simply no more tears.

When he was certain life was returning to normal in Velikoe Selo, Arseny decided to leave. He said goodbye to its residents on a fine

January morning, not allowing anyone to escort him beyond the outskirts. But Arseny's great renown—the source of which may be found in Velikoe Selo—could not confine itself to that one locality.

Arseny's renown spread, independent of his will, through burgs and hamlets, overcoming dank dampness and roadlessness. Arseny moved on to the village of Lukinskaya, but his renown greeted him right at the first house. It stood in the form of an old peasant woman leaning against a carved doorframe and holding a ceremonial loaf of bread.

Art thou Arseny? asked the woman.

I am, answered Arseny.

The woman thrust the bread at him and he mechanically pinched some off. The bread was hard because (as Arseny gathered) it had been baked long ago.

Do helpe us, O Arseny, for we are dying the death.

If it so please God, I will help, Arseny muttered, not looking at the woman.

He did not understand where she had learned about him; he silently followed her around the village. Mud squished underfoot, and large, wet snowflakes floated down on them through awkwardly angled birch branches. The snowflakes were invisible against the backdrop of the white tree trunks but their faces keenly sensed them. The snow melted instantly on their cheeks but lingered on their eyelashes, hanging for a short time.

How does she know me? Arseny asked Ustina, but Ustina remained silent.

Arseny paused and then said, I'm afraid she takes me for someone else. And that her expectations are too high.

Sometimes he got ahead of the old woman and looked her in the eyes. They reflected a gray sky with no ray of light. He took the woman by the shoulder and abruptly stopped her. She turned her head but looked beyond him.

You know full well your grandson died so why are you taking me to him? said Arseny.

And why, one must ask, am I alive? said the woman, indifferent.

Arseny did not know how to respond, and it had not been a question anyway. At least not a question for him. He silently watched the woman disappear beyond the snowflakes. Once she was no longer visible, he headed toward the nearest house. Work already awaited him there.

Arseny spent more time in Lukinskaya than in Velikoe Selo. There were more patients here. There were also more dead. Apathy reigned in Lukinskaya and it turned out to be much more complicated to get people to help each other. But Arseny dealt with that, too.

He worked to convince the peasants that their recovery depended in large part on they, themselves. With the wish of awakening the vitalizing force within them, Arseny proved to them that God's help often comes in the form of hard workers. The peasants nodded because they took Arseny to be one of those hard workers. But they did not want to become hard workers. Or perhaps could not. Hope awakened within them when a few of the sick they had already mourned recovered.

And so the recovered began to help the sick and gather up the deceased. They brought bread to orphaned children, washed houses and burned incense for purification, and cleared out yards and streets that had suffered from neglect during the time of the pestilence. Arseny left the village of Lukinskaya and moved on after seeing this.

The village of Gory was the next spot Arseny came to on his journey. After spending some time in Gory, he went around Lake Kishemskoye, ending up in the village of Shortino after walking ten versts. From there his route took him to Kuligi, from Kuligi to Dobrilovo and from there to Zagorye. People already awaited Arseny everywhere and the local residents were already aware of how they should help him, the doctor. His words, like his renown, preceded him and everyone now knew what Arseny would say to them upon arrival, meaning he could speak ever less. This became a significant relief for Arseny: of all his work, it was the uttering of words that took the most effort.

Frost finally struck when Arseny was in Zagorye. It was a hard frost: less than a week passed before it had frozen the Sheksna River over with a thin but solid ice. Arseny now continued his travels along the frozen surface of the Sheksna. His feet sometimes slipped, sometimes got caught on reeds frozen in the ice, but it was still easier to walk along the river than along roadlessness.

And so he arrived in the large village of Ivachevo, a wealthy village that lived off fishing. In Ivachevo there stood a large stone church named for Andrew the First-Called, who was a fisherman before his apostlehood. The smell of nets and salted fish blended with the smell of decaying bodies in the houses of Ivachevo. The pestilence had arrived long ago, as in all the river villages that took in boatmen and travelers.

Arseny, who grew up far from watery expanses, sensed the river's presence with every hour. The Sheksna was not large, but the depth of its flowing water radiated a certain unusual energy of motion, even under the ice. This force was new in Arseny's life and it made him uneasy. It awakened in him the thought of pilgrimage.

Spring found Arseny in Ivachevo. The frosty weather, which had made the pestilence a bit less ferocious, had given way to thaw. Arseny expended all his strength on thwarting a second wave of the pestilence scourge. He prescribed that the residents of Ivachevo eat ground sulfur in egg yolk, drinking it down with an extract of rosehip juice. He ordered them not to eat pork or drink any milk or wine on the days they took the remedy. In the afternoons, Arseny went around to patients' houses and at night he prayed they be bestowed with health and also that the illness not spread.

When Arseny found himself on the banks of the Sheksna, he thought about how the river's ice would soon begin melting. He needed to cross the river to another village before the onset of warm days. He was already planning to head out on that journey when a sledge arrived in Ivachevo one morning over the ice of the Sheksna. Someone among Ivachevo's residents called the sledge "princely" upon seeing its beauty. This turned out to be the truth. The sledge had been sent from Belozersk by Prince Mikhail. And it had been sent for Arseny.

For me? asked Arseny. He was surprised when they told him of the sledge's arrival.

For you, confirmed those who had come from Belozersk. Pestilence's sores have come to bear on the princess and her doughter. Your renown is great, O Arseny, in the Land of the White Lakes. Show thy doctorly wisdom and thou shall be esteemed by the prince.

I await rewarde from only our Savioure Jesus Christ, answered Arseny, and why need I esteem from the prince?

Turning aside, he said to Ustina:

I shall see, my love, what I can do for these people. The disease will not become easier simply because they belong to a princely line. Nor more severe, either, that is true.

With those words, Arseny boarded the decorated sledge. The seat was covered with down pillows that lent their softness to the body with the emphatic readiness of expensive items. They wrapped Arseny in a coverlet and he felt awkward before the residents of Ivachevo who gazed at him. Never before had he ridden in such a sledge. And he had not imagined the passage could be so comfortable. Or the motion so fast.

The runners moved along the ice with a quiet, crystal-clear sound and the water responded to them from its depths like a heavy bell. Blowing snow swirled behind the runners in well-worn ruts. Frightened fish scattered every which way under the ice. Whenever there were bends in the Sheksna, the forest changed to villages.

There was a shorter route to Belozersk, too. It was not as convenient as the river route and it went through villages that flashed by, one after another. But the travelers did not know if it had been cleared. They were in a hurry and so decided not to risk anything, knowing the river route to be quick and reliable. Perhaps they did not want to ride into those villages because the pestilence raged there. They had (the sledge driver looked sternly at Arseny) plenty of pestilence in Belozersk.

The icy expanse began to broaden after the sun had lost its brightness. As he looked around, Arseny realized that now there was only a riverbank to the left. Instead of a right riverbank, endless versts of ice extended as far as the eyes could see. This was Beloozero, White Lake. The lake's ice turned out to be flatter than the river ice and the ride quickened. When it was already completely dark, the lake gradually changed to city. Belozersk, the principal city in the princedom, greeted them.

The sledge glided through dark streets. Arseny had never before seen such long streets and such tall buildings. He could judge the tallness of the buildings by the glow in upper-storey windows. People were already waiting when they pulled up to the prince's residence. Arseny was plucked from the sledge and quickly led along the staircase to the second floor. After racing through two half-darkened rooms, they ended up in a third. It was brightly lit, and a person stood there. This was Prince Mikhail.

I have hearde thou art a wise doctor, said the prince. He came closer to Arseny and began speaking quietly, almost directly into his ear. From above, for he was tall. My wife and daughter, they took ill last night, do you understand? The doctors here can do nothing. Nothing. Even treating teeth...

That is obvious, said Arseny. You have fetid breath.

Help my dear ones, O Arseny. I think that you can.

Why do you think so? Arseny asked. A rather large number of those I have treated died.

The prince sat down on a massive carved chair. When he was sitting, a bald spot was visible on the top of his head. He looked at Arseny, twisting his head unnaturally.

Because you yourself did not die. They told me you went through many plague villages and did not die. In that I see your blessedness.

Arseny was silent.

The prince brought him to the female half of the residence. Arseny stopped the prince when they arrived at the room where the ill lay.

I will go further by myself.

He bent his head and entered.

Two beds stood side by side. A young woman lay on one (she was much younger than the prince) and a girl of six lay on the other. The girl was unconscious. The princess nodded weakly to Arseny. He went first to the child and took her by the wrist. Then he touched her forehead.

What wilt thou saye, O Arseny? asked the princess.

Thou knowest my name, said Arseny, surprised.

He sat down on her bed. Even in the room's duskiness, it was apparent the princess had blue eyes. Her eyes must sparkle with a heavenly blueness in the sun, thought Arseny. The Lord has such a color. He carefully lifted her head from the pillow and felt her neck.

What wilt thou saye? she repeated.

Pray, O princess, and the Lord will show his mercy.

Arseny went out and closed the door behind him. The prince silently approached him. He looked away.

You saw them?

I saw them, said Arseny. They are gravely ill but life is not leaving them. With the Lord's help, I think they will feel better by morning.

The prince laid his head on Arseny's shoulder. Arseny felt tears on his neck.

Arseny returned to the ill and remained with them until morning. He watched as life battled with death and he understood he needed to help life. He treated the pestilent sores of mother and child. He gave them much to drink because water washes what is foul from the body. He held their heads over the wooden tub when they vomited. Most important, he released his vitalizing strength into them when he felt they did not have enough of their own.

Arseny was particularly apprehensive about the little girl since children withstand the plague worse than adults. He held her hand, not letting go, whenever he could. From her pulse he discerned changes in her condition and controlled her battle for life. Arseny could feel when he had to intervene decisively. At those moments, he mustered everything he had, leaving nothing behind, and delivered to the child everything vitalizing that he could find within himself. He feared only the depletion of his own strength.

When people came into the room to see them in the morning, Arseny was sitting motionless on the floor and holding the child by the hand. Those who entered thought he was dead. That the princess and her daughter were dead, too. But Arseny was alive. And though the princess and her daughter were still very weak, they were healthy.

That event became the beginning of Arseny's rise. The prince doted on his family, so the recovery of his loved ones made a deep impression on him. He gave Arseny a sable fur coat as a gift. The gift's value was obvious despite the warm season. The prince decided to make Arseny the court doctor and house him in his own palace.

It should be noted that princely chambers in this time long gone do not fully correspond to current notions of palaces. The Russian nobility's palaces were usually wooden. They differed from the houses of simple townsfolk in terms of size more than anything: they were taller and broader. Construction never finished. It might be interrupted, but it would be resumed when the first necessity arose. New quarters were added to the main building with new marriages in the family. New additions appeared when kitchens, rooms for servants, and service areas were expanded. The structures became larger but not more beautiful.

They resembled bee hives or a colony of mollusks. Their primary merit was that they suited the owners.

After living at the prince's for several weeks, Arseny appealed to him, requesting that he be let go. No, Arseny did not want to leave Belozersk—there were still many people there who needed treatment—he asked only to be provided other housing. The request surprised the prince at first but Arseny explained that he visited other patients and was afraid of bringing the pestilence into the prince's chambers. This was the truth but it was not the whole truth. Life in the palace weighed upon Arseny.

I feel you less strongly when I am amid luxury, he admitted to Ustina, in tears. And there it is impossible to accomplish the task I now live for.

The prince did not even consider hindering Arseny, for Arseny's word meant a great deal to him. It was important for the prince that Arseny not leave Belozersk. He gave him a house not far from the palace and let him live as he saw fit. As Arseny saw fit was, of course, to deal with the affliction that gripped the city. Within a short time, he was able to arrange for the recovered to help the ill in Belozersk, too. He could not have dealt with the entire city's ill all by himself.

Arseny left his house at daybreak and made the rounds to the houses of the plague-stricken. He examined them, determining their conditions and prospects for life. He stayed for long hours in places where his help could turn out to be decisive, persuading the sad angels of death to wait a bit. At times, when he thought his powers had completely abandoned him, he went to Beloozero.

It was already the end of May, but the lake was still under ice, its boundless leaden expanse standing in contradiction to the green-covered shores. Arseny felt the coldness of the lake's depths as he walked along the ice. A waft of that coldness felt to him like a waft of death, as if the lake's abyss contained everyone from Belozersk who had ever departed. He could gaze at the ice for hours, studying what had frozen into it over the winter: shards of a pot, charred pieces of campfire wood, a fallen wolf, remnants of bast shoes, and items that had lost their initial appearance and transformed into pure matter after resting for so long.

Arseny thought he was by himself but that was not the case. He could not hide anywhere from his renown. Unbeknownst to Arseny, Belozersk observed him from the shore. The city understood that the strain on Arseny would be unbearable for a regular person, so its people did not prevent him from gathering his strength in solitude.

But one day a speck broke free from the shore and began rapidly moving toward Arseny. He paid it attention when it became obvious that the speck was headed directly toward him. At first he thought the person was still far away but it only appeared that way because the person was so small. When the boy approached, Arseny saw he was around seven years old.

I am Silvester, said the boy. I have come, for my mother is sicke. Helpe us, O Arseny.

He took Arseny by the hand and pulled him in the direction of the shore. Silvester's hand was cold. Arseny moved along silently behind him. Silvester slipped on the ice several times and hung ludicrously from Arseny's hand. But neither laughed, since their walk was not joyful. Their motion was accompanied by the crackling of ice beneath their feet; above their heads there bellowed birds who had returned from warm lands. From time to time, waves of warm shore air flowed over them, offering its heat as they walked over the icy expanse.

My father died two years ago, said Silvester. Also from the pestilence. My mother's name is Kseniya.

Seeing that Silvester was looking at him, Arseny nodded.

Silvester's house stood by a swampy pond near the very edge of the city. Despite Arseny's expectations, it was a nice home, without orphanhood or abandonment.

When did she get sick? Arseny asked before crossing the threshold.

Yesterday, said the boy.

Arseny went in. Silvester followed him despite a cautionary gesture.

She's my mama, whispered Silvester. Nothing wicked can come to me from her.

But she belongs to the illness now, not to herself, said Arseny, whispering too, as he led the boy outside.

Kseniya lay with her eyes closed. Arseny watched her in silence for several minutes. Even the swelling from the illness had not distorted her balanced facial features. Arseny touched her forehead with his hand, surprised at his own timidity. He pressed on her forehead with his palm to shed his indecisiveness. Kseniya opened her eyes. They expressed nothing then slowly closed: Kseniya had no strength to resist sleep. Arseny felt her pulse. He drew his hand along her jugular artery. He pressed several times on the place under which her heart was beating. He could feel nothing in her but the waning of life.

In the entry room, Silvester looked at Arseny, questioning. Arseny knew that look very well but had not seen it before on a child. He could not fathom what he should say to a child who wore that look.

Things look bad, you know (Arseny turned away). I feel pained that I cannot save her.

But you saved the princess, said the boy. Save her, too.

Everything is in God's hande.

You know, for God, it would be such an easy thing to heal her. It is very simple, Arseny. Let us pray to Him together.

Let us. But I do not want you to blame Him if she dies anyway. Remember: she is likely to die.

You want us to ask Him but not believe that He will grant this for us?

Arseny kissed the boy on the forehead.

No. Of course not.

Arseny made a bed for Silvester in the entryway and said, you will sleep here.

Yes, but we will pray first, said Silvester.

Arseny went to the room and brought out icons of the Savior, His Virgin Mother, and the great martyr and healer Panteleimon. He took dippers off a shelf and put the icons in their place. He and the boy knelt. They prayed for a long time. When Arseny finished reciting prayers to the Savior, Silvester tugged at his sleeve.

Wait, I want to say it in my own words. (He pressed his forehead to the floor, which made his voice sound more muffled.) Lord, let her live. I need nothing else in the world. At all. I will give thanks to you for centuries. You know, after all, that if she dies I will be left all alone. (He looked out from under his arm at the Savior.) With no help.

Silvester did not fear for himself when he informed the Savior of these possible consequences: he thought of his mother and chose the weightiest arguments in favor of her return to health. He hoped he could not be refused. And Arseny saw that. He believed the Savior saw it, too.

Then they prayed to the Mother of God. Arseny glanced back when he did not hear Silvester's voice. Still kneeling, Silvester slept, leaning against a storage chest. Arseny carefully carried him to the bed and prayed, now alone, to the healer Panteleimon. At around midnight he went in to begin taking care of Kseniya.

For several days, Kseniya did not improve. But she was not dying, either. In this Arseny saw a display of God's boundless mercy and an encouragement to fight for her life. And he continued to fight. He lifted Kseniya's head a little, pouring into her mouth remedies for the plague as well as infusions to strengthen her flesh during her struggle with death. He held Kseniya by the hand, whispering a prayer and feeling how the help from Him to Whom he appealed poured into his patient through him.

When Arseny left her room, Silvester greeted him in the entry room. They went to the lake for a short time after praying for Kseniya's good health. The days in Belozersk had become hot, so the coolness of the lake was pleasant. They did not go out onto the ice because it was already unreliable: underwater springs had created melted patches and pools in the ice. The ice had changed from dark blue to black, from stable to fragile.

You will marry my mother, won't you? asked Silvester as they walked along the shore.

Arseny stopped from the unexpectedness.

I want for us to always be together, said Silvester.

You see, Silvester...

After walking a bit ahead, the boy slowly returned to Arseny.

Do you have another woman?

You ask very adult questions.

That means there is?

One might say so.

Arseny saw the boy's eyes fill with tears. Silvester kept himself in hand, and the tears would not roll down his cheeks.

What is her name?

Ustina.

Does she live in your village?

No.

In Belozersk?

She does not live on this earth.

The boy took Arseny's hand and they walked on, silent.

On the fifth day of her illness, Kseniya began to recover. She had no strength whatsoever but death no longer threatened her. She looked with gratitude at Arseny, who helped her drink, fed her porridge with a spoon, and brought her the chamber pot.

I do not feel embarrassed around you, she said. This surprises even me.

The flesh loses its sinfulness during illness, said Arseny, after thinking. It is becoming known that the flesh is only a shell. So there is no need to feel embarrassed about it.

I do not feel embarrassed around you, said Kseniya at another time, because you have become close to me.

Kseniya improved. On one of the following evenings, she got up and boiled a turnip. She cut the turnip into regular little circles and placed them in bowls. She watched the men with a happy gaze. Arseny looked at Silvester: the boy was hardly eating. It began to worry him that Silvester had been listless all day.

After supper, Arseny took Silvester by the wrist. As he approached the boy he already knew things were bad but he did not understand how bad until he felt Silvester's pulse. Arseny felt as if his own blood had reversed its flow and would now gush from his nostrils, ears, and throat. Kseniya still kept talking but Arseny could not even part his lips, distinctly feeling his inability to help. He looked at the child and again he wanted to die.

Silvester did not sleep that night. He thrashed around in his bed, seized by an inexplicable restlessness. He tossed and turned and could not find a comfortable position for sleep. The muscles in his arms and legs ached. After falling asleep for a few minutes, he would quickly wake up and ask if Kseniya and Arseny were there. He thought they had gone. But they were beside him: they sat by his bed and never ceased watching over him. Kseniya did not speak; tears ran down her cheeks. Toward morning, Silvester lost consciousness.

Kseniya lifted her head.

Save him, O Arseny. He is my life.

Arseny fell to the floor next to her, buried his head in her knees, and sobbed. He wept from the fear of losing Silvester and from his inability to help him. He wept for all those he had not succeeded in saving. He felt his own responsibility for them, a responsibility he had to bear alone. He wept from his own loneliness, which now burned at him with an unexpected sharpness.

In trying to cure Silvester, Arseny used every measure against the plague that Christofer had ever taught him. He employed several methods whose usefulness he had discovered himself, through observation. He sat the child on his lap and held him that way, not letting him go. Arseny feared the angel of death might come for Silvester in his absence. Arseny knew that, at the crucial moment, he would press the child to himself, pushing waves of life from his heart to Silvester's. He felt dread when Silvester began coughing. When he wiped the bloody slime from the boy's lips, Arseny feared Silvester's soul would fly out with the dreaded cough, for the position of the soul within the body was not stable.

Arseny remembered what Silvester had said and appealed to God:

Help him, this is so easy for You. I understand that my request is impertinent. And I cannot even offer my life for the boy's because my life is already devoted to Ustina, before whom I am guilty for the ages. But still I trust in Your boundless Mercy and beg You: save the life of Your servant Silvester.

Arseny did not sleep for five days and five nights: another reason he could not let Silvester out of his arms was that the boy needed to be held in a semi-sitting position. When Silvester lay down, his lungs quickly filled with phlegm and he began violently coughing it out. On the sixth day, Arseny sensed changes: they were not yet outwardly visible but they did not escape Arseny.

Without explaining anything, he ordered Kseniya to pray harder. Falling down from exhaustion and lack of sleep, Kseniya prayed harder. She genuflected before the icons in the sacred corner and remained that way for hours. Her hoarse voice now intoned continuously. Her hair came loose from under her headscarf but she had no strength to neaten it. And her tears came to an end, no longer flowing down her cheeks. On the seventh day, the boy opened his eyes.

Arseny collapsed on a bench after uttering a prayer of thanksgiving. He slept for two days and two nights but still did not feel rested. He understood that he needed to get up, and he dreamt that he was getting up. He wanted to examine Silvester and he dreamt that he was examining him: the examination showed that everything was fine with Silvester. Arseny knew that he was dreaming but he knew that he was dreaming the way things truly were. Otherwise, something else would have come to him in his dream.

A cool touch to Arseny's hand woke him. Kseniya's lips. Seeing that Arseny had opened his eyes, Kseniya pressed his palm to her forehead. Silvester stood behind her. The boy was pale and thin after the illness. He was transparent, almost spectral. A crease in his shirt stuck out from behind his back as if it were an angel's wing. He smiled at Arseny, not trying to come closer. Letting his mother go first.

~5

The city warmed as soon as the ice on the lake had melted. The plague began abating with the onset of hot days. The residents' unease gradually dissipated as Belozersk returned to normal life. Arseny's great renown, however, did not dissipate: it had already resounded throughout the entire princedom. People appealed to Arseny for all manner of medical reasons, sometimes even appealing without any reason. The city dwellers sensed obvious grace from God when speaking with him. Arseny spoke little but his very attention, smile, and touch filled people with joy and strength.

Prince Mikhail invited him to dinner from time to time. He again asked Arseny to live in his chambers but Arseny gently refused several times. The prince wanted to build him a large home beside his chambers but Arseny rejected that, too. Arseny would have refused the dinners as well but the prince would have taken that as a personal offense.

The prince was an intelligent person and was not zealous in his attempts to draw Arseny closer to himself. When Prince Mikhail grasped that Arseny needed a particular variety of independence, he did not consider imposing his company on him. The prince understood that this *particular variety* of independence was an independence whose boundaries he, the prince, could set himself. Letting Arseny live in the city as Arseny saw fit, the prince limited him in only one way: by denying him the right to leave. He politely but firmly made that plain.

Dinners with the prince were not the only complications Arseny faced. Dinners at Kseniya's turned out to be more frequent and torturous for his soul. Silvester came for him nearly every day and pulled him to his mother's house. It was even harder to refuse those dinners than the prince's. It especially troubled Arseny that he did not want to refuse them.

He would come to Kseniya's and see how she set the table. He delighted in her calm and precise motions. He and Kseniya barely spoke. Silence was not heavy with her and Arseny liked that, too. Sometimes Silvester spoke but more often he tried to leave them by themselves. After dinner, he would see Arseny home. That was pleasant for Arseny, too. Sometimes he thought Silvester feared he would turn and go into some other house.

Ustina cannot be your wife, said Silvester one day as he was seeing Arseny home.

Why? Arseny asked.

Because she does not live on this earth.

I answer for her everywhere, O Silvester.

Arseny placed his hand on Silvester's shoulder but Silvester turned away.

Silvester was not alone in his unhappiness. Arseny was beside himself, too. He could not avoid visiting Kseniya because there were no apparent reasons to do so. Beyond that, he had started noticing that he awaited those visits as if they were holidays, and so he began experiencing shame. Arseny was also ashamed that he could not hide from his renown in Belozersk. But he was not allowed to quit the city.

The people of Belozersk now came to him on their own. He treated them for the same afflictions as he had treated residents of Rukina Quarter. He never asked anyone to pay for treatment but few were willing to be treated for free. Unlike the residents of the quarter, the city dwellers rarely paid in kind, preferring money. And they paid far more. Sometimes Prince Mikhail made generous gifts, too.

Arseny used the money to buy several small books that he chanced upon: they described the healing properties of herbs and stones. One of them was a doctor book from abroad, and Arseny paid the merchant Afanasy Flea, who had visited German lands, for a translation. Flea's translation was extremely approximate, which limited opportunities for using the book. Arseny employed the book's prescriptions only when they coincided with what he knew from Christofer.

By following along as the merchant read the unfamiliar symbols and translated the words they composed, Arseny grew interested in the correlations between languages. Thanks to the story of the confusion of tongues, Arseny knew of the existence of seventy-two world languages, but he had yet, in his whole life, to hear a single one of them beyond Russian. His lips moving, he repeated the unaccustomed combinations of sounds and words to himself, after Flea. When he learned their meanings, it surprised him that familiar things could be expressed in such an unusual and—this was the main thing—awkward way. At the same time, the multitude of opportunities for expression entranced and attracted Arseny. He tried to memorize correlations between Russian and German words, along with Flea's pronunciation, which probably did not correspond to authentic German pronunciation.

The enterprising Flea quickly noticed Arseny's interest and offered to give him German lessons. Arseny readily agreed. Essentially, these new lessons were nothing like the usual notions of teaching, because Afanasy Flea was unable to say anything intelligible about language in general. He had never thought about its structure and certainly did not know its rules. At first the lessons consisted of nothing more than the merchant reading more of the doctor book aloud and translating it. These language lessons differed from their previous translation sessions only because at the end of each section, Flea asked Arseny:

Got that?

This allowed the merchant to charge Arseny a double fee: for translation and for lessons. Arseny did not begrudge the money so he did not grumble. He valued Afanasy Flea as the only person in Belozersk familiar to any degree with speech from abroad. Understanding that he would achieve little by merely reading the doctor book, Arseny decided to make use of one of his instructor's undeniable merits: Flea possessed a good ear and a tenacious memory.

During his time spent on lengthy trips in the land of Germany, Flea had mastered phrases to be uttered in various situations and could repeat those words when asked probing questions. Arseny described these situations for Flea and asked what to say in those cases. The merchant (this is so easy!) waved his hands around, surprised, and reported all the versions he had heard. Arseny wrote down what Flea said. When he was alone, he put his notes in order. He extracted the unfamiliar words from the expressions he heard from Flea and registered them in a special little dictionary.

One time Arseny bought a German chronicle when a foreign merchant's items were sold off after he died while on the road. It was a thick and fairly tattered manuscript. Arseny and Flea could not tear themselves away when they opened it at random.

They read about people called satyrs that cannot be overtaken when they run. They go around naked, live with wild animals, and their bodies are covered with fur. Satyrs do not speak, they only shout shouts. Arseny and Flea read about athanasias who live in the northern part of the Great Ocean. Their ears are so large they can easily cover their entire bodies. They read of shchirits who, on the other hand, have no ears, only holes. They read of manticores who live in Indian lands: they have three rows of teeth, human heads, and the body of a lion.

The world is so varied, thought Arseny, remembering similar descriptions in the *Alexander Romance* and asking himself about the place of all these listed phenomena in the overall scheme of things. After all, their existence could not, could it (he asked himself), be an irrationality in a world that is constructed rationally?

The greater part of the money Arseny earned went, however, not toward books or even lessons. Arseny primarily bought roots, herbs, and minerals he needed to make remedies. He gave out expensive remedies to those who had no opportunity to buy them. The most expensive were medicinal remedies brought in from other countries. Among them were items Arseny had only heard about from Christofer or read about in the German doctor book. Now an opportunity had arisen for Arseny to try them out, too, thanks to the generosity of the citizens of Belozersk.

First off, he bought a few pearls and finely ground them. He then mixed that with sugar from rosehips and gave it to someone weakened after the illness of the pestilence. According to Christofer, this remedy returned strength. The ill man's strength really did return, just as strength returned to other surviving patients. The role of the ground pearl in the matter remained unexplained for Arseny. All Arseny could say with certainty was that the pearl had not harmed the patient.

Arseny also bought a marvelous emerald stone, the sort brought from Britain. Those who often look at emeralds, Christofer had said, will strengthen their vision. Ground emerald that is dissolved in water helps treat lethal poisons. Arseny had never once used it as an antidote but looking at an emerald truly was pleasant.

He also tried out oils the likes of which he had never before seen. Arseny applied turpentine oil to heal up fresh wounds and it seemed efficacious to him. For joint pain, he rubbed the black oil petroleum on bothersome places. Patients felt better from Arseny's touch. When all was said and done, it did not matter to them what oil Arseny rubbed in. It was important to them that it was Arseny himself who did it because when they rubbed on the petroleum themselves, the curative effect seemed considerably weaker. They did not, however, deny the positive effect of the petroleum.

Arseny was content after trying out remedies previously unavailable to him. It cannot be said he completely lost faith in them, if only because he had faith in Christofer. Arseny, though, took into consideration the fact that even Christofer formed opinions of many medicines without personal experience. This enabled him to subject them to testing and reach his own opinions. Over all, Arseny felt ever more strongly about his long-time supposition that, when all is said and done, medicines are of secondary significance. The primary role belongs to the physician and his doctoring power.

Meanwhile, the short northern summer was already coming to an end. The evening coziness of stoves and the light of splinter lamps had returned. There were even frosts at night. Arseny would stay up late at Silvester and Kseniya's, reading Christofer's manuscripts to them.

Vasily the Great sayde: virtue that is in old age is not virtue, but infirmitie in acting on luste of the flesh. Alexander, upon seeing a certain person with his same name, a horrifying creature, sayde, Yonge man, change either thy name or thy morals. When a certain bald man insulted Diogenes, Diogenes said: I will not render insult for insult but I will praise the hairs of your head because they ran off after seeing its madness. Some young man at the market, proud, said he was wise because he had conversed with many wise people, but Democritus answered him: Well, I have conversed with many rich people but that did not make me rich. When Diogenes was asked how to live with the truth, he answered: Do as with fyre: do not go so exceadyngely close that it will burn, but do not go so farre away or the colde will reache you.

З

Meanwhile, cold weather was already close. The wind was tearing leaves from Belozersk's trees and flinging them into the lake. Gusts of wind were growing ever stronger, and the leaves' connection to the branches was already extremely tenuous. Leaves that had flown off into the river seemed to resemble flocks of small birds that were hurrying north for some reason.

Arseny continued treating patients, but not all were residents of Belozersk. Drawn by news of the Doctor, people from the entire Belozersk princedom now streamed to Arseny. At first he seated them in an entry room. When there was not enough space in the entry room, he ordered that several benches be placed in the yard. When the visitors no longer fit there, either, Arseny began limiting times he would see patients. He only took those who managed to find space on the benches. The rest, however, did not leave. They wandered the yard and patiently awaited the Doctor's kindness. They knew he would examine them anyway if they waited it out.

There were many patients, and they were very highly varied.

People with broken bones were brought to him. Arseny aligned their bones and stretched pieces of linen and a medicinal ointment over the injured places, to cover them. This was the flower *mallow*, which had been boiled in wine from another land. He gave them *blackthorn* juice with ground *cornflowers* to drink. These ailing people patiently wore their dressings and drank the remedy every morning for eight days. And their bones knitted together.

People burned in fires and scalded by boiling water were brought to him. Arseny applied linen with ground cabbage and egg white to the burns. He sprinkled the burns with cinnabar when changing the dressings. He gave an infusion of the magical herb known as *ephiliya* to those with burns. Their burns began to heal over and scar after a short time.

People tormented by worms came. For them, he prescribed wild radish ground with pure honey. He prescribed almond nuts. And young nettles, boiled in vinegar with salt. If a person still had any sort of worms after all this, Arseny gave him a pinch of vitriol on a full stomach, so the worms would leave for good. There were many worms in the Middle Ages.

Arseny also treated those suffering from hemorrhoids. He ordered them to dust the painful places with ground dill seed or antimony. People with itchy chests came to him. He prescribed that they obtain herring, an ocean fish, from merchants—it was well known that herring goes around in schools and its eyes glow in the dark. The herring should be cut lengthwise and applied to the chest. People with sore gums came to Arseny, too. He advised them to firm up their gums by frequently holding an almond in the mouth.

As before, Silvester came for Arseny and brought him to his mother. Knowing that Arseny was busy with patients all day, the boy would appear late in the evening. Without noticing it himself, Arseny would begin hurrying toward the end of the day, doing all he could to be free before Silvester's arrival. Arseny's patients noticed this and tried not to come in the evening. Arseny finally noticed this himself, too. His heart sank the day he made this discovery. He was silent until sunset and did not take out the manuscripts to read that evening.

Arseny began wavering when Silvester arrived. The boy looked at him, wordless, and Arseny could not withstand that look.

Shall we go, O Silvester?

They did not speak along the way. The boy could feel some changes had taken place within Arseny's soul but was afraid to ask. Kseniya already had everything on the table. Arseny did not want to eat; he ate so as not to offend Kseniya. He did not have any manuscripts from Christofer with him and the conversation did not go well. When Silvester disappeared into the entry room, Arseny said:

I should not be here, O Kseniya.

Kseniya's expression did not change. She had been waiting for those words and was prepared for them. Those words inflicted suffering on her.

I know that you are faithful to Ustina, said Kseniya, and I love you for that. But I am not seeking Ustina's place.

It makes me joyful and happy to be with you, said Arseny. But Ustina is my eternal bride.

If it makes you joyful to be with me, be my brother. Let us live together under a perfect love. Just to be with you, O Arseny.

I am weak so I cannot live with you under a perfect love. Forgive me, for God's sake.

God will forgive you, said Kseniya. You serve your memory and display boundless devotion, but know, O Arseny, that you are destroying the living in the name of the dead.

The whole point, shouted Arseny, is that Ustina is alive, too, and the baby is alive and they crave to be atoned for. Who will atone for them if not I, who has sinned?

We will. The two of us and Silvester, who will be happy to share a prayer with you. And he will be happy to return your serenity to you. His prayer is pleasing to the Lord. The three of us, together, will pray to the Lord on all dayes, from morning until evening. Just do not leave us, O brother mine Arseny.

Kseniya was pale and thus inexpressibly beautiful. Arseny felt a lump growing in his throat. As he left, he saw Silvester in the entry room; his gaze was achingly lonely. Arseny burst out sobbing from that gaze. He covered his face with his hands and flung himself from the house. He walked along the pine fencing and sobbed loudly. Nobody saw him because it was already night in Belozersk. The people of Belozersk only heard his sobs and wondered whose they might be, for they had not previously been familiar with this voice of Arseny's.

As he arrived home, Arseny wiped away his tears and told Ustina:

And so you see, my love, what is happening. I have not spoken with you, my love, for several months and I have no excuse. Instead of atoning for my sin, I am ever more mired in it. How can I pray for your atonement before God, my poor girl, when I myself am sinking into the abyss? It would not be so regrettable, you know, if I alone were to be lost forever, but who will atone for thee and the babe? I am the only one here who prays fervently for you and that is the sole reason that I still do not despair.

That is what Arseny said to Ustina. He gathered Christofer's manuscripts in a bag, showed it to Ustina, and added:

Here is the bag with Christofer's manuscripts, essentially the most treasured thing that I have. I would take it and go wherever I feel like, away from my renown. My renown has overcome me: it is driving me into the ground and preventing me from conversing with Him. I would leave here, my love, but the prince of this cyte will not release me, though the main thing that keeps me here is Kseniya and Silvester. They would be happy to pray with me for you and the baby but they do not understand that only I can do that. I am the only one on this earth who is still united with you and it is as if you continue to live through me. But Kseniya thinks I am destroying the living in the name of the dead and wants to pray for you as if you were dead, though I happen to know you are alive, only in a different way.

Arseny began thinking. He stroked the bag with the manuscripts and they answered him with a birch-bark rustle.

You know, I am going to the city gates. They are shut at this tyme but yf it will be necessary, an angel will lead me from this cyte.

His gaze fell on the fur coat the prince had given him. He had never even worn it. Despite its grandeur, the fur coat was neither heavy nor cumbersome. Arseny put on the fur coat and strolled around the room. He liked the fur coat. Arseny grew uneasy because he thought he was beginning to value the comfort of expensive things. He stood in the fur coat for about a minute but decided not to take it off after all. If he truly had a journey ahead of him, this sort of fur coat might come in handy. He noticed several more of Christofer's manuscripts on the bench by the door. He did not feel like untying his well-packed bag. Arseny shoved the manuscripts into the pocket of the fur coat and left the house.

Snow was blowing and drifting outside. Arseny felt its prickly touch on his cheeks but saw nothing in the darkness. Not one light was shining in the windows, and that was a good sign: in Arseny's life, lights at night accompanied illnesses and deaths. The darkness did not prevent him from walking. He could have made his way to the city gates with his eyes closed.

It was a little brighter in the open area near the gates. Arseny noticed movement in one corner of the square. After wavering, he went over there. A horse and rider gradually became visible, against the background of a freshly planed fence. Arseny did not know if angels rode horseback. Another horse stood alongside.

Ready? the horseman quietly asked.

Ready, Arseny replied, just as quietly.

The horseman silently motioned to the other horse, and Arseny jumped into the saddle. The horseman started off in the direction of the gates. Arseny followed him. At the gates, the horseman dismounted and knocked at the guard booth. Something sleepy was uttered in response. The horseman entered. A quiet conversation accompanied by the jingle of coins could be heard from the booth. A minute later, several people, the horseman among them, came out of the booth. He got in the saddle again. Two people put a key in a lock and turned it with an unexpectedly loud clank that rolled through the hushed city. Three others pushed on the gates. They opened them, again with a creak, to exactly the distance needed for a horse to pass through. The night wayfarers disappeared through that crack.

The guards are venal, said Arseny's traveling companion, once they were far from the gates.

Arseny nodded, though nobody saw it. His traveling companion said nothing more to him. They soon entered the forest. Only there did it become completely obvious what true darkness is. They were forced to ride slowly; the horses had to feel around to place their hooves. One time a branch hit the stranger's face and he cursed foully. Arseny realized he was not accompanied by an angel. He had suspected that from the first moment they met.

A quarter of an hour later, a second branch knocked the horseman from his saddle. As he fell, he awkwardly splayed his leg, injuring it.

He tried to get up right away, stood on the injured leg, and collapsed to the ground with a groan.

My leg… Son of a bitch, did myself in with all that riding.

Arseny jumped from his horse and went over to the fallen man. He carefully felt his leg.

It's nothing serious, just a dislocation. The main thing is the bone is intact.

The stranger tensed at the sound of Arseny's voice. Arseny felt the leg jolt.

This is easy to deal with, Arseny said to liven him up.

Without saying a word, the other man grabbed Arseny by the hair and pulled him toward himself. Arseny felt a knife at his throat.

Who are you? wheezed the stranger.

Me? Arseny.

I'll slice you up, you lowlife.

Why? asked Arseny.

The question seemed pointless, even to him.

Because my man Stinge was supposed to be in your place. The stranger shook Arseny and the knife lightly cut the skin on his neck. What, you telling me you're Stinge?

No, said Arseny.

Then how'd you end up here, you nit?

You were the one who asked if I was ready.

And what of it?

And I was ready.

Oh, jeez, you… Stinge is going to slice me up next time I see him. Son of a bitch, I didn't just bring you, I brought our money, his and mine… Now he's sitting there thinking I skipped town on him, that's what's so shitty. That's what's so shitty, is what I'm saying!

He shook Arseny again but the knife no longer touched his throat.

Just explain to him that everything is all my fault, said Arseny.

Right, like he's just waiting for my explanations. No, no, I wouldn't even have a damn chance to open my mouth. But I'm going to slice you up before that, you got it?

A certain calming could be felt in his bitter words, though. His change in tone offered a chance for the travelers to reconcile themselves to their circumstances. Arseny gently took away his traveling companion's knife and got to work on his leg. He reset the leg with one jerk as the man briefly shouted.

You could have at least warned me, complained the patient.

It works better without a warning.

The other man got off the ground with Arseny's help and carefully stood on the reset leg:

Seems a little better.

Ride on horseback and do not walk for the time being, said Arseny. It will be completely healed in a few days.

The forest was no longer so dark. This was not yet dawn itself, only its portents. Arseny's traveling companion looked at him with interest.

Maybe this is what had to happen, for Stinge to stay in Belozersk, he said pensively. Maybe it's all for the better.

He took both horses by the bridle and began moving into the depths of the forest.

And you know what, you go the hell away, too. Son of a bitch, I get twitchy when I'm not alone. I'm going to go take a rest away from the road, then tonight I'll slowly be on my way. And you, brother, just leave me the fur coat, you have a nice fur coat.

What? Arseny did not understand.

Take off the fur coat and you can go. You set the leg for me, I'll let you out of this alive. What are you gawking at me for?

The knife glinted in his hand again. Arseny took off the fur coat and held it out to the stranger. The man took off his homespun coat and tossed it to Arseny.

Here, wear this.

He put on the fur coat, checking that it was not tight in the shoulders. He spun around ludicrously in front of Arseny. After thinking a minute, he went to the horse Arseny had been riding and unfastened the leather bag from the saddle, taking a long time. The straps would not come undone. He slit them with a knife and the small bag fell to the ground with a jingle. He picked up the bag and winked.

This is mine, that (he tossed the reins to Arseny) is yours. I don't need the second horse. Go wherever you like, even to Belozersk. You can get some sleep along the way. The horse is from Belozersk, she'll take you right there. And forget about me, you got that?

Arseny did not go to Belozersk. The gates of that city had closed behind him. He knew he would enter them no more. He had felt comfortable in Belozersk and that was exactly why he had fled. That city distanced him from Ustina. Arseny came onto the road and headed in the opposite direction to Belozersk.

He felt downcast as he rode along. Despite his former traveling companion's request, Arseny could not forget him. Arseny was not upset with how his companion had treated him. He was not even upset by the obvious fact that it was not an angel who had led him from the city, something he had, truth be told, dreamed about. Arseny felt agitated as he advanced slowly in an unknown direction. The agitation was seemingly unfounded, but with each minute it grew clearer that the agitation was swirling around the person he had left behind. Arseny knew he could not return, for that person had sent him away. And that person was alone, so he was not twitchy.

After riding for about another hour, Arseny remembered that a few of Christofer's manuscripts, the ones he had put in his pocket at the last minute, were still in the fur coat. He began feeling regret about the manuscripts: it was unlikely they held any value for the new owner of the fur coat. He could have returned them. Arseny grasped that he now had an excuse to see his traveling companion again. And so he turned his horse. He rode back and the agitation intensified.

Arseny dismounted by the place where he needed to leave the road. He tied the horse to a tree and headed into the forest. He already noticed some sort of motion far off, beyond the bare trees. A person was walking around in his fur coat between two horses, but Arseny recognized that he was not the person who had ridden with him that night. They had never met but Arseny recognized the person must be Stinge. Stinge held a cudgel in his left hand. He was most likely a leftie. A few steps later, Arseny saw his traveling companion, too.

He was lying in an unnatural pose on the ground behind one of the horses. He was turned so his face looked up and, for some reason, he was holding one arm behind his back and his legs were convulsively scraping at the ground. One of his heels had dug a shallow trench edged with pine needles. He looked at Arseny with unseeing eyes and in them Arseny could read what awaited this person.

Arseny paid no attention to Stinge as he bent over the dying man. He was no longer moving. Stinge thought for a moment and lowered the cudgel on Arseny's head.

It was darkish in the forest. And difficult to determine if it was sunset or sunrise. Only when it began to lighten a bit was it clear that it was sunrise. Arseny gathered his strength and was able to separate his head from the hard thing it rested upon. It was his traveling companion's body. It was just as cold as the ground.

But I am warm, Arseny said to Ustina. I, who am guilty of his death, am warm and alive. Now I have been saved—only for your sake—but he, like you, is on my conscience. I doomed him with one spoken word. If I had not told him I was ready, he would not be lying here so cold. Arseny remembered Arsenius the Great, who more than once regretted the things he said but never once regretted his silence. From now on, I do not want to speak with anybody but you, my love.

Arseny held onto a tree and stood. There were no horses now. Stinge had most likely taken them. Arseny plodded toward the road. The horse he had tied there still stood in the same place. He untied her and led her into the depths of the forest, grasping the mane so as not to fall. He reeled from side to side.

Arseny sat down to rest when they got to the dead body. Arseny gathered his strength and dragged the dead man toward the horse and tried to lay him across the saddle. The slain man, who would no longer bend, slid off several times. He fell to the ground with a dull, hardened sound. By sheer force of will, Arseny threw the man's arms on the saddle and pressed his head against the man's legs, pushing the body upward. Indifferently balanced, the slain man began wobbling in the saddle. The gaze in his open eyes expressed indifference, too. He had the look of a man who wanted to be left alone.

Arseny managed to sit the corpse in the saddle and turn his face forward. When Arseny could not find anything with which to tie him to the horse, he checked the dead man's boots. In one of them lay the knife the man had threatened him with just the day before. Arseny took off the homespun coat he had been given and began cutting it into thin strips. By tying them together he came up with a fairly long cord. He bound the deceased's legs to the saddle using the cord.

Arseny led the horse onto the road.

You are from Belozersk, he said. Take him there, for there they will commit him to the earth.

The horse gave Arseny a long look and would not get going.

I am not going, said Arseny. He needs you more. He smacked the horse lightly on the rump.

The horse got going, heading in the direction of Belozersk. The dead horseman rode, nestled into her mane. Arseny watched them as they grew more distant and transparent, turning into one large circle that disintegrated into small circles. The circles floated, not coming into contact. When they met, they simply passed through one another. Arseny vomited. His feet no longer held him.

....
....,........................
.... they thought: he is dead, since he did not look alive ....
....
....

Ten days later, Stinge was approaching Novgorod. He himself sat atop one horse; a second horse, without a rider, trotted a little behind him. Four pairs of hooves clopped on the frozen earth with an exaggerated loudness. He rode unhurriedly because he had nowhere to hurry. Stinge thrust his hand into the pocket of the fur coat and pulled out Christofer's manuscripts. He read them, his lips moving.

David sayde: misfortune shal slaye the ungodly. Solomon sayde: your close one will praise you, not your lips. Kirik asked bishop Nifont: should a prayer be carried out over a defiled clay vessel or only over one of wood, and should the rest be smashed? Nifont answered, a prayer may be carried out over anything, the same over a wooden vessel as over clay, or over brass or glass or silver. He who holds to worthy actions cannot be without many enemies. Wealth does not bring a friend but a friend brings wealth. Remember your absent friends when you are with those who are present, that they may hear and know you do not forget them either. All Stinge's friends were absent so he had to remember them alone.

He opened his eyes, they said over Arseny.

He realized, too, that he had opened his eyes. The crossed branches floating above Arseny seemed like a dream. Someone's face sprang up in front of him. It was so big that it blocked the astonishing arch of sky that was floating above him. Arseny saw each of the face's wrinkles and the beard framing the face. A mouth moved within the beard and asked:

What is your name?

So that is how sounds are formed, Arseny thought.

What is your name? the mouth asked again.

He pronounced those four words separately, as if he did not trust the hearing of the man lying there.

Ustin, Arseny said, barely audibly.

Ustin. The face turned to someone. His name is Ustin. What befell thee, O Ustin?

Arseny had tired of looking at the face and so closed his eyes. His whole body sensed soft straw. His hand felt the wooden side of a cart.

Leave him alone, said another voice. We'll bring him to the nearest village, let them sort it all out there.

Arseny opened his eyes again but no longer felt the cart rattling. It was cold. He was lying on something hard. It was similar to firewood. He dragged a log out from under himself and looked at it for a long time. Light through a door ajar. Light and squeaking. A woodshed.

After raising himself a little on his elbow, Arseny saw he was completely undressed. Alongside him lay his bag and some sort of rags. Hesitating, Arseny extended a hand toward the rags but pulled it right back. He felt disgusted. It was not just the filth of the rags that repelled him. It was unbearable to think the person who had undressed him had most likely worn them. That person had not taken—and this was even insulting—the bag with Christofer's manuscripts. Overcoming his revulsion, Arseny extended his hand toward the pieces of fabric, which turned out to be a shirt, trousers, and a belt.

Arseny needed more than clothing, he also needed shoes, for his boots had been taken from him, too. After some thought, he tore the bark off two birch logs and fit the pieces against his feet. He gave the birch bark the proper shape using his teeth. Then he pulled the belt from the rags and began rubbing it against the door frame. When the shabby belt had frayed through into two pieces, Arseny used it to bind the birch bark to his feet. Shod, he caught himself putting off the moment he would dress. He was slow to get dressed, despite shivering.

But he could not leave the shed naked. Arseny took what had once been a shirt and held it against his chest. Hesitating, he put his arms into the sleeves and his head through the hole: the collar had been torn off. The shirt hung on his body like a formless rag. Patches livened up its colorlessness.

It was most difficult to put on the trousers. They turned out to be a bit more intact than the shirt but that only made things worse. As Arseny put on those tatters, he thought that they had touched the thief's indecent member. His trousers were like a bodily closeness to him, and Arseny convulsed with loathing. The theft dispirited him not for the loss of his own clothes but for acquiring someone else's. Arseny was scared that he would abhor his own body from now on; he wept. And then, after it had dawned on him that from now on he would abhor his own body, Arseny began laughing.

He emerged from the shed in an elated mood. After taking several steps in his new clothes, he said to Ustina:

You know, my love, these are essentially my first steps in the right direction since I came to Belozersk.

The shed stood on the edge of a village. Arseny approached the nearest house and knocked at the door. Andrei Magpie lived in the house with his family.

Who are you? Magpie asked Arseny.

Ustin, answered Arseny.

Hey, Ustin, just wait till the trees turn green, Magpie smirked and slammed the door.

Then Arseny knocked at Timofei Pile's door. Timofei looked Arseny over and said:

You will bring in lice: in your position, you cannot not have lice. Or fleas. I think you have a whole bag of them.

The bag contained only Christofer's manuscripts but Arseny did not consider untying it in front of Timofei.

Next was Ivan Skinanbones's house. Ivan remembered the hospitality of Abraham and did not want to send away a pilgrim. But he did not want to let him in, either. He led him to the other end of the village, to the old woman Yevdokia, who was afraid of neither lice, nor fleas, nor strangers.

Yevdokia was chewing the soft part of some bread when they entered. She had no teeth so chewed the soft bread with her gums, which made her entire face move. It just plain bobbed up and down, folding and unfolding, looking like an old leather wallet.

After observing Yevdokia's face for a bit, Ivan said:

Here you go, woman, a guest who says nothing except that he is Ustin. You have to agree that is at least some sort of information.

I am of the opinion that is plenty, nodded Yevdokia.

She tore off half the soft part of the bread and held it out for Arseny.

Eat, O Ustin.

Ivan and Yevdokia silently watched as Arseny ate.

He is hungry, said Ivan.

That is a fact, confirmed Yevdokia. He can stay.

After warming up a little, Arseny could feel his head start to itch. The clothing he had inherited was full of lice. They had come to life in the warmth and begun crawling into Arseny's hair. He sat, feeling the motion of the lice along his neck, from bottom to top. Arseny knew it was difficult to get rid of lice and began feeling sorry for Yevdokia. He did not want to multiply the difficulties in her life. He decided he should not stay here. As Arseny stood, he bowed to Yevdokia from the waist. Yevdokia continued chewing. He went outside and closed the door behind him.

The cold hit Arseny. He was still holding on to the door ring. The desire arose to pull on it and go back inside the warm house. After stepping down from the front steps, though, he realized he was not going back. An early dusk was thickening. Arseny walked, experiencing fear and the cold. And he himself did not understand why he had stepped out of the warmth. All he understood was that a difficult journey awaited him—and it might not even be surmountable. And he did not know where that journey would take him.

Arseny walked along a forest road that was growing ever darker. His legs would not bend in the cold, so he walked as if he were on stilts. Then snow began to fall. It was the first snow of the year and it was falling somewhat uncertainly. At first there were individual snowflakes, few but large. Their fluffiness seemed to make it a little warmer. The snowflakes came down ever more, until they turned into a complete wall, a blizzard. When the blizzard ended, the moon came into sight and everything grew bright. Each bend in the road was visible.

The coldness seemed to intensify when the moon appeared. Arseny thought the moon itself was pouring out the silvery cold that was spreading across the land. He took pity on his chilly body for a while but the pity left him when he suddenly remembered his body was defiled by another's clothes and lice. This was no longer his body. It belonged to the lice, the person who previously wore his clothes, and, finally, the cold. But not to him.

As if I were dwelling in the body of another, thought Arseny.

However much sympathy one might have for another's body, its pain cannot be perceived as one's own. Arseny knew that, having helped infirm bodies. Though he had lived in the pain of others in order to ease it, he could never fathom all its depth. And now the matter at hand concerned a body he did not even sympathize with very much. A body that, for the most part, he despised.

Arseny was no longer cold, for someone dwelling in another's body cannot be cold. Quite the contrary, he markedly felt how his (not his) body had filled with strength and was confidently moving along toward dawn. He was surprised at how firmly he strode and broadly he swung his arms. Waves of warmth rose in spurts from somewhere below and flowed to his head. After he'd fallen to the ground, Arseny did not even notice that his tireless motion had ceased.

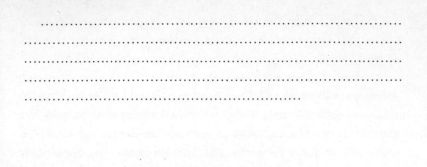

Do I want, thought Arseny, to forget everything and live from now on as if there had been nothing in my life before, as if I had just appeared on earth right now, as a grown-up from the start rather than as a child? Or perhaps: remember only what was good from what I have already lived, since it is typical for the memory to rid itself of what is torturous? My memory keeps abandoning me and next thing you know, it will abandon me forever. But would being freed of my memory become my absolution and salvation? I know it would not and I will not even pose the question that way. Because what kind of salvation would I have without the salvation of Ustina, who was the primary good fortune in my life as well as the primary misery? And so I pray to You: do not take away my memory, where there is hope for Ustina. If you summon me to Yourself, be merciful: pass judgment on her not based on our doings but on my hunger to save her. And register as hers the bit of kindness, which I haue made.

. . . .
. . . .
. . . .

A cow's tongue is soft and does not scorn the lice-ridden. Its rough caress partially replaces human warmth. It is not easy for a person to take care of the festering and lice-ridden. He who enters can leave a crust of bread and a mug of water alongside the ill person, but one can only count on a cow for a true, unsqueamish caress. The cow quickly got used to Arseny and considered him one of her own. She licked dried clumps of blood and pus from his hair with her long tongue.

Arseny observed the sway of her udder for hours and sometimes pressed his lips upon it. The cow (how shall I udder your name?) had nothing against that, though all she took seriously were her morning and evening milkings. Only her mistress's hands brought genuine relief. There was strength in them, unlike Arseny's lips. The urge to squeeze all the milk out into a tightly woven birch-bark container, leaving nothing. The milk burst out of the udder with a loud gurgle, first delicate, almost chirring, but taking on fullness and range as it filled the container. Some of the milk flowed down the mistress's fingers. Watching those fingers twice a day, Arseny remembered them better than the woman's face. He knew what each individual finger looked like but had never once felt their touch.

Sometimes the cow would stand motionless and lift her tail a bit (it quivered), then warm patties would slap onto the cowshed floor right under the tassel of her tail. From time to time, those patties spattered in all directions under a strong stream. Arseny used a clump of hay to wipe off the drops that ended up on his face.

. . . .
. . . .
. . . .

The wound on his head had almost healed but then he had bouts of headaches. The pain came not from the wound but from somewhere in the very depths of his head. It felt to Arseny as if a worm had taken up residence there and that its movements were inducing this torture so difficult to endure. During these bouts, he would grasp his head with his hands or bury his head between his knees. He rubbed his head, frenzied, and the resulting external pain removed the internal pain for a moment. But the internal pain came on right away with new force, as if it had caught its breath. Arseny wanted to split his skull in two and toss out the worm along with his brains. He pounded himself on his forehead and on the top of his head but the worm sitting inside understood perfectly that it could not be reached. The worm's invincibility allowed it to swagger, driving Arseny to wit's end.

....

....

.... They asked Arseny who he was but he kept silent. And he discovered, surprised, that the cow was no longer alongside him.

But where is the cow? Arseny asked the closest of those present. The cow was a splendid comrade and showed me heaven-sent mercy.

Nobody answered him because those who seemed present were absent. The one closest to Arseny—small, hunched, and gray—turned out, upon careful examination, to be a plow handle. The others were also curved and bony. Horse yokes of gigantic sizes. (On whom, one might ask, do they ride here?) Sledge runners. Shafts and milkmaid's yokes for buckets. But the room was completely different.

Interesting, said Arseny, feeling a wagon wheel underneath himself. Interesting that time moves along but I am lying on a wagon wheel, not thinking the slightest bit about the supertask of my existence.

Arseny laboriously stood and went outside the door, stepping unsteadily. The houses in the unfamiliar village lined up before him, their roofs like fluffy hats. Smoke extended from each, into completely calm air. It looked to Arseny as if the smoke plumes had evenly affixed all the houses to the sky. The connecting threads took on an unusual soundness once they lost the mobility characteristic of smoke. Wherever they were a bit shorter than necessary, the houses rose a few *sazhens*. Sometimes they rocked a little. There was something unnatural in that and Arseny's head spun. As he grasped the doorframe, he said:

The connection of sky and earth is not as simple as they have apparently grown used to considering it in this village. This sort of view of things seems excessively mechanistic to me.

Arseny headed right out of the village, squeaking along the freshly fallen snow. A short while later that sound attracted his attention and he looked at his squeaking feet: they were wearing bast shoes.

And they were in birch bark before, Arseny remembered. Now that is transformation for you.

The bag with Christofer's manuscripts was swinging behind his back.

Arseny went from village to village and his memory did not abandon him again. His head ached less; sometimes it did not ache at all. Arseny answered all questions by saying he was Ustin, for that was all that seemed essential at present. It was, however, also obvious to everyone what sort of person he was and how he could be helped. Arseny was no longer the former Arseny. During his time of wanderings, he acquired an appearance that required no explanations whatsoever. Without saying a word, people would give him— or not give him—a place in a shed (a cowshed). They would bring him a piece of bread from warm houses, or not bring it. More often, they brought it. And he grasped that life was possible without words.

Arseny did not know what direction he was moving in, or even if he was moving in one direction. Strictly speaking, he did not need a direction because he was not striving to go anywhere specific. He also did not know how much time had passed since he left Belozersk.

Judging from the easing of the cold weather, spring was coming. Then again, that did not particularly concern him, either. As if dwelling in the body of another, Arseny had grown used to the cold. When he was given a holey but warm homespun coat in the village of Krasnoe, he was already unsure if this thing was necessary. He left the coat by one of the houses in the village of Voznesenskoe, saying to Ustina:

You know, with all this hoarded junk, we will not rise in the wake of our risen Savior. A person has, my love, a lot of unnecessary property and attachments that drag him down. If you happen to be concerned regarding my health, then I am pleased to inform you that—though it may still be cold now—a warming spring is already on the way.

Arseny correctly recognized spring's arrival as he traveled along a road that was softening but not yet fully thawed. He was remembering the joy he had experienced in his previous life at the change in the air. And from the sunbeams, filled with strength, that he felt falling on his face.

One time he began to weep when he saw his own face in a spring puddle. His snarled hair no longer had any color. Clumps of beard were emerging from his sunken cheeks. It was not even a beard but tangled fluff that stuck to his skin in some places, and hung like icicles in others. Arseny cried not for himself but for a time gone by. He understood that now it would not return. Arseny was not even certain of the existence of the earth where he had lived during previous springs. It did, however, still stand in its former place.

Weeping, Arseny came to the city of Pskov. This was the largest of the cities he had seen. And the most beautiful. Arseny did not know its name for he did not ask anyone. As residents of a large city, the Pskovians did not ask Arseny anything, either, and that gladdened Arseny. He had the sense he could get lost here.

He walked along the wall of Pskov's kremlin (*krom*) and was surprised at the might of the wall. Behind a wall like that, Arseny thought, life would go on, by all appearances, calmly and placidly. It was difficult to anticipate that an external enemy could get over its walls. I cannot picture ladders of dimensions large enough for these walls. Or, let us imagine, weapons capable of breaking through that thickness. But (Arseny threw back his head and it felt as if the wall had slowly begun bending toward him) even a wall like that did not preclude the danger of an internal enemy if he were to appear behind that wall. You might say that would be the worst possible thing: now that would truly be a critical situation.

The wall led Arseny to the Velikaya River. Chunks of ice were still drifting along the river, but it was generally open. Ferrymen were assembling people on the shore. Arseny felt drawn to the other shore and boarded the ferry, too.

And did you pay the fare? one of the ferrymen asked Arseny.

Arseny did not answer.

Do not ask him for money, people said to the ferryman, for this is a person of God before you, can you not see?

So I see, acknowledged the ferryman, I asked just in case.

He pressed his pole into the shore and the ferry cast off, its bottom rasping along the sand. In the middle of the river, Arseny lifted his head. Cupolas that had not been visible before showed from behind the kremlin's walls. The setting sun gave them a double gilding. When the main bell struck, it became clear it was ringing from the water because the cupolas on the water were more alive than the cupolas in the sky. Their fine quivering reflected the strength of the sound they generated.

For a long time after getting off the ferry, Arseny admired the view that unfolded in front of him.

You know, my love, I had simply grown unaccustomed to beauty in my life, he told Ustina. And it unfolds so unexpectedly when crossing a river that I cannot even find the right words. And so on one side of the river I am wallowing in scabs and lice, but on the other there is this beauty. And I am glad to accentuate its grandeur with my wretchedness, since in doing so it is almost as if I am a party to its creation.

After it had grown dark, Arseny wandered along the shore. Finally, he stumbled upon a wall. He began walking along the wall and noticed it had a narrow gap. The darkness in the gap was even thicker than the surrounding darkness. Arseny crawled through, groping at the edges of the gap. In front of him there glimmered several oil lamps. The outlines of crosses could be discerned in their dull light. It was a cemetery. What a wonderful place, all the same, thought Arseny. You could not come up with anything better. It is just the right thing for the moment. He took one of the lamps and held his hands over it. The warmth spread through his whole body. Arseny placed his bag under his head and went to sleep. He shuddered in his sleep for a while but then Christofer's manuscripts rustled under his cheek.

He was woken by birdsong. This was real spring singing, though spring's arrival was not yet obvious. Snow lay on some graves. The birds assisted the thaw. To the sound of their song, snow turned to water and seeped down to the deceased, bringing glad tidings of spring to them, too. Spring came earlier to Pskov than to Belozersk. Residents of Belozersk have always considered Pskovians southerners. To this day they continue to consider them southerners.

The cemetery where Arseny had spent the night belonged to a convent. He grasped that when he saw nuns walking around the cemetery. When the sisters asked him who he was, Arseny called himself Ustin, in his usual way. Of course he said no more to them. The sisters informed him that he was on the land of the Convent of the Nativity of Saint John the Baptist. They were not certain Arseny understood them. After conferring, they brought Arseny a dish of fish soup. After Arseny had eaten the soup, they took him by the arms and led him outside the fence.

Arseny wandered along the bank of the Velikaya River all day. When he saw an approaching ferry, he decided to cross the river in the other direction. This time the ferryman did not ask him for money. He said:

Ride, yf thou wylt, O man of God. Me thinketh your visit is good fortune.

Holy fool Foma greeted Arseny on the other shore.

Aha, shouted Foma, I see you are the realest of holy fools. Real. You can rest assured that I have a first-class nose for matters of this sort. But did you know, my friend, that each part of the Pskov soil supports but one holy fool?

Arseny kept quiet. Holy fool Foma then grabbed him by the arm and dragged him away. They were nearly running along the kremlin walls but Arseny saw no chance to halt their movement: Foma turned out to be very tenacious. Another river appeared before them. This was the Pskova, whose waters carried into the Velikaya River.

Out there, beyond the Pskova, said holy fool Foma, lives holy fool Karp. His speech is meager and unintelligible. Sometimes he only announces his name in quickspeache: Karp, Karp, Karp. A very worthy person. Even so, I have to pound his face in, on average, once a month. This occurs on the days when he crosses the river and comes to the city. And I, by inflicting bloody wounds on holy fool Karp, induce him not to leave Zapskovye, the area beyond the Pskova. That is your lot, I teach him, to stay in the Zapskovye part of town. Keep in mind, I tell him, that Zapskovye would be like a lonesome orphan without you, and you'd create an excess of our sort in my part of town. And excess is depravity that leads to spiritual devastation... Come he must, collecting no dust!

Holy fool Foma folded his arms on his chest and looked at the opposite shore. Holy fool Karp threatened him with a fist from the other side.

Go ahead and threaten, you shithead, threaten, shouted holy fool Foma, without malice. If I shall ever see thee here one daye, I will mercilessly smash your members. Like as the smoke vanisheth, so shall you be driven away!

He takes me for a holy fool, Arseny told Ustina.

And who else could you be taken for? said Foma, surprised. Just take a look at yourself, O Arseny. You really are a holy fool, for thou hast chosen a life for yourself that is wild and disparaged by people.

And he knows my christened name.

Foma began laughing:

How could I not know when it is written all over every christened person's face? Of course it is more complicated to guess about Ustin but you yourself are informing everybody about him. So go ahead and holyfool it, dear friend, don't be shy, otherwise they'll all get to you with their reverence in the long run. Their deference is not compatible with your goals. Remember how things were in Belozersk. Do you need that?

Who is this one who knows my secrets? Arseny turned to Foma: Who are you? Who?

A prick wearing one shoe, answered Foma. You are asking about things of secondary importance. But I will tell you the main thing. Go back to Zavelichye, the part of town beyond the Velikaya River, where the John the Baptist Convent stands on the future Komsomol Square. I suspect you already spent the night in the convent cemetery. Stay there and believe me: Ustina could have been in that convent. I think she just never got that far. Though you made it here. Pray for her and for yourself. Be her and be yourself, simultaneously. Be outrageous. Being pious is easy and pleasant, go ahead and make yourself hated. Don't let the Pskovians sleep: they are lazy and incurious. Amen.

Foma drew his arm back and hit Arseny in the face. Arseny silently looked at him, feeling the blood flow from his nose and run down his chin and neck. Foma embraced Arseny and his face got bloody, too. Foma said:

By giving yourself to Ustina, you are, I know, exhausting your body, but disowning your body is only the half of it. As it happens, my friend, that can lead to pride.

What else can I do? thought Arseny.

Do more, Foma whispered right into Arseny's ear. Disown your identity. You have already taken the first step by calling yourself Ustin. So now disown yourself completely.

ΑΙ

Arseny settled in at the cemetery that same day. Near one of its walls, he saw two oaks that had grown entwined: they became the first wall of his new home. The cemetery wall became his second wall. Arseny constructed the third wall himself. While walking along the river, he gathered logs that were lying around, bricks from demolished walls, scraps of nets, and many other objects essential for building. Arseny did not need a fourth wall: there was an entrance there instead.

The nuns kept an eye on the work but said nothing to Arseny. They never heard any words whatsoever from his end, either. The construction was conducted under a mutual tacit agreement. When construction concluded, the convent's abbess, accompanied by several sisters, came to Arseny's home. When she saw Arseny lying on last year's yellow grass, she said:

He who lives here has the earthe as a bed, the heavens as a roof.

Indeed, this cannot be called full-fledged construction, the sisters confirmed.

It is simply that he is building his main home in the heavens, said the abbess. Pray to the Lord for us, O man of God.

By order of the abbess, they brought Arseny a bowl with porridge. Arseny's hands loosened as soon as they felt the warmth of the bowl. The bowl fell with a dull thud but did not smash. The grass slowly swallowed the porridge. The first greenery that made its way through the yellow clumps was noticeable.

This grass, Arseny told Ustina, requires feeding, too. May it grow and bring glory to our little boy.

Afterwards, they brought him porridge more than once, and the same thing happened to it each time. Arseny finished eating only what the grass left for him. He carefully extracted remainders of the food from the grass, raking through it with his fingers. Sometimes dogs ran into the cemetery through the gap and lapped up the porridge with their long, red tongues. Arseny understood that they needed to eat, too, so he did not chase away the dogs. Besides, they reminded him of Wolf, from his childhood. It was as if Arseny was feeding him by feeding the dogs. The memory of him. The dogs ate up what Wolf had not had time to finish. When they would leave, Arseny yelled words of parting after them, asking them to say hello to Wolf.

You are all kin, Arseny shouted, so I think you know how to do it.

When they saw the particulars of Arseny's eating habits, the sisters began laying food out on the grass for him. He would bow, not turning toward them, and he did not watch as they walked away. He was afraid he would not see Ustina's features in the sisters who came to him.

During the first weeks of his life in Pskov, Arseny would get up at sunrise and head out for a walk around Zavelichye. He sized up the people who lived there. He would stop and then fix a special gaze on them: it was the gaze of someone whose state of mind differs from what is generally accepted. He peered behind fences. He pressed his forehead to windows and observed the innermost life of Pskovians. This generally failed to inspire delectation in him.

Smoke mixed with steam inside the houses of Zavelichye. Clothes dried and cabbage soup boiled there. They beat children, yelled at old people, and copulated in the house's common space. They prayed before meals and sleep. Sometimes they collapsed to sleep without a prayer—they had worked so much they lost their strength. Or drunk so much. They cast booted feet on old rags their wives laid on their sleeping benches. Loudly snored. Wiped away spit that trickled when they slept and shooed away flies. Ran a hand over a face, making a grater-like sound. Cursed. Fouled the air with a crackle. All that without waking up.

As he walked along the streets of Zavelichye, Arseny threw stones at pious people's houses. The stones bounced off the logs with a dull wooden thud. Arseny crossed himself and bowed to the residents when they came out of their houses. He walked right up to the houses of the depraved or those who behaved themselves inappropriately. He sank to his knees, kissed the walls of those houses, and quietly said something. And when many people showed surprise at Arseny's behavior, Foma said:

Really, though, what's so surprising here, when it comes right down to it? Our brother Ustin is profoundly correct, for he throws stones only at the houses of the pious. Angels exiled demons from these houses. They are afraid to enter and, as practice has shown, they cling to the corners of houses. Holy fool Foma pointed at one of the houses. Do you see all those demons on the corners?

We do not, answered those who had gathered.

But he does, he answered. And he pelts them with stones. Demons sit inside the houses of the unrighteous because the angels assigned to protect the human soul cannot live there. The angels stand near the house and weep for the fallen souls. So our brother Ustin appeals to the angels and requests they not abandon their prayer, that the souls not perish completely. And you, you sons of bitches, think he's talking to walls...

Holy fool Foma noticed holy fool Karp among his listeners. Karp was sunning his face. He was listening to Foma and smiling vacantly. He was enjoying the warm spring day and his presence in this part of the city. After catching Foma's irate look, Karp remembered he had violated the ban. He tried to hide on the sly, though he understood that was not the simplest of missions. As he hied off to make his way toward the bridge over the Pskova River, Karp began sidestepping to skirt the crowd. He seemed to think sideways motion could conceal his true intentions. Just a few moments later, he noticed Foma had cut him off from the bridge.

Karp, Karp, Karp, blubbered holy fool Karp and went sidestepping off in the opposite direction.

But holy fool Foma turned out to be faster than holy fool Karp. His palm descended on the transgressor's neck with an unnaturally loud slap.

What else could I possibly have expected from this one? Karp shouted, as he set off running toward the bridge.

Foma urged him on with kicks. Karp stopped running after he had reached the middle of the bridge. When his pursuer neared, Karp gave Foma a powerful wallop. Holy fool Foma took it meekly, for this was already holy fool Karp's land.

You are my faithful friends in my struggle with the flesh, Arseny told the mosquitoes. You do not allow the flesh to dictate its conditions to me.

There were a multitude of mosquitoes on the bank of the Velikaya River, where the convent stood. There were even more mosquitoes beyond the cemetery wall, which the shore breeze did not reach, than at the water itself. Nobody had ever seen so many of them. The blood-suckers were the outcome of an unusually hot spring.

A medieval person left only his face and hands uncovered but even that turned out to be enough to deprive Pskov's residents of their patience. Pskovians scratched, spat on their palms and smeared the saliva on their skin, thinking it would ease the suffering caused by the bites. Unwilling to settle for uncovered body parts alone, the raging insects even bit through thick clothing.

The mosquitoes did not distress Arseny, though. On damp, warm nights, when the air turned into a humming blob, he stripped naked and stepped onto the gravestone in front of his house. He experienced an unusual sensation when he ran his hand along his body. It felt as if his skin was covered with thick fur, like Esau's. The growth turned to blood when he touched it. Arseny did not see the blood in the dark but he sensed its scent and heard the crunch of crushed insects. Mostly, though, he paid them no mind, since he diligently prayed for Ustina when he stood there at night.

He stood like that only during the dark hours, times of brief duration, but long enough for a full bloodletting. Arseny, however, was not drained of blood. Whether the mosquitoes had tired of his blood or the bloodsuckers had decided—on account of Arseny's exceptional generosity—to show restraint, his nocturnal standing did not take his life. He was found lifeless on more than one morning, but he ended up recovering each time.

Remove your earthly apparel and clothe thyself with passionless garmentes, said the abbess on those days, turning away from his nakedness.

There were fewer mosquitoes with the passage of time, but Arseny's nocturnal vigil did not cease. It could not cease because night remained Arseny's only tranquil time for prayer. The day was full of cares and worries.

Arseny made the rounds of Zavelichye, keeping an eye on life's flow. He pelted demons with stones and conversed with angels. He knew about all christenings, weddings, and burials. He knew about births of new souls in Zavelichye. When he stood near the home of a newborn, he could foresee its fate. Arseny would laugh if the lifetime appeared to be long. Arseny would weep if the baby must soon die. In those days, nobody but holy fool Foma knew yet why Arseny laughed and wept. Foma was in no rush to explain it to anybody and besides, he was rarely in Zavelichye.

One day holy fool Foma came to Zavelichye and demanded that Arseny follow him across the river.

I need your advice, he told Arseny. This is no simple matter, which is why I am bringing you to my part of the city.

The military officer Perezhoga's baby, Anfim, had taken ill. He was lying in his cradle, silently looking up. Ten pairs of eyes moved in time with the cradle's mute swinging. Close kin had flocked around Anfim's cradle. The child began wailing in despair when Arseny took him in his arms. Arseny's eyes filled with tears and he placed Anfim back in the cradle and lay on the floor. Crossed his arms on his chest. Closed his eyes.

Our brother Ustin sees the child will die, said holy fool Foma. Medicine is powerless.

Anfim stopped breathing at twilight. Holy fool Foma gave Arseny a wallop as he saw him off at the ferry.

That's for showing up in my territory. But it makes you feel better, doesn't it?

At the middle of the river, Arseny nodded. Of course he felt better. In the dim light, dull, flashing sparks were visible on the river's ripples. The largest shaft of light slowly moved along the peak of a wave and Arseny thought this was the departed child's soul, which had come out of the small body so late in the evening.

You still have three nights here ahead of you, Arseny told the soul. It is thought that souls spend their first three days in the place they lived. You know, Pskov is a good city so why not depart the world from here? Take a look: lights are burning in houses on the riverbank, people are getting ready for bed. And the sky is still bright in the west. The clouds are frozen there and their uneven edges are scarlet. They have no intention now of moving until morning. Linden trees are gently quivering in a refreshing evening breeze. In short, it is a warm summer evening. You are leaving all this and that might be scary for you. It was, after all, because of that fear that you wailed when you saw me, right? My look told you death was near. But do not be afraid. I will spend these three days with you, do you want me to, so you will not feel all alone? I live at the convent cemetery, it is a very quiet place.

And so Arseny brought Anfim's soul to the cemetery.

He recited prayers for three days and three nights. As the third day elapsed, Arseny's lips no longer moved but his feeling of love for the child had not waned. And that feeling was telling Arseny: stand vigil. It said: you will fall asleep if you sit on the ground. Arseny did not sit down, though he permitted himself to rest an elbow on the oaks that had grown entwined and formed a wall for his house. He did not want to leave the child alone with his death.

As he parted with Anfim's soul, Arseny whispered:

Listen, I want to ask you a favor. If you meet a little boy there, he is even smaller than you… You will recognize him easily, he does not even have a name. He is my son. You tell… Arseny pressed his forehead to an oak and felt its woodenness pour into him. You give him a kiss for me. Just give him a kiss.

5̄I̅

Here is how mornings began for holy fool Karp. He would stand outside Samson the loaf baker's house, his arms folded behind his back.

Karp, Karp, Karp, holy fool Karp would say to passersby.

When Samson came outside with his hawker tray hanging around his neck, Karp grasped a half-coin loaf with his teeth and sprinted away. He ran very fast for a person holding a loaf in his teeth. He was, by necessity, silent. And did not unlink his arms, which were behind his back. People of modest means ran behind the holy fool because they knew the loaf would eventually fall. When the loaf fell, they would pick it up. Whatever remained in the holy fool's mouth was his daily food.

Baker Samson did not run after holy fool Karp. Even if he had wanted to run, it would have been impossible with his hawker tray. But the baker did not want to run. He was not angry with holy fool Karp:

business was good after his encounters with the holy fool, and his loaves sold out very quickly. If the holy fool was late due to his busyness, loaf baker Samson patiently waited for him by his home in Zapskovye.

Loaf baker Prokhor from Zavelichye was different. He was reputed to be a rather gloomy person and not inclined to hand out loaves. Since Zavelichye was within Arseny's sphere of responsibilities, Arseny happened to run across loaf baker Prokhor. This occurred in late summer.

Arseny was deeply rattled when he saw Prokhor with his loaves. He looked at Prokhor up close and his look grew ever more bitter.

What dost thou need, O holy fool? asked Prokhor.

Without uttering a word, Arseny struck Prokhor's hawker tray from below. The loaves jumped off the tray, all at once, thudding into the August dust. Passersby wanted to brush off the loaves and take them for themselves, but Arseny would not allow it. He began breaking loaf baker Prokhor's goods into small pieces, kicking and stomping them into the dust. Only when the loaves had been transformed into clumps of dirt did Prokhor seem to come to life. He moved slowly toward Arseny and each blow was like a loaf. He struck Arseny in the face with those blows, without making any special preparatory swings. Arseny fell to the ground and the loaf baker kicked him.

Do not touch him, he is a man of God, shouted passersby.

And scattering my loaves around, does a man of God do that? And stomping them with his feet, does a man of God do that?

With each question, loaf baker Prokhor struck Arseny with his foot. Arseny lay there, bouncing like a pile of rags with each strike. He might well have been a pile of rags, for hardly any of his body remained. Shrieking, the loaf baker jumped on Arseny's back with both feet and everyone heard ribs crack. The gathered men then threw themselves at loaf baker Prokhor and twisted his arms behind his back. Someone bound them with a belt. The strong Prokhor tried to shake off those who had bound him so he could go after Arseny again.

Go away, O man of God, the people told Arseny.

But Arseny did not go away. He did not move. He lay there, his arms stretched out, and a reddish-brown puddle spreading under his hair. Everyone was watching loaf baker Prokhor, who was calming down, bit by bit. Holy fool Foma was walking from the direction of the ferry.

From now on, your name is not loaf baker but blow-maker, Foma shouted at Prokhor. And now I will acquaint you, you shits (he looked around at those standing there), with the following facts. Yesternight, this mutt copulated with his wife. Then he kneaded dough and shaped his loaves without cleansing. In the morning he wanted to sell this impure product to Orthodox people and, if it had not been for our brother Ustin, he would have sold them, as sure as certain.

Is that true? asked those present.

Loaf baker Prokhor did not answer but his silence was already an answer. Everyone knew holy fool Foma spoke only the truth. They decided to take Prokhor away to the cellar prison. They postponed his punishment until Arseny's fate had been determined. They said:

Yf a man of God dies, this sinne shall be on thee.

They laid Arseny on bast matting and headed for the John the Baptist Convent.

The sisters wept upon meeting them at the convent gates, for they had become attached to Arseny. They already knew of the misfortune that had occurred. Taking the mat by its edges, the sisters carefully carried Arseny through the convent so as not to inflict needless pain upon him. But Arseny was not in pain: he felt nothing. The sisters tried to walk with small steps and in rhythm as they carried him; Arseny's head jiggled slightly.

The abbess said:

A stranger to your own people, you endured everything with joy for the sake of Christ, searching for an ancient, perished fatherland.

The abbess's face was covered by her hands and her voice was muffled but intelligible.

They had emptied a remote cell for Arseny, where the presence of a male could not embarrass any of the pilgrims. The sisters themselves were not embarrassed since the holy fool Ustin was sexless in their eyes and, to some extent, incorporeal. As they carried the patient to the faraway cell, they hoped for his recovery and prepared for his departure.

It should be stated, with some bitterness, said the abbess, that the injured person's injuries are extremely critical. Death, however, is not a completely unfamiliar topic for our brother Ustin: our brother Ustin is already deade within his living body. The holy fool Ustin goes about, worthie already of mourning, however the person within him has been restored to life. After living without a home, he, our brother, will have his tentes pitched in heven.

In the event of a mortal outcome, the sisters had designated for Arseny the spot by the cemetery wall where he had settled back in the spring. To them, Arseny's dwelling almost seemed to be a ready crypt. A cozy and habitable structure.

31

But Arseny survived. He regained consciousness a few days later and his bones began knitting together, bit by bit. Arseny felt their knitting just as unmistakably as he had felt them break earlier. It was soundless but obvious.

The sisters fed Arseny with a spoon. He silently opened his mouth and tears streamed down his cheeks. Tears streamed down the sisters' cheeks, too. They asked the carpenter Vlas to wash Arseny, who could not stand.

On the first of September, holy fool Foma came to see Arseny and wish him a happy new year. He brought a dead rat as a gift: Foma held the rat by the tail and it swung sorrowfully back and forth.

After laying the rat at Arseny's headboard, holy fool Foma pressed its front paws against its snout and turned to the patient:

I am heartily glad, colleague, that you did not take on a wretched appearance such as this. After all, everything was headed in that direction. And so I wish you a happy new year, 6967, which we are celebrating for old time's sake on this bright September day, thirty-three years before the seven thousandth year.

The sisters were displeased by the arrival of the rat but they dared not object to Foma. And their anger ceased when they saw Arseny's smile. This was his first smile in many months. He sneezed when holy fool Foma tickled his nostrils with the tip of the rat's tail.

The patient needs fresh air, Foma shouted, but—and do forgive me—it's as stale in here as inside the Devil's ass. Haul him to the river. Water and air flow there. It will aid his recovery.

The abbess turned away and rolled her eyes but signaled to the sisters to carry out the holy fool's instructions. They moved the patient (Arseny began moaning) onto a piece of canvas that they (he moaned again) carefully lifted.

Whimper and whine, bitch and moan, snorted holy fool Foma, and the abbess turned away again.

The sisters carried Arseny out to the river. Foma indicated the place where they should position the patient. Taking all precautions, they settled Arseny on the grass.

And now get your asses out of here, you tarts, holy fool Foma told the sisters.

The sisters headed in the direction of the convent without a word. The wind fluttered the hems of their habits and Arseny and Foma watched them go. The way the sisters retreated showed they were not, essentially, offended by holy fool Foma. Almost not offended.

After the sisters had disappeared behind the gates, holy fool Foma said:

I carried out your request with regard to Prokhor. If I understood you correctly across the river, you did not want the authorities to punish him.

I simply prayed for him, Arseny told Ustina. I requested: O Lord, laye not this synne to his charge, for he knoweth not what he creates. You pray for him, too, my love.

Holy fool Foma nodded:

As far as your prayer goes, people in Zavelichye are already well aware of what's going on, I told them about it. (He motioned with his hand toward the Zavelichye residents who had managed to gather, and they confirmed what had been said.) I'm just afraid this isn't the last of these prayers for you. Your clock will be cleaned again, my friend, more than once.

Not necessarily, objected the residents. Everyone in Rus' knows that you're not, like, you know, allowed to beat holy fools.

Foma burst into loud laughter.

I will resort to a paradox to illustrate my thought. People beat holy fools precisely because they are not supposed to beat them. It's common knowledge, after all, that anyone who beats a holy fool is a bad guy.

Well, who else could they be? agreed the residents of Zavelichye.

That's exactly it, said holy fool Foma. And a Russian person is pious. He knows a holy fool should endure suffering so he goes ahead and sins to supply him with that suffering. Somebody has to be the bad guy, right? Somebody should be capable of beating or maybe, let's say, killing a holy fool, what do you think?

Well, like, you know, said the concerned Zavelichye residents. Beating might not always be so bad, but killing, is that really piousness? It is a mortal, if it can be put that way, sin.

Screw that, exclaimed holy fool Foma in a fit of pique. A Russian person, after all, is not simply pious. Just in case, I can report to you that he is also senseless and merciless and anything he does can easily turn into a mortal sin. But the line here is so fine that you, you bastards, wouldn't understand.

The residents of Zavelichye did not know how to respond. Holy fool Karp, who was standing in the crowd, did not know, either. He was listening to holy fool Foma in utter bewilderment, his mouth agape.

Aha, and you're here, you sinner, shouted holy fool Foma, and then holy fool Karp began weeping. I haven't popped you in the face for a while.

Foma began making his way toward Karp but Karp was already walking backward, in the direction of the convent, and the crowd parted in front of his back.

O, wo is me, shouted holy fool Karp.

Once he'd broken away from the crowd, he rushed off toward the convent gate. The gate turned out to be closed. Karp drummed on it with all his might and watched in horror as Foma drew closer. Karp put his hands behind his back and rushed off for the river before the gates had opened. Foma ran past after the gate opened. Foma stuck out his tongue at the sisters, who were peering from the gate, and ran along. The sisters exchanged looks; they were used to not being surprised.

Didn't I tell you to sit tight in your Zapskovye? holy fool Foma yelled to holy fool Karp.

Karp covered his face with his hands and kept on running. His bare feet slapped noisily on the grass. He stopped at the very edge of the river. When he took his hands away from his face, he saw Foma was catching up to him.

Karp, Karp, Karp, shouted holy fool Karp.

He stepped onto the water's surface and carefully began walking. The waves on the Velikaya River were not high that day, despite a blustery wind. At first Karp walked slowly, as if he were uncertain, but his stride gradually quickened.

Foma ran up to the river and tested the water with one of his big toes. He shook his head in distress but also stepped onto the water. Arseny and the Zavelichye residents silently observed the holy fools walking, one after the other. They bounced lightly on the waves, ludicrously waving their arms to maintain their balance.

Apparently they can only walk on water, said the residents. They have not yet learned to run.

Holy fool Karp stopped in the middle of the river. He waited for holy fool Foma and then struck him on the cheek with all his

might. The slap's resonance floated along the water to those standing on shore.

He has the right, the Zavelichye residents said, shrugging. This is
his territory, after all.

Holy fool Foma turned around without saying a word and headed
toward his part of the city. The rays of a low autumn sun emphasized
the uneven flow of the river. A mirror-like surface alternated with
ripples and waves. If one gazed at the water long enough, the river
seemed to begin flowing in the opposite direction. Perhaps because it
reflected the flight of clouds. The two small diverging figures glided
in time with the overall movement of the river's surface. Only Arseny
and the residents of Zavelichye surrounding him remained in their
places.

As winter drew closer, Arseny was already walking well. His bones had
knitted together and all that reminded him of his illness was the weakness that sometimes seized him. Arseny returned to his home at the
cemetery when he began feeling better. The sisters tried to convince
him to stay in the faraway cell but he was adamant.

Blessed be thou, O pilgrim and homeless one, the abbess said, and
let Arseny go to his chosen place of residence.

When Arseny returned to the entwined oaks, he realized he had
become unaccustomed to a difficult life. He mourned as lost the weeks
he spent in the cell, for they had forced him to pay attention to his body.
They had, in essence, left Arseny cold and he could not find a way to

get warm in the first days after his return. He tirelessly whispered to himself that it was as if he were in the body of another, but that was of no immediate help. It helped four days later.

On the seventh day, loaf baker Prokhor came to him. He silently took a loaf out from under his shirt and fell to his knees before Arseny. Arseny, who was standing next to his residence, approached loaf baker Prokhor. He knelt alongside him and embraced him. And he took the loaf from his hands.

I fasted for seven days, said Prokhor.

Arseny nodded because he knew this from the form of the loaf and its fragrance.

Forgive me, O blessed Ustin, wept loaf baker Prokhor.

Arseny touched Prokhor's cheek and one of Prokhor's tears remained on his index finger. He rubbed the edge of the loaf with it. Arseny took a bite from the loaf where it had absorbed Prokhor's tear. After chewing what he had bitten, Arseny stood up and helped the loaf baker up. He made the sign of the cross over him and sent him homeward. After loaf baker Prokhor had disappeared through the gap, Arseny took the loaf and made his way outside. People of modest means stood at the convent wall. Arseny broke the loaf into pieces and gave it to them.

From that day on, loaf baker Prokhor called on Arseny fairly frequently. He brought a loaf each time, sometimes more than one. Arseny took the loaves gratefully. After Prokhor left, he took them to the convent wall and gave them to people of modest means.

With time, however, it was not only they who awaited the loaves from Arseny. People came from the city and from Zapskovye and many of them were considered well-to-do. These people were not tormented by hunger but they knew the loaves from Arseny's hands were unusually tasty and wholesome. They had observed that these loaves imparted strength, stopped bleeding, and improved the metabolism.

One day Pskov's mayor, Gavriil, came to Arseny after hearing about the distribution of loaves. Gavriil received half a loaf and headed back home with it. He, his wife, and their four children of various ages ate the bread he had received. They liked the bread and they felt better, though, essentially, they had felt pretty good before the bread, too.

Now this is a phenomenon worthy of all kinds of support, said Mayor Gavriil.

He set off to see Arseny and, in the presence of the sisters, presented him with a wallet of silver. To Mayor Gavriil's surprise, Arseny accepted the wallet. As he left, the mayor had someone remain at the convent to see how the holy fool would handle the funds that had been presented to him. In the evening of that same day, the person came to Mayor Gavriil and reported to him that holy fool Ustin had gone straight to merchant Negoda. It was noted separately that the holy fool entered the merchant's with the wallet in his hands but left without the wallet.

Mayor Gavriil then went to visit Arseny again and asked why he had given the money to a merchant rather than a beggar. Arseny looked silently at the mayor.

What's not to understand here? asked a surprised holy fool Foma, who stood in the gap in the wall. Merchant Negoda is broke and his family is wasting away from hunger. And he's ashamed to solicit alms because of his uprightness. He'll put up with it, the damn tomcat, until he kicks the bucket—he and his family. And so Ustin gave him the money. Paupers can feed themselves: begging, after all, is their profession.

Mayor Gavriil marveled at Arseny's wisdom and asked:

And you, O brother Ustin, what is necessary for thy life? Ask me and I will geue you a good rewarde.

Arseny was silent and then holy fool Foma said:

If I chose for him, will you geue the rewarde?

Mayor Gavriil answered:

I will geue it.

Then geue him the great burg of Pskov, said holy fool Foma. And sufficient it shall be for his sustenance.

The mayor did not utter another word, for he could not give the entire city away to Arseny. And holy fool Foma began laughing when he saw Mayor Gavriil's distress:

Take it easy; jeez. If you can't give him the city, then don't. He'll get it without you anyway.

The ensuing winter was dreadful. Neither the Pskovians nor, even more so, Arseny could remember a winter like it. Admittedly, Arseny did not remember how many winters had passed since his arrival in Pskov. Maybe one. Or maybe all the winters had blended into one and no longer had anything to do with time. They just become winter.

First, snow covered the city. The snow fell day and night, and its abundance in the air and on the earth was stunning. It turned God's world into a single milky clump. Cowsheds, houses, and even small churches were snowed under. They turned into huge snowbanks, sometimes with crosses visible at the top. The snow crushed the roofs of old houses and they collapsed with a dry crack. People found themselves under open skies from which the snow unceasingly floated, filling the damaged houses in the course of a day. Snow fell for three weeks and then a cold snap hit.

The cold snap was relentless. The wind, which could not be escaped, tripled the force of the cold. The wind knocked pedestrians off their feet, stole in through door cracks, and whistled from between logs that had not been firmly set. Birds perished from the wind in mid-air, fish froze to death in small rivers, and wild animals fell in the forests. Even people who had warmed themselves with fire could not tolerate the bitter cold, the body being feeble. Many people and cattle froze at that time, in the city, the surrounding villages, and on the roads. In enduring great adversities, beggars and those who were pilgrims for the sake of Christ lamented from the depths of their hearts and wept bitterly and shivered unceasingly and froze.

By order of the abbess, they moved Arseny into the faraway cell, where he was commanded to wait out the ferocious bitter cold. After three days elapsed, Arseny left the faraway cell and returned to his home in the cemetery. He responded with silence to all attempts to persuade him to stay inside.

You understand, he told Ustina, my flesh warms up in the faraway cell and begins making its own demands. There's no use starting anything, my love. If you give your flesh a finger, it will grab an entire hand. It really is better, my love, that I spend some time in the fresh air. I guess I will go walking around Zavelichye to keep from freezing. I will watch what is happening in this big wide world of ours, though it looks less wide than white, more than ever before.

So Arseny began walking around Zavelichye. And when he encountered freezing people or drunk people or those inclined to fall asleep in a snow bank, he led them off to their homes. If someone had no home, he brought that person to a home for the impoverished, which had been set up for the cold spell in an old shed near the walls of the convent.

One day, as he was walking along the frozen river, Arseny saw holy fool Foma on the river, and Foma said to him, from the ice:

My kind friend, the border between the city's various parts has now been erased by natural means. It should be stated that the barrier that divided us is hidden temporarily under ice of an unprecedented thickness. If you wish to gather up these frozen elements on my territory, too, I shall saye nothinge against it.

After hearing holy fool Foma's statement, Arseny stopped limiting himself to Zavelichye. He went to the city and even to Zapskovye, where holy fool Karp resided. Prints of bare feet radiating from the John the Baptist Convent spoke to this. The new tracks that revealed themselves each morning showed Pskovians where Arseny had been the night before.

One time, Arseny brought a night wanderer back to his home. The man was leaving a tavern and his strength was almost gone. He sat down in the road often, demanding Arseny leave him alone. When that happened, Arseny had to use force and drag the unknown man through the snow. This was no smooth glide: the unknown man, laughing, scraped at the snow with the toe of his boot during the first part of the journey. An hour later he was chilled to the bone and merriment had deserted him. He silently trudged after Arseny, mean and significantly sobered.

They walked in circles through the hamlets outside the city in search of his dwelling. As midnight neared, the moon settled matters by showing itself in the sky. After identifying one of the drifted snowbanks as his house, the unknown man decisively headed for the front steps. He went up the steps and slammed the door behind him just as decisively.

Arseny looked around. All the roaming had disoriented him and now he could not figure out which direction the city was in. The moon clouded over again. Arseny understood that even the house would be lost to him if he took a few steps away. He sensed that he could also no longer get by without warmth.

Now is the sort of moment, my love, when I need to stay in the warmth, even if only for an hour, Arseny told Ustina. You need not worry about me: as you can see, nothing terrible is happening. I need only catch my breath, my love, and then I can make my way back.

Arseny tried to smile but realized he could not feel either his lips or his cheeks. He wavered and then returned to the house and went up the icy front steps. He knocked at the door. Nobody opened it so he knocked again. The door opened. His acquaintance stood on the doorstep. He stepped back as if freeing the space for Arseny. Arseny was despondent when he realized this person truly needed a running start. The man ran up with a shriek, knocking Arseny from the front steps with both arms.

The moon was shining again when Arseny came to. He took a handful of snow and rubbed his frozen face. The snow he tossed away was bloody. Arseny caught sight of the silhouettes of distant houses in the moonlight. He set off for them, staggering. The houses were rundown and Arseny knew poor people lived in them. When he knocked, people came out with sticks. They said:

Go away and die, O holy fool, we find no way to save ourselves from you here.

Arseny left after finding no compassion among these people. He set off, walking past houses, and noticed a ramshackle shed at the end of the street. Once his eyes had grown used to the dark, he could make out several pairs of eyes in the corner of the shed. The eyes reflected the moonlight penetrating through gaps in the roof. Several large dogs were watching Arseny, who got on all fours and crawled toward them. The dogs growled, muffledly, but brought Arseny no harm. He laid down between them and dozed off. There were no dogs alongside him when he awoke.

That is how vile I have become, Arseny told Ustina. God and man have left me. And even the dogs want nothing to do with me, either, so they left. My body, all dirty and turned blue, is loathsome, even for me. This all indicates that my bodily existence is pointless and nearing its end. Meaning, my love, you will not be pardoned because of my prayers.

Arseny crouched, grasped his head in his hands, and buried it in his knees. He was aware that he could no longer sense either his head or his hands or his knees. All he could feel, weakly, was his heart. Only his heart had not been shackled by the cold, because it was located deep within his body. It is good, Arseny thought, that I have already bid farewell to a part of my body. From the look of things, it will be far easier to bid farewell to what has not yet frozen.

As Arseny had that thought, he sensed warmth gradually filling him from within. After opening his eyes, he saw before him a young man with a splendid appearance. His face shone like a sunbeam and in his hand he held a branch scattered with scarlet and white flowers. The branch did not look like branches from the decaying world and its beauty was unearthly.

The splendid young man asked, holding the branch in his hand:

O Arseny, where dost thou now endure?

I sit in darkness, shackled by iron in the shadowe of death, answered Arseny.

Then the young man struck Arseny on the face with the branch and said:

O Arseny, take invincible life for your whole body and the cleansing and the ceasing of your sufferings from this great bitter cold.

And with those words, the fragrance of the flowers and life— granted to him a second time—entered Arseny's heart. When he raised his eyes, he discovered the young man had become invisible. And Arseny understood who that young man was. He remembered the life-giving verse: Wher the Lord wills it, the natural order is overcome. Because according to the order of nature, Arseny should have died. But he was scooped up and returned to life as he was flying off toward death.

From then on, time definitively began moving differently for Arseny. More precisely, it simply stopped moving and remained idle. Arseny saw events taking place on earth but also noticed that events had, in some strange way, diverged from time and no longer depended on time. Sometimes events came one after another, just as before; sometimes they took a reverse order. Rarer still, events arrived in no order whatsoever, shamelessly muddling prescribed sequences. And time could not cope with them. It refused to govern those sorts of events.

It has become known here that events do not always flow along in time, Arseny told Ustina. Now and again they flow on their own. Uprooted from time. Of course you, my love, already know this very well but I am encountering it for the first time.

Arseny observes the spring snow melting and the cloudy waters flowing down to the Velikaya River through the gutter the sisters have hollowed from wood. The sisters clear out this gutter every spring because it clogs with leaves—oak and maple—in autumn. The wind sweeps leaves into Arseny's home, too, but Arseny does not object to this sort of feather bed since he considers it not made by human hands.

Arseny sees how an early June sun peers out after a night rain. Water is still quivering on leaves. Water detaches, as clouds of steam, from the John the Baptist cupola and disappears in an improbably blue sky. Sister Pulcheria leans on her broom and observes the water evaporate. A warm wind touches the wheaten locks of hair that have come out from under her wimple. Sister Pulcheria is pensively scratching a beauty mark and dying from blood poisoning. She is lying in a fresh grave a few *sazhens* from Arseny's home. Her grave is drifted with snow.

The abbess approaches Arseny at the height of the autumn leaf season. She says:

The time commeth for me to departe from this vayne worlde for the never old, eternal dwellinge. Bless me, O Ustin.

Leaves glide along her vestments with a rustle. Arseny gives his blessing to the abbess.

Even as he does so, he tells Ustina, I have no right to bless someone. And so, my love, I am doing this not because I have the right but from impudence, since this woman requests it. Beyond that, her journey truly is distant, and she knows it.

The abbess is dying.

On a hot summer day, Sister Agafya leans on her broom, standing by the church of John the Baptist. She looks at the church's cupola and her hand stretches for a beauty mark on her face. Arseny stops Sister Agafya's hand halfway. He did so in time.

She will live, Arseny thinks as he walks away.

With a steady gait, he walks into the building, to priest John. He jolts the door open. The rough tongue of bitter cold barges in behind Arseny. Priest John and his family are sitting at the table. The priest's wife is preparing to put food on the table. She peers out the blurry window: there is nothing outside but snow. Priest John stares straight ahead, as if he is trying to spot his own impending fate. The priest's wife gestures silently, inviting Arseny to share the meal with them. The gesture separates itself from the priest's wife and flies out the open door. Arseny does not notice it. The children squeeze onto the bench and focus their gaze on their hands, which rest on their knees. Then their fingers tug at the coarse linen of their shirts. To them, Arseny is similar to the lightning ball their father once saw. Their father taught them that when a lightning ball flies in, it is best not to move and not to give yourself away. Best to exhale and be still. They are still. Arseny grabs a knife off the table and lunges at priest John. Priest John continues staring ahead, as if he does not notice Arseny. In reality, he sees everything but considers it unnecessary to resist fate. Arseny waves the knife right in front of priest John's face. As before, the priest does not move; perhaps he is thinking about the lightning ball. About how it found him anyway. Arseny tosses the knife to the floor and runs out of the house. Priest John feels no relief. He understands that what has happened is prophesy. It is only heat lightning but he is waiting for the lightning bolt to arrive. And he guesses that this time it will not be so easy for it to miss.

Arseny is walking around in Zapskovye, where little boys lie in wait for him. They knock him down, onto the boards of the roadway. Several pairs of hands press him into the boards, though he does not resist. The boy whose hands remain free nails the edges of Arseny's shirt to the boards. Arseny watches the boys laugh and then he laughs, too. He laughs along with them each time the boys nail his shirt to the roadway. And he silently asks God not to cast blame on them for this. He could neatly tear his shirt away from the nails but does not. Arseny wants to do something nice for the boys. He abruptly stands and the hem of his shirt tears away with a loud rip. The boys are rolling on the ground with laughter. For the rest of the day, Arseny searches the trash for scraps of fabric and sews them on to replace the torn-off hem. The boys laugh even more when they see the new patches on his shirt.

It gets quiet when they run away. Only one boy remains, and he approaches Arseny and embraces him. And weeps. Arseny's heart sinks because he knows this boy pities him but is embarrassed to show it in front of the others. He wants the boy to be joyful because he recognizes the features of another child in this boy's features. And Arseny weeps, too. He kisses the boy on the forehead and runs away because his heart is ready to burst. Arseny chokes on his sobs. He runs and the sobbing shakes him and tears fly from his cheeks in all directions, sprouting all sorts of humble plants on the roadside.

The Velikaya River rises in the spring and the wooden roadways float in places. It is muddy in Zapskovye. The priest John wades through the mud on his way home. He hears the juicy squishing of mud behind his back. He slowly turns. In front of him stands a person covered in mud, holding a knife. Priest John silently presses his hand to his chest. A recollection of Arseny's premonition flashes in his head. In his heart there sounds a prayer that he has no time to pronounce. The person inflicts twenty-three knife blows. With each swing of his arm, he grunts and groans from the strain. Priest John is left to lie in the mud. The person's tracks are lost in that very place. They say it is as if there was not even a person, only a muddy splash. Which leapt up behind priest John's back and immediately spread along the road. A short while later an inhuman shriek is heard. It floats across the Velikaya River and the Pskova River, extending over the entire city of Pskov. It is the priest's wife shrieking.

People come from Mayor Gavriil. They say:

You, O Ustin, are an unusual person and your visits are salutary. The mayor's wife's teeth have been aching for three weeks now, might you help her? Many doctors have already come to her but brought no real relief. The mayor asks you to come to his house, too, hoping for your help.

Arseny looks at his visitors from Mayor Gavriil. They are waiting. They say the mayor's wife could have come to the cemetery herself but, as it happens, she does not feel like coming to the cemetery. Arseny shakes his head. He thrusts his hand into his mouth, pulls a wisdom tooth out of his gums, and presents it to the visitors. They understand that this is, itself, the blessed man's answer to their request. Taking all due care, they bring Arseny's tooth to the mayor's wife. The mayor's wife places it in her mouth and the toothache goes away.

Mayor Gavriil and his suite come to see Arseny. He brings expensive clothing to Arseny and asks him to don it. Arseny dons it. He and Mayor Gavriil are each given a goblet of wine from another land. The mayor drinks and Arseny bows, turns to the northeast, and slowly empties his goblet onto the ground. The flowing wine forms a spiral as it falls, its polished facets glimmering. The grass thirstily soaks up the precious liquid. The sun is at its zenith. Mayor Gavriil scowls.

How can it be, holy fool Foma asks the mayor, that you don't understand why God's servant Ustin emptied your wine to the northeast?

The mayor does not understand and is not even inclined to hide that fact.

Well now, my dear man, says holy fool Foma, you are simply not aware of the news that on this daye there is a fire in Novgorod and God's servant Ustin is striving to extinguish it, using makeshift methods.

Mayor Gavriil sends his people to Novgorod to make conclusive inquiries regarding what occurred. Upon their return, these people report to Mayor Gavriil that on the morning of the aforesaid day, an extremely powerful fire truly did break out but then died down around noon, through some power unfathomable to the Novgorodians. The mayor does not answer at all. He signals to the visitors to go out and they leave, bowing. The mayor lights an icon lamp. The muffled words of his prayer carry to those standing outside the doorway.

Arseny is walking to a hostelry in the clothes that were given to him. The hostelry's patrons undress Arseny with the intention of drinking for three days and three nights with the money the clothing fetches. Arseny has a small bundle of old clothes with him and puts them right on. He sighs with relief. The hostelry guests order their first mug. When Arseny sees this, he knocks the mugs out of their hands. The mugs roll with a tinny sound, spilling their contents on the floor. The guests order a second round but Arseny again does not let them drink. One of them wants to hit Arseny in the face but the hostelry keeper bids him not to do so. The hostelry keeper knows he would be the one answering for beatings and so kicks the patrons out. The patrons call it a night and go home, sober and with money in their pockets. When they return home, their kin take away the money and are unable to find any rational explanation for its appearance. They remain completely bewildered.

And do you know, holy fool Foma asks Arseny, how many years have passed since you showed up here?

Arseny shrugs.

Well, you don't need to know that anyway, says holy fool Foma. Live outside time for now.

Arseny tosses clods of mud at several venerable residents of Zapskovye. He can faultlessly discern small and large demons behind their backs. The residents are displeased.

There is consolation only in the fact, Arseny informs Ustina, that the demons are even more displeased.

Sometimes he throws stones at church doors. Ample quantities of demons throng there, too. They do not dare enter the churches and so huddle around the entrance.

When she sees how Arseny prays at night, the new abbess says:

During the dayes, God's servant Ustin laughs at the worlde, at nyghte he mourns the same worlde.

Evpraksia, a carpenter's daughter, is brought to Arseny at the monastery. A ceiling beam in the granary fell on her two months ago and she has been lying motionless ever since. Her affliction does not allow her to return to life but does not release her into death, either. And those around Evpraksia cannot understand which of those conditions she is closer to.

Evpraksia is assigned to a guest cell and prayers are recited over her there. On days with nice weather, she is carried out into the monastery yard, where prayers are recited in fresh air. The wind blows at Evpraksia's hair but she herself remains motionless. Arseny approaches Evpraksia's bed in the yard. He takes Evpraksia by the hand.

Life has not fully left her, Arseny tells Ustina. I sense that she may wake up. She only needs help to do so.

Arseny places his palm on Evpraksia's forehead. His lips move. Evpraksia opens her eyes. She sees Arseny and the sisters surrounding her. It is a warm summer day. The shadows of the trees are sharply drawn. They shift in time with the sun's movement. The linden leaves are sticky and barely tremble in the wind.

We are celebrating Evpraksia's return, says the new abbess, but we remember, too, that it is temporary, for everything on this earth is temporary.

I had wanted to speak with her at least one more time, says carpenter Artemy. And now I will speak with her constantly. Meaning, of course, temporarily. I weep at the thought of the boundless mercy of God and the grace that has descended upon God's servant, Arseny. And all of us standing here (without exception) are capable of inhaling the smells of a warm summer day and hearing the birds chirp. All of us, without exception, because my daughter Evpraksia might have been that exception if not for Arseny.

Carpenter Artemy kneels before Arseny and kisses his hand. Arseny pulls his hand back and crosses the Velikaya on the ice and ends up in Zapskovye. Loaf baker Samson takes out his goods in the early morning. He waits for holy fool Karp, who should steal one of his loaves. Holy fool Karp shows up, grasps a half-coin loaf and, with his arms behind his back, dashes off, away from loaf baker Samson. The loaf baker smiles a kind, loafy smile. The steam from his mouth settles on his beard like frost. He runs his hand through his beard and says:

A man of God, you understand. A blessed man.

The loaf baker lacks the words (as always) to fully express his feelings. Holy fool Karp (as always) drops the loaf and people of modest means pick it up. Karp chews what remains in his mouth.

When his mouth is freed up, he shouts:

Who will be my traveling companion to Jerusalem?

The people picking up the loaf are perplexed. They say:

Our Karp is holyfooling it. Who would go from Pskov to Jerusalem?

Who will be my traveling companion to Jerusalem? holy fool Karp yells to those gathered.

Those who have gathered answer:

Jerusalem, that is, like, you know, really far. How do you get there?

Holy fool Karp looks at Arseny, unblinking. Arseny is silent but does not turn. He has a lump in his throat. He wants to get a good look at holy fool Karp, that is what he came for. Karp cringes, shrinks his head down into his shoulders, and leaves.

Karp, Karp, Karp, he says pensively.

The weakened Davyd is being carried to the monastery. Davyd has been sick since the dayes of his youth. He is unable to move and cannot even hold up his head. Davyd's head must be lifted when he is fed porridge. Sometimes the porridge falls from his mouth. Then it is picked from his chin with a spoon and again directed toward his mouth. They are carrying Davyd to the monastery cemetery. They carefully place him on the burial mound next to Arseny's home. They say:

Helpe us, O Ustin, if thou canst.

Arseny does not reply. With his bare hands, he picks nettles from the graves, gathering them into a bunch. When the bunch is ready, Arseny lashes the visitors on their faces and on their hands. They feel their presence here is undesirable. They leave and Davyd remains, lying on the grave. Arseny thinks a bit and then lashes him with nettles, too. Davyd winces but continues lying there since he has no other option. The sun is setting faster than usual. The moon appears in the sky.

Arseny kneels next to Davyd and touches his hand. He examines Davyd's white and almost lifeless skin. This skin was created for moonlight. Arseny strokes it with his fingers and begins kneading firmly. He switches to the other hand. He turns the weakened man onto his stomach. He kneads his deadened flesh with all his strength, as if pumping vitalizing forces into it. He rubs Davyd's back along the spine. He kneads at Davyd's legs, making Davyd's arms, which dangle off the burial mound, shake. The patient is reminiscent of a large doll. The new abbess comes out to the cemetery twice during the night and twice sees Arseny's unceasing work. Davyd rises to his feet at dawn's first light. He takes several wooden steps in the direction of the cathedral, where his kin are already waiting for him. Davyd's strength leaves him because his muscles are still unaccustomed to walking. His kin rush to him and grasp him under the arms. They understand that the first steps are the most important. But also the most difficult.

What is this? the new abbess asks those present, herself most of all. Is this the result of our brother Ustin's therapeutic measures or the Lorde's miracle, appearing independently of human action? Essentially, the abbess answers herself: one does not contradict the other, for a miracle can be the result of effort multiplied by faith.

Arseny gathers plants by the Velikaya River and in the Pskov forests. The Pskov lands are more southerly than Belozersk and produce greater quantities of herbs. There are even herbs that Christofer did not describe in his time. Arseny surmises their effects from the smells and shapes of their leaves. He dries plants like this in the monastery shed and experiments with them on himself. He dries other plants, too.

Some good believers in Christ catch a large fish in the Velikaya River and give it to priest Konstantin. The priest's wife, Marfa, prepares fish for dinner. She warns her husband that a large fish has large bones and appeals to him to be careful. Priest Konstantin, a carefree person, absentmindedly eats the fish, not thinking about its bones. He is thinking about the parish church that is being built. He is trying yet again to calculate the quantities of purchased materials and worries there will not be enough. Priest Konstantin does not immediately notice that an arch-shaped bone with a fragment of the fish's backbone has entered his throat along with the fish's tender flesh. He coughs and pieces of fish—everything but the bone—fly out of his mouth.

The bone is stuck in his throat in three spots. It goes no further down but is not coming up, either. It has gone too deep to reach with fingers. Marfa, the priest's wife, pounds on her husband's back but the bone sits there, immovable. Priest Konstantin lies down, his belly on the table and his head hanging almost to the floor, trying to cough out the bone. Saliva and blood run out of his mouth but the bone does not move, not one *vershok*.

The doctor Terenty is brought to priest Konstantin. Terenty asks the patient to open his mouth and brings a candle toward it. The bone is not even visible under candlelight. Terenty tries to stick his long fingers down the patient's throat but even he is unable to happen upon the bone. Priest Konstantin silently shakes from retching movements and finally breaks out of the doctor's arms. Marfa, the priest's wife, throws Terenty out of the house.

They refuse medical assistance, the doctor Terenty tells those gathered on the street. And, with hand on heart, I say they are correct, for the depth of the embedded bone is beyond the bounds of modern medicine.

After a night of suffering, they bring priest Konstantin across the river to Zapskovye. When they arrive at John the Baptist Convent's cemetery, they place the priest in front of Arseny. The patient sits on a gravestone because he is no longer able to stand. His throat has swelled and he is gasping for breath. Suffering and grief are in his eyes: he thinks they are already going to bury him. He fears his pain will never pass, even in death.

Arseny crouches in front of priest Konstantin. He feels his neck with both hands. The priest quietly moans. Arseny suddenly grabs him by the feet and lifts him off the ground. He shakes priest Konstantin with unexpected strength and fury. Arseny's fury is directed at the ailment. A wail, red mucus, and a bone issue from the patient's throat.

The priest is lying on the ground and breathing heavily. His half-closed eyes gaze at the cause of his suffering. Certain among those who happen to be at the cemetery want to lift him, but he motions to stop them: he needs to catch his breath. The priest's wife Marfa kneels before Arseny. Arseny bends and grasps her by the legs, trying to lift her, too. The priest's wife shouts. She is too heavy and Arseny does not have that much strength.

Pretty much unliftable, those present whisper to each other, shaking their heads.

Arseny leaves Marfa and departs the cemetery. The priest's wife wraps the bone in a handkerchief, as a family keepsake of gratitude.

Mayor Gavriil's daughter Anna is dead. At fifteen years olde. After slipping on the ferry, Anna falls into the water and sinks to the bottom like a rock. Several people plunge in after her. They dive in various directions, trying to figure out where the maiden's body has been dragged off to. They resurface, gasping for breath, gather more air in their lungs, and submerge into the water again. They have difficulty reaching the bottom of the Velikaya River and when there they cannot locate the mayor's daughter. The water is cloudy. The water is swift and full of whirlpools. One of the divers nearly drowns but their efforts are in vain. They find the drowned girl's body downstream several hours later, after it has washed up in the reeds.

Mayor Gavriil is beside himself with grief. He wants to bury his daughter at the John the Baptist Convent and goes to see the abbess. The abbess tells him it would be better to bury Anna in the potter's field. Mayor Gavriil grabs the abbess by the shoulders and shakes her for a very long time. The abbess looks at the mayor not with fear but with sorrow. She allows the mayor to bury his daughter at the convent. The mayor orders Anna be adorned in gold and silver jewelry, that she not lose her beauty even when dead. The residents of Zavelichye and other parts of Pskov greet the ferry carrying the body. Everyone is in tears. They commit Anna to the earth, the sobs makynge a funeral dirge. All leave but the mayor. He remains and lies on the fresh grave for several hours. The mayor is led away when night falls. Only Arseny remains at the cemetery, leaning against the entwined oaks. He seems to have become entwined with them, too, having taken on the color of their bark and their immobility.

This impression is mistaken because Arseny's essence is human and prayerful, not of wood. A heart beats inside him and his lips move. He prays for heavenly gifts for the newly departed Anna. His eyes are opened wide. They reflect a candle flame that uncertainly traverses the cemetery. The small flame skirts the crosses and climbs atop the hillocks. It stops upon reaching Anna's grave. An unseen hand affixes the flame to a stump alongside the grave. Another hand breaks off a branch of quaking aspen and uses it to hide the flame on the convent side. A shovel appears within the flickering circle the candle forms. The shovel slices effortlessly through the burial mound. Fresh earth requires no effort. The digger is already standing up to his knees in the grave. Standing up to his waist. His face is at the same level as the candle. Arseny recognizes that face.

Stinge, he says quietly.

Stinge shudders and lifts his head. He sees nobody.

If you, Stinge, enter that grave up to your chest, you will never leave it, Arseny says. Is it not stated in the manuscripts you stole? Death is fierce for sinners.

Stinge is shaking. He looks into the dark sky.

Art thou an angel?

Does it really matter who I am, answers Arseny, an angel or a man? You used to steal from the living, but now you have become a grave robber. It turns out that you are taking on earthly properties even while you are alive, thus you can become of the earth in no time.

So what am I supposed to do, Stinge asks, if I am a burden to my own self?

Pray unceasingly and, for starters, fill up the grave.

Stinge fills up the grave.

If you were not an angel, you would not know my name, he says to someone above. Because today is my first day in this burg of Pskov.

Little by little, the renown of Arseny's doctoring gift spreads through all of Pskov. People come to him with the most varied of illnesses and ask him to give them relief. They look into the holy fool's blue eyes and tell him about themselves. They feel their troubles drown in those eyes. Arseny says nothing and does not even nod. He hears them out attentively. They think his attention is special, for he who refuses to speak expresses himself by hearing.

Sometimes Arseny gives them herbs. After rummaging around in his bag, Sister Agafya finds the appropriate manuscript from Christofer and reads it aloud to the patient. The one who receives the herb *corncockle* is prescribed to boil it in water with its root: it will draw pus from the ears. They give the plant *quack grass* to those stung by bees and order them to rub it on. Arseny silently takes notice of Sister Agafya's reading though he is not inclined to overestimate the significance of the herbs offered. Doctoring experience tells him medicaments are not the most important part of treatment.

Arseny does not help everyone. He hears out the patient but turns away from him when he feels powerless to help. Sometimes he will press his forehead to the patient's forehead and tears will flow from his eyes. He shares the patient's pain with him and, to some degree, his death, too. Arseny's heart fills with grief because he understands that the world does not remain the same after a patient passes away.

If I had the light within me, I would have cured him, Arseny says to Ustina about patients like that. But I cannot cure him, because of the gravity of my sins. These sins do not allow me to rise to the height where that person's redemption lies. I, my love, am the culprit in his death and thus I weep for his passing and for my own sins.

But even the patients Arseny cannot cure feel benefit from interacting with him. They think their pain reduces after meeting with Arseny, and their fear lessens along with the pain. Incurable patients see in him a person capable of understanding the depth of suffering, for in his exploration of pain he gets to the very bottom of things.

It is not only the ill who come to Arseny. Pregnant women also show up at the cemetery. He looks at them through his tears and places his palm on their bellies. They feel better and birthing is easy after seeing the holy fool. Nursing mothers whose milk has dried up come, too; Arseny gives them the herb *celandine*. If the herb does not help, Arseny takes the woman to one of Zavelichye's cowsheds and tells her to milk a cow. He watches as the white liquid dribbles through fingers red from tension. How the cow's taut udder sways. The cow's owners stand in the back, in the doorway. They watch, too. They know the arrival of the holy fool and the woman is a blessing. Arseny signals for the nursing mother to drink some milk. She drinks and feels her own nipples swell. And she hurries off to her child.

Arseny crosses the Velikaya River. Along the way, he notices that the ice is already gone but the water is still cold. An unwarmed river breeze has been blowing on Zapskovye since early morning, chilling that part of the city. Holy fool Foma squints and looks off into the distance somewhere. His beard twists in the breeze. Holy fool Karp stands, covering his face with his hands. He is half-turned toward holy fool Foma. Loaf baker Samson does not make them wait long: he shows up with his tray of loaves. And a kind smile on his lips. Holy fool Karp wearily takes his hands from his face and clasps them behind his back. A blue vein beats on his temple. He is, in his essence, no longer young. His facial features are delicate. Holy fool Karp approaches loaf baker Samson with a soft, balletic gait and grasps the closest loaf with his teeth. Holy fool Karp turns after taking a step away from the tray. He looks pitifully at Samson. Samson's facial expression never changes as he takes the strap off his neck and carefully places the tray on the ground. He takes several steps in holy fool Karp's direction. The loaf baker's well-proportioned body folds. His hand drops to the top of his boot. Something there gleams, cold and sharp. The loaf baker walks right up to Karp. Karp stands to attention. He is taller than the loaf baker and senses the baker's breath on his neck. The knife slowly enters the holy fool's body. Oh, ye hosts of heaven, whispers loaf baker Samson, I have waited so long for this day.

THE BOOK
OF JOURNEYS

Ambrogio Flecchia was born in a little place called Magnano. To Magnano's east, a day away on horseback, lay Milan, the city of Saint Ambrosius. The boy was named in honor of that saint, too. Ambrogio. Which is what it sounded like in his parents' language. Perhaps it reminded them of ambrosia, nectar of the immortals. The boy's parents were wine-makers.

As he grew up, Ambrogio began helping them. He obediently did everything he was instructed to do, but there was no joy for him in the labor. The older Flecchia, who had secretly observed his son more than once, was ever more convinced of this. Ambrogio remained serious even when stomping on grapes in the vat with his bare feet (and what could be merrier for a child?).

The older Flecchia, who descended from a family of wine-makers, did not himself like excessive mirth. He knew the fermentation of wine was an unhurried, even melancholy, process, and thus he permitted a certain degree of pensiveness in winemaking. But his son's aloofness toward wine production was something else: in his father's eyes, it bordered on disinterest. Only a person who is not indifferent is capable of making real, true wine (the older Flecchia sighed as he brushed press cake from his fingers).

The boy's assistance to the family business came from an unexpected angle. Five days before a big grape harvest, Ambrogio announced that the grapes should be harvested right away. He said this in the morning—after he had opened his eyes but before he had fully woken up. A vision of a thunderstorm had come to him. It was a dreadful thunderstorm and Ambrogio described it in detail. His description included a darkness that suddenly thickened, a howling wind, and hailstones the size of a hen's egg whistling through the air. The boy told of ripe bunches of grapes that beat, tattered and soaked, against their stems, and of balls of ice that fell, drilling holes in thrashing leaves and finishing off grapes that had fallen to the ground. On top of that, a blue, ringing cold descended from the heavens and a thin coating of snow covered the site of the catastrophe.

The older Flecchia had seen a thunderstorm like that only once in his life, and the boy had never seen one. All the specifics of the story, however, coincided exactly with what the father had seen back in the day. The older Flecchia was not inclined toward mysticism but, after some wavering, he heeded Ambrogio's advice after all and set to harvesting the grapes. He said nothing to the neighbors because he feared ridicule. But when a dreadful thunderstorm really did come down on Magnano five days later, only the Flecchia family ended up with a harvest that year.

Other visions visited the dark-complexioned adolescent. They affected various and sundry aspects of life but were fairly remote from winemaking. And so, Ambrogio predicted the war that developed between the French kings and the Holy Roman Empire in the territory of Piemonte in 1494. The wine-maker's son clearly saw the forward French troops marching from west to east, past Magnano. The French hardly touched the local population, taking only small livestock to supplement their provisions, as well as twenty casks of Piemonte wine that seemed pretty fine to them. This information came to the older Flecchia in 1457, meaning it was far, far in advance, and would not, in essence, let him reap any possible benefit. A week later, he had already forgotten about the predicted military operations.

Ambrogio also predicted that Christopher Columbus would discover America in 1492. This event did not attract his father's attention, either, since it would have no substantial influence on winemaking in Piemonte. The vision put the boy himself into a dither, though, for it was accompanied by the ominous luminescence of the outlines of all three of Columbus's caravelles. This disagreeable light even touched the explorer's aquiline profile. The Genovese man named Colombo, who had switched to Spanish service by force of circumstances, was, in essence, Ambrogio's countryman. One would not want to think that on October 12, 1492, a person of this sort would do something unseemly, and thus the child was inclined to explain the light effects as excessive electrification within the Atlantic atmosphere.

After Ambrogio had grown up a little more, he expressed the desire to go to Florence and study at the university there. The older Flecchia did not impede him. By this time, he was already conclusively convinced that his son was not cut out for winemaking. Everyone in Magnano already knew that Flecchia the younger was, essentially, his own man, so they had been expecting his departure from the small town any day. Ambrogio himself, though, decided to postpone his departure: he was able to foresee that the plague would rage in Florence for the next two years.

The young man did finally end up in Florence. Everything was different in that city: it bore no resemblance to Magnano. Ambrogio arrived as Florence was recovering from the plague, and the city's grandeur still mingled with dismay. Ambrogio studied seven liberal arts at the university. After mastering the trivium (grammar, dialectics, and rhetoric) he moved on to the quadrivium, which covered arithmetic, geometry, music, and astronomy.

As was often the case at universities in the olden days, the education process ended up lasting a long time. It included several years of rigorous instruction interspersed with years of similarly rigorous interpretation of what had been studied, during which Ambrogio's attendance at the university ceased and he would set off and travel around Italy. In practice, though, the student's ties with his alma mater were never cut, not even during his trips to the most distant corners of his native country, which, happily, was not that large.

Ambrogio came to love history more than anything else he happened to be introduced to during his studies. The university did not consider history a distinct subject: it was studied within the trivium, as an element of rhetoric. The young man was willing to spend hours sitting over historical writings. With their focus on the past, they (and this connected them with Ambrogio's visions of the future) were an escape from the present. Movement away from the present—in both directions—became something Ambrogio needed as much as air, because it removed time's unidimensionality, which caused him to gasp for breath.

Ambrogio read ancient and medieval historians. He read annals, chronicles, chronographs, and the histories of cities, lands, and wars. He learned how empires formed and collapsed, how earthquakes happened, and how stars fell and rivers overflowed their banks. He took particular note of fulfilled prophesies, too, and how omens appeared and came true. In this surmounting of time, he saw confirmation of the nonrandomness of everything that took place on earth. People encounter one another (thought Ambrogio), bumping into one another like atoms. They do not have their own trajectories and so their actions are random. But when taken together, those random events (so thought Ambrogio) were their own form of consistency, which could be predictable in certain parts. Only He Who created everything knows this in full.

A merchant from Pskov once came to Florence. The merchant's name was Therapont. With a long beard split into two tails and a huge pocked nose, he stood out from the local populace. Besides his bundles of sable pelts, Therapont brought the news that Rus' awaited the end of the world in 1492. On the whole, people in Florence took this information calmly. In the first place, Florentines were busy with routine matters galore and many simply had no time to think about things that posed no immediate threat. In the second place, very few people in Florence could picture the location of Rus'. In view of Therapont's own unusual appearance (it was unclear if everyone in his homeland had similar beards and noses) it was presumed there was a possibility Rus' was located outside the inhabited world. This gave the populace hope that the conjectured end of the world would be limited to just Rus'.

Of all the people living in Florence, merchant Therapont's announcement only seemed truly important to one person: Ambrogio. The young man sought out Therapont and asked him about the basis for this conclusion that the end of the world was coming in 1492. Therapont replied that this was not his conclusion but that he had heard it from competent people in Pskov. Unable to substantiate the fatal date, Therapont jokingly proposed that Ambrogio head to Pskov for clarification. Ambrogio did not laugh. He nodded pensively for he did not rule out that possibility.

After this conversation, Ambrogio began taking Russian (old Russian) lessons from the merchant. The older Flecchia had no inkling how his money was being spent. For his part, Ambrogio wisely said nothing to his father: the existence of Rus' would have seemed even more dubious to the older Flecchia than the specifics of the 1494 war his son had once described.

It was at this same time that Ambrogio Flecchia met Amerigo Vespucci, the future mariner. Looking at Vespucci's eyes, Ambrogio had no trouble realizing where his course lay. It was obvious Amerigo would head to Seville in 1490, where he would help finance Columbus's expeditions through his work at Giannotto Berardi's trading house. Beginning in 1499 and inspired by Columbus's successes, the Florentine himself would undertake several voyages and all so very successfully that the newly discovered continent would be named for him rather than Columbus. (In that very same 1499—and Ambrogio could not help but tell the merchant Therapont about this—archbishop Gennady Novgorodsky would compile the first full Holy Scripture in Rus', which was subsequently called Gennady's Bible.)

Ambrogio directed Amerigo Vespucci's attention to a strange convergence of events foreseen for 1492. On the one hand, a new continent would be discovered, on the other, the end of the world was expected in Rus'. How much (Ambrogio's quandry) were those events connected, and, if they were connected, then how? Could it be (Ambrogio's guess) that the discovery of the new continent was the beginning of a lengthy, drawn-out end of the world? And if that is the case (Ambrogio takes

Amerigo by the shoulder and looks him in the eye), is it worth giving your name to a continent like that?

Meanwhile, Arseny's lessons with the merchant Therapont continued. Ambrogio read a Slavonic Psalter the merchant had with him and, it must be said, understood much of it, because he knew the Latin text of the Psalms by heart. He listened to Therapont's readings with no less interest. At his request, each Psalm was read through multiple times. This allowed Ambrogio to remember not only the words (he had already learned them during the reading) but also the specifics of pronunciation. To Therapont's surprise, little by little, the young man became his phonic twin. The Russian originals of the words Ambrogio pronounced could not always be discerned immediately, but at times— and this happened ever more frequently—Therapont involuntarily shuddered as the purest intonations of a Pskov merchant issued from the Italian's lips.

The day arrived when Ambrogio knew he was ready to head for Rus'. The last thing the Florentines heard from him turned out to be a prediction of a horrifying flood, fated to descend upon the city on November 4, 1966. As he pleaded with the city dwellers to be vigilant, Ambrogio pointed out that the Arno River would overflow its banks and that a body of water with a volume of 350 million cubic meters would gush onto the streets. Florence subsequently forgot about this prediction, just as it forgot about the predictor himself.

Ambrogio headed for Magnano and informed his father of his plans.

But the boundary of the inhabited expanses is there, said the older Flecchia. Why are you going there?

Perhaps on the boundary of the world, replied Ambrogio, I will learn something about the boundary of time.

B̃

Ambrogio did have his regrets about leaving Florence. A considerable number of worthy people (Sandro Botticelli, Leonardo da Vinci, Raffaello Santi, and Michelangelo Buonarroti) whose roles in cultural history were already clear to him were passing their time there. Not one of them, however, could contribute the slightest clarity to the only issue meaningful for Ambrogio: the issue regarding the end of the world. That issue does not disquiet them, Ambrogio noted to himself, for they are creating for eternity.

In the last days of his life in Florence, Ambrogio was favored with several visions, large and small. The visions were not completely comprehensible to him and he did not tell anyone about them. They were not related to world history. The events he saw related to the histories of individual people, and it is they, or so it seemed to Ambrogio, who ultimately form world history. One of the visions—the least understandable for him—touched on the large country to the north, where he aspired to go. After some deliberation, Ambrogio decided to tell the merchant Therapont about the vision. What follows is the short version.

In 1977, Leningrad State University sent Yury Alexandrovich Stroev, who was right on the verge of becoming a candidate of historical sciences, to Pskov for an archeological expedition. Yury Alexandrovich's dissertation, which was devoted to early Russian chronicle writing, was nearly finished. It lacked only a conclusion containing findings, but the dissertator just could not write it. Whenever he sat down to work on his findings, Stroev began thinking they were incomplete, trivialized his work, and, in some sense, nullified it. It's possible he was simply burnt out. That is, in any case, what his research advisor, Ivan Mikhailovich

Nechiporuk, thought. And Nechiporuk, as it happened, was the person who had included Stroev in the archeological expedition's team. The professor figured the findings would fall into place on their own after Stroev got some needed rest. The professor had tremendous experience as an advisor.

The members of the expedition were housed in private apartments in Pskov. Stroev's apartment was in Zapskovye, on Pervomaiskaya Street, not far from the Church of the Image of Edessa, which was built during the great pestilence of 1487. The apartment consisted of two rooms. A young woman with a five-year-old son lived in the large room, and they settled Stroev into the small room. They told him the woman's name was Alexandra Muller and that she was a Russian German.

The German woman introduced herself as Sasha. Her son, who greeted the guest along with her, was Sasha, too. The boy hugged her leg, turning Alexandra's cotton print dress into tight-fitting pants. Despite being immersed in thought about his dissertation, Stroev noticed Alexandra's shapely legs.

Stroev liked their building. It was an old red-brick merchant's home. In the evenings, the windows glowed with a yellowish electrical light. When he came home from the excavation for the first time, Stroev stopped at the front steps to admire their glow. This glow was reflected on the Pobeda automobile that stood in front of the building. And on the round cobblestones in the roadway, too.

When he went in, Stroev saw Alexandra was drinking tea with her son. And he drank tea with them.

What is your expedition working on? Alexandra asked.

Someone began playing the violin on the other side of the wall.

We're studying the foundation of the Saint John the Baptist Church. It has sunk considerably over the centuries. Stroev slowly brought his palm closer to the table.

The boy's palms also nearly touched the table. When he noticed Stroev's glance, he began drawing his fingers along the patterns on the oilcloth. The patterns were small and complex but the boy's fingers were even smaller. He could handle this geometry easily.

A holy fool named Arseny, who called himself Ustin, lived around the John the Baptist Convent, said Alexandra, by the cemetery wall.

There's no wall there now.

There isn't even a cemetery. Alexandra topped up Stroev's tea. The cemetery became Komsomol Square.

But what about the deceased? the boy asked. Did they all become Komsomol members or something?

Stroev bent right to the boy's ear:

That will be determined during the excavations.

They went out for a walk the next evening. They crossed Trud Street, came to the Thundering Tower, and sat there on the bank of the Pskova River. The boy tossed pebbles into the river. Stroev found several shards of tile and launched them so they skipped like a frog along the river's surface. The largest piece hopped along the water five times.

Another time they went to Zavelichye. They crossed the Velikaya River over the Soviet Army Bridge and headed to the John the Baptist Convent. They came to the church and stood for a long time at the rim of the excavation site. They cautiously went down the stairs. They stroked ancient stones warmed by the August evening. Warmed for the first time in many centuries. And someone was stroking them for the first time in many centuries. That's what Alexandra was thinking. She was imagining an ancient holy fool near those stones and could not answer her own question about whether or not she actually believed what she had read. Had a holy fool even really existed? And, one might ask, had his love existed? And if so, then what had that love turned into during those hundreds of years gone by? And who, then, could feel that love now, if those who had loved had been reduced to dust long ago?

I like being with both of them, Stroev said in his heart, because I feel a certain something kindred in both of them. A definite consonance, you might say, despite her German heritage. She is calm, dark blonde, and her facial features are well balanced. Why is she a single mother to her boy, and where is her husband? What is she doing here in the Russian provinces among windows sunken into the ground that have little view, old automobiles, untucked linen shirts (with patch pockets), and the wrinkled, yellow-faced, dust-strewn photographic denizens of honor boards (a breeze blows, ever so slightly, through the feather grass under them)? I don't know, he answered himself, what she's doing, for she is not organic to this world. And his heart faltered when he imagined Alexandra Muller on a teeming Leningrad street or, for example, at the Kirov Opera and Ballet Theater, with her face flushed just before intermission's third bell: it was within his power to take her there.

Then they returned home and drank tea, and the violin began plinking on the other side of the wall.

That's Parkhomenko playing, said the boy. We love listening to him.

Alexandra shrugged.

Stroev imagined himself gazing from the street and tried to see them—all three of them—in the window, in the yellow electric light. Maybe he was even gazing from Leningrad. He already knew, now, that he would yearn for that kitchen, for the automobile by the window, the cobblestone roadway, and Parkhomenko's unseen violin. He was already scrutinizing them, sitting there, as if they were themselves a cherished photograph: the window frame was its frame and the chandelier's light flooded it with the yellowing of time. Why am I (thought Stroev) yearning in advance, predestining events, and moving ahead of time? And how is it that I always know in advance about my yearning? What is it inside me that gives rise to this vexing feeling?

I teach Russian language and literature at a school, said Alexandra, but that's not of much interest to anyone here.

Stroev took a cookie from the dish and pressed it to his lower lip.

And what does interest them?

I don't know. After a silence, she asked:

So why did you choose medieval history?

It's hard to say… Maybe because historians in the Middle Ages were unlike historians these days. They always looked for moral reasons as an explanation for historical events. It's like they didn't notice the direct connection between events. Or didn't attach much significance to it.

But how can you explain the world without seeing the connections? said Alexandra, surprised.

They were looking above the everyday and seeing higher connections. Besides, time connected all events, even though people didn't consider that connection reliable.

The boy was holding a cookie by his lower lip. Alexandra smiled: Sasha's copying your body language.

Stroev went home two weeks later. The semester started and, contrary to his expectations, he didn't feel any yearning at first. He didn't feel it later, either, because he was so busy that autumn, finishing his dissertation and preparing for the defense of it that he would be expected to present. Stroev successfully gave his defense at the very end of the year. Everyone was satisfied with his dissertation, especially Professor Nechiporuk, who was convinced the decision to send the dissertator to the excavation had turned out to be the one and only correct thing to do. Stroev entered January of the new year by tossing off the burden that had been weighing on him for so long and, let's be honest, making his life thoroughly miserable. His soul felt lighter. And in that weightless, almost soaring condition, it sensed the absence of Alexandra Muller.

This doesn't mean Stroev began thinking constantly about Alexandra, let alone took steps to see her: action was not his strong point. But he remembered Alexandra before going to sleep, in that flickery instant when daytime matters have already receded and dreams aren't yet drawing close. Her kitchen drifted in front of him, with the fabric lampshade over the table and the tea pot painted with leaves. As he lay in his bed, Stroev inhaled the scent of the old Pskov building. From outside the window, he heard pedestrians' footsteps and snatches of their conversations. He saw the boy's body language, which turned out to be his own body language. Stroev calmed and fell asleep.

One time he told Ilya Borisovich Utkin, his friend and colleague, about Alexandra.

It's possible that's love, said Utkin, wavering.

But love (Stroev flapped his arms around) is such an overpowering feeling that, as I understand things, it just convulses you. Practically makes you high. But I'm not feeling that. I miss her, yes. I'd like to be with her, yes. Hear her voice, yes. But not behave like a madman.

You're talking about passion that really is a form of insanity. But I'm talking about love, which is sensible and, if you like, predestined. Because when you miss someone, we're talking about lacking a piece of you, yourself. And you're looking to be reunited with that piece.

That sounds very romantic, thought Stroev, but how do notions like that fit into real life? And so Alexandra, let's say, has a son, a very sweet little boy. But he's not my son. I know nothing about his father. Stroev bit his lips. And, when it comes down to it, I don't want to know. I can't rule out that there are some bleak stories connected with this person. Some sort of, for all I know, gulfs in Alexandra's life. For the most part, though, this isn't about him. I'm just afraid I wouldn't be able to get along with the boy.

About a month later, he said to Utkin:

I keep thinking about the kid. Would he get in the way between me and Alexandra?

Has she really already said she'll marry you?

What, you think she won't?

I don't know that. Call her, ask.

Things like that aren't resolved over the phone.

So go there.

Oh, come on, Ilya, what are you talking about?! I'm not ready for that yet.

I don't know myself what I want, Stroev admitted to himself. I have lots of different thoughts and feelings, but, yet again, I can't reach conclusions.

In March, it was Utkin who asked Stroev about Alexandra.

I'm afraid, Stroev said, she might marry me just to get out of the provinces. Or so her kid has a father.

What, and you don't want her to leave the provinces or for her kid to have a father?

Why are you asking me about this?

Because you still haven't looked at what's happening from her perspective. If you can manage to do that, it means you love her and you have to go see her.

At the end of May, Stroev told Utkin:

You know, Ilya, I think I'm going to go.

Stroev got on the train and headed for Pskov. Poplar fluff was bursting through the windows. As Stroev rode, he thought he wouldn't even find Alexandra there again. He'd go to the door and nobody would open it for him. He'd press his forehead against the kitchen window and, after he'd placed his palms to his temples so the reflections wouldn't get in the way, see remainders of his former happiness. The lampshade, the table. An empty table. His heart would shrink. A reproachful Parkhomenko (and I played for you, you know) would come out of the neighboring door, all big shoulders and short legs. And that, it turns out, is what was behind the music. They're not here, Parkhomenko would say, they went away forever. For. Ever. It took too long for you to get yourself together. Essentially, what's happening here isn't really about time, because true love is beyond time. It can, after all, wait an entire lifetime. (Parkhomenko sighs.) The cause of what's happening here all lies in the absence of an internal fire. Your trouble, if you will, is that reaching final conclusions just isn't your thing. You're afraid the decision you make will deprive you of further choice, so that paralyzes your will. Even now, you don't know why you've come. Meanwhile, you've missed out on the best thing life had arranged for you. You had, I can report to you, all the conditions that nature could present a person: a place to live on a quiet Pskov street, old linden trees outside the window, and good music on the other side of the wall. You didn't take advantage of any of the things I just listed, so this trip is, just like your previous trip, a complete waste of time.

A complete waste of time, Ambrogio said pensively.

A complete waste of time, repeated the merchant Therapont.

Ambrogio Flecchia turned up in Rus' in either 1477 or 1478. The Italian was met with reserve—but without hostility—in Pskov, where the merchant Therapont sent him. He was received there as a person whose goals are not entirely clear. People began treating him more warmly when they were convinced he was only interested in the end of the world. Determining the time the world would end seemed like an estimable pursuit to many, for people in Rus' loved large-scale tasks.

Let him determine it, said Mayor Gavriil. Experience tells me that signs of the end of the world will be most obvious here.

Mayor Gavriil became the Italian's patron after getting to know him better. Ambrogio did not manufacture anything or trade anything, so he would not have had an easy time of things without that patronage. Essentially, he completely owed his rather decent life in Pskov to the mayor's generosity.

Gavriil liked talking with Ambrogio. The Italian told him about past prophesies in history, about indications of the end of the world, about famous battles, and just about Italy. When he talked about his homeland, Ambrogio was crushed that he could not convey the undulating blueness of the mountains, the damp saltiness of the air, and many other things that made Italy the most wonderful place on earth.

But were you not sorry to leave a land like that? Mayor Gavriil once asked him.

Of course I was sorry, answered Ambrogio, but the beauty of my land did not allow me to concentrate on what is most important.

Ambrogio devoted all his time to reading Russian books, attempting to find in them an answer to the question that was troubling him.

Many people who knew about his quest asked when the end of the world would come.

Me thinketh it be knowne only to God, Ambrogio answered, evading. I have ofte read in books of what is sayde, morover, there is not any numeric agreement within them.

The contradicting sources flustered Ambrogio but he did not abandon his attempts to determine the date of the end of the world. It surprised him that there was no sense this menacing event was approaching, despite the indication that the end of the world was most likely to come during the seven thousandth year. Things were precisely the opposite: Ambrogio's small and large visions concerned much later years. Essentially, he was even glad of this, though it increased his perplexity.

The birth of the Antichrist in the year 6967 was approaching (Ambrogio read) and there will be created an erth quake soche as has never been before this woeful and fierce time and there will then be great mourning, on all the land of all times and places.

Yes (thought Ambrogio), the Antichrist should make an appearance thirty-three years before the end of the world. But year 6967 from the Creation (this was year 1459 since the Birth of Christ) had passed long ago and indications of the coming of the Antichrist were still not tangible. Did it follow that the end of the world was being indefinitely postponed?

One day, Mayor Gavriil said to him:

I need someone willing to go to Jerusalem. I want him to hang an icon lamp in the Church of the Holy Sepulcher, in memory of my perished daughter Anna. And that person could be you.

Well sure, Ambrogio said, I could be that person. You have done a lot for me so I will take the icon lamp in memory of your perished daughter.

Mayor Gavriil embraced Ambrogio.

I know you are waiting here for the end of the world. I think you will be able to return before then.

Do not worry, mayor, said Ambrogio, for if the expected does occur, it will be conspicuous everywhere. And a visit to Jerusalem is auspicious.

Loaf baker Samson was being led down the street, bound.

My glorious, lovely bread products and baked goods, said the loaf baker, weeping. I loved ye more than life, my own or anyone else's, for I could nurture you like nobody else in this entire burg of Pskov. That holy fool Karp grabbed you with his unclean mouth, dragged you along the ground, and gave you away to people who were not worth your heel, and they all smiled, trustinge he was doing a good deed. And I smiled, for what else could I do when everyone considered me a good person and, yes, I was a good person, when it comes right down to it. It's just that the level of what was expected from me exceeded the level of my kindness—and that does happen, no surprises there. And so, I do report to you, that a malice as heavy as lead simply filled the gap inside me, between the kindness expected and the kindness possessed. The gap increased and the malice increased and the smile that bloomed on my lips was, if you can believe it, a sort of spasm.

Do you know how long you have already been in Pskov? holy fool Foma asked Arseny.

Arseny shrugged.

Well, I know, exulted holy fool Foma. You have already worked things out for Leah and for Rachel and some third person, too.

Only not for Ustina, Arseny said in his heart.

Foma pointed at loaf baker Samson, who was being led away by guards, and shouted:

There's no more point in your silence now that Karp's gone. You could be silent because Karp spoke. You don't have that opportunity now.

So what am I supposed to do now? asked Arseny.

Karp invited you to Heavenly Jerusalem but you didn't become his traveling companion. Which is understandable: you wouldn't go there without Ustina. But go to earthly Jerusalem and pray for her to the Almighty.

But how will I get to Jerusalem? asked Arseny.

I have this one idea, said holy fool Foma. But for now, buddy, give me the bag with Christofer's manuscripts. You won't be needing them anymore.

Arseny handed the bag with Christofer's manuscripts to holy fool Foma but he felt mournful inside. As he handed over the bag, Arseny thought about how his attachment to property seemed to have stayed with him, and he was ashamed of this feeling. Holy fool Foma grasped what was happening within Arseny's soul and told him:

Do not mourn, O Arseny, for Christofer's collected wisdom will enter you in an unwritten way. As far as the descriptions of the herbs go, I reckon that's already ancient history for you. Heale the ill by taking their sins upon yourself. Herbs are not required for that sort of treatment, as I hope you understand. And also: from now on you are not Ustin but Arseny, like before. Prepare, comrade, for the journey.

Shortly thereafter, all of Pskov knew that Ustin had begun speaking. That his name was not Ustin but Arseny. And they all came to look at him but they could not see him because he was no longer living in the cemetery but in a guest cell at the John the Baptist Convent.

What do you think this is, a circus or something? the abbess asked the visitors. A person lived outdoors for fourteen years, so let him come to his senses.

Ambrogio came to see Arseny on one of those days.

Mayor Gavriil sent me to see you, said Ambrogio. He wants you to be my traveling companion for a journey to Jerusalem. I am presuming the end of the world will arrive no earlier than the year 7000, 1,492 years from Christ's birth. So if everything works out right we can make it back.

What are you basing your calculations on? Arseny asked him.

It is all very simple. I will liken days to millennia for it was said in the ninetieth psalm: A thousande yeares in thy sight are but as yesterdaye that is past. Since there are seven days in a week, it results in seven millennia of human lyfe. It is now year 6988: we have another twelve years at our disposal. I think that should be plenty for repentance.

Are you sure, Arseny asked him, that it is now that precise year, I mean are you sure that it has been exactly 6,988 years from the Creation until now?

If I were not sure of it, Ambrogio answered, I probably would not have invited you to come with me to Jerusalem. Judge for yourself: Hellenic and Roman chronicles have been documenting all the emperorships ever since the year 5500, when Jesus Christ our Savior was born. Add up the years the Roman and Constantinople emperors ruled and you will get the sought date.

But why—forgive me, O you from other lands—do you think that precisely 5,500 years, no more and no less, passed between the Creation and the birth of our Savior? What served as the source of that conclusion?

Only that I read the Holy Scripture carefully, Ambrogio responded, and it is my principle source. For example, the Book of Genesis indicates the age of each of the forefathers at the time his firstborn arrives. Beyond that, there are also mentions of the number of years the forefathers lived after the arrival of their firstborn, as well as the overall sum of the forefathers' years of life. As you see, O brother Arseny, the two final items are even redundant to my calculation. In order to find the overall number of years that have passed, it is sufficient to add up the forefathers' years before the arrival of their firstborn.

But the letters that denote the numerical figures are subject to flaws, Arseny objected. For a long tyme what is wrytten has been erased and unknown. And yf just one of the two lines that form the letter т is erased, then it cannot be understonded if it was originally the letter т or rather the letter п, which has three lines, and that would be the difference between a quantity of eighty or three hundred, methinketh. Tell me, Ambrogio, how do you prove that your calculations are infallible and that the birth of our Savior Jesus Christ really happened in the year 5500? Using what harmony, one might ask, will you prove all this algebra?

The figures, O Arseny, have their own higher meaning, for they reflect that heavenly harmony you are asking about. Now listen carefully. The Passion of Christ fell on the sixth hour of the sixth day of the week and that indicates that the Savior was born in the middle of the sixth millennium, meaning the 5,500th year since the Creation. This is also indicated because the sum of the measures of Moses' ark, according to the twenty-fifth chapter of the Book of Exodus, totaled five and a half cubits. Thus Christ, like a true Ark, should also have come in the year 5500.

This person is capable of sound reasoning, Arseny told Ustina. It truly is possible to go to Jerusalem with a person like this. If I am to believe his calculations (and I am inclined to do so), we have at least ten years for the journey. And so I, my love, am going to the very center of the earth. I am going to the point that is closest of all to Heaven. If my words are destined to fly all the way to Heaven, then it will happen there. And all my words will be about you.

That day, Arseny and Ambrogio began preparing for the journey to Jerusalem. Mayor Gavriil allotted a purse of Hungarian gold ducats to each of them for the trip. The ducats were recognized over the entire distance from Pskov to Jerusalem and pilgrims eagerly took them on the road. The mayor could have given even more but he knew coins rarely lingered very long with travelers in the Middle Ages. Like money, items also had trouble going the distance. Their possessors often returned home without one or the other. Even more often, they did not return.

Letters of recommendations and personal connections were sometimes more useful to wayfarers than money. In this epoch, which was anything but simple, it was important that someone in a certain place was either waiting for someone or doing the opposite: sending someone someplace, vouching for him, and asking that his travel be facilitated. In some sense, this was a confirmation that the person had a place in life before, too, and that he had not come out of nowhere and was traveling honestly around an expanse. In the most general sense, journeys confirmed to the world the continuity of the expanse, a concept that continued to evoke certain doubts.

Arseny and Ambrogio were issued letters of recommendation for several cities. These were letters to personages of princely rank, spiritual figures, and representatives of the merchantry: any of them could help if need be. Each man was granted two horses and two riding caftans. The pilgrims sewed the ducats into the hems of the caftans. They inserted small strips of leather between them so the coins would not jingle or be detectable. Dried meat and fish were purchased, too, as much as two unsaddled horses were capable of carrying. Ambrogio, who had experience in distant wayfaring, led the preparations.

They limited themselves as they gathered food and clothing. It was a warm time of year in Pskov but of course it was always a warm time in the land of Palestine. Warm and abundant, for in this lande watery brooks and sprynges flow from the depths along valleyes and hilles, watering grapes, fig trees, and dates, this land streams with olive oil and honey for truly this land is blessed and belongs to the Lord's Heaven.

On the eve of their departure, Mayor Gavriil summoned Arseny and Ambrogio and presented them with a six-faceted silver icon lamp.

The icon lamp was small, so as not to attract unwanted attention. For that same reason, the mayor presented them, separately, with six adamants. Upon arrival at the site, the adamants should be placed in the spots intended for them on each of the icon lamp's facets. Place them and squeeze the pins, which bend easily. The mayor showed them how the pins bent.

There is nothing complex.

They were silent.

I thought for a long time about who to send to Jerusalem and chose you. You are of varying faiths but both are true. And you seek the same Lord. You will be going to Orthodox and non-Orthodox lands and your differences will help you.

Mayor Gavriil kissed the icon lamp. He embraced Arseny and Ambrogio.

This is important to me. This is very important to me.

They bowed to Mayor Gavriil.

5

The horses shifted from one foot to another on the shore and were afraid to step onto the vessel. Moving in water was not what frightened them: they had swum across and waded through rivers more than once in their lives. Moving *on top* of the water frightened them. It seemed unnatural to them. The horses were dragged by the reins along the gangways. They neighed and knocked their hooves on the deck's wood. As he gazed at the horses, Arseny did not even notice they had set sail.

The crowd on shore set sail, too, beginning to shrink in size and sound after the rowers had begun rowing their oars. The crowd simmered, turning into a whirlpool that spun around the mayor, who stood at its center. He did not even wave. He stood motionless. Alongside him fluttered the robes of the abbess from the John the Baptist Convent. Sometimes the heavy black fabric even touched the mayor's face, but he did not shift. The abbess seemed far wider than usual in the wind; she seemed lightly inflated. She blessed the departing vessel with slow, broad crosses.

The shores moved in time with the oar strokes. They tried to catch up to the clouds gliding through the sky but clearly lacked the speed. Arseny inhaled the river breeze with delight, understanding it was the breeze of wayfaring.

So many years, he said to Ustina, I sat here for so many years without moving and now I am sailing directly south. I feel, my love, that this motion is beneficial. It draws me closer to you and further from people whose attention, to tell the truth, had begun to weigh on me. I have, my love, a good traveling companion, a young, cultured person with a broad range of interests. Dark-complexioned. Curly hair. Beardless, for they shave beards in his part of the world. He is attempting to determine when the world will end and though I am not sure this is within his competence, attention to eschatology, even on its own, seems worthy of encouragement. Some Pskov boatmen are with us. They are taking us along the Velikaya River to the boundaries of the Pskov land. The river is wide. The residents of the shores that we pass watch us leave, if they notice us. Sometimes they wave as we pass. We wave to them, too. What awaits us? I feel an inexpressible gladness and fear nothing.

Toward evening, they moored at the shore and started a fire. They did not take the horses off the vessel because they had already grown used to being there. A late Pskov night was setting in.

In our lands, said the boatmen, nothing is unexpected. But, according to some sources, there will be people with dogs' heads further along. We do not know if that is true, but this is what people say.

Do not be too proud, answered Ambrogio, for there is plenty of everything in this land, too. Suppose you go into the kremlin: there are lots of people like that there.

From time to time, one of the boatmen would go to the nearby forest and gather fallen branches. Arseny watched the fire flare up. He pensively added branch after branch, using them to build a pyramid. At first the fire licked them. It was as if the fire was tasting them with its tongue before taking them entirely. Some of the brushwood crackled as it burned.

They are damp, said the boatmen. It is still damp in the forest.

Mosquitoes and gnats circled the fire. They were flying in a translucent swarm, almost like smoke. They drew circles and ellipses within the swarm, making it look as if someone was juggling them. But nobody was juggling them. They scattered when the smoke shifted in their direction. Arseny was surprised to note that the mosquitoes' escape gladdened him.

Can you believe, he said to Ustina, that I have gotten squeamish and am afraid of these bloodsuckers? I feared nothing when I was living as if in the body of another. And that, my love, does frighten me. Did I lose in an instant what I was gathering for you all those years?

We heard, said the boatmen, that the fire that comes upon the Holy Sepulcher at Easter does not singe. You have set out on your journey after Easter, though, so it works out that you will not see this fire's unusual properties.

But should not every day of the Lorde become Easter for us? asked Arseny.

He stretched his palm over the very fire. Tongues of fire came through his separated fingers, illuminating them from below with a rosy light. In the middle of the night that had fallen, Arseny's palm glowed brighter than the fire. Ambrogio stared steadily at Arseny. The boatmen crossed themselves.

3

The next day they reached the southern limits of the land of Pskov. The boatmen had been ordered to transport the pilgrims to these limits. The Velikaya River was becoming small and turning to the east.

The river is nearing its sources, said the boatmen, and there are more and more sandbars, which are just one more huge headache to deal with. We are, truth be told, sorry to part ways with you, but at least there is some consolation that we will be floating with the current on the way back.

It has long been observed, confirmed Ambrogio, that it is much easier to float with the current. So go in peace.

The horses were led to shore and Ambrogio and Arseny embraced the boatmen in parting. They felt disquiet as they watched the vessel grow distant. From now on, the wayfarers were left to the Lord and their own devices. A difficult journey awaited them.

They headed south. They rode unhurriedly, Arseny and Ambrogio in the front and the two pack horses in the rear, tethered with the reins. The road was narrow, the locality hilly. They dismounted to eat. They cut off strips of dried meat and washed it down with water. The horses hurried to nibble grass at their stopping places. When they crossed brooks, they lowered their lips to it and drank, snorting.

Toward the end of the day, they arrived in the town of Sebezh. Upon entering, they asked where they could stop for the night. They were directed to a hostelry. The hostelry reeked of either spilled beer or urine. The keeper was drunk. After seating the visitors on a bench, he himself sat on another. He looked at them for a long time, unblinking. He sat, his legs spread, arms resting on his knees. He did not answer questions. After touching him on the shoulder, Arseny realized the hostelry keeper was sleeping. He was sleeping with his eyes open.

The hostelry keeper's wife turned up and led the horses to a stall. She showed the guests to a room.

Hey, Ladle, she called out to her husband, but he did not stir. Ladle! She gave up on him with a wave of her hand. Let him sleep.

Close his eyes, said Ambrogio. It is much better to sleep with the eyes closed.

No, no, it is better like this, said the hostelry keeper's wife. This way, he will see you if you start prowling around the hostelry.

The Ladle he sleeps—The Ladle the hostelry keeps, said the keeper, with a belch. Don't try anything clever. The big thing is, do not trespass on my wife, for she will trespass on you herself. He lifted his feet onto the bench and covered himself with a bast mat. You cannot even imagine the things I have to close my eyes to.

In the middle of the night, Arseny felt something warm moving on his belly. He thought it was a rat and jolted to toss it off.

Shh, whispered the hostelry keeper's wife. The big thing is not to make any noise, my fees are low, just a token amount, you might say, I would not charge anything, but my husband—an animal, as you have seen for yourself—thinks there should be an economic component to any matter, and changing his mind is impossible, the scoundrel, and you want it, you want it...

Go away, he whispered to her, barely audibly.

She continued stroking Arseny on the belly and he felt himself lose all his will under the hand of this woman who was neither young nor pretty. He wanted to tell Ustina that everything that had been forming all those years might now be broken, but then the hostelry keeper's wife croaked out, at almost full voice:

And I know your type inside and out...

Her hand glided down toward the very bottom of his belly and Arseny jumped up, hitting his head on something hard and resonant that fell from the wall, rolled, bounced, and flew out of the room along with the hostelry keeper's wife.

The fire began smoldering in the next room.

No, just have a look, will you, have a look, shrieked the hostelry keeper's wife, pointing at Arseny. He started coming on to me.

He was using my moment of weakness, said the hostelry keeper, who was nearly sober and thus mean.

He was coming after me, Ladle! My garment is left in his hands. But I got away.

Arseny extended his hands and they were empty:

I have nobody's clothing.

The hostelry keeper's wife looked at Arseny and shouted, more calmly now:

Look at you, could not keep your hands to yourself, you are not in your Pskov. Pay a gold coin for this dishonor.

This is the Grand Duchy of Lithuania, said the hostelry keeper, and I, in other words, will not allow anyone...

Arseny began weeping.

Listen, Ladle, said Ambrogio, I have a document that I will present to your local authorities. But I will inform them orally (Ambrogio walked right up to the hostelry keeper) about how guests are received in Sebezh. I do not think they will be pleased.

And what about me? said the hostelry keeper. I know of this only from what she says. You need not pay for the dishonor if you wish.

The tavern keeper's wife cast a stern look at him:

Oh you, Ladle. This one sayde to me, I will revell in youre beauty. And I did denye him. At least give me something, even if it is not gold coin.

To pay you for your beauty, asked Ambrogio.

We will pay her because she rejected me, said Arseny. For if she rejected me in words, then she is capable of doing the same in deed. And I am to blame for all, and this is my fall. Forgive me, kind woman, and you forgive me, too, Ustina.

Without saying a word, Ambrogio took a ducat and extended it toward the hostelry keeper's wife. The woman stood, eyes cast down. The hostelry keeper shrugged. His wife looked at her husband and took the ducat, embarrassed. It was getting light outside.

They rode silently from Sebezh to Polotsk. Arseny rode a bit ahead and Ambrogio did not catch up.

After so many years of silence, said Ambrogio, it is difficult for you to get used to speech again.

Arseny nodded.

When they dismounted yet again, Ambrogio said:

I understand why you took the blame upon yourself. He who holds the world within answers for everything. But you did not think about how you deprived that woman of feeling the blame. Thanks to you, she is convinced everything is permitted for her.

You are wrong, said Arseny. Look what I found in my pocket.

He took his hand from his pocket and unclenched his fist. In his palm there lay a ducat.

In Polotsk they dismounted by the Spaso-Evfrosinevsky Monastery. Ambrogio tied the horses to an old elm. Arseny pressed his forehead to the monastery fence and said:

Hello, O Saint Evfrosinia. As you likely know, my traveling companion Ambrogio (Ambrogio bowed his head) and I are going to Jerusalem. It is not our place to tell you just how complicated is the journey there, for you have made it and we are at its very beginning. And it would be even more inappropriate for us to tell you how complicated is the journey back: we have not even begun it. And you, saintly one, totally forewent it and, with God's favor, found your resting place in the Holy Land. We are going there to pray for two women and are counting on your help very much. Bless us, O Saint Evfrosinia.

The pilgrims bowed and rode away.

Ambrogio addressed a pedestrian on the outskirts of Polotsk:

We are looking for the road to Orsha.

Orsha is on the Dnepr, said the pedestrian. The Dnepr is a big river and that, correspondingly, opens up great possibilities.

He showed the direction to Orsha and went about his business.

I have noticed, said Ambrogio, watching the pedestrian leave, that the people of ancient Rus' prefer a water route because of unfit roads. By the way, they do not yet know that Rus' is ancient but they will figure that out over time. Certain skills of foresight allow me to assert this. And this, too: the condition of the roads will not change. Basically, the history of your land will unscroll in a rather unusual way.

Does the history of my land truly unroll as a scroll unrolls? asked Arseny.

All history is, to a certain extent, a scroll in the Almighty's hands. Some people (me, for example) are granted the opportunity to peek every now and then, to see what lies ahead. There is just one thing I do not know: if that scroll will suddenly be thrown away.

Do you mean the end of the world? asked Arseny.

Yes, the end of the world. And the end of the dark underworld at the same time. This event, you know, has its own symmetry.

They rode for several hours without uttering a word. The road ran along the Dvina. The road followed the river, looping, fading, and sometimes even getting lost. But the road invariably turned up somewhere further on. They rode into a pine wood and the sound of hooves became more ringing.

Arseny asked:

If history is a scroll in the hands of the Creator, does that mean that everything I think and do is my Creator's thinking and doing, rather than mine?

No, that is not what it means: the Creator is good but not everything that you think and do is good. You were created in God's image and likeness, and your likeness consists, among other things, of freedom.

But if people are free in their intentions and actions, then it works out that they create history freely.

People are free, Ambrogio replied, but history is not free. As you say, there are so many intentions and actions that history cannot bring them all together, and only God can holde them all. I would even say that it is not people that are free but the individual person. I liken the confluence of human wills to fleas in a container: their movement is obvious but do they really have a common purpose? That is why history has no goal, just as humanity has none. Only an individual person has a goal. And even then, not always.

It was already their second day riding along the river. As they were riding through a forest, they saw a glade with a slope leading down to the water. Ambrogio dismounted to water his horse. He slipped on the clay at the very edge of the river and fell into the water. It turned out to be unexpectedly deep, almost to his throat. Ambrogio laughed as he spat out river plants. His long, black hair resembled river plants, too, streaming down his laughing face. Ambrogio's laughter splashed on the water's surface like sunny glints.

Today is warm, almost hot, said Arseny. We can wash some of our clothes and they will dry before evening.

After gathering some birch bark and branches, Arseny began starting a fire. He got a steel and flint out of his bag. He got tinder he had made from a bracket fungus, which was wrapped in a separate cloth. He struck the flint on the steel until one of the sparks lit the tinder. He noticed this because of a small plume of smoke. Then a barely perceptible spot of smoldering appeared on the tinder and began broadening. Arseny placed dried pine needles and the thinnest layers of birch bark on it. He began fanning the flame with a wide piece of birch bark. Once it had flared up, Arseny placed some thin branches on it. Then some fatter branches.

All we have to do now is wait for the wood to turn to ash, said Arseny. We need the ash for laundering.

Ambrogio was still standing in the water. His hands were tracing two frothy semicircles on the water.

Jump in here, he shouted to Arseny.

After wavering a bit, Arseny undressed and jumped into the river. He sensed the water as if it were someone's touch. A gentle, cool touch upon his entire body, all at once. Arseny felt happiness and was ashamed of it, for Ustina could not come into the Dvina's waters with him. He went on shore. Embarrassed at his nakedness, he wound himself in a wide sash he was not planning to launder.

After some of the branches had burned down, Arseny raked the ashes to the side and poured on water. He spread a rag on the ground and arranged the ash on it. He tied the ends of the rag then tested it. The little bundle had come out tight. He noticed a rock jutting out of the water and brought over the items that had been designated for laundering. Ambrogio had difficulty taking off his wet caftan after coming out of the water. He added some of his clothing to the caftan and placed it all on the heap Arseny had collected.

After thoroughly wetting the clothes and linens, Arseny rubbed them on the rock with the bundle of ashes. He was crouching. The ducats sewn into the caftans dully knocked when they touched the rock. Ambrogio rinsed what had been laundered and hung it on low tree branches. He hung it on rosehip bushes and pine saplings that bent under the weight of their wet medieval clothes.

Arseny lay down not far from the water. He felt the heat of the sun on his back and the softness of the grass on his stomach. Each of them was curative for his body. He himself became the grass. Small nameless creatures crawled along his arms. They conquered the tiny hairs on his skin, cleaned their little paws, and pensively flew off. Ducks beat their wings in the water. The wind stirred in the tops of the oaks, turning the leaves inside out. Arseny fell asleep.

When he awoke, he discovered he was already lying in shade. The sun had gone behind him and hidden beyond the trees. Sometimes, when the wind gusted, the sun made an appearance in openings in the crowns of the trees. The wind caught ashes from the fire, onto which Ambrogio had laid two dried-out birch trunks crosswise. The tree trunks burned slowly and dimly but dependably: the wind could not put them out. Ambrogio had managed to take the linens off the branches and was now feeling the caftans. They were all still damp.

I think we will stay here and spend the night, said Ambrogio.

We will stay, nodded Arseny.

He wanted to stay here forever but he knew that was impossible.

It grew cool at dusk. They brought some dry branches from the forest and laid them by the fire. Clouds began floating along the sky and then it finally darkened. The moon and stars were gone. The forest and river were gone. All that was left was the fire and what little it illuminated. A misshapen pyramid of logs. Two sitting wayfarers. Many-armed shadows on the trees.

Is it true there are many-armed monsters? asked Arseny.

I have not heard of them, answered Ambrogio, but one of my countrymen saw monsters when he was traveling east from Rus', and they had only one arm, and it was in the middle of their chest. Plus only one leg. Because of their peculiarities, it took two of them to shoot with one bow. But they got around so quickly the horses could not keep up with them even though they hopped on just one leg. When they got tired, they walked on the arm and the leg, turning somersaults. Can you imagine?

Ambrogio sat so his head was thrown back and his face was not visible. Based on the Italian's voice, Arseny thought the other was smiling.

Arseny was serious. He was staggered by the huge, black world that was sprawled out behind their backs. That world contained much that was unknown, that hid dangers, murmured its foliage in the night wind, and agonizingly creaked its branches. Arseny no longer knew if that world existed at all, at least for now, in that shaky time when the world dwelled in darkness. Had the forests, rivers, and cities been removed for the dark time of the day? Was nature taking a rest from its own orderliness so it could gather its strength and transform chaos into cosmos once again in the morning? The only one who had not betrayed himself in this strange time was Ambrogio, and Arseny felt a warm gratitude toward him for that.

They reached Orsha a few days later. Their supplies proved to have diminished considerably during their journey and now they did not need the pack horses. Two horses were sold in Orsha. It was easier to consider water routes with only the two remaining horses. Two days later they found a vessel bound for Kiev and boarded.

The Dnepr River was not yet wide in Orsha. It was no wider than the Velikaya, whose very name even spoke of greatness. Arseny and Ambrogio surmised, though, that it would broaden: they had heard the Dnepr truly was great, unlike the river in Pskov. Ambrogio showed some interest in learning more about this river but the boatmen turned out to be gloomy and did not keep up their end of the conversation. They knew they were being paid to carry people and cargo. And apparently surmised that they were not being paid for conversation.

They did not even converse when they gathered in a tight circle in the evenings and shared some sort of murky drink. Neither Arseny nor Ambrogio knew what, exactly, these people were drinking, only that the drink did not make them cheerier. Their backs got even more hunched. Sitting, these people brought to mind large, unattractive flowers that close up for the night. Every now and again they would begin singing something in low voices. Their songs were as joyless and murky as what they drank.

Lots of Russians are gloomy, said Ambrogio, sharing an observation.

It is the climate, nodded Arseny.

Three days later, they docked in Mogilev. Neither the city nor, particularly, its name, sounding almost like the grave itself, improved the boatmen's mood. That evening they drank more than usual but did not go to bed. A cart pulled up to the pier at around midnight. Someone whistled from the cart. The boatmen exchanged looks and went ashore. They returned with tightly tied sacks. People from the cart helped them drag the sacks onto the ship. With the curiosity and openness of one from abroad, Ambrogio wanted to ask them what was in the sacks but Arseny put his finger to his lips.

Arseny approached one of the boatmen after the ship had set sail. He took him by the neck with two hands and asked:

What is thy name, O boatman?

Prokopy, responded the boatman.

You, O Prokopy, have a tumor in your respiratory tract. Your condition is dangerous but not hopeless. If you decide to ask the Lord's help, dispose first of what burdens you.

Boatman Prokopy did not respond to Arseny but tears flowed from his eyes.

The river became significantly wider in Rogachev.

Prokopy approached Arseny in Lyubech and said:

Nobody knows of my illness yet but I am already beginning to feel short of breath.

You are short of breath because of your sins, answered Arseny.

As they were approaching Kiev, boatman Prokopy told Arseny:

I have perceaved what thou hast spoken and will do as thou hast sayde.

Upon seeing Kiev's mountains on the starboard side, boatman Prokopy shouted out:

O ye saints of the Kiev Caves, pray to God for us!

Prokopy's comrades looked at him gloomily. His unexpected piety put them on guard. When the vessel entered the Pochaina River to moor at Kiev's Podol district, Prokopy said to them:

Run from this ship that I may repente of my synnes and delyuere myself to those holding power.

If the ship had not stood at a crowded Kiev dock and if there had not been two guests on board, boatman Prokopy might not have managed to leave the ship so easily. It is entirely likely that he would not have managed to leave it at all. But circumstances were on Prokopy's side.

He went ashore and gave his final orders to his former comrades from there. He advised them not to wallow in sin and, after repenting, to go upstream on the Dnepr, to the city of Orsha, and look for honest work there. The boatmen listened silently, for how could they object to Prokopy's reasonable speech? As they followed the movement of his lips, they regretted, to a certain extent, that they had not wrung his neck somewhere outside Lyubech and tossed him into the deep waters of the Dnepr River.

The port authorities approached the ship. Boatman Prokopy told them, of his own free will, that the vessel had delivered stolen goods from Mogilev to Kiev, along with linen shirts, clay crockery, the pilgrims, and their horses. He told them that the merchant Savva Chigir was killed three weeks ago in Mogilev. Savva's property had been transported, by water, to Kiev because it could not be sold in Mogilev, where there was a danger it would be recognized. Other Mogilev merchants' property had been transported earlier using the same route; boatman Prokopy had known nothing about this, having been hired into service without any special explanations. Though he was surprised, of course, that loading took place in the dead of night, with unusual precautions for mere shirts and crockery. But Prokopy immediately suspected something amiss this time when he discovered jewelry, as well as the murdered Savva's goblet (his name was engraved on the silver goblet), in one of the bags instead of crockery. And the worsening of his health did not seem accidental to him, so he saw in the words of the pilgrim Arseny instructions from God and was, thus, repenting in the presence of everyone. Prokopy exhaled. And his next breath seemed easier to him than the one before.

After hearing the boatman's confession, the port authorities went aboard but found no people there. They found several bags that were, indeed, stuffed with valuables. They then began questioning Prokopy about his comrades and he told everything he knew. He spoke in a weakened voice because he could not get enough air.

Arseny approached Prokopy and again placed his hands on his neck. He felt it and squeezed, his index fingers resting on the larynx. The boatman had a coughing fit. He bent in half and a bloody spittle came out of his mouth. It caught on Prokopy's beard and hung over the ground like a thin pink icicle.

Considering the boatman's sincere repentance, his lack of involvement in the matter, and the sorry state of his health, the authorities released him.

Now take Communion and you will be on the road to recovery, Arseny told him. Believe me, O brother Prokopy, you have gotten off easily.

ตี

Arseny and Ambrogio had a letter from Pskov mayor Gavriil, addressed to Commander Sergy in Kiev. Gavriil asked Sergy to facilitate matters for the pilgrims and, if possible, attach them to one of the merchant caravans that left Kiev from time to time. When the pilgrims began asking where they could find the commander, local residents directed them to the Castle. That is what they called the part of the city that was on a small plateau and enclosed by a wall.

The Castle was visible everywhere. Arseny and Ambrogio took their horses by the bridles and slowly began climbing along one of the streets. The street looped but the travelers knew they would not get lost. The blackened logs of the Castle's walls hung above them.

The horde, a pedestrian told them, pointing at the darkened wall. Since I recognize you are wayfarers, I will explain the reason for this blackening to you: Mengli-Girei's horde. It was, quite frankly, a big headache.

He smiled a wide, toothless smile and went about his business.

Russians are not as gloomy as you seemed to think, after all, Arseny told Ambrogio. Sometimes they are in a good mood. After a horde leaves, for example.

A guard greeted them at the entrance to the Castle. They were admitted after giving their names. The homes of Kiev's nobility and several churches were located within the Castle. They approached Commander Sergy's house and introduced themselves to other guardians. One of them disappeared into the house after hearing what they had to say. He returned a few minutes later and signaled for the visitors to be searched. Arseny and Ambrogio were let inside after a brief pat-down.

Commander Sergy was bald with thick eyebrows. His eyebrows made his uninteresting face expressive. Thanks to his eyebrows, the slightest emotional impulse, which would go unnoticed in any other person, became a facial expression. After sternly greeting the pilgrims (brows knitted), the commander accepted their letter from Mayor Gavriil. His face smoothed as he read, depending on his level of immersion in the letter, until his brows extended into one even, fat cord. After finishing the letter, he placed it on the table and pressed his hand to it. The fingers of his other hand were tucked under the left edge of his caftan. They were moving.

I know the mayor and will help you, said Commander Sergy. I will send you with the next caravan of merchants. You will live in a guest house while you wait.

Will we need to wait long? asked Ambrogio.

Maybe a week, replied Commander Sergy. Or maybe even a month. It is anybody's guess. He took a drink from a swan-shaped dipper and drew his palm across his forehead. It is hot.

It was clear their audience was over. When they were already in the doorway, Arseny said:

You know, commander, the problem is not with your heart. It is with your spine. Basically, a lot depends on the spine. A lot more then we are sometimes inclined to suppose.

Commander Sergy's eyebrows crept upward.

You know about my heart disease?

I repeat: it is not your heart but your spine, replied Arseny. One of your veins is pinched and you think it is your heart. Undress, commander, and I will see what can be done.

After a brief hesitation, Commander Sergy began pulling off his clothes. His shoulders and chest were covered with hair. Stooped and with a large belly, he resembled the dipper from which he had drunk. Arseny pointed to a bench:

Lie down on your belly, commander.

Sergy lay down on his belly as if it were something separate from him. The bench squeaked melodiously under him. Arseny's fingers plunged into the commander's shaggy back. They ran from top to bottom, feeling vertebra after vertebra. They stopped on one of them, kneaded slightly and then let the lower part of the palm take their place. Arseny placed one palm on top of the other and began power-fully and rhythmically pressing on the spine. Ambrogio watched the patient's fatty nape shake. A light crack sounded and the commander screamed.

Okay, said Arseny. From now on the heart pain and all pain will ease for you.

Commander Sergy stood from the bench and rubbed his back. Straightened. Nothing hurt. He asked:

What dost thou ask for your doctorly help?

I ask one thing, Arseny answered after thinking a bit: that you be very wary of drafts and of lifting heavy loads. They are a sharp knife for you.

Commander Sergy accommodated them in his own chambers and did not let them go to the guest house. Many people visited them over the next three days.

The commander's father-in-law, Feognost, who had lost his flex-ibility long ago, came. It seemed he was constantly in a half-bowing position and he leaned on a low cane. Arseny settled the patient on the bench. After going over Feognost's spinal column, vertebra by vertebra, he found the reason for his inflexibility. Feognost left Arseny without his cane.

The commander's pregnant wife, Fotinya, came, complaining of the child's restlessness inside the womb. Arseny placed his hand on her belly.

You are in your eighth month, he told her, and a boy will be born. As far as his restlessness, well, he is the commander's son after all, how could he be calm?

The commander's mother-in-law, Agafya, came because a broken bone in her wrist had not knitted together after a winter fall. Arseny bandaged Agafya's wrist tightly with pieces of linen and held it in his hand.

Grieve no more, O Agafya, for you shall be whoale before the byrth of your grandson.

Among Arseny's visitors were the steward Yermei with his painful teeth, the priest's wife Serafima with the shaky head, the urban tradesman Mikhalko with the festering wound on his hip, and several other people who had heard of the astonishing help provided by this person from Pskov. And he healed the ailments of those who came to see him or gave them relief by strengthening their ability to overcome illnesses, because simply interacting with him felt curative. Still others sought to touch his hand because they felt a vitalizing strength from it. And then his first nickname—Rukinets—inexplicably flew in from Beloozero. Everyone who came to see Arseny now knew he was Rukinets. They did not learn his primary nickname until later: Doctor.

During the third night of their stay in Kiev, Arseny and Ambrogio left the city limits and went to the Kiev Monastery of the Caves. They walked along a mountain overgrown with trees as the Dnepr, a dark mass, slumbered below. It was not visible, but it breathed and made itself known, just as the sea or any other abundance of water makes itself known. Day was already breaking when Arseny and Ambrogio reached the monastery. The gently sloping left shore was visible from the mountaintop. Nothing broke the view to the east: the vista soared over a plain and reached Rus', which lay in the distant distance. A huge red sun was visible from where they stood, and it was even rising, as if in fits and starts.

They were questioned for a long time at the monastery gates, about who they were. There were doubts about letting them in when they learned Ambrogio was Catholic. Someone was sent to the abbot. He gave his blessing for both to enter, deciding a visit to the monastery could benefit the foreigner.

They were given one candle each and then a monk led them into the Caves of Saint Anthony and the Caves of Theodosius. They saw the relics of the Venerable Anthony and Theodosius. There were many other saints there, too, some of whom Arseny knew about, and occasionally some he did not know about. The monk accompanying them walked ahead. He turned at one of the twists and each of his eyes began burning as if it were a candle.

Evfrosinia Polotskaya (the monk indicated one of the reliquaries). She returned here from where you are headed. Her relics were transferred here during the times of discord in the Holy Land.

Peace be with you, O Evfrosinia, said Arseny. And we did stop in Polotsk, though of course we did not catch you there.

She will return to Polotsk in 1910, Ambrogio surmised. The relics will be transported to Orsha along the Dnepr and then carried by hand from Orsha to Polotsk.

The monk said nothing and walked on. Arseny and Ambrogio began following behind him, feeling for the uneven floor with their feet. Dawn and summer were sparkling overhead, outside, but only three candles tore into the darkness here. Darkness slipped away from the candles, though rather uncertainly and not very far. It would stay still under low arches only an arm's length away and then swirl, ready to close in again. It was already hot outside at this early hour but cool reigned here.

Is it always so cool here? asked Ambrogio.

Here there is never the frost nor the heat that are the manifestation of extremes, answered the monk. Eternity is tranquil and so it is characterized by coolness.

Arseny drew a candle toward the inscription near one of the shrines.

Salutations, O beloved Agapit, Arseny quietly uttered. I had so hoped to meet you.

To whom are you wishing health? asked Ambrogio.

This is the Venerable Agapit, an unmercenary physician. Arseny dropped to his knees and pressed his lips to Agapit's hand. You know, Agapit, all my healing, it is such a strange story… I can't really explain it to you. Everything was more or less obvious, as long as I was using herbal treatments. I treated and knew God's help came through the herbs. Well then. Now, though, God's help comes through me, just me, do you understand? And I am less than my cures, far less, I am not worthy of them, and that makes me feel either frightened or awkward.

You want to say you are worse than herbs, asked the monk.

Arseny raised his eyes to the monk.

In a certain way I am worse, for the herb does not sin.

But it does not sin because it has no consciousness, is that not so? said Ambrogio. Can this truly be a merit of the herb?

It means one must consciously rid oneself of sins, shrugged the monk. And that's all there is to it. One must be more like God, you know, not expound on things.

The three men walked on and were met by ever more new saints. The saints were not exactly moving or even speaking, but the silence and immobility of the dead were not absolute. There was, under the ground, a motion that was not completely usual, and a particular sort of voices rang out without disturbing the sternness and repose. The saints spoke using words from psalms and lines from the lives of saints that Arseny remembered well from childhood. When they drew the candles closer, shadows shifted along dried faces and brown, half-bent hands. The saints seemed to raise their heads, smile, and beckon, barely perceptibly, with their hands.

A city of saints, whispered Ambrogio, following the play of the shadow. They present us the illusion of life.

No, objected Arseny, also in a whisper. They disprove the illusion of death.

A caravan of merchants set off for Venice a week later, and Arseny and Ambrogio joined them. In releasing them for their journey, Commander Sergy did not hide the sadness he was experiencing. The commander was sorry to part with such a wonderful doctor. He was sorry to part with good conversation partners. During the short time the pilgrims had been his guests, he had managed to learn a lot about life in Pskov and in Italy, about world history, and about methods for calculating how long until the end of the world. Commander Sergy weakly endeavored to hold back his guests but made no serious attempts to stop them. He knew the reason Arseny and Ambrogio had undertaken this journey.

A caravan of forty merchants, two Novgorod envoys, and thirty guardians had formed. Money for the guards was gathered from all the travelers, including Arseny and Ambrogio, whom they charged four ducats, taking into consideration that they hardly had any cargo. Each of the merchants had brought several pack horses and many brought their cargo in wagons harnessed with oxen. When all assembled, the caravan filled the entire square in front of the Saint Sophia Cathedral. Sounds could be heard everywhere: the squeak of wagons, the neighing of horses, the bellows of oxen, and the cursing of the guardians protecting the caravan. They were angry people, as befits guardians.

The caravan set off after two hours of formation and monetary calculations. It narrowed after reaching the Golden Gates and began heavily seeping outward, as if it had come through the neck of a bottle. Those traveling with goods had to make payments to exit the city. Arseny and Ambrogio were not charged because they were traveling without goods. The only valuable object in their possession was the silver icon lamp, but nobody knew about that.

The merchants, though, were carrying furs, hats, belts, knives, swords, locks, plow iron, linen, saddles, lances, bows, arrows, and jewelry. From the perspective of the men standing at the Golden Gates, the merchants had something to pay for. Money was charged per wagon, not per individual good. They thus loaded each wagon with as much as it could hold, sometimes even more. In situations like that, if the wagons broke, their cargo, according to law, became the property of the Kiev commander. Items that fell (what might fall is windfall) were also ruthlessly taken away. The road through the gates was pitted with potholes. If the potholes smoothed over time, they were carefully gouged out again. In the Middle Ages, just as in later times, customs officers knew how to work with travelers.

The caravan stopped after traveling a considerable distance from the city walls. Ten wagons awaited them here, so they could transfer a portion of the cargo they'd brought from the city. The goods would not have made it to Venice the way they were arranged when they went through the gates, and the merchants understood that. Redistributing the goods required several hours. The sun was already low when the caravan got underway for good.

They spent the night not far from Kiev. The caravan was so large they needed to seek shelter in several villages at once. As they were being taken into the villages, the guardian Vlasy approached Ambrogio and Arseny. He held a flail in his hands and a battle ax hung from his belt.

Are you from Pskov? asked the guardian Vlasy.

We are from Pskov, the travelers replied.

I am also from there, I earn money as a guard. Let us go, I will give you good lodging.

Arseny and Ambrogio were housed in the same hut as the Polish merchant Vladislav, who was going to Krakow. He had seven bundles of sable pelts purchased in Novgorod. Vladislav piled all seven bundles by the bench where his bed had been made.

The pelts were fresh and gave off a pungent odor. The merchant held onto the lobes of his large ears, taking each in turn as he told about his goods. His ears burned from the warmth in the hut, making their unusual size even more noticeable. Several rings with gemstones shone on his fat fingers. From time to time he thrust his hands into the sable fur, as if into grass, and the precious stones twinkled from inside the bundle like hefty, inedible wild strawberries.

They are excellent pelts, summed up the merchant Vladislav.

Are there no pelts like this in Krakow? Ambrogio asked out of politeness.

But why not? There are, said the merchant, offended. Though at different prices. There is everything in the Kingdom of Poland.

He spoke with a noticeable accent, so it was difficult to make out certain words.

People's speech is no longer as reliable as it was at the beginning of our journey, Arseny told Ustina as he lay down on a bench. Words are more and more shaky now. Some slip away without being identified. To be honest, my love, this disquiets me a little.

An instant later, Arseny was sleeping.

The caravan set off again at dawn. Its formation resembled the previous evening's but did not repeat it precisely. The line-up finally took shape outside the furthest settlement where the travelers had stayed. The caravan's movement was slow: the speed was determined by the oxen, animals that are unhurried by nature. The oxen had a contemplative look, though they were not actually contemplating anything. The caravan left no tracks as it moved because there had not been any rain in a long time. Only swirls of dust, floating in the dry air, were left behind.

Arseny and Ambrogio saw the guardian Vlasy a bit ahead. He had seemed older yesterday; now he looked almost like a boy. He had dark blond hair. Gray eyes. He waved to them and said something. They could not hear over the noise of the caravan. Ambrogio pointed to his ear.

I lived in Zapskovye, shouted the guardian Vlasy. In Za-pskov-ye. He smiled. Do you know that spot?

They knew and nodded: but of course they knew Zapskovye.

The road was narrow and Arseny's horse lightly brushed against Ambrogio's horse from time to time. Arseny took his traveling companion's horse by the reins and said:

For many years, I have been attempting to devote myself to saving Ustina, whom I killed. And I still just cannot understand if my effort is beneficial. I keep waiting for some sort of sign that could show me I am going in the right direction, but I have not seen a single sign in all these years.

It is easy to follow signs, and that requires no courage, replied Ambrogio.

If this were about saving me, I would not be getting impatient. I would keep moving on and on, as long as my feet would walk, for I do not fear movement and exertion. I only fear I am not going in the right direction.

But I should think the main difficulty is not in the movement (Ambrogio met Arseny's glance), but in choosing the path.

The caravan was riding through a forest. Arseny rocked silently in the saddle and it was unclear if he was nodding as a sign of agreement with Ambrogio or was shaking his head in time with the horse's gait. When they rode onto a field, Arseny said:

I am just afraid, Ambrogio, that everything I am doing is not helping Ustina and my path is leading me away from her, not toward her. You have to understand that I have no right to go astray, what with the end of the world coming up. Because if I have gone down the incorrect path, I will not have time to return to the correct one.

Ambrogio unfastened the top buttons of his caftan.

I am going to tell you something strange. It seems ever more to me that there is no time. Everything on earth exists outside of time, otherwise how could I know about the future that has not occurred? I think time is given to us by the grace of God so we will not get mixed up, because a person's consciousness cannot take in all events at once. We are locked up in time because of our weakness.

Does that mean you think the end of the world already exists, too? asked Arseny.

I am not ruling that out. Of course death of individual people exists, and is that not, really, a personal end of the world? In the long run, history over all is just a part of personal history.

You could say the opposite, too, noted Arseny, after thinking a bit.

Yes, you could: inherently, these two histories cannot exist without each other. And here, O Arseny, what is important is that the end of the world for each individual person will come a few decades after birth—each gets however much time is allotted. (Ambrogio leaned toward the horse's neck and exhaled into his mane.) The overall end of the world worries me, as you know, but I do not dread it. Meaning I dread it no more than my own death.

The road was now wider and the merchant Vladislav pulled up alongside them.

I heard you were talking about death, said the merchant. You Russians really love talking about death. And it distracts you from getting on with your lives.

Ambrogio shrugged.

So, do people just not die in Poland? asked Arseny.

The merchant Vladislav scratched the back of his head. There was a doubtful expression on his face.

Of course they die, but ever less and less frequently.

He spurred his horse and galloped to the head of the caravan. Arseny and Ambrogio silently watched him.

I keep thinking about what you said about time, said Arseny. Do you remember how long the forefathers lived? Adam lived 930 years, Seth 912, and Methuselah 969. So tell me, is time truly not a blessing?

Time is more likely a curse, for it did not exist in Heaven, O Arseny. The forefathers lived that long because a heavenly timelessness still glowed on their faces. It was as if they had grown used to time, see? They had a little eternity in themselves, too. And then their age began to decrease. And when the pharaoh asked the elder Jacob how old he was, Jacob answered: the dayes of my pilgremage are an hundred and thirty yeres. Few and evil have bene the dayes of my lyfe, not attayning the dayes of the yeres of my fathers' pilgremage.

But Ambrogio, you are speaking of general history that you consider predestined. Perhaps that is how things really are. But personal history is something entirely different. A person is not born ready-made. He studies, analyzes his experience, and builds his personal history. He needs time for that.

Ambrogio placed a hand on Arseny's shoulder.

O friend, I do not question the necessity of time. We simply need to remember that only the material world needs time.

But we can only act in the material world, said Arseny. That is where the difference lies now between me and Ustina. And I need time, at least for her, if not for both of us. I, Ambrogio, am very afraid that time might end. We are not ready for that, neither she nor I.

Nobody is ready for that, Ambrogio quietly said.

13

The caravan reached Zhitomir a few days later. After leaving Zhitomir, it headed for Zaslav. From Zaslav its path lay to Kremenets. When they left Kremenets, the merchant Vladislav said:

The Kingdom of Poland begins after this.

He pronounced this so loudly and slowly that those around him turned. They wanted to expect something special from the Kingdom of Poland: after all, this was the first kingdom to appear along the caravan's route. The mood was animated. The caravan was making progress but the same forest, fields, and lakes that had been accompanying the wayfarers along their route continued to stretch along both sides of the road. Some of them supposed the forests, fields, and lakes were already different. Others, though, noticed a resemblance to what they had seen earlier and explained it by saying the Kingdom of Poland had not yet begun.

Night found the caravan in a deserted territory and nobody, including the merchant Vladislav, was capable of determining if this was already Poland or still Lithuania. A group of horsemen galloped past the caravan. They asked the horsemen what land the caravan was in but they did not know or did not want to answer. These were fairly gloomy horsemen.

They stopped in a field by a forest and built fires. Arseny and Ambrogio ended up by the same fire as the merchant Vladislav and the guardian Vlasy. Before lying down to sleep, the guardian Vlasy asked those present if there exist people with dogs' heads. The guardian was young and loved edifying conversations.

In traveling east from Rus', said Ambrogio, the Italian monk

Giovanni da Pian del Carpine saw many of those people. Or was told about them, which, of course, is not the same thing.

The merchant Vladislav cleared his throat and joined the conversation.

In the Kingdom of Poland, people have been seen who have a completely human appearance but the ends of their feet were like a bull's and even though the head was human, the face was like a dog's, and they would say two words like a human but yelp the third like a dog.

The Kingdom of Poland is extremely interesting, said Ambrogio, and we can only regret that we are passing through without making any lengthy stops.

They have also seen people, the merchant Vladislav went on, whose ears are so great they cover their entire body.

Arseny involuntarily looked at the merchant Vladislav's ears. They were not so very small, either, but it would be impossible to cover oneself with them.

The guardian Vlasy asked:

And are there people in the Kingdom of Poland who live only by smell? I've heard tell about them.

The Kingdom of Poland has everything, replied the merchant Vladislav. There are people with small stomachs and small mouths: they do not eat meat, they only boil it. After boiling up the meat, they lie down on the pot, soak up the steam, and sustain themselves with only that.

And what? marveled the guard Vlasy. Do they not eat anything at all?

If they eat, it is not much at all, the merchant said modestly.

The fire burned down and nobody added any new wood. Everyone, including the guardian Vlasy, began settling in to sleep. Vlasy was not on guard duty that night. The other fires went out, too, little by little, all but one, where several guardians sat. They were supposed to keep vigil until morning. A while later that fire went out, too.

Arseny pulled up some soft grass and ferns and piled them into a bed. He placed his saddle at the head. The saddle smelled of leather and horse sweat. This was especially unpleasant on a sultry night. A vague sense of alarm was entering into his soul. A full moon shone into his eyes. Arseny began turning on his side but then the saddle pressed on his cheekbone. He hesitated and turned onto his back again.

Saddles were invented for a different spot, whispered Ambrogio when he saw how Arseny was settling in. I have something a little better.

He held out a wide, soft sash for Arseny. Arseny wanted to refuse it at first but stopped himself in time. He ached with a feeling of gratitude toward Ambrogio, for looking after him. Arseny lay and thought he was, for the first time in so many years, not alone. He could feel how much he had tired of his loneliness. He began weeping. And went to sleep in tears.

$$\overline{51}$$

Arseny dreamt of screams. The screams were simultaneously warlike and blood-curdling. It was clear to Arseny that various people were producing them. It was possible they were not even people. Perhaps they were the forces fighting over Ustina. Two opposing forces pulling the soul of the deceased in various directions.

Arseny opened his eyes and knew he had not dreamt the screams. They were coming from the far end of the field where their camp had been pitched. Arseny saw guardian Vlasy run past him, unstrapping the battle ax from his belt. The guardian was running to the place the screams were coming from. Everything in the air was still drenched in darkness and it had only begun to brighten in the east, the direction from which the caravan had come.

They attacked the caravan, screamed someone close by.

And so it was. The highwaymen had chosen to attack during pre-morning sleep, when a body ripe with warmth is will-less and defenseless. They concentrated first on the guardians sitting night duty. They put up no resistance because they were not keeping vigil but were, instead, embraced by a deep sleep. They were hacked right away, in their sleep, next to the lifeless fire. One of them, who was fatally wounded, managed to shout and awaken the other guardians. The guardians, who were sleeping clothed that night, quickly rushed into action.

The highwaymen did not expect resistance. They were used to guards scattering in these situations, leaving all the goods for the attackers. But these guards did not scatter. They silently and fiercely resisted the highwaymen, fully waking up as the battle unfolded. The villains saw there would be no swift victory, and victory at any cost had not entered their plans. They decided to retreat after several of their men were lost, slain. A quiet command sounded and the highwaymen began leaving the caravan's location. Several minutes later, the group of horsemen was already rushing east. Nobody pursued them.

Only when dawn fully broke was it clear how horrible the battle had been. Four slaughtered guardians lay beside the lifeless fire. There were no weapons in their hands, they simply had not managed to wake up. The bodies of three highwaymen were also found. Based on the form of the crosses they wore, it was determined that they were Russians.

The field of battle resounded with frantic screams. They would abate then begin again with an unhuman strength, for there was nothing human in those screams. Arseny headed toward the screams. A crowd surrounded the person who was screaming but nobody had resolved to approach him. The person was writhing in pain and rolling on the bloody earth, his guts fallen out and dragging behind him, gathering dust and pine needles. When the person straightened for a moment, from a spasm, Arseny saw the screaming person was the guardian Vlasy.

The crowd parted before Arseny when he took a step toward Vlasy. They had been waiting to see who would take that step. The fervent desire to help was embodied in the speed with which a path was made for Arseny, and how broad it was. Arseny stooped over the injured man. Vlasy, a man of few words, the kindly Vlasy, had turned to suffering flesh weakened from screaming. And Arseny asked himself if there was now a spirit in that flesh, and answered himself that it could not be that there was not.

Arseny cut the suffering man's clothing with a sharp knife, baring his torso. He asked for some water. When a pitcher of water was brought, he ordered those around him to hold Vlasy by the arms and by the legs. He then lifted Vlasy's guts from the ground and began washing them with a stream of water. He felt clots of blood and mucus on their slippery surface. Vlasy began screaming as he had never screamed before. Ambrogio touched Arseny's back to support him but looked away because he did not have the strength to watch what was happening to Vlasy. Arseny placed the guts in Vlasy's belly and wrapped it in linen. Several men lifted the wounded Vlasy and laid him on one of the carts, on top of the pelts. His head hung lifelessly. Vlasy had lost consciousness.

I see he will die in a short time, Arseny told Ustina, and I, my love, am powerless to help him. But now it will be easier for him to live out that time.

They decided to bury the dead guardians in the nearest Russian village, for the merchant Vladislav informed them that the Kingdom of Poland had Russian villages as well as Polish villages, particularly near the border. After thinking things through, they decided to take the highwaymen's bodies, too, though they would be committed to the earth separately.

The caravan set off. The guardian Vlasy came to from the motion of the cart and began moaning. The jostling caused him suffering. Arseny approached the cart and took the miserable man by the shoulder. Vlasy lost consciousness again. When Arseny took his hand away, Vlasy came to and began screaming again. And so Arseny walked alongside him and did not remove his hand.

The caravan stopped when it reached the nearest village. Vlasy was exhausted from the jostling so they decided to leave him there. The merchant Vladislav went into the village because it was Polish. After several unsuccessful attempts to find a place for the wounded man, the merchant managed to come to an agreement with two elderly people. Their names were Tadeusz and Jadwiga and they had no children. These merciful people were willing to look after the wounded man.

Vlasy opened his eyes when they carried him into Tadeusz and Jadwiga's house. When Vlasy saw Arseny at his bedside, he took him by the hand, for the pain slackened as long as Arseny was holding his hand. With only his lips, Vlasy asked:

Thou leavest me, O Arseny?

The merchants from the caravan looked at Vlasy, their eyes filled with tears. They understood that everyone had to leave with the caravan.

Lament not, O Vlasy, said Arseny. I wyll byde with you.

Arseny turned to Ambrogio. Ambrogio bowed his head. He went outside with the merchants and returned a short while later, leading two horses. Arseny and Ambrogio watched from Tadeusz and Jadwiga's yard as the caravan solemnly went on its way.

Jadwiga wanted to cook porridge for Vlasy but Arseny stopped her. He would only allow the injured man to be given water. Ambrogio brought an earthenware mug to his lips again and again. Vlasy drank thirstily, not letting go of Arseny's hand. He spent the afternoon in semi-consciousness. In the evening, he opened his eyes and asked:

Will I die?

Sooner or later we all die, answered Arseny. May that be a consolation to you.

But I am dying sooner.

A film slowly covered Vlasy's eyes. Leaning over him, Arseny said:

The words *sooner* and *later* do not determine the content of occurrences. They relate only to the form in which they flow: time. Which Ambrogio reckons does not, in the final analysis, exist.

Arseny glanced back at Ambrogio.

I think, said Ambrogio, that it is not time that runs out, but the occurrence. An occurrence expresses itself and ceases its own existence. The poet dies at, say, thirty-seven years old, and when people lament over him, they begin debating about what he might yet have written. But perhaps he had already accomplished what he had to and expressed all of himself.

I do not know who you have in mind but that is something to think about. Arseny pointed at the dozing Vlasy. Do you want to say this boy has expressed himself already?

Nobody can know that, replied Ambrogio. Except God.

Vlasy squeezed Arseny's hand with unexpected strength.

I am afraid to leave this world.

Do not be afraid. That world is better. Arseny wiped the sweat from Vlasy's forehead with his other hand. I would leave myself but I need to finish something.

I am afraid to leave by myself.

You are not by yourself.

My mother and brothers are still in Pskov.

I am your brother.

So I came here to serve in the guard. To earn money. Why?

You have to live on something.

But now I do not have to. Do not let go of my hand.

I will hold it.

To the very end.

The dying man closed his eyes.

The first roosters, do you hear them?

No, said Arseny, I do not.

But I hear them. They are calling to me. It is bad that I am leaving without Communion. Without repentance.

Confess to me. I will take your Confession to Jerusalem and, I do believe, your sins will turn to dust.

But that will happen only after my death. Will that really count for me?

I am telling you: the very existence of time is open to question. Maybe there simply is no *after*.

Vlasy then began making his Confession. Ambrogio went out to the entryway, where Tadeusz and Jadwiga were sitting. They said something to him in Polish. Ambrogio did not understand what they said, but he nodded. He agreed with anything they said because he saw there were kind people.

Just do not forget any of my sins, Vlasy whispered to Arseny.

I will not forget, O Vlasy. Arseny stroked his hair. Everything will be fine, do you hear?

But Vlasy no longer heard anything.

31

Arseny and Ambrogio set off after committing Vlasy to the earth. They rode quickly, in hopes of catching up with the caravan. Caravans are unhurried, so they actually did catch up with it around midnight. The next morning, Arseny and Ambrogio hit the road along with the caravan.

The forests again gave way to fields, and small Polish towns gave way to Russian towns. Primarily Poles lived in Busk, Russians in Neslukhov, and in Zapytov, one must suppose, half and half. It was unclear who lived in Lvov. The caravan met up with the urban tradesman Stepan on a Lvov street. Stepan was not sober and his language could not be determined. He shook his fist at the riders. He went rolling under one of the guardians' horses after slipping in manure. The horse's hoof came down on Stepan's hand and broke a bone. They laid Stepan on a wagon and sent for Arseny.

What is your name, O man? Arseny asked, as he bound Stepan's hand in linen.

Stepan motioned with his healthy hand and mumbled some gibberish.

Judging from his gesture, his name is Stepan, surmised the merchant Vladislav.

Listen, Stepan, said Arseny, God's world is bigger than your small town. You should not shake your fist at people. Or you might lose a hand.

After Lvov they went through Yaroslav, and then Zheshov after Yaroslav.

In Zheshov, Arseny said to Ustina:

These Zheshovites' speech surely does shine with shushing sufficient for the inspiration of sensations of sheer satiation.

After Zheshov was Tarnov, Bokhnya was after Tarnov, and Krakow was after Bokhnya. Arseny and Ambrogio parted with the merchant Vladislav in Krakow. The merchant invited them to stay and visit his city but they gratefully declined. They needed to move on. They embraced in parting. There were tears in the merchant's eyes:

I do not like parting.

Life consists of partings, said Arseny. But you can rejoice more fully in companionship when you remember that.

But I would (the merchant Vladislav blew his nose) gather up all the good people I've met and never let them go.

I think then they would quickly become mean, smiled Ambrogio.

On the way out of Krakow, the caravan traveled along the Vistula. The river was not yet wide there. Winding along with the river, they reached the small town of Oświęcim. Ambrogio said:

Believe me, O Arseny, this place will induce horror in centuries. But its gravity can be felt, even now.

Silesia began further on. Arseny was still questioning the merchants about Silesia when it turned, unnoticed, into Moravia. He hurried to learn everything about Moravia, for nothing in Moravia heralded that it was any larger than Silesia. Slavic speech was equally interspersed with German and Hungarian in the mouths of those who lived there. German was ever more frequent as they progressed further to the southwest, until it completely displaced everything else. And then Austria began.

German speech was not alien to Arseny. In the utterances of the people he met, he divined the words he himself had once attempted to read in Belozersk, when he studied with the merchant Afanasy Flea. The pronunciation of German speakers turned out to differ significantly from Afanasy Flea's pronunciation. Afanasy, however, was only partly to blame for that. Even at the time, residents of Austria were trying to speak German in their own way. At the end of the fifteenth century, Austrians still did not know for sure if they were different from Germans and— if they were—how. In the end, the specifics of pronunciation gave them answers to both questions.

In Vienna, Ambrogio went to St. Stephen's Cathedral to take Communion. Arseny decided to accompany him. He went with Ambrogio feeling ever more certain of his decision, since there was no Orthodox church in Vienna anyway. He wanted to see a huge cathedral from within. Beyond that—and this was likely the most important thing—he had never been to a Catholic mass.

It makes a twofold impression, Arseny reported to Ustina from St. Stephen's Cathedral. On the one hand, there is the sense of something kindred because we have common roots. On the other hand, I do not feel at home here: after all, our paths diverged. Our God is closer and warmer, theirs is higher and grander. Perhaps, my love, this impression is superficial and caused by my ignorance of Latin. But throughout the entire service I just could not determine if the Austrians themselves know it.

Hugo, a Franciscan monk from Dresden, joined the caravan in Vienna. Brother Hugo had been in Bohemia for some monastery matters and was now on his way to Rome. He was riding a donkey and even explained—counting on his fingers—why he was doing so. In the first place, Christ had ridden a donkey (the monk made the sign of the cross over himself). In the second place, a donkey is smaller than a horse and, correspondingly, requires less tending. In the third place, a donkey is a stubborn animal, exactly what a true monk needs for humility.

Everything the brother said was true. The customary donkey stubbornness was intensified by the fact that the donkey did not like Brother Hugo as a rider. The brother was good-natured and genial but also fat and impatient. He constantly drove the donkey, knocking him in the sides with his heels even though the animal most valued deliberateness and quiet. It was not surprising that Hugo's talkativeness openly irritated him. Whenever Brother Hugo began speaking, the donkey hastened to bite him on the knee.

After speaking with various people in the caravan (this cost him several painful bites), the Franciscan latched onto Arseny and Ambrogio. Unlike many of the others, they understood German, more or less anyway. This was most likely the reason Brother Hugo felt at ease when talking with them, far more at ease than he felt with the traders in the caravan. Beyond that—and this was not insignificant—he began to think his donkey was calmer and bit him far less in the presence of the two pilgrims.

After leaving Vienna, the caravan began riding along the Alps. Fields spread between the road and the mountains. There was something soothing, almost lazy, in how the mountains lay. Despite the apparent calm, though, their motionlessness was illusory. Unlike the fields, which conscientiously stayed in their places, the mountains moved. The mountains accompanied the caravan on the right, neither nearing it nor distancing themselves. They rushed ahead at the same pace as the caravan, and those walking thought it was impossible to overtake them.

The mountains' movement began on the far side of the fields, where wind combed at the rye, against the grain. These expanses, which remained a plain, were already moving, along with the mountains. The mountains changed as they went along. They became taller and steeper, the forest became rock, and the rock was snow-covered. Arseny saw tall mountains for the first time and now could not stop admiring them.

And so the caravan reached Graz after Vienna, then set a course from Graz to Klagenfurt. The road was already running through the mountains here, winding and adapting itself to the giant folds of the rock. Crags came together, ever more densely, over the road. Sometimes they almost joined overhead and it would get dark. Then the mountains would part again for a while, and they would make their camp in those places because there was less danger of ending up under a rockslide.

Each time, Brother Hugo sprinkled the camp site with Irish road dust that kills snakes, for he knew that Ireland had been rid of reptiles, thanks to prayers from Saint Patrick. That country's soil is so unbearable for those scaly creatures that even toads carried in on a ship burst as soon as they are tossed onto the Irish shore. The dust, which the forward-thinking Franciscan had gathered in Ireland, continued to work, protecting the travelers in the Alps, too.

After tying the donkey to some distant bushes, Brother Hugo had a chance at camp to calmly tell how the Apennines suppress the heat of a southern wind and how the Alps' crags stop the cold northern winds, Boreas and Arktos. He also knew a little something about the Hyperborean Mountains in the Far North: their surface is as smooth as glass, allowing them to easily reflect the sun's rays. The mountains' dish-like form forces the rays to converge in one point, warming the air. The height of the mountains does not allow that air to mix with the Arctic cold, and it is precisely that which makes the climate remarkably pleasant. This is why the Hyperboreans who reside there reach such an age that they tire from life naturally and then throw themselves into the sea from high cliffs for no apparent reason whatsoever, thus putting an end to their existence, which is, of course, a sin.

When he found an opportune moment, Hugo would tell his new acquaintances about other mountains, too. He shared his knowledge about Olympus, which beholds the clouds from on high; about Mount Lebanon, which is covered by forests; and about Mount Sinai, with its peak reaching the very clouds, making it impossible for regular people to climb. As a Franciscan, of course the monk reminisced about Mount La Verna, where Saint Francis came for a retreat, blessing the mountain just as he had formerly blessed birds. Brother Hugo's attention did not overlook a mountain that Alexander the Great had passed: it turned men of courage into cowards and cowards into men of courage. Alexander was a selfless traveler and the road simply unrolled beneath his feet.

Sometimes I feel like Alexander, Arseny told Ustina, and the road unrolls itself under my feet. And like Alexander, my love, I do not know where it leads.

One day a rockslide came down on the caravan. Rocks flew, echoing a thousand times in the gorge, and that was frightening. When everything had quieted, they all saw a horse thrashing and wheezing in the bushes beside the road. The horse was frantically kicking her hooves in front of herself, and they could hear the sound of branches cracking under her rump. Arseny stopped those who intended to kill the horse to spare her suffering. Approaching the horse from the side of the bush, he placed a hand on her mane. The horse stopped pounding her legs. Blood was visibly running from a front leg. Arseny walked around the horse and felt the wounded leg.

This is not death throes, said Arseny, the horse is thrashing not because it is dying but from unbearable pain. Her leg is badly bruised but not broken. Give me some pieces of linen and I will wrap the leg to stop the bleeding.

Take it but be careful, they shouted to him from the caravan, because she could kill you with a hoof. Keep in mind, too, that the caravan cannot wait for a horse to recover.

Arseny wrapped the horse's leg and carefully drew his hand along the linen as he sat beside her. The horse got up a little while later. She walked with a limp, but walked. The merchants thanked Arseny, not so much for saving the horse as for giving them something unusual to witness. They understood this was not about the horse. The caravan moved along.

In the wide, bright gorges where the road allowed three horsemen to ride abreast, Brother Hugo's small donkey invariably ended up between Arseny and Ambrogio's horses. A staccato clopping reminiscent of a toy drum accompanied the horses' measured gait. Brother Hugo's cheeks and chins joggled in time with that staccato. The horses and the donkey walked side by side, despite the difference in their strides: this was a matter of honor for the donkey. For the brother, it was important only that both conversation partners could hear him equally well.

When it rained, Brother Hugo would tell them about the nature of various clouds; in good weather, he spoke of belts in the heavens, where daytime and nighttime luminaries float. When observing quick changes in the Alpine weather, the Franciscan did not hide from Arseny and Ambrogio his knowledge of how climate influences a person's character. Based on the climactic particularities of lands, he concluded validly that Romans were gloomy, Greeks fickle, Africans crafty, Gauls fierce, and Englishmen and Teutons sound of body. The strong mistral in the Rhône Valley led to people being flighty, airheaded, and not keeping their word. The migration of peoples, along with a change in climate, inevitably led to a change in disposition. Thus the Lombards who moved to Italy lost their severity in part, of course, because they married Italian women but mostly, one might think, because of climactic conditions.

Brother Hugo, there are many useful things, said Arseny, that we would never have learned had we not met you.

Moving around within an expanse enriches our experience, the brother modestly said.

It compacts time, said Ambrogio, and makes it more spacious.

A person journeying in the Alps is similar to a person moving through a labyrinth. He zigzags along the bottom of gorges, following their form, and his route is never direct. Gorges merge together at times, giving the traveler an opportunity to transit, unimpeded, from one to the other. But mountains, which are primarily an ordeal for a person, do not always offer the convenience of transitions. Situations where mountains completely shut off a gorge are not uncommon. In those situations, there is only one route: up.

That was exactly what lay ahead for the caravan. The road went along the gentlest of slopes and the caravan was slowly gaining altitude. Whenever the ascent was not too steep, Brother Hugo told of the astonishing nature of glaciers, which not only slip down between cliffs but are also in constant internal motion, meaning their upper parts gradually sink and their lower parts rise to the surface, causing the bodies of those who have fallen into crevasses or deep cracks to be discovered only afterwards, when they have risen to the surface of the ice. Brother Hugo also imparted knowledge of avalanches set loose by the slightest shout, speeding away, growing like an enormous, shapeless lump, and rolling into themselves everything that comes across their path—people, horses, and carts—and then nothing that was caught up in the avalanche can come to the surface, for an avalanche stops for the ages after its descent.

The incline grew ever steeper with each hour, making the ascent not only difficult but also unsafe. The air was already appreciably colder. The road narrowed. A sheer cliff rose to the walkers' right; to the left, a stream roared at the bottom of the gorge, a rainbow glistening in its spray. Snow began to fall after they'd climbed higher, and drops and vapor from the stream settled and froze on the road, making it slippery.

Brother Hugo's donkey's legs kept splaying and even the shod horses were slipping noticeably. The donkey fell on its front legs several times and Brother Hugo dismounted. He was no longer telling stories and he walked, panting, ahead of Arseny and Ambrogio. The width of the road now only allowed two to ride abreast. A little later, those who rode horses dismounted and led their horses by the bridle. Those who owned wagons pushed them from behind because the oxen's legs had begun helplessly scrabbling at the ice.

On yet another bend in the road, the donkey's legs went off to the right, he fell on his side, and ludicrously began to slip, taking Brother Hugo along behind him. The donkey was slipping downward and slowly rolling, as everyone stood motionless, watching: his rather-too-large white stomach, onto which the travel bags had fallen, was shaking, and his legs were helplessly twitching, which only sped the downward motion, all as Brother Hugo slipped along with him, powerless to let go of the rope...

The Franciscan let go of the rope when Ambrogio grabbed him by the scruff of the neck at the very last moment, but the animal continued slipping, making a horrible whooshing sound on the iced rocks, and sliding all the way to the edge of the precipice. The donkey hung in the air. He fell into the stream, his bellow diminishing.

Brother Hugo rose to his feet. He silently cast his gaze over everyone. He took a few steps toward the precipice, and those standing nearby were already prepared to grab him, thinking he had lost his senses. But Brother Hugo fell to his knees. It was unclear if he was praying or if his legs simply could not hold him. And when he stood, there was a clump of donkey fur in his hand. He held the clump in front of everyone and tears flowed from his eyes.

Brother Hugo wept for the rest of the descent from the mountain pass. He held onto one of the wagons along with everyone else, so it would not roll too fast, and tears streamed down his face. He kept taking out the clump of fur he had picked up and pressing it to his eyes. In a flat area, two Kiev merchants sat Brother Hugo in a cart with furs because he was short of breath from the fast walking. In mourning his dead comrade, he unexpectedly noticed that nothing was biting him any longer. That could not reconcile him with the loss, though it did ease his pain to some degree.

K̃

The way out of the final Alpine gorge was narrow. It was reminiscent of an archway, with its upper part formed by young saplings that had grown along both sides of the road on the cliffs and bent toward one another. It was in that archway that a group of horsemen appeared, blocking the caravan's way. The caravan's tail end was still continuing to make its way through the ravine, though the guards at its head were no longer moving. They stood some distance from the horsemen, making no attempt to near them, for their appearance presaged nothing good.

They are highwaymen, said Brother Hugo, sitting on the furs; those around him could not help but agree.

The highwaymen spoke amongst themselves in Italian. After brief deliberations, Ambrogio was entrusted to negotiate with them. Several guardians offered to go with him but Ambrogio refused. He pointed to Arseny, who was riding toward him, and said:

The two of us are enough.

Three, Brother Hugo intervened. Three. I speak Italian, too, after all. Besides, as of today I have nothing to lose.

They then gave Brother Hugo a horse so he would be on the same level as the highwaymen rather than speaking to them from a lower position. Those in the caravan thought the monk's appearance was capable of softening even the hardest hearts. The three riders slowly headed toward the highwaymen.

Peace be with you, shouted Brother Hugo, still far away.

No answer followed, and the brother repeated his greeting from closer range.

You don't speak our language so well, stranger, said a highwayman on a white horse. You must pay for that.

The other highwaymen began laughing. The speaker seemed to be the ringleader. He was heavyset and not young. His face was as crimson as a glass of Piemonte wine and a sable scar was engraved into his skull on his deeply receding hairline. His horse was pawing at the ground, clearly expressing the horseman's impatience.

To the Lord, there are no strangers, objected Brother Hugo.

Then we will send you to Him, the ringleader said, and you can be among your own people there. And your stuff will be left for us.

The highwaymen laughed again, this time with more restraint. They themselves still did not know to what extent that was a joke.

We have good guards and they will not run away, said Ambrogio. This has been proven.

Proven but not by us.

The ringleader pulled the reins and his horse neighed.

Ambrogio shrugged.

You will have losses, no matter how this all ends.

Without answering anything, the ringleader and several of the highwaymen rode off to the edge of the path. They deliberated for a fairly long time. These people were not the type to fight for the sake of fighting, so they understood the outcome of the battle was not foregone. After steering his horse toward Ambrogio, the ringleader said:

You bring us ten ducats per person, including guards, and no blood will be shed.

Ambrogio became pensive.

One ducat per person, said Brother Hugo. Infidels charge two ducats for the opportunity to go to the Holy Sepulcher in Jerusalem, which is a total rip-off. In this case, it is the Christians who are robbing us, so I believe it ought to be possible to limit it to one ducat.

We appear to be bargaining, said the surprised ringleader.

I am trying to ease your conscience as much as I can, said Brother Hugo.

After an extensive discussion, they reached a sum acceptable to all: five ducats from each in the caravan. When Brother Hugo rode off to the caravan to announce the result of the negotiations, Arseny said to Ambrogio:

The person who was speaking with you is in danger. There is a loud noise in his head. Blood is pressing on the vessels in his head and they are ready to burst. I see, Ambrogio, that they are swollen from too much blood. They look like fat, coiled-up worms. Blood circulation can still be improved in that head, but believe me: nothing will work out unless there is a change of thought in there.

After hearing what Arseny had to say, Ambrogio addressed the ringleader:

The noise you hear in your head is the consequence of thoughts that have settled in there. The noise is life-threatening but my comrade could still help you.

The highwaymen, who knew nothing about the noise in the ringleader's head, began laughing again. But the ringleader remained serious. He asked:

And what does your comrade ask for that?

He is a person of the Greek-Russian belief and asks that you alter your thinking; put another way: that you repent, for repentance in Greek is *metanoia*, which literally means a change in thoughts.

You are bargaining again, smirked the ringleader. But only money can be the object of bargaining.

This is not bargaining, it is a condition, said Ambrogio, shaking his head. A necessary condition, so that my comrade could help you.

Carrying the money, Brother Hugo rode up to the men as they conversed. The ringleader took the small bag with the gold coins from his hands and tossed it to one of the highwaymen to be counted. He turned to Arseny and Ambrogio as they were riding away:

You know, I have not yet accepted anyone's conditions. He pointed at a piece of sky closed off by the cliffs. Not even His.

The caravan silently watched as the highwaymen left the gorge. The caravan began moving, too, after the last highwayman had disappeared behind the cliff. Everyone understood they had gotten off easy this time, though that gave them no joy.

There are so many different kinds of people in the world, sighed one of the Kiev merchants.

What did he say? Brother Hugo asked Ambrogio.

He said that people are very dissimilar.

What is true is true, confirmed Brother Hugo.

He again climbed onto the wagon with the furs. After settling in comfortably on the sable pelts, Brother Hugo continued:

There are all kinds of people. They say there are people known as androgyns. They have a body that is masculine on one side, feminine on the other side: a person like that has a masculine right nipple but a feminine left nipple. And there are people known as satyrs. Their dwellings are in mountain forests and their movement is quick: nobody can catch up when they run. They go around naked and their bodies are covered with hair. They speak no human language, they just shout shouts. As we know, there are also sciapods, people who rest in the shade of their own feet. Their feet are so big (Brother Hugo raised his own feet) that in hot weather they cover themselves with them, like an awning. There are, I can report to you, many various creatures born into the world: some have dog heads, some have no heads, teeth on the chest, eyes on the elbows, some have two faces, some have four eyes, some have six horns on their heads, and some have six digits on their hands and on their feet.

If they truly exist, asked Arseny, turning, what is the purpose of their existence?

Brother Hugo grew pensive.

There is no purpose, only a reason. The whole thing is that after the Tower of Babel, God let everyone live as their hearts desired. And so some went astray. They chose their paths to conform to their desires, and their outward appearances began to correspond to their ways of thinking. It is all very logical.

Ambrogio began laughing:

Logical? I have known people whose ways of thinking were such that, according to this logic, they should have looked very frightening. But they looked totally fine nevertheless.

Ambrogio spurred his horse and galloped ahead without waiting for an answer. Arseny followed him after reflecting a bit.

There are no rules without exceptions, Brother Hugo shouted to them as they rode off. They tell, for example, of antipodes who live on the other side of the earth. And, just imagine, many of them look exactly the same as us.

But Ambrogio could no longer hear him.

How do you like that? Brother Hugo said to the Kiev merchants.

The merchants nodded. They did not understand a word of German.

But I do not much believe the stories about antipodes, continued the brother, encouraged, and do you know why? Well, because to take them seriously, one must be willing to declare that the world is round! I am not even saying that this is funny or that it is blasphemy—it is, above all, ridiculous. As soon as we acknowledge that the world is round, we will simply be obligated to acknowledge that people on the other side of the earth walk upside down!

Brother Hugo began loudly laughing. The Kiev merchants also started smiling as they looked at him. Brother Hugo's laugh proved so infectious that within just a minute the entire caravan was laughing. Thanks to that laugh, the anxiety that everyone felt after being subjected to mortal danger over the last several days departed. That laughter contained the joy of people for whom Venice, the most wonderful city on earth, awaited ahead.

As the caravan was leaving its nighttime campsite the next morning, two horsemen rode up from the Alps side. Members of the caravan recognized them as the highwaymen they had met the day before. When the highwaymen saw Arseny and Ambrogio, they approached them.

Our leader is in a very bad way, the highwaymen said to Ambrogio. He was stricken yesterday and is lying motionless. Can your comrade help in some way?

Ambrogio interpreted for Arseny what they had said.

Inform them that I am now powerless to help, Arseny answered. This person's hours are numbered and he will die in the evening. There is mercy in the quick death the Almighty has presented to him.

After hearing Arseny's reply, the highwaymen said:

When he was still able to speak, he asked to give you this.

One of the highwaymen took out the little bag with the gold coins and gave it to Ambrogio. Right then and there they returned the money to the people who had given it the day before. The caravan set its course for Venice.

Guards stopped the caravan upon its arrival into Venice. They asked everyone for traveling papers that could prove the wayfarers were arriving from the north, not the southeast. The plague was raging in Asia Minor and the authorities feared its entry into the Venetian Republic. Everyone had letters except Brother Hugo, who had lost his along with his bags and donkey, but the caravan unanimously confirmed the brother had crossed the Alps with them.

I crossed, sighed the Franciscan, though he was not convinced it had been the right decision.

They all parted ways in Venice. The parting was marked with an especial cordiality, for many knew they were parting forever. In this lay a particularity of partings during that era. The Middle Ages rarely presented opportunities that brought people together twice during the course of an earthly life.

Brother Hugo invited Arseny and Ambrogio to spend the night at the Franciscan monastery. With no other shelter in Venice, they gratefully accepted the invitation. Brother Hugo's memory of the route was shaky, so it took some time to reach the monastery. He rode the same horse as Ambrogio, pointing out which way to go. Streets looped, turned into dead ends, or led back to previous spots. Thrice they found themselves on Piazza San Marco and twice at the Rialto Bridge. The horses went one after the other, the clopping of their hooves overpowered by its own echo. Sometimes they had to press right up against walls to let through horsemen riding in the opposite direction. Ambrogio looked at Arseny with a smile. It was the first time he had seen his friend so amazed.

Arseny truly was amazed: he had never seen anything like this. One time he even stopped on a bridge to watch as an elderly Venetian woman stepped directly down from the doorway of her own home into a gondola. The gondola began rocking under her foot. Arseny turned away. He cautiously turned his head when he heard the splash of an oar. The woman was sitting calmly in the stern. She had been leaving her house just like this for the last half-century, so never suspected Arseny was alarmed.

The travelers were received affably at the monastery. Brother Hugo informed the prior that Arseny was not a Catholic and the prior answered with an elaborate gesture. That gesture could be interpreted in various ways, but it did not indicate a direct ban on staying at the monastery. That, at least, was how Brother Hugo perceived it. He brought Arseny and Ambrogio to a cell intended for three, where water for washing and beds had been prepared for them. They would be expected at evening table in an hour.

None of the three went to table. Brother Hugo and Ambrogio sank into a deep slumber after the road, but Arseny was experiencing deep excitement over his encounter with Venice. It would not let him sleep.

It would not even let him stay in the cell. He quietly went downstairs and stepped outside after bowing to the porter.

The monastery stood on a canal. It seemed like a regular house from the street, no different from the other houses built right up against one another. A thin strip of a roadway ran between the houses and the canal, so here one need not walk straight onto the water from a house. Arseny took several steps toward the canal. He crouched and watched seaweed billowing on a mooring post. The water here smelled different from that of other places he'd visited. The smell was putrid. Arseny felt happy when he remembered it afterwards, for this was the smell of Venice.

Evening was falling. The sun was not visible because of the buildings, but the walls that the sun's last rays still reached had turned ocher and yellow. Arseny walked along the canals—in the places it was possible to walk—and crossed arch-shaped little bridges. At first he tried to remember the route he had taken so he could return, but after just a few streets he could not even determine the direction in which the Franciscan monastery lay. Never in his life thus far had he found himself in such an astonishing place, and now he could not commit it all to memory. Arseny had developed a feel for the expanse of the forest and the expanse of the field, the icy emptiness of Beloozero and the wooden streets of Pskov, finding his way around everywhere without difficulty. But now, after ending up among overlapping water and stone, it occurred to him that he had no sense of this expanse. He was alone in a strange and wonderful city and did not know its language. The only one who could help him was asleep, exhausted, in a monastery that was in some unknown place. And Arseny grew calm.

He set off at random and no longer tried to remember his way. Several streets at the beginning seemed familiar to him. But then, the next instant, he would discover balconies and bas-reliefs he had not seen before and understand that similarity was brazenly passing itself off as repetition. After it had grown completely dark, Arseny came upon Piazza San Marco. The rising moon brightened the basilica, which in the murk resembled a dark mountain. Ambrogio had told Arseny it was made of stones from sacked Constantinople. He touched a marble column and sensed the warmth it had absorbed during the day. He thought this was likely the warmth of Byzantium.

Arseny sat down to the right of the entrance and leaned against a column. He could feel that he was tired. As he was settling in more comfortably, Arseny touched on something soft. A young woman was sitting in a niche between the columns, and her child-like face seemed to be one of the bas-reliefs, perhaps because it was motionless. Arseny brought his hand to her eyes and she blinked.

Peace to thee, childe, Arseny uttered. I wanted only to know that life had not left you.

She looked at him, unsurprised.

My name is Laura and I do not understand your language.

I see you are somehow dispirited but I do not know the reason for your sorrow.

Sometimes it is easier to speak when people do not understand you.

Maybe you are pregnant and your child will not be legitimate because its father has not become your husband.

Because when you live in despair, you want to express your pain but are afraid it will become known to everyone when it leaves your lips.

You know, there is nothing irreparable about that. The child's father can still become your husband. Or another person might become your husband, that does happen. Believe me, I would take you as my wife to help you, but I cannot because I have an eternal love and an eternal wife.

But you could say I am no longer afraid. I know of a way to reconcile all my problems. If things get completely awful for me, my despair will give me the strength to use it.

In my life, I had Ustina and I had a little boy without a name, but I did not keep them safe.

A few days ago I heard that I am sick, with leprosy. When the spots appeared on my wrists, I did not know, at the time, what they meant. And I did not figure things out when the tickle started in my throat in the middle of the summer, either. But some chance person on the street saw me and said: why, you have leprosy. He said: abandon this city and go to the leper colony, so you do not become a curse upon your house. And I went to a doctor and the doctor confirmed that person was correct.

I have been trying to talk with them ever since, but they just cannot seem to answer me. The boy was small when he died so he cannot answer. But even Ustina is not answering. Of course in their position, things are not all that simple. How could I not understand that? I understand... but I am still waiting. Maybe not for a word but for a sign. Sometimes this is very difficult for me.

And I have not gone back home since. I knew my loved ones would not let me go and would prefer to slowly die with me.

But I am still not giving in to despair. And I do try, to the best of my ability, to tell Ustina about what happens here. She did not live out her life, after all, so I am trying to somehow fill in what was left unlived. But that is very difficult. You just cannot tell about an entire life in all its details, you know?

A wall has been built between me and the rest of the world. It is glass for now because nobody knows about my troubles. But it will be noticeable later. The doctor told me everything. It seemed like that gave him satisfaction. Or maybe he wanted to rid me of hopes and disappointments.

All you can truly convey to them there is a general idea, the main things that are happening. My love for her, for an example.

They will send me to a leprosarium. In time, I will have a saddle nose. Leonine facies. I will be ashamed that the sun that belongs to everyone falls on this face. I will know that I have no right to it. I have no right whatsoever to what is beautiful. It is possible to die while still living.

Arseny took Laura by the hands, looked her in the eye, and then the essence of what was happening was revealed to him. He kissed Laura on the forehead.

Be in good health, childe. Much is reparable as long as a person is on this earth. Know that not every illness remains in the body. Even the most terrible. I cannot explain this with anything but the mercy of the Almighty, but I see the leprosy will leave you. So you return to your loved ones and embrace them and do not ever part with them.

When he saw that Laura had no more strength, Arseny helped her stand and brought her home. A light nocturnal rain began to fall. The sky was still free of clouds in the part where the moon was. Wet gondolas glistened, rocking, in the moonlight. Water splashed at the gondolas' hulls with a resonant smacking sound. On the threshold of her home (in the embraces of her parents), Laura turned to Arseny.

But Arseny was not there. The spectral city was made so one could vanish within it. Dissolve in the rain. Laura knew this and was not surprised. Arseny had not seemed like a real creature to her even when he was alongside her. Laura could not have repeated his words but they had filled her with endless joy, for their main meaning had already been disclosed to her. She now perceived recent days as a dreadful dream. She herself did not understand what had happened to her and she wanted, more than anything on earth, to awaken.

Arseny walked toward the monastery. It had become more or less clear to him which direction to take now that the sky had completely clouded over and rain was falling like a solid wall. Brother Hugo and Ambrogio did not know of his absence. They were sleeping and dreaming.

Brother Hugo was dreaming of his donkey—affectionate, with a groomed mane, and elegantly decorated. He slowly soared over a precipice, his appearance reminiscent of Pegasus. A white horsecloth fluttered ever so slightly on his back. I always knew that nothing of what has been disappears, Brother Hugo whispered in his sleep. Not a person, nor an animal, nor even a sheet of paper. *Deus conservat omnia.* His face was wet with tears.

Ambrogio dreamt of a street in the city of Orel. A group of five people was being photographed on the steps of the Russian Linen store. Left to right: Nina Vasilyevna Matveyeva, Adelaida Sergeyevna Korotchenko (top row); Vera Gavrilovna Romantsova, Movses Nersesovich Martirosian, Nina Petrovna Skomorokhova (bottom row).

May 28, 1951. Director Martirosian had suggested the group organize a celebration in honor of the Russian Linen store's fifth anniversary. The women made jellied meat, stuffed cabbage, beet salad, and rice pilaf at home. They brought all that to work in pots and set it out in dishes and salad bowls. They licked the spoons after stirring up the beet salad and rice pilaf, one after the other. Movses Nersesovich brought two bottles of Champagne and a bottle of Ararat cognac. He arrived wearing medals. The women smelled of perfume and ironed dresses. There was the smell of a sunny May day. They said toasts (Movses Nersesovich), it was lots of fun. The medals on the store director's chest jingled pleasantly when he raised his glass. Then the photographer came and took pictures of them, with the store in the background. When she examined the yellowed photograph in 2012, Nina Vasilyevna Matveyeva said: Then Movses announced the store would close early that day. Of everyone you see in the photograph, only I am still alive. I cannot even visit their graves because I moved to Tula and they stayed in Orel. Could that all really have happened to us? It's as if I'm looking at them from the great beyond. Lord, how I do love them all.

A week later, Arseny and Ambrogio boarded the ship *Saint Mark*. During that week, Brother Hugo was able, through the monastery prior, to solicit traveling papers for them from the Venetian doge, signor Giovanni Mocenigo. This letter had the purpose of protecting them throughout the Venetian Republic, which extended along both sides of the Adriatic Sea. Arseny and Ambrogio had to sell their horses during those same days. A long sea journey lay ahead and nobody knew how the animals might withstand it. Besides, transporting horses was not cheap.

Arseny and Ambrogio had orders to be on the ship by midnight. Brother Hugo saw them off to the dock. He left Venice the next day, too, and headed for Rome. The Franciscan brothers had given him another donkey, but he did not consider it a worthy replacement. After giving it a meticulous inspection and chucking it on the withers, Brother Hugo said:

This animal lacks real character and I fear it will not keep me humble.

Fear not, Brother Hugo, replied the Franciscans. Leave your worries behind, for this animal will keep you humble. He has an attitude, and that explains, to a certain degree, our desire to part with him.

Wishing as he did to help Arseny and Ambrogio bring their luggage to the dock, Brother Hugo loaded their bags on his new donkey. Essentially, the load was not that large but the donkey did not want to carry even that. He angrily bucked the whole way, trying to throw off the leather bags that had been tossed over the saddle. He rubbed the bags against walls and caught them on the stirrups of horsemen riding past. Brother Hugo calmed a bit when he saw that. He realized he still had a chance of being kept humble.

Brother Hugo embraced the sea travelers at the dock. He wept and said:

Sometimes you wonder if it is worth getting attached to people if it will be this difficult to part with them later.

Arseny slapped Brother Hugo on the back as he embraced him:

You know, O friend, any meeting is surely more than parting. There is emptiness before meeting someone, just nothing, but there is no longer emptiness after parting. After having met someone once, it is impossible to part completely. A person remains in the memory, as a part of the memory. The person created that part and that part lives, sometimes coming into contact with its creator. Otherwise, how would we sense those dear to us from a distance?

After boarding, Arseny and Ambrogio asked Brother Hugo not to wait for them on the dock, since nobody knew exactly when the vessel would set sail. The Franciscan nodded but did not leave. In the weak lights of the ship, it was not immediately obvious that the rope kept pulling in Brother Hugo's hands or that the donkey resisted desperately because he did not want to leave the dock. The animal observed the embarkation of 120 infantrymen the Venetian doge was sending for service in Crete. They arrived in full uniform and the women accompanying them were doubly sad to let them go when they were looking so smart. This, thought the women, is the first time we have seen them like this. And perhaps the last, too.

The vessel raised anchor at four o'clock in the morning, just before dawn. It slowly left port; the contours of San Marco's Basilica could already be divined against the backdrop of a brightening sky. Even as all the other travelers slept below in hammocks, Arseny did not leave the deck for several hours. He listened with delight to the mast creaking and the sails flapping: this was the sweet music of wayfaring. Arseny observed as the water gradually turned from black to pink and from pink to emerald.

It seemed to Arseny that—compared to the water he had seen previously in his life—sea water was a liquid with a completely different composition. He tasted the salinity of the waves' spray when he licked it off his hands. Seawater was another color, and it smelled different and even behaved in another way. It did not have fine river ripples. It varied from river and even lake water as much as a crane varies from a sparrow. In reaching that comparison, Arseny did not mean to imply size so much as the character of the respective motions. Seawater rolled in large billows and its motions were grand and smooth.

The ship's captain, a puffy man with large lips, approached Arseny when he saw his interest in seawater. The captain had heard Arseny's conversation with Brother Hugo and so began speaking with him in German:

Sea and river water are two different elements. I would never agree to do this work on fresh water, signor.

Arseny lowered his head as a sign of respect for the captain's point of view. Drawn by the discussion of water, two pilgrims from Brandenburg drew closer to Arseny and the captain.

It is completely obvious, the captain was continuing, that fresh water is weaker than salt water. If anyone doubts that, then let them explain to me why, for example, seawater is capable of pushing back a powerful flow of fresh water, like the Seine in Rouen, and forcing it to flow in the reverse direction for three days.

It is possible, said pilgrim Wilhelm, that fresh water thinks salt water is disgusting and so retreats when faced with it.

But I think, objected pilgrim Friedrich, that a river expresses its deference to its father—the sea—by yielding the road to it. And when the tide begins to go out, the river follows him just as deferentially.

In speaking of fatherhood, are you, foreigner, presuming there is a kinship between such differing elements? asked the surprised captain.

Of course, said pilgrim Friedrich. After all, the sea is the source of all rivers and springs, just as the Lord Jesus Christ is the source of all virtue and knowledge. Do not all pure aspirations, every last one of them, stream from one and the same source? And just as spiritual streams rush to their source, all waters return to the sea.

What do you think about the circumrotation of waters? pilgrim Wilhelm asked Arseny.

Our earth is reminiscent of the human body, replied Arseny, with canals running all through the inside, just as blood vessels run through the body. No matter where a person starts to dig up the earth, he will certainly strike water. That is what my grandfather Christofer said, and he felt water under the earth.

I had two grandfathers but never saw either one, sighed the captain. Both were sailors and both drowned.

Everyone was quiet for a while after the captain said that.

The flow of fresh water into salt water, the pilgrim Friedrich softly said, is something I liken to how the sweetness of this earth ends up turning to salt and bitterness.

ΚΓ

A day and a half after setting sail from Venice, the *Saint Mark* had crossed the Adriatic Sea and cast anchor a quarter-mile from the city of Parenzo. Cliffs prevented approaching the city any closer, but there was no possibility of moving further anyway: the sea was dead calm. Numerous travelers were on deck.

Parenzo is a beautiful city, Arseny told the captain.

It is beautiful because Paris founded it, said the captain. So they say.

They are mistaken, said pilgrim Wilhelm.

So then why do Paris and Parenzo sound similar? The captain's puffy lips sprayed saliva as he pronounced the two proper nouns. Paris, I can report to you, founded the city when the Greeks stole Helen.

The Greeks did not steal Helen, said pilgrim Friedrich. That is just a heathen tall tale.

And maybe Troy is a tall tale, too? the captain asked maliciously.

Troy is a tall tale, too, confirmed pilgrim Friedrich.

The captain raised his hands in a helpless gesture and licked his wet lips. He most definitely had nothing to add.

I am not sure you are right, my dear Friedrich, said Ambrogio. I have a hunch that someone will find Troy one fine day. Perhaps it will even be someone from your part of the world.

Fair winds began blowing toward evening of that same day. They sailed for a full day with that wind but then had to enter the Dalmatian port of Zara because an opposing wind, known to Italians as the sirocco, began blowing. The travelers needed to prepare themselves to remain patient because this wind could blow for several days. One hundred and twenty infantrymen indifferent to coastal cities started playing dice together. All the rest of the travelers went ashore.

They were met on the dock by the Venetian pretor, who inquired if the ship had come from healthy air or not. They assured him the ship had arrived from Venice and not from the East. The pretor was also shown their traveling letters from the Venetian doge, and he permitted all who wished to go into the city and its fortress.

The city of Zara was famous because the relics of a pious elder rested in the Church of Saint Simeon. Arseny and Ambrogio went to bow to Simeon. As they sank to their knees before his incorruptible relics, Arseny said:

Now lettest thou thy servant departe in peace, acordinge to thy promesse, for myne eyes have sene my salvation. You know, O Simeon, I am not expecting any reward comparable to yours. And my salvation consists of salvation for Ustina and the baby. Take them in your arms as you took the Christ Child and bring them to Him. That is the gist of my entreaty and prayer.

Arseny touched Simeon's relics with the upper part of his forehead so as not to dampen them with tears. But one tear found its way from his lashes anyway and fell on the relics. Fine, let it abide there, thought Arseny. It will remind the elder of me.

The next day, Arseny, Ambrogio and the two Brandenburg pilgrims took a walk around the fortress in the city of Zara. Before returning to the ship, they stopped to eat at a tavern, where people representing the Croatian population of the Venetian Republic were celebrating something or other. These residents of Zara pricked up their ears when they saw guests in traveling clothes. The Turkish threat was no longer just empty noise, so they did not rule out that the strangers could turn out to be enemy infiltrators. Suspicion changed to certainty as their consumption of beverages increased. The final thing that reinforced this certainty was the pilgrims' German, which was quickly taken for Turkish. The revelers all stood at once, overturning, with a crash, the benches they had been sitting on.

Arseny and Ambrogio, who generally understood Slavic speech, grasped the sense of what was happening before the others. But it became clear, even to the Brandenburg pilgrims, who did not understand Slavic speech, that events were taking a dangerous turn. A tin mug flew at pilgrim Wilhelm, because he was speaking an incomprehensible language.

Arseny took several steps in the direction of the attackers and extended his hand. For a moment, it appeared that this gesture had calmed them. They froze and stared, rapt, at Arseny's hand. Arseny said to them in Russian:

We are pilgrims who are going to the Holy Land.

His language seemed understandable, albeit strange, to the residents of Zara. The revelers' own speech was already garbled, too, so they regarded it with a fitting tolerance. Calmer already, they said to Arseny:

Go on, then, cross yourself.

Arseny crossed himself.

The storm resumed in the same breath:

He cannot even cross himself properly! Could we have expected anything else from the Turkish infiltrators?

For a while, Ambrogio attempted to explain that Catholics and Orthodox cross themselves differently and demanded they be taken to the Venetian pretor, but nobody would listen to him any longer. The residents of Zara were discussing how they should handle the captured men. After a brief but heated argument, they came to the conclusion that the infiltrators should be hung. Further, the residents of Zara were not inclined to postpone the matter to a later date, since they were well aware that time is the arch-enemy of decisiveness.

They demanded rope from the tavern keeper. He initially would not give it to them since he feared the offenders would be hung right in his tavern. When he learned the rope was only needed, at this point, for tying (who would hang people in a tavern, anyway?) he gladly gave it to them and even poured a last round, on the house, for the infiltrators' captors. After tying up the captured men, despite their resistance, they drank quickly since the task before them was onerous and required time. They were already in the doorway when they asked for more rope but—more importantly—for some soap, which they had completely forgotten after the last toast, which they drank to the ruin of all infiltrators.

Our death will be so stupid, Ambrogio said to Arseny in a quiet voice.

But what death is not stupid? asked Arseny. Is it not stupid that coarse iron enters the flesh, violating its perfection? He who is not capable of creating even a fingernail on a little finger is destroying a most complex mechanism, something inaccessible to human comprehension.

It was decided the sentence passed at the tavern would be carried out in the port. There were many suitable beams and hooks there, and the space was open, too, meaning it was accessible for viewing, as an edifying lesson to all prospective infiltrators.

Ambrogio again attempted to get through to the hearts and minds of the residents of Zara. He shouted to them that the pilgrims had traveling papers from the Venetian doge and had offered more than once to cross themselves in the Catholic way, but all was in vain. The hearts and minds of these people were impaired by alcohol.

Arseny was surprised at the mistrust of Zara's residents. Perhaps (he thought) infiltrators truly had tormented them here. Arseny also did not rule out that these people simply felt like hanging someone.

They finally stuffed a gag in Ambrogio's mouth. After conferring, they untied all the prisoners' legs so they could walk, but left their hands tied. Now Ambrogio could neither shout nor cross himself.

He walked alongside Arseny and looked at the pair of Brandenburg pilgrims striding in front of them. Despite the high drama of what was happening, their appearance could not help but evoke smiles. They walked, swaying from side to side, and their tied hands behind their backs gave them a solemn, almost professorial, appearance. They also resembled the pair of penguins that Europe would become acquainted with in another ten or fifteen years. Friedrich and Wilhelm still understood nothing and hoped the misunderstanding would be cleared up very soon. Arseny did not want to dissuade them of this notion, nor did Ambrogio, either, though of course he could not speak anyway.

My love, Arseny said to Ustina in the port, it is very possible that my journey—but not my love for you—will come to an end right here. Stepping back from the sad side of all this, I can be glad that my journey is concluding in such a beautiful place: with a view of the sea, a distant island, and all the grandeur of God's world. Most important, though, I am glad my last hours are elapsing alongside the devout elder Simeon, whose aspiration, unlike mine, was fulfilled. I am sorry, my love, that I managed to do so little, but I firmly believe that if the All-Merciful takes me now, He will accomplish everything we did not accomplish. Without that belief, there would be no point in existing, either for me or for you.

The sun was already low. It had sketched a journey for itself from a mooring in the port to the horizon. It left no doubt that it also intended to set there, at the most distant point. The sun beat right into Arseny's eyes but he did not squint. The sun beat in the captain's eyes as he stood on the deck of the *Saint Mark*; he went to the opposite side. From that side, he noticed people tossing a rope with a noose over the piling of a port winch.

They are planning to hang someone, the captain told those standing on deck. Whoever is interested can watch.

They were all interested, including the infantrymen. They all scrutinized the people standing by the winch, particularly the one whose neck was being fitted with the noose.

Is that Arseny? the captain asked, uncertain. Arseny!

He turned to the spectators on deck and they nodded.

That is Arseny, the captain shouted to the residents of Zara. He held his hands like a megaphone, and everyone in port heard him. This person is under the personal protection of Giovanni Mocenigo, the doge of Venice, and anyone who lays a finger on him will be punished!

The residents of Zara paused. They knew the captain and turned to the *Saint Mark* to be certain of what they had heard, but the captain was already running down the gangplank. All 120 infantrymen—thoroughly exhausted from throwing dice—watched from aboard the ship.

Did you hear me? the captain shouted again along the way. Anyone laying a finger will be punished!

But the residents of Zara were no longer laying a finger on Arseny. Even earlier, they had begun to suspect that their accusations were not altogether correct, meaning they had most likely been hanging Arseny out of inertia. They had lacked only the tiniest of reasons for stopping, and now it had been found. Their rage ran out just as suddenly as it had arisen.

We are no longer hanging anyone, said the residents of Zara. Your words cleared up all the issues and resolved the situation for us.

The captain ran up, pulled the noose off Arseny, and removed the gag from Ambrogio's mouth.

My comrade Wilhelm and I just could not figure out what they wanted from us, cried out the pilgrim Friedrich, appealing to everyone. We would like to know the gist of their claims about us and why they suddenly decided to hang Arseny. We see no guilt whatsoever in that person.

Arseny answered them with a grateful bow. Ambrogio began laughing and said:

I just remembered an Irish monk who joked that German was the most important Eastern language for him. His joke turned out to be prophetic: your speech was taken for Turkish!

Once on board the *Saint Mark*, Arseny asked:

Tell me, Ambrogio, did your gift of foresight tell you we would be saved?

It is hardest of all, O Arseny, to foresee the future of one's own life, and that is good. But of course I hoped to be saved. If not in this world, then in the next.

$$\overline{K\epsilon}$$

The Sirocco quietened two days later and the ship raised its sails. Standing on the port side, Arseny said to the devout Simeon:

Glory to thee, O elder. I think that my waiting has been extended, thanks to your prayers. So pray again, will you, so my waiting will not be in vain.

The next large cities on the ship's route were Spalato and the won-derful Ragusa. Winds continued to be favorable, though, so they did not stop in either. The *Saint Mark*'s captain trusted water far more than dry land and did not go ashore unless there was the utmost need.

They first sensed strong rocking motions after entering the Mediterranean Sea. The captain asked those with weak guts to stay very close to the railing: it took a long time to air out the hold after the spewing of seasickness. The *Saint Mark* tried not to lose sight of shore despite having entered the large sea.

When coming into harbor on the island of Corfu, they successfully avoided a sand bar known to anyone who was involved with navigation in any way. They stopped a half-mile from the island and replenished their supplies of fresh water and provisions. The island-dwellers deliv-ered everything on large barques, shouting as they loaded it onto the ship. Arseny watched as the sailors carried the items into the hold. In addition to greens, they delivered about two dozen crates of live chickens to the ship. The captain personally sampled the flavors of the water and the greens. He sampled the chickens by touch. After drinking half a mug of the water that had been delivered, the captain said:

Fresh water is completely flavorless but, to my great regret, salt water cannot be drunk.

On the Greek island of Cephalonia, where the ship came in to dock, they bought three bulls to replace what had been eaten along the way. One bull gored a sailor when they attempted to drive the bulls into the hold. Arseny examined the sailor and saw the wound was not serious, despite an abundance of blood. The bull's horn had pierced the soft tissues of the sailor's buttocks but had not grazed any vitally important organs. Because of the peculiarity of the wound, the sailor could no longer lie in a hammock, so Arseny settled him onto a large kitchen storage chest. The captain thanked Arseny and told the sailor that he should now lie on his stomach more. The sailor knew that—he simply could not lie any other way—but thanked the captain anyway. Arseny most certainly enjoyed the atmosphere of the trip.

It must be said that the captain had taken a liking to Arseny, too. The captain had been watching over Arseny ever since he had managed to save him from certain doom. Once, in a free moment, the captain told Arseny how salt water forms. It turned out that it simply evaporates from regular water in the tropical ocean—thanks to help from the sun's hot rays—and spreads from there, with the current, into other seas. The changes that the water undergoes are strikingly visible in the example of a lake in the county of Aix, not far from Arles. The water in this lake turns to ice, thanks to help from the winter cold, and then naturally to salt, under the influence of the summer heat. This proves that it is impossible to sail around the world: the ocean that bathes it will freeze in the north but turn to salt in the south.

In essence, we are sailing in a narrow crevice between ice and salt, summarized the captain.

Arseny thanked the captain for the information. Beyond gratitude for being saved, he felt respect for him as a seaman who soberly gauged the limits of his own abilities.

On the approach to Crete, the captain introduced those present to the story of how Zeus kidnapped Europa. The Brandenburg pilgrims protested, accusing the captain of being gullible. Paying no mind to their objections, the captain also expounded on his available bits of knowledge about the Minotaur, Theseus, and Ariadne's thread. To help them visualize it better, he even ordered a sailor to fetch a skein of thread and unwind it on deck, weaving it between the masts and rigging. The pilgrims offered skeptical commentary to these actions. The captain went on speaking in an unnaturally calm tone, and it was clear to everyone who knew even the slightest thing about people that his nerves were at breaking point. The pilgrim Wilhelm, who knew nothing about people, said:

These are all pagan tall tales and it is shameful to believe in them during our time.

Without saying a word, the captain swept the pilgrim Wilhelm into his arms and took a step toward the side of the ship. The pilgrim Wilhelm, who may have wished to suffer in this confrontation with paganism, put up not the slightest resistance. Everyone else was just far enough from the captain that they simply lacked the time to come to the unfortunate man's assistance: the distance from the captain with the pilgrim in his arms to the side of the ship really was measly. They saw Wilhelm already flying over the side, for the captain's intentions were written on his face and contained no secrets. They saw Wilhelm hanging over the deep sea. All of them, including Arseny, saw him being swallowed up there.

But Arseny saw it an instant before the others: no sooner had the captain lifted the pilgrim Wilhelm over the side, than Arseny stood before him. He clutched at the pilgrim with all his might, not allowing him to be tossed overboard. The battle for the body of Wilhelm, who limited himself to being an external observer, as before, turned out to be brief. The captain was not a bloodthirsty person, so he released the pilgrim Wilhelm when his momentary rage subsided. Deep down in his heart, the captain felt no malice toward the pilgrim.

Have a look, my love, Arseny told Ustina, I managed to forestall time just now, and that shows that time is not all-powerful. I forestalled time by only an instant, but that instant was worth an entire human life.

After calming somewhat, the captain proposed that he and the Brandenburg pilgrims go ashore together and go to a labyrinth that was, according to him, still in existence. The pilgrims refused, regarding it as a waste of time, but someone standing on deck—Brother Jean from Besançon—confirmed the labyrinth's existence.

Not very long ago, he and some other monks had even visited there when they were in Crete. According to Brother Jean, the labyrinth's difficulty came not so much from the intricacy of its caves as from its darkness, and so one brother immediately lost his way when his candle was extinguished by a flittermouse flying past. They could not find the brother for three days and it was only thanks to the local population, who were more or less familiar with the labyrinth, that the brother was finally discovered, tormented by hunger, thirst, and a temporary lunacy that went away, however, as the result of good care. The labyrinth itself had not made any real impression on Brother Jean; it reminded him of an abandoned quarry.

The captain then repeated his proposal to the Brandenburg pilgrims, but they again rejected it. The pilgrims announced that they had seen countless quarries, for life had done nothing but bring them to quarries, though nowhere else had the extraction of stone been accompanied by such quantities of tall tales.

The infantrymen left the ship upon arrival in Crete. They were met at the dock by no fewer than 120 women.

Are those the same women who saw them off in Venice? asked Ambrogio.

Yes, they look like them, replied Arseny, but they are different women. Completely different. As it happens, I thought in Venice about how there is no repetition on this earth: only similarity exists.

K͞S

Cyprus came after Crete. They arrived in Cyprus late in the evening and did not go ashore. They saw the contours of a mountain range and the tops of cypresses. They heard the singing of unfamiliar birds, one of which was even sitting on the mast. The bird liked to sway as it sang.

Who are you, bird? the captain asked, joking.

There was no answer, it sang what it wanted, interrupting itself only to groom its feathers. It observed, from above, the replenishment of supplies of water and provisions. The *Saint Mark* set sail when the contours of the mountains began to brighten.

It was already swelteringly hot in the early morning. The travelers did not even want to think about what the afternoon would be like. The captain hastened their departure, hoping it would be cooler at sea. To cheer passengers drooping from the heat, he shared more of the knowledge of natural science that he possessed in such great quantities. As he looked at the sun blazing in the heavens, the captain told of waters that bathed the atmosphere and cooled the luminaries. He had no doubt those waters were salted. In his view, he was talking about the most ordinary of seas, which, for certain reasons, was located over the heavenly firmament. Otherwise why is it, the captain asked, that people in England recently left church and discovered an anchor that had been lowered from the heavens on a rope? And after that they heard, from above, the voices of sailors who were attempting to raise the anchor and when some sailor finally descended on the anchor rope, he died just after reaching earth, as if he had drowned in water.

The only lack of clarity here concerned whether the waters that lie over the firmament are joined to the waters in which we sail. One might say the safety of seagoing depended upon the answer to that question because the captain (he wiped away the sweat that had broken out on his forehead) could not guarantee to anyone that he could successfully drop his ship into the lower sea again if he were to unknowingly ascend to the upper sea.

Danger was much closer that morning, though. It was located under the heavenly firmament and issued from the same sea where the captain had sailed the *Saint Mark* for many years. Heat gave way to stuffiness after noon. The wind calmed and the sails sagged on the masts. The sun disappeared in the hazy heat. It lost its intensity and crept along the sky in an immense, formless mass. Leaden clouds formed on the horizon and quickly began approaching. A gale was coming from the east.

The captain ordered the sails be taken down. He hoped the gale would pass to the side but he understood they would not have time to take in the sails at the last minute. It appeared the clouds actually were veering more to the south instead of coming toward the ship. And though a wind had come up and whitecaps were now visible, the gale itself was developing fairly far away, off the starboard side. Over there, halfway between the ship and the horizon, the leaden clouds had released rays just as leaden into the water: the union of the waters the captain had spoken of had come into being. Lightning kept appearing against a black and blue backdrop but no thunder could be heard, which meant it truly was far away. Light was still pouring down from the heavens to the port side. The *Saint Mark* stood at the very edge of the gale.

Arseny felt nauseous from the rocking of the ship. He made several swallowing motions. He bent over the side, vacantly observing the dribbling fluid that stretched from his throat. The dribble got lost below, where the seawater raged. Where it frothed and swirled in maelstroms. Playfully flexed the muscles of its waves. Arseny sensed a huge mass of water behind him, too. He regarded its slow swooping even without seeing it, as someone's back feels a murderer approach. This was the first large wave that flew up (Ambrogio raised his head) over the stern. It froze (Ambrogio attempted to take a step toward Arseny) over the deck and lowered itself (Ambrogio attempted to shout) on Arseny's back, easily tearing him from the railing and pulling him overboard.

Ambrogio leans over the railing. There is nothing below but water. Arseny's face gradually shows through the water. Set free in the water, his hair glows like a rippling halo. Arseny looks at Ambrogio. The captain and several sailors run to Ambrogio. Ambrogio sits on top of the railing, throws his second leg over it, and pushes off. Swallows air as he flies. Arseny looks at Ambrogio. The captain and sailors are still running. A wave covers Ambrogio. He comes to the surface and swallows air once again. Arseny is not visible. Ambrogio dives. A thought slowly rises toward him from the leaden depths: the ocean is mighty and he will never find Arseny. That he will find him only if he drowns. Only then would he have time to search. That thought releases him from the fear of drowning. Fear had fettered his movement. Ambrogio rises to the surface and inhales. Dives. Senses the slippery surface of the side of the ship with his hand. Inhales. Dives. Feels Arseny's hand with his hand. Clings to it with all his might. Resurfaces and lifts Arseny's head above water. A rope with a log is tossed from above. Arseny grasps the log and they begin pulling him up. Arseny falls. Ambrogio helps him grab the log again. The log slips out of Arseny's hands. A log tied to a rope ladder is tossed from the side of the ship. Ambrogio slips the ladder on Arseny's legs as if it were a swing. Arseny grasps at the ropes. Ambrogio seizes Arseny with one hand and holds the ladder with the other. Ten pairs of hands pull them up. They are swinging back and forth over the water. They will be battered (they are no longer afraid) if they hit the side of the ship. Sailors' sad eyes. A wave rolls away from the side of the ship (the last of the water flows down over the seaweed and shells that have been revealed) and the whole sea leaves with it. The ladder hangs over the abyss that has emerged. The next wave comes up to Ambrogio and Arseny's waists and swallows the side of the ship whole. Half the sky is still free of clouds. They are pulled on deck.

The sea was agitated but this was not yet the gale. The gale, which had initially gone south, had undeniably changed its course. The captain silently watched a leaden wall move in the direction of the *Saint*

Mark. Its movement was slow but steadfast. The bright part of the sky grew ever smaller and thunder began to accompany distant flashes of lightning.

It got dark. Not as dark as night because nighttime darkness has its own tranquility. This was a restless gloom that devoured light, contradicting the established changes from day to night. It was not uniform: it swirled, thickened, and dissolved depending on the density of the clouds, and its border was at the horizon itself, where a thin ribbon of sky still shone.

Arseny and Ambrogio were brought to the hold. Arseny turned before going down. Lightning struck as if it had noticed his motion, and then came a clap of thunder unlike anything he had ever heard. With that sound, the heavenly firmament split, and its crack stretched along a line of lightning that resembled a root with countless branches. Water gushed from the crack. Perhaps this was water from the upper sea.

Seawater gushed out of Arseny, too, until it had all gone. He and Ambrogio were thrown from their hammocks and rolled along the floor. Both were semi-conscious. The candle toppled and went out. Arseny was turned inside out but there was no longer anything left to come out, so only bile came. He thought that at least he would stop vomiting if the ship sank. The sea's cold tranquility would seize him there, below.

It was dark and stuffy for Arseny in the hold. Two disasters had come together and deepened one another. Dark stuffiness. Stuffy darkness. They were one indivisible essence, one entity. Arseny thought he was dying. That he would die right now if he did not swallow some air. Ambrogio did not see him grope for the door that led to the stairs and the deck. He pushed the door. He slipped on the stairs. Crawled up on all fours. Slid down and crawled again. He was knocked into the banisters. He crawled up to the door onto the deck and opened it. The hurricane stung him.

Horrified at what he had seen, he began shouting but did not hear his own shout. It was the grandeur of the elements—rather than impending death—that horrified. The hurricane ripped Arseny's shout from his lips and instantly carried it a hundred miles off. That shout could sound only in a place where there was still a ribbon of clear sky. But that thin ribbon was already pink, making it clear that night was falling and that this last strip of sky would disappear. And Arseny began shouting again because the all-encompassing gloom that was advancing carried hopelessness.

Waves pounded at the side of the ship and everything on the vessel shook, and after each blow Arseny was surprised that the vessel was still intact. Huge waves alternately propped up the vessel and came out from under it. It tipped awkwardly onto its railing: its side bowed to the waves and the tops of its masts nearly touched them. It spun in the maelstroms, bobbed, and dove.

Arseny was still standing in the doorway. Two sailors were making their way past him along the deck. They moved, hunched, their feet set widely apart. And spreading their arms as if for embraces. They were pulling some sort of rope from the mast to the side of the ship, attempting to tighten it, but they themselves were tied to the mast with ropes. They kept slipping and falling to their knees. Their work, which was incomprehensible to Arseny, resembled either a dance or supplication. Perhaps they actually were praying.

Arseny saw an enormous frothy wave moving along the port side of the ship. The wave was very visible despite the darkness, and its crest glistened in a light that seemed to come out of nowhere. This glimmering was the most frightening thing. The wave was much higher than the deck. The ship seemed small, almost toylike, compared to the wave. Arseny soundlessly shouted to the sailors, telling them to flee, but they continued their strange motion. Their hoods, pulled low, made them look like astonishing creatures from the *Alexander Romance*. And the ropes dragged behind them like tails.

The wave did not strike the ship, it simply crushed it under itself and swept over it. Arseny was thrown below, where he could no longer see what was happening on deck. When he recovered, he again attempted to climb up toward the exit. The captain was standing in the doorway.

He was praying. The deck was empty. Much of what Arseny had seen before from this vantage point was missing. Cannons, rails, masts. The two sailors who had been pulling the rope were missing. Arseny wanted to ask the captain if they had saved themselves in time but he did not ask. The captain sensed his presence and turned. He shouted something to Arseny. Arseny did not catch what he said. The captain bent right to Arseny's ear and yelled:

Did you see Saint Germanus?

Arseny shook his head, no.

Well, I did. The captain pressed Arseny's head to his own. I believe we can be saved by his prayers.

It was not that the gale had quietened—it had stopped intensifying. The ship was still being tossed from side to side, but that was no longer so frightening. Perhaps because the last light had disappeared with the arrival of night and the huge waves were no longer visible. The ship was no longer resisting its element: it was a part of it.

The sun was shining in a cloudless sky when Arseny went on deck in the morning. A light wind was blowing. Two of the three masts were broken and everything that had been on the deck had been washed away or mangled. The sailors and pilgrims said a memorial prayer. Their arms and faces were covered with scratches.

Arseny did not see several familiar faces. He did not know the names of the dead sailors and had barely heard more than a sentence or two—simple greetings—from them when they were alive, but their absence was gaping. He knew that from now on he would be deprived of their greetings forever.

Forever, whispered Arseny.

He remembered their final dancing motions. He imagined the sailors floating now in the seawater. At a depth where they would be inaccessible to any storms.

After the prayer, the captain told those gathered on deck:

This night past, I saw Saint Germanus seven times. He appeared, as always, as a candle flame that could be described, if one wishes, as a distinct star. The flame might be bright one minute, then muted the next, the size of half the mast, always prominent. If you want, for example, to take the flame, it goes away; if you motionlessly recite *Oure Father* it will stay in place for about a quarter-hour, half an hour maximum, and when it appears, the wind always grows quieter and the waves smaller. When ships sail in a caravan, the ship to which Saint Germanus appears will be saved but he who does not see him will be wrecked. If two candles appear, which is a rarity, then the ship will certainly be lost, for two candles is a ghost, not an appearance from the saint.

That, said the pilgrim Wilhelm, is because demons never appear one at a time, but always in multitudes.

All that is Divine and true is one, said the pilgrim Friedrich, all that is demonic and false is in multiples.

The Brandenburg pilgrims no longer argued with the captain, for which he was glad.

Ambrogio was looking pensively to the north. He saw a gale in the White Sea on October 1, 1865. The Solovetsky Monastery's steamer *Faith* was sailing from Anzer Island to Big Solovetsky Island. It was carrying pilgrims from Verkhny Volochok. Dinghies were ripped from the side of the boat and the bilge pump broke down. The ship was flung around like a twig. The pilgrims were nauseous. The gale was astonishing in that it arose under conditions of full visibility. A hurricane-force wind blew but there were neither clouds nor rain. And Big Solovetsky Island looked like a glistening white dot off the starboard side. One of the pilgrims asked the captain:

Why are we not sailing straight for the island?

Without moving from the ship's wheel, the captain indicated that he could not hear the questioner.

Why are we sailing away from the island instead of sailing toward it? the pilgrim shouted directly into the captain's ear.

Because we are tacking, answered the captain. Otherwise a lateral wave will smash us.

The *Faith* captain's long beard fluttered in the wind.

The crew, composed of Solovetsky monks, was calm. This was the calm of those who do not even know how to swim. Sailors in the White Sea do not generally know how to swim. They do not need to know anyway. The water of the White Sea is so cold they could not endure for more than a few minutes.

The *Saint Mark*'s captain brushed aside a tear because he was mourning the lost mariners so immeasurably. The captain gave thanks to God and Saint Germanus that he had remained alive. He stood on the sun-drenched deck, delighting in the length and sharpness of a morning shadow. He inhaled the scent of drying wood. He felt like falling on the deck's boards, lying there, and feeling their roughness on his cheek but he did not. As captain, he must be in possession of his own feelings. A captain should generally never be sentimental, he thought, otherwise the crew would mutiny. He took the decision to bring the ship to the nearest shore on her one remaining sail. The captain had no other choice. The *Saint Mark*, all gilded by the evening sun, approached the port of Jaffa after a day of quiet sailing.

КИ

This was the East. The East Arseny had heard so much about, though he had no definite image of it. He had seen goods from the East in Pskov. He had even seen Eastern people in Pskov, but those people had adapted to a northern-Russian way of life that was neither showy nor loud. Eastern people in Pskov were meek and well-groomed. They spoke in soft voices and smiled enigmatically. The smell of non-Russian herbs and fragrances accompanied them. They turned out to be completely different in Jaffa.

The Jaffaites who flocked around the travelers were primarily Arabs: they were noisy, guttural, and seemed to have many hands. They kept grabbing at the arrivals' clothing, attempting to attract attention. They would open their holey robes and beat themselves on the chest. They wiped sweating foreheads and necks with grimy sleeves.

What do these people want? Arseny asked Ambrogio.

Ambrogio shrugged:

I think they want the same as everyone else: money.

One of the Arabs led a camel to Arseny and attempted to insert the camel's reins into Arseny's hand. He pressed on Arseny's fingers with both hands but the reins kept slipping out because Arseny would not hold them. The Arab showed the price for the camel with his fingers. The number of fingers decreased each time he raised his hands. Arseny looked at the marvelous animal, and the animal looked at Arseny, from somewhere above. This creature sure has a haughty gaze, thought Arseny. The Arab pounded himself on the chest, finally inserting the reins in Arseny's hands, and pretended to walk away.

Arseny tugged at the reins for some reason and the camel looked at him pensively. He was, in terms of character, the antithesis of his master, who seemed to have rather worn him out. The animal took the Arab's unexpected disappearance as a blessing and did not look in the departed man's direction. When he saw Arseny's hand move, the Arab appeared again next to the camel and again showed his price. All the fingers that had been bent were back in their places. Arseny smiled. The Arab thought a bit and also smiled. The camel showed his teeth, too. Despite life's less-than-simple circumstances, they were all capable of finding a reason to smile.

Life in Jaffa truly was less than simple. The city, which the Mamluks had turned into a heap of ruins two centuries ago, simply could not revive itself. It led a spectral, almost otherworldly, existence at the expense of occasional vessels that, for some reason or other, moored in what remained of the port. No, Jaffa was not a dead city. Spending two days in Jaffa, Arseny and Ambrogio noticed that a life with its own adventures and passions flowed along here, too, in the evenings. They also discovered that the residents of Jaffa, whose energy had struck them so much on the first evening, were no strangers to contemplation.

It was contemplation that defined Jaffaites' lives during the daytime hours. These people spent the sweltering days in small yards outside earthen homes, their softened bodies catching faint sea breezes. They lay on the damaged port's parapets and observed fishing boats and (much rarer) ships as they entered the bay. Sometimes they helped unload them. But only in the evenings were Jaffaites truly active and animated. The energy and warmth they accumulated during the day spilled over, spreading to one another and out-of-towners. All sales, barter, agreements, and murders were completed during the two hours preceding sunset.

During the pre-sunset time the next day, Arseny, Ambrogio, and the other pilgrims managed to come to an agreement with the Arabs about their passage to Jerusalem. They proposed the travelers hire a camel or donkey, their choice, for half a ducat. Many, including Arseny and

Ambrogio, wanted to walk but they were told they would lag behind the caravan.

A caravan usually moves slowly, Ambrogio told the Arabs, through an interpreter.

Usually but not now, answered the Arabs. You will be there before you know it.

The proposal to hire donkeys and camels was obviously not a topic for discussion. Remembering Brother Hugo's two donkeys, Arseny and Ambrogio had chosen camels. Friedrich and Wilhelm decided to ride donkeys, though.

There was still some time before the caravan's departure but the pilgrims stayed in port rather than returning to the city. Several slept, leaning against stones that had warmed during the day. Others conversed or mended clothing that had worn through during their wanderings. Ambrogio took out the icon lamp and installed the adamants. He was already in the Holy Land and had decided to restore the lamp's initial beauty. He placed each of the six stones in the bottom of the groove and squeezed the pins, as Mayor Gavriil had shown him.

The Arabs that the pilgrims had hired to protect the caravan wordlessly observed Ambrogio's work. They had demanded half a ducat from each traveler for their services, which seemed too expensive to the pilgrims because the journey to Jerusalem was not really that long.

The journey is not long but it is dangerous, retorted the Arabs. Death lurks everywhere here. And life has its costs.

Getting on a camel is not the same as getting on a horse. The Arab made the camel drop to its knees as he helped Arseny get on. Arseny was surprised at the animal's ability to kneel; he took a seat between the two humps. Arseny nearly fell to the ground when the camel stood. A camel's hind legs are the first to straighten, which tosses the rider forward. The camel looked at Arseny with sadness after it stood. What made it sad and what premonitions did it have?

The caravan set off at dawn. Contrary to the Arabs' promises, it moved unhurriedly. The pilgrims' faces reflected all the colors of the brightening desert. The sun rose improbably fast and coolness gave way to heat at the same rate. The pilgrims' faces were covered with sweat and dust from the hooves of the Arabian horses that preceded the caravan.

Two hours into the journey, the Arabs demanded each person add another ducat. They explained this by saying they had seen a band of Mamluks off in the distance and protection from Mamluks cost extra. As they were bargaining, one of the Arabs galloped off ahead, saying he would check the road. They each added another ducat for the Arabs.

From time to time, the Arabs lagged behind the caravan and conferred about something. Their behavior, along with the band of Mamluks they had sighted, troubled the Brandenburg pilgrims, so they began insisting on returning to Jaffa. The Arabs refused to return and, as far as the Mamluks were concerned, they hastened to admit they were a mirage that quite often pursues travelers in the desert. Then the Brandenburg pilgrims, followed by the others, began demanding that the additional ducats they had paid to their escorts be returned, but the Arabs also refused to refund them.

I have this burdensome feeling, said Ambrogio, but I cannot say anything definite about our future, for these events lie too close. There was no reason to expect an easy journey, nobody promised us that anyway, and things were not easy before, either. We are approaching the holy city and the opposition to our approach is tripling.

It would be a shame not to enter the city when we are only a half-day's journey away, said the pilgrim Friedrich.

Moses was fated to see the Promised Land from a distance, but he was not fated to enter it, retorted the pilgrim Wilhelm.

Do any of us really resemble Moses? asked the pilgrim Friedrich.

Everyone who seeks the Promised Land resembles Moses, said Ambrogio. Is that not so, brother Arseny?

Arseny looked silently at Ambrogio and it seemed that Ambrogio's head had risen above his body. The head was still speaking but it obviously no longer belonged to the body. A hazy shroud had enveloped Ambrogio's body; it first became translucent and then dissolved completely. The others' bodies were still showing through the haze but their futures were not obvious. They began wavering, too, revealing their transparent properties, as Ambrogio's body had. Arseny feared he would lose consciousness. But he retained it.

The caravan's movement grew even slower. Gusts of hot wind flung sand into the riders' eyes. The camels kept stopping to munch on camel thorn and the donkeys stopped for no apparent reason. The sky was now as yellow as the earth because the sun had filled the sky's entire expanse. Their eyes watered from the sand and sun but their tears dried on their lashes, before they had a chance to fall on their cheeks. This is why the pilgrims took the band of Mamluks for a clump of sun and sand.

At first, the clump truly was indistinguishable from a patch of sunlight or a sandy whirlwind, and it seemed to move just as irregularly. But it only seemed that way: the whirlwind was being carried right to the caravan. This band of Palestine's Egyptian masters rode at full gallop and it looked as if they knew what they were seeking. Once the

Mamluks had come closer, the pilgrims noticed among them the Arab who had gone off to check the road. The riders surrounded the caravan.

The Mamluks were dressed in padded red robes; yellow turbans towered on their heads. This saved the Mamluks from the sun's rays, but obviously did not save them from the heat. The stale smell of their robes could be sensed even in the open air. The pilgrims, surrounded by Mamluks, inhaled the stench. The Arabs huddled at a distance, following the proceedings and smiling. They did not make even the slightest attempt to interfere.

The Mamluks' chieftain—his gold-embroidered sash distinguished him—ordered all the pilgrims to dismount. Only those riding donkeys could do this immediately: it turned out not to be so simple for the rest. Brother Jean from Besançon, who was sitting on a camel, attempted to climb down to the ground but could not. He hung, holding onto the camel's hump. Brother Jean was afraid to jump and his legs swung helplessly in the air. The Mamluks and Arabs laughed loudly. One of the Mamluks struck the monk on the hands with a whip and he flopped to the ground. The camel began roaring from the unexpectedness. It began stamping its front feet, landing a hoof on the head of Brother Jean, who was lying on the ground. This evoked another outburst of laughter. Only the Mamluks' chieftain barely cracked a smile. Perhaps his rank did not allow him to laugh using his entire mouth. Brother Jean fumbled in the dust with his hands, as if he were drunk. His gray hair quickly soaked with blood.

The camels' masters approached. The camels dropped to their knees when their legs were rapped with sticks. The pilgrims climbed down from the camels, not without some difficulty, and stretched their numbed legs. Arseny began approaching Brother Jean but was sent reeling by a punch. Arseny felt his nose begin bleeding. The stunned monk continued his strange motions. When he tried to get up, he looked like a beetle that had fallen on his back. He genuinely did amuse the prancing horsemen, so nobody was allowed to stop the entertainment.

Arseny grew frightened when he looked at the chief Mamluk. The Mamluk's smile had transformed to a grimace. This grimace expressed neither laughter, nor hatred, nor even disdain. A hunter's unbridled passion for his victim pulsed in time with a swelled vein on his temple. Even when sated, a cat will pounce on a bird with a broken wing because that is how the cat and all her ancestors were made: the bird acts like a victim and the sweetness of harsh punishment for the victim is, for the hunter, stronger than hunger and more demanding than lust.

The chief Mamluk flicked his arm with a sultry wail and then a spear shuddered in Brother Jean's chest. Brother Jean gripped the spear so it would not shudder and would not break his ribs, then he turned on his side along with the spear. He began screaming, too, and that scream drove the Mamluk to ecstasy. The Mamluk extended his hand and was given a new spear; he hurled it with a new scream, landing it in Brother Jean's side. The monk began screaming and pounding in the dust and the Mamluk again extended his hand and again hurled a spear, landing it in Brother Jean's back. Brother Jean did not scream this time. He jolted and breathed his last. And it seemed to Arseny that the slain man's face was Ambrogio's face.

They began searching the pilgrims. After Brother Jean's death, nobody dared protest. The Mamluks divided into pairs and took the pilgrims aside, one by one. Those who had been searched were ordered to move to the head of the caravan. Habit and experience were palpable in the Mamluks' approach to their work. They first rooted around in bags, then moved on to body searches. The Mamluks knew well where coins were hidden. They ripped open linings and the double bottoms of bags, turned cuffs inside out, and tore off boot soles. Money was not made of paper in the Middle Ages and it was not at all simple to hide.

Arseny's turn came. The Mamluks took only his money, which they cut out of his caftan's lining with one slice of a knife. What lay in his traveling bag did not interest them. They motioned to Arseny to move forward with his camel. Arseny did not move because he saw Ambrogio's severed head on the ground. The head's eyes looked intently at Arseny. The tongue was visible in the half-open mouth. Blood oozed from the nostrils. Arseny was nudged forward with a kick. Arseny made several wooden steps. He went forward, even as he continued looking back. Powerless to tear his gaze away from Ambrogio's head.

A pair of Mamluks now took Ambrogio aside. They made him raise his hands and searched him. (Arseny pushed away the Mamluk who was escorting him and took a first step in Ambrogio's direction.) Ambrogio calmly observed as the golden coins were cut from his caftan. They checked his traveling bag, like Arseny's, with no particular thoroughness. They had almost let Ambrogio go when an Arab came over, exchanged glances with the Mamluk, and nodded at his traveling bag.

The Mamluk pulled the icon lamp out of Ambrogio's bag. Its embedded stones blazed in the midday sun. Ambrogio grabbed the lamp from the Mamluk and said something to the interpreter. (Arseny moved in Ambrogio's direction, shaking off the arms that twisted around him.) The interpreter translated, watching sunbeams play on the stones. The Mamluk reached again for the lamp but Ambrogio drew his hand away, not allowing the Mamluk to touch the lamp. Ambrogio did not see that the Mamluk in the embroidered sash had ridden up behind him, and that he raised his sword, and that Arseny kept pace with the Mamluk and grasped onto his leg with all his strength.

Ambrogio saw an angel with a cross slowly lowering himself onto the bell tower of Peter and Paul Cathedral in Saint Petersburg. The angel hovered for a moment, gauging how to make a precise landing, then slowly submerged the base of the cross into a gilded ball on the spire. The angel was returning to his usual place after renovation and restoration work. An Mi-8 helicopter spread its blades over him, creating a downward air current. It was under these less-than-simple conditions that industrial climber Albert Mikhailovich Tynkkynen affixed the base of the cross with bolts of a particularly durable alloy. The mountain climber's long hair blew in all directions, getting in his eyes and mouth. Tynkkynen regretted that he had forgotten his cap in the helicopter—he always put it on when installing something under a rotorcraft—before descending onto the cupola with the angel. Annoyed, he reproached himself for his forgetfulness and reproached himself, too, for the long hair that he always promised himself to cut when he was in the heavens, breaking the promise back on earth every time because he was secretly proud of his hair. He scolded himself with sincerity, though his choice of utterances did not overstep certain boundaries: he was, after all, constrained by the presence of an angel. Despite all the interference, Albert Mikhailovich could see a lot from the height of 122 meters: Zayachy Island, Petersburg, and even the country in its entirety. He could also see that an ungilded but absolutely real angel in distant Palestine was raising the Italian Ambrogio Flecchia's soul to the heavens.

THE BOOK
OF REPOSE

It is generally held that Arseny returned to Rus' in the mid eighties. It is known for certain that he was already in Pskov by October 1487, since that was the beginning of the great pestilence the city suffered. Some people had already managed to forget Arseny before he returned to Pskov. That happened not because so much time had passed (not that much had really passed) but due to the weakness of human memory, which retains only those near and dear. Those considered not near and dear (as was true of Arseny) rarely remain in the memory. People lose sight of one who has gone away and do not usually resurrect his image under their own power. In the best case, a photograph jogs the memory. But there were no photographs in the Middle Ages, so oblivion became complete.

Many residents of Pskov did not recall Arseny, even when they saw him, because they did not recognize him. The person who had returned did not resemble either the holy fool who had first arrived in the city or the pilgrim who had left the city. Arseny had changed. Alongside his dark face, tanned in a way that was not Russian, was light hair that had become even lighter. It might have initially appeared that his hair had faded under the hot Eastern sun but upon closer scrutiny it became clear that Arseny's hair was no longer light: it was white.

Arseny had returned gray-haired. A scar above the bridge of his nose stretched along his entire forehead; it looked like a deep, bitter wrinkle. Coupled with the real wrinkles that had made their appearance, the scar lent his face the dolefully impassive expression of an icon. And it might have been that expression, rather than the gray hair or the scar, that meant the people of Pskov did not recognize Arseny.

He did not tell anyone anything after he returned. He generally spoke very little. Not as little, perhaps, as in his time as a holy fool, but his words these days rang with a quietness that was not characteristic of even the deepest silence. When he came to see Mayor Gavriil, he said:

Peace be with you, O mayor. Do forgive me.

Mayor Gavriil saw Arseny's entire difficult journey in his eyes. He saw Ambrogio's death. And he asked no more about anything. He embraced Arseny and wept on his shoulder. Arseny stood, not stirring. He could feel the mayor's hot tears on his neck but his own eyes remained dry.

Do dwell in my home, said Mayor Gavriil.

Arseny bowed his head. He placed little importance now on where he stayed.

Arseny wanted to go and see holy fool Foma but by this time Foma was no longer of this earth. Foma had predicted his own death shortly after Arseny's departure, and he had managed to say goodbye to everyone. Wearied by the burden of his approaching death, Foma found the strength within to make one final round of the city and pelt the most shameless of the demons with some last stones. Everyone knew Foma was dying so the whole city went along behind him, accompanying him on that final round. Foma's legs were unsteady but people helped him move them.

The dark of death has taken me, and the light wente awaye from myne eyes, Foma began shouting as he circled half the city.

They placed the stones in his hands since he could no longer see anything, and he used his last strength to cast them at the demons; he circled the second half of the city that way because his physical blindness had only sharpened his spiritual vision.

When the city had been cleansed of demons, Foma said, reclining in front of the church:

You don't really think I drove them out forever, do you? Maybe about five years, ten maximum. And what will you do then? you might ask. Well, write this down. A great pestilence awaits you but God's servant Arseny will help you, when he's back from Jerusalem. And then Arseny will leave, too, for he will need to leave this burg. And then you'll have to display some spiritual fortitude and internal focus. You're not children anymore yourselves, after all.

Holy fool Foma closed his eyes and died after he had made sure everything had been written down. Then he opened his eyes for a moment and added:

Postscriptum. Arseny should keep in mind that Abba Kirill's monastery is expecting him. That's all.

After saying that, holy fool Foma died forever.

B̃

Arseny grew pensive after reading Foma's missive. For seven days and seven nights, he had not left the annex of Mayor Gavriil's house that had been given to him as lodging. He might have stayed even longer, but news of the pestilence began spreading through Pskov on his eighth day of sitting around. When the mayor came to Arseny, he said:

What Foma has spake is coming true. We trust in God's mercy and, O Arseny, in your great gifte.

Arseny was genuflecting, with his face to the icons and his back to Mayor Gavriil. He was praying and it was unclear if he heard what the mayor had said. The mayor stood a little longer but did not bother repeating his words, for he guessed Arseny already knew everything anyway. Mayor Gavriil left carefully, so as not to squeak the floorboards. After Arseny finished his prayers the next day, he left, too.

A crowd awaited him by the front steps. He glanced at the crowd and said nothing. The crowd was silent, too, understanding that there was no need to say anything here. Remembering Foma's prediction, the crowd knew that Arseny was the only person capable of helping during the coming misfortune. Arseny knew his abilities were limited and the crowd knew of his knowledge, and the crowd's knowledge was transferred to Arseny. They looked at each other until the crowd had no more unjustified expectations and Arseny lost his fear of betraying their expectations. After all this took place, Arseny walked down the steps and went off to the pestilence.

He made the rounds of home after home, examining the sick. He treated their buboes and gave them ground sulfur in egg yolk, cleansed their bodies of vomit, and filled their residences with smoke from juniper twigs. Even the doomed did not want to let him leave: as long as he was with them, they did not feel so pained and hopeless. They clung to Arseny's hand and he could not find the strength within to break free of their hands and so he sat up with them for nights on end, until their very deaths.

It seems, Arseny told Ustina, that I have gone back many years in time. The very same festering bodies are in my hands and, can you believe this, my love, they are almost the very same people I treated at one time. Did time go backwards or—let us phrase the question differently—am I myself returning to some starting point? If that is so, perhaps I will meet you in this journey.

Arseny's hands quickly remembered their forgotten work and now they treated the pestilent sores on their own. As he watched the deft motions of his own hands, Arseny began to fear their actions would become routine and frighten off the astonishing power that flowed through them into the patients but had no direct relation to the art of medicine. Arseny noticed ever more frequently when he was healing people that their recoveries came from that power, not from the ground sulfur and egg yolk. The sulfur and egg yolk did no harm but (or so it now seemed to Arseny) they did not substantially help. It was Arseny's inner work that was important: his ability to concentrate on prayer while simultaneously dissolving himself within the patient. And if the patient recovered, it was Arseny's recovery.

If the patient died, though, Arseny died with him. And when he sensed he was alive, he would shed tears and feel ashamed the patient was dead and he was alive. Arseny came to the understanding that blame for a death lay not in the power of the illness but in the weakness of his prayer. He began considering himself a direct culprit in those deaths that occurred and he went to Confession daily, lest the weight of blame become overwhelming for him. And he came to each next patient as if that person were his first, as if he had not examined hundreds of people before this one. So his astonishing power came to the ill as if untouched, for that was all that gave hope for recovery.

Arseny battled human fear as well as illness. He walked around the city and prevailed on people not to fear. As he advised them to take precautions, Arseny warned against panic, which is ruinous. He reminded them that not one hair would fall from a person's head without God's will, and called on people not to lock themselves away in their homes and forget about helping those nearby. Many had forgotten.

During the first weeks of the pestilence, Arseny thought he was not up to the task. He was ready to drop from fatigue. He often lacked the strength to get home and so would stay and nap at a patient's. A while later, Arseny would notice, surprised, that he felt a little better.

I am apparently growing accustomed to what one cannot grow accustomed to, he told Ustina. This proves yet again, my love, that, although there is cowardice, there is no shortage of strength.

Arseny slept for two or three hours each day but could not free himself from the sorrow around him, even when he slept. He saw swollen patients in his colorful dreams and they asked him for cures but he could not help them at all because he knew they had already died. There were no more fantasies in his dreams: these were true dreams, dreams about what had been. Time truly was going backwards. It did not accommodate the events designated for him—those events were too grand and raucous. Time was coming apart at the seams, like a wayfarer's traveling bag, and it was showing its contents to the wayfarer, who contemplated them as if for the first time.

Г

Here I am, O Lord, and here is the life I have already been able to live before coming to see you, Arseny had said at the Empty Tomb. And also that part of my life that, by Your ineffable kindness, I may still live. After all, I had not even thought I would be here, for I was robbed and slashed by a sword near the very city of Jerusalem and I consider it Your great favor that I stand before You. My unforgettable friend Ambrogio and I were bringing You an icon lamp in memory of the Pskov mayor's daughter, Anna, who drowned in the ryver. My hands are now empty and I do not have the icon lamp nor do I have my friend Ambrogio or a number of others I met along the way but lost, also due to my sins. Here I remember the guardian Vlasy, who laid down his lyfe for his frendes. I promised Vlasy I would confess his sins before You, for he himself is lying in Polish soil, awaiting the universal resurrection. Give repose with the Just, O our Savior, unto Thy servants. Establish them in Thy courts, as it is written. Disregard their transgressions, both voluntary and involuntary, committed in knowledge or in ignorance, for Thou art good and lovest mankind. I appeal to You also with the primary entreaty of my life, regarding Your servant Ustina. I ask You not through my right as her husband, for I am not her husband, though I could have been him, had I not fallen into the clutches of the prince of this world. I ask through my right as her murderer since my crime has bound us together for this lifetime and the coming times. By destroying Ustina, I deprived her of the possibility of discovering what You placed within her, of developing that, and compelling a Divine light to shine. I wanted to give up my life for her, or rather to give my life *to her* for the life I took from her. And I could only have done that through mortal sin, but who would need a life like that? So I decided to give that life to her using the only means available to me. I attempted, as best I could, to serve as a substitute for Ustina and perform, in her name, good deeds that I could never have done in my own name. I understood that every person is irreplaceable so I had no grand illusions, but how else, do tell me, could I give form to my own repentance? The only trouble is that the fruits of my labors turned out to be so small and ridiculous that I have experienced nothing but shame. The only reason I did not give up is that I would have been even worse at anything else. I am not certain of my path and that makes it ever more difficult for me to progress further. One can walk an unknown road for a long time—a very long time—but one cannot walk it eternally. Is this redemptive for Ustina? If I could have just any sign, just any sort of hope… You know, I do talk with Ustina constantly, I tell her about what's happening in the world and about my impressions of things, so she can always be, as they say, in the loop about what's going on. She does not answer me. This is not the silence of unforgiveness; I know her kindheartedness and she would never torment me for all these years. Most likely she has no means to answer me or perhaps she is simply sparing me the bad news for, I say in all sincerity, could I count on good news? I have faith that I can save her in the afterlife with my love, but I need at least some grain of knowledge about this along with that faith. And so, O Savior, give me at least some sign that I may know my path has not veered into madness, so I may, with that knowledge, walk the most difficult road, walk as long as need be and no longer feel weariness.

What sign do you want and what knowledge? asked an elder standing by the Empty Tomb. Do you not know that any journey harbors danger within itself? Any journey—and if you do not acknowledge this, then why move? So you say faith is not enough for you and you want knowledge, too. But knowledge does not involve spiritual effort; knowledge is obvious. Faith assumes effort. Knowledge is repose and faith is motion.

But were the venerable not aspiring for the harmony of repose? asked Arseny.

They took the route of faith, answered the elder. And their faith was so strong it turned into knowledge.

I want only to know the general direction of the journey, said Arseny. The part that concerns me and Ustina.

But is not Christ a general direction? asked the elder. What other kind of direction do you seek? And how do you even understand the journey anyway? As the vast expanses you left behind? You made it to Jerusalem with your questions, though you could have asked them from the Kirillov Monastery. I am not saying wandering is useless: there is a point to it. Do not become like your beloved Alexander who had a journey but had no goal. And do not be enamored of excessive horizontal motion.

Then what should I be enamored of? asked Arseny.

Vertical motion, answered the elder, pointing above.

In the center of the church's cupola there gaped a round, black opening reserved for the sky and stars. Stars were visible but they were fading from sight. Arseny understood day was breaking.

By February, the pestilence had begun to abate. Winter's end was so cold the plague simply froze. And though Arseny began having noticeably less work, it was also in February that he began to feel his strength near its end. Months of fighting the plague had completely run Arseny into the ground, and the usual weakness that comes with the arrival of spring added to that. It became ever harder for him to get up in the morning. When he went out to call on the sick, he would sit to rest several times along the way. When Mayor Gavriil saw Arseny's exhaustion, he said:

Citizens of Pskov, he has expended all his strength on your numerous recoveries, so look after him, for God's sake.

By the end of February, cases of plague infection had completely ceased. And when the opportunity came for Arseny to rest, he fell asleep. He slept for exactly half a month: fifteen days and fifteen nights. Arseny knew the strength he had given out during the pestilence had been borrowed from his future, so now he was making up for what had been used up out of turn. Sometimes he woke up to quench his thirst but then he would fall right back to sleep because his eyes would not stay open. He continued to dream of Jerusalem and the journey to Palestine and Ambrogio, who was still completely alive. Arseny's great sleep ended on the sixteenth day and he felt his strength gradually return.

When Arseny woke up, he understood that spring had arrived. He had become used to measuring the years in springs. Spring differed from the other seasons because its onset was the most noticeable and strident. Arseny usually awaited spring's appearance, but this time he had awoken in the middle of a spring that had already arrived, just as people suddenly awaken on a lovely day, see the sun is already high, contemplate its glints fluttering on the floor and the silver of a cobweb in a sunbeam, and weep tears of gratitude. At first Arseny thought, based on the smells and overall condition of the air, that this spring was identical to one from his childhood, but he gave himself a talking to right then and there. Arseny was completely different now, so this spring had nothing in common with his childhood spring. Unlike that spring, this one was not filling his whole world. It was a wonderful flower in his world but Arseny had known for a long time that this garden had other plants.

The roadways resounded woodenly in time with Arseny's movement as he walked through Pskov. Buds were swelling on the trees and the first dust after the winter was floating in the air. As he approached the John the Baptist Convent, Arseny searched for the gap in the wall and found his way into the cemetery. He shed some tears when he saw his trees by the wall because they were trees from a past and irretrievable life.

The abbess and sisters already awaited Arseny in the cemetery. The abbess said:

Foma's prophesy possesses a quality of necessity. This means it may not be avoided, no matter what your wishes. So you, O man, should head for the Kirillov Monastery. And the sooner the better.

In Pskov's kremlin, Mayor Gavriil just lifted his hands in dismay. He remembered what Foma had said but deep down inside he had counted on Arseny residing in Pskov until the presumed end of the world. He would feel calmer that way. The mayor was not certain of the practicability of Arseny's continued presence.

In theory, we are ready to take him in, was the word from the Kirillov Monastery. Tell Mayor Gavriil, would you, that he shouldn't grumble or put a spoke in the traveler's wheel, if, that is, we are not talking about travel on foot.

Who would send him on foot after he has been so exhausted? said the surprised Mayor Gavriil. Most likely we will knock together some means of travel commensurate with his services to the burg of Pskov and its environs.

They wanted to offer the mayor's own wagon to Arseny but he chose a horse. Wagons predominantly served those weak of body, and also women and children. Knowing that, everyone understood Arseny wanted to ride as befitted a man. Though he was not fully healthy, nobody attempted to convince him to refuse to ride on horseback. Mayor Gavriil insisted only on giving Arseny an escort of five men, in the event of unforeseen circumstances. Essentially, the majority of circumstances were unforeseen in this not-so-simple time.

Nearly the entire population of Pskov came out to see Arseny off. He was pale, almost transparent, but he held himself in the saddle well.

Being on the road will bring him back to health for good, said the abbess of the John the Baptist Convent. The road is the best medicine.

Mayor Gavriil, who was usually reserved, did not hide his tears. He knew he was seeing Arseny for the last time. Pskovians were a little frightened by Arseny's departure. The only thing that calmed them was that the pestilence was over and familiar life had returned to the city, if not forever, then for at least the next five years. In light of the possible end of the world, the residents of Pskov no longer expected a new pestilence.

~Е

Arseny truly did feel better on the road. Recovery entered him with the undulation of the fields and the sounds of the forest. The expanses of the Russian land were curative: they were not yet boundless at that time, so they gave, rather than demanded, strength. The drumming of hooves gladdened Arseny. He did not look around at his traveling companions but imagined that his dear friend Ambrogio was riding a little behind him and behind Ambrogio was the caravan and in the caravan were all those he had parted with at one time.

The horsemen rode quickly. Not because they were hurrying somewhere (Arseny was riding into timelessness, why should he be in a hurry?) but simply because the fast movement corresponded to Arseny's inner state and raised his spirit. Arseny's great renown traveled faster than the horsemen, however. It outstripped them and sent crowds of people out to greet them. Arseny dismounted. He attempted to listen to everyone who wanted to appeal to him.

Many awaited help with an illness. Arseny took them aside and examined them carefully. He determined if it was within his power to help these people. If he felt it was within his power, then he helped. If he was unable to help, he searched for possible words of encouragement. He would say:

Your illness exceeds my power, but the Lord's mercy is far greater than human powers. Pray and do not despair.

Or:

I know you fear pain more than death. And so I tell you that your passing will be peaceful and pain will not torment you.

Many asked questions unrelated to illnesses. They simply wanted to speak with a person they had heard a lot about. Arseny touched them with his hand but did not enter into conversation with them. His contact was deeper than any words. It produced an answer inside the head of the inquirer himself, for he who asks a question often knows the answer, too, even if he cannot always admit that to himself.

Finally, there were a great many people who did not want treatment and did not ask anything, since in any nation the majority of people are healthy and have no questions. These people had heard that simply beholding Arseny was auspicious, and so they came to have a look at him.

Those meetings on the road took time and significantly extended the journey for Arseny's procession. Arseny, though, did not attempt to speed up his movement.

If I do not hear out all these people, he told Ustina, my journey cannot be considered traveled. Our good deeds, my darling, will save you, but could they be enacted within oneself? No, I answer you, no can do, they are only for other people, and praise the Lord that He sends us these people.

Arseny's arrival would become known several days in advance and residents would decide then who he would stay with. These people based their decisions on the greatest convenience for Arseny as well as a hope for their own welfare. Along with Arseny's renown, after all, there also spread the opinion that his lodging in someone's home portended of great benefit to the owner. Sometimes, instead of being housed in the place that was offered to him, Arseny would look out at the crowd to choose a person and then ask him:

And would you, O friend, allow me to stay with you?

The life of the person Arseny chose would change from that day on, too, at least in the eyes of his townsmen. Arseny also sensed his own life was changing. He had never before experienced such a gain in strength. Despite not sparing himself when helping those who asked, he gained more strength than he lost. And he never tired of being amazed about this. Arseny could feel that the hundreds of people he met gave him strength. He only imparted that strength to those who needed it most.

The travelers rode through places where Arseny had been many years ago, when he set off for Pskov from Belozersk. He recognized hills, rivers, churches, and houses he had seen before. It felt like he even recognized people, though he was not fully certain of that. People do change quickly, after all.

Arseny thought back to the sorrowful events of his youth, but his thoughts were warm. These were already thoughts about someone else. He had long suspected that time was discontinuous and its individual parts were not connected to one another, much as there was no connection—other than, perhaps, a name—between the blond little boy from Rukina Quarter and the gray-haired wayfarer, almost an old man. Strictly speaking, his name changed, too, over the course of his life.

In one of the wealthy homes, Arseny saw himself in a Venetian mirror: he was, indeed, an old man. This discovery staggered him. Arseny was not at all sorry about his bygone youth and, yes, he had felt before that he was changing. Even so, that glance in the mirror made a strong impression on him. Long gray hair. Sharp cheekbones that absorbed his eyes. He had not thought the changes had gone so far.

Just take a look at what has become of me, he said to Ustina. Who would have thought? You, my love, would not recognize me like this. I myself do not recognize me.

Arseny rode and thought about how his body was no longer as flexible as it had once been. Not as invulnerable. Now it felt pain not only after being struck but also without being struck. More specifically, now and then his body felt as if it had been struck. It reminded Arseny of its presence, aching maybe in one place, maybe in another. Before, though, Arseny had not remembered his own body, for he was treating the bodies of others, caring for each as if it were a vessel containing a spirit.

Once, along the way to Kirillov Monastery, he saw a body whose spirit had already almost departed. The body belonged to a man of advanced age: he looked at Arseny with blue eyes but no expression. The old man's kin had brought him to Arseny, saying the man was weak. Arseny looked into the blue eyes of this man of advanced years and was surprised that they had not faded as everything in the man's soul had faded.

Dost thou want to live, O olde man? asked Arseny.

I want to be deade, answered the old man.

Well, he died long ago but his body will not let him go, and so you are clinging to a shell, Arseny told his kin. What you loved in him is no longer here.

Well that, as they say, is noticeable, acknowledged the relatives. No more of his former spiritedness is left. If you say to him, maye thou live many more yeares, Grandfather... he says, scram, you. It is a horrifying metamorphosis. But really, what can we do with him, under the circumstances?

There is nothing for you to do, answered Arseny. Everything will be resolved within forty days.

And that is what happened. The old man passed away the day Arseny arrived at Saint Kirill's cloister.

5̄

A multitude of people greeted Arseny when he rode up to the monastery toward evening. When Arseny saw the monastery's walls, he remembered his childhood trip with Christofer. He remembered the nighttime cart and the peasant men from the quarter speaking in hushed tones over his head. He thought about how bones were all that remained of Christofer, who had loved him. And he was delighted that he was now nearing those bones. Arseny began feeling their kindred warmth. He attempted to imagine Christofer's face but could not.

After dismounting from his horse, Arseny sank to his knees and kissed the ground by the monastery gates.

I have returned home after long travels, my love, Arseny told Ustina.

Your travels are just beginning, objected Elder Innokenty. But now they will proceed in a different direction.

Arseny raised his head and looked up at the elder.

I think I recognize you, O elder. Might it have been you I spoke with in Jerusalem?

Quite possible, answered Elder Innokenty.

He took Arseny by the arm and led him through the monastery gates. Once inside the monastery, the elder said:

Monks usually take their vows and are shorn about seven years after they arrive. But the story of your life, O Arseny, is known to us and it has been monastic hitherto, so there is no real need for you to undergo additional trials. And the overall circumstances, as you know, do not exactly lend themselves to a lot of procrastination. If the end of the world truly does await us, well, it is better that you greet it shorn. Though maybe that will hold off.

The elder winked.

The crowd that accompanied them began buzzing. The issue of the end of world was extraordinarily agitating for them. They saw before them two people who lived holy lives, and awaited their explanations. Those who had come knew Arseny had been granted the gift of healing, but they did not rule out that he possessed the gift of prophesy, too. Essentially, knowledge about the end of the earth was more important to them than healing because, as they saw things, acknowledging the nearness of doomsday canceled out the need for healing.

So the question is, the crowd shouted, when is the end of the world? Forgive our directness but this is important to us, both in terms of planning one's work and in terms of saving one's soul. We have appealed to the monastery for specifics many times but have never received a straight answer.

Elder Innokenty took in the crowd with a severe gaze.

It is not for man to know times and deadlines, he said. What dates are you waiting for? Every Christian should be ready to meet his end at any hour. Even the youngest of those standing here will live no more than seventy years, well, perhaps eighty. (The young began weeping.) And nobody you see here will still be around in one hundred years. Is that delay great in comparison to eternity? This is why (the elder looked at the young) I tell you: weep for your own sins. But the main thing is: remain vigilant and pray. And be glad you have acquired yet one more man to pray fervently for your souls. And now we shall bid farewell to Arseny, for ye dost now acquire Amvrosy.

After saying that, Elder Innokenty brought Arseny to the abbot. According to custom, a monastic name is chosen that begins with the same letter as the secular name. And Arseny already knew what name would be offered to him and he delighted in that name to the depths of his soul.

We are choosing a name for you in memory of the saint and bishop Ambrosius of Mediolanum, said Elder Innokenty. We have also heard a lot—things always seem to work out this way—about your devoted friend who pronounced this saint's name in another manner.

May this name in its correct pronunciation serve as a remembrance of your friend. How many more lives will you spend henceforth simultaneously?

With the bishop's blessing, the abbot confirmed Arseny's new name. Arseny was shorn after seven days of strict fasting.

3̃

Do not seek me among the living under the name Arseny, but seek me under the name Amvrosy. That is what Amvrosy told Ustina. Do you remember, my love, that you and I talked about time? It is completely different here. Time no longer moves forward but goes around in circles because it teems with events that go around in circles. And events here, my love, are tied primarily to worship. In the first and third hours of each day we remember Pilate's trial of Our Lord Jesus Christ, in the sixth hour it is the Way of the Cross, and in the ninth hour, the suffering on the cross. And that composes the worship cycle for the day. But each day of the week, like a person, has its own face and its own dedicated purpose. Monday is dedicated to incorporeal forces, Tuesday to the prophets, Wednesday and Friday to the remembrance of Christ's death on the cross, and Saturday to prayer for the deceased, and then the main day is dedicated to the resurrection of the Lord. All that, my love, composes the seven-day worship cycle. But the largest of the cycles is annual. It is determined by the sun and moon, to which you are, I hope, closer than all of us here. The great feasts and the saints' days are tied to the movement of the sun, and the moon tells us about the time for Easter and the holidays that depend on it. I wanted to tell you how long

I have already been at the monastery but, you know, somehow I cannot get my thoughts together. Apparently I can no longer understand this myself. Time, my love, is very shaky here because the cycle is closed and it corresponds to eternity. It is autumn now: that may be the only thing I can say with anything approaching certainty. Leaves are falling and clouds are rushing above the monastery. They nearly get caught on the crosses.

Amvrosy was standing on the lake shore, where the wind was covering his face with a fine spray. He watched as Elder Innokenty slowly approached him, along a wall. A robe hid the elder's feet so his steps were not visible, making it impossible to say he was walking. He was approaching.

Monastic time truly does lie close to eternity, said Elder Innokenty, but they are not equal. The path of the living, O Amvrosy, cannot be a circle. The path of the living, even if they are monks, has been opened up because, as one might ask, how could there be freedom of will if there is no way out of a vicious circle? And even when we replicate events in prayer, we do not simply recall them. We relive those events once again and they occur once again.

The elder, along with a swirl of yellow leaves, passed right by Amvrosy and disappeared behind a curve in the wall. The shore by the wall was once again unpeopled. Exaggeratedly deserted (as if nobody had even walked through here) and not intended for walking. Only Amvrosy's immobility made his presence on that shore possible.

So you think time here is some sort of open figure rather than a circle? Amvrosy asked the elder.

That's exactly it, answered the elder. After I have become enamored of geometry, I will liken the motion of time to a spiral. This involves repetition but on some new, higher level. Or, if you like, the experience of something new but not from a clean slate. With the memory of what was experienced previously.

A weak autumnal sun appeared from behind some clouds. Elder Innokenty appeared from the opposite side of the wall. He had managed to walk around the monastery during the time he spent talking with Amvrosy.

And you, O elder, are making circles, Amvrosy told him.

No, this is already the spiral. I am walking, as before, along with the swirl of leaves but—do take note, O Amvrosy—the sun came out and I am already a little different. I feel as if I am even taking flight, ever so slightly. (Elder Innokenty broke free of the ground and slowly floated past Amvrosy.) Though not very high, of course.

Oh, no, that's fine, Amvrosy nodded. The main thing is that your explanations are straightforward.

There are events that resemble one another, continued the elder, but opposites are born from that similarity. The Old Testament opens with Adam but the New Testament opens with Christ. The sweetness of the apple that Adam eats turns into the bitterness of the vinegar that Christ drinks. The tree of knowledge leads humanity to death but a cross of wood grants immortality to humanity. Remember, O Amvrosy, that repetitions are granted for our salvation and in order to surmount time.

Do you mean to say I will meet Ustina again?

I want to say that no things are irreparable.

Once he had become accustomed to monastic life, Amvrosy asked to work in the kitchen. Service in the kitchen was considered one of the most difficult responsibilities at the monastery. Many had gone through service in the kitchen but far from everyone did so eagerly. And even those who went into the kitchen of their own volition looked upon their labor there as some sort of ordeal. Amvrosy did not consider the kitchen an ordeal. He was fond of this sort of work.

Amvrosy liked carrying water and splitting wood. He was not used to the work, so at first he got blisters. The blisters burst, leaving dark, damp spots on the ax handle. The blisters disappeared after he began wearing gloves when preparing the firewood. Later he split wood without gloves, too, but no longer got blisters. The skin on his palms had coarsened. And Amvrosy no longer tired so much. He had learned to hit the middle of the log with the ax, splitting it apart with a short, fine sound so it opened up like two petals of a large wooden flower. When he did not hit the middle, the sound was different. Thin and false. The sound of poor work.

In the middle of the night, as the brethren slept, Amvrosy would light a candle from an icon lamp in the church and carry it around the monastery yard, sheltering it with his palm. He walked slowly, inhaling the nocturnal freshness and the candle's honeyed scent. From a distance—sheltered by Amvrosy's palm and not illuminating him—the candle seemed like an independent essence. It moved through the air, carrying its fire into the kitchen.

It was from that fire that the fire in the enormous stove was lit. A short while later, the stove would glow red. It was so hot that it was difficult to stand next to. But Amvrosy prepared food for the brethren with that stove. He set down and took away pots, poured some water, and threw on firewood. The fire singed Amvrosy's beard, brows, and eyelashes.

Endure this fyre, O Amvrosy, he would tell himself, for this flame will delyver you from the eternal fyre.

Amvrosy simmered cabbage soup in large clay pots. He put cabbage in it—either fresh or soured, sometimes with beets or wild sorrel. He would add onion and garlic, and mix in hemp oil. He cooked porridges from peas, oats, and buckwheat. On non-fasting days, boiled eggs were served with the cabbage soup, two per brother. On those days he would also fry, in a skillet, fish the brothers had caught in the lake. Or make fish soup. During the fast at Assumption, he fed them cucumbers served with honey. On usual days during Great Lent, he served cabbage with oil, diced radish, and bilberry ground with honey, and on Saturdays and Sundays there was black caviar with onion or red caviar with pepper. When he was serving the brethren, he usually ate after them, by himself in the kitchen, rather than at table. Amvrosy ate bread, washing it down with water, not touching the dishes he had prepared for them. Sitting by the fire.

Sometimes he would see his face in the fire. The face of a light-haired boy in Christofer's home. A wolf curled up at the boy's feet. The boy looks into the stove and sees his own face. Gray hair, gathered on the back of his neck, frames it. The face is covered with wrinkles. Despite the dissimilarity, the boy understands this is a reflection of himself. Only many years later. And under other circumstances. It is the reflection of someone who is sitting by the fire and sees the face of a light-haired boy and does not want the person who has entered to disturb him.

Brother Melety shifts from foot to foot at the threshold and, placing a finger to his lips, whispers to someone over his shoulder that Amvrosy, Doctor of All Rus', is now busy. He is observing the flame.

Let her in, Melety, says Amvrosy, not turning. What do you want, O woman?

I want to lyve, O Doctor. Helpe me.

And you do not want to die?

There are those who want to die, explains Melety.

I have a son, O Amvrosy. Take pity on him.

Is he like that one? Amvrosy points at the mouth of the stove where the image of a boy is discernible in the contours of the flame.

There is no reason for you to kneel, my lady (Melety is agitated and gnawing his nails), he does not like that.

Amvrosy tears his gaze from the flame. He approaches the kneeling princess and sinks to his knees alongside her. Melety walks out, backwards. Amvrosy takes the princess by the chin and looks into her eyes. He wipes away her tears with the back of his hand.

You, O woman, have a tumor in your head. This is why your vision is worsening. And your hearing is dulling.

Amvrosy embraces her head and presses it to his chest. The princess hears the beating of his heart. The labored elderly breathing. Through his shirt, she feels the coolness of the cross he wears around his neck. The rigidity of his ribs. She herself is surprised she notices it all. Behind the closed doors, Melety is cutting splinters from logs so they may be used as lamps. There is no expression on his face.

Believe in the Lord and His Most Blessed Mother and ask their helpe. Amvrosy's dry lips touch her forehead. And your tumor will shrink. Go in peace and grieve no more.

Why do you weep, O Amvrosy?

I weep from joy.

Amvrosy wordlessly turns to the wolf. The wolf licks away his tears.

And so, in the kitchen, Amvrosy was granted the gift of tears and when he was alone, tears perpetually washed his face. The tears flowed along the wrinkles on his cheeks but there were not enough wrinkles for the tears. So tears then carved new paths for themselves and new wrinkles appeared on Amvrosy's face.

At first they were tears of sorrow. Amvrosy mourned Ustina and the baby and after them he mourned everyone he had loved in his life. He mourned those who had loved him, too, since he believed his life had not given them any joy. Amvrosy also mourned those who had not loved him and had vexed him at times, as well as those who had loved but vexed him, for that was how they expressed their love. He mourned himself and his life and did not know precisely what might be at issue.

With his hope to live out Ustina's life so it would be counted as her own, Arseny no longer understood where *his* life dwelled since he, after all, had not died. Finally, he wept bitterly for those he had not managed to save from death: there were certainly many of them.

And then his tears of sorrow changed into tears of gratitude. He was grateful to the Almighty that Ustina was not left without hope and that he, Amvrosy, could make pleas for her while he was alive and labor for her spiritual benefit. Amvrosy's tears of gratitude came because he was still alive, which meant he was capable of good deeds. Amvrosy was also grateful to the Lord for a great many recovered people, for the opportunity afforded to them to be alive at a time when they should have been dead and no longer capable of good deeds.

The tears cleansed his soul as well as his face. For the first time in his life, Amvrosy felt his soul was finding peace. Amvrosy's gradual sense that he was finding that peace was born not from overall reverence (his renown was greater than at any time before) but also not from the indifference that seizes many worthy people as they near old age. His sense of peace was tied to a hope that strengthened ever more and more in Amvrosy with each day he lived in the monastery. He no longer doubted the correctness of his path: he was satisfied that he was walking the only possible path.

He did not sense his previous alarm when he looked into the raging flames. More accurately, the alarm remained but at times the thought of an impending eternal flame ceded its place to memories of the past. Now he did not just see his childhood. He saw his life in Pskov and his wanderings. Amvrosy imagined Jerusalem when he closed his eyes by the hot stove.

Low trees in the Garden of Gethsemane. With broad, cracked trunks. With branches like twisted fingers. As crooked and broken as a frozen scream. The stone slabs of roadways, polished by many centuries of walking to Him. They retain the sun's warmth all night. One can lie on them without the fear of catching cold. Amvrosy grasped that, when he lay on the warm slabs to sleep. When there was nowhere else to sleep. When he was still Arseny.

He was nursed back to health outside Jerusalem after a blow from a Mamluk's sword. Two elderly Jews, he and she. They lived outside Jerusalem for fear of Mamluks. And it was clear from their faces that they had no children. Their names were Tadeusz and Jadwiga. And they cared for him. No, they were the ones who cared for the dying Vlasy, others cared for the dying Arseny. Perhaps they were Abraham and Sarah. The elderly always care for someone. As it happened, the dying Arseny survived. The elderly couple gave him oatcakes, water, and a little money for the road, and he set off for Jerusalem.

The ill continued to come to Amvrosy. There were many of them, though there could have been more visitors, had circumstances been different. Several factors contributed to reducing the flow. The primary factor was Elder Innokenty, who forbade disturbing Amvrosy for no real reason. He did not consider treating teeth, removing warts, or other such things worthy grounds for appealing to Arseny, for they distracted him from other, more serious, cases.

I request, announced the elder, that individuals resolve issues of this nature within their local communities.

The abundance of visitors was not just a distraction for Amvrosy. It also bothered the monastery's brethren, who had withdrawn from the world. Beyond that, it disturbed many that people frequently went straight to Amvrosy, without ever giving thought to prayer, repentance, and salvation.

These people, said the steward father, forget it is our Lord in the heavens who brings recovery, not Brother Amvrosy.

Brother Melety was the first to greet those who came for help: he decided how to handle each case. He sent some home immediately without even hearing them out. This included the great majority, who had lost or never had virility. Melety saw no necessity to restore it, stating that, in his own experience, it was far more difficult to achieve the opposite effect. The exceptions were those living in a childless marriage: after an appropriate prayer, Melety brought these people to Amvrosy. Bedroom thoughts were bestirred after visiting the monastery. After the birth of a child, however, those thoughts quickly disappeared with the aid of Melety's prayers.

The strictness of Elder Innokenty and Brother Melety was not the only reason the flow of visitors to Amvrosy dwindled rather than increased. Many residents of the Belozersk region did not appeal for help because—in light of the possible end of the world—they perceived no critical need. They thought they could tough out the short time left until that dreadful event. Or, at the very least, simply die, for a deferment of the fatal hour seemed insignificant to many.

There were, however, those who not only did not want to come to terms with death but also reflected on ways to overcome it, even in the case of a universal end. It was among these people that a rumor began to spread, saying Amvrosy possessed the elixir of immortality. That Amvrosy, when he was still Arseny, had allegedly brought that elixir from Jerusalem.

Despite the absurdity of the rumor, its emergence surprised no one at the monastery.

Some peoples' nerves give out when waiting for the end of the world, said Elder Innokenty. And there is a certain logic that they await the elixir of immortality from Amvrosy. In seeking immortality for the flesh and blood, who else might they turn to if not a doctor?

Brother Melety attempted to explain to many of them that Amvrosy had no elixir, but they did not believe him. Fearing that there would not be enough elixir for everyone when the time came, some people settled in by the monastery walls and built themselves some semblance of housing. They imagined the monastery could function like a new ark that might take them in if the necessity arose.

Amvrosy came to see these people when their numbers topped one hundred. He looked at their squalid housing for a long time and then signaled to them to follow him. After entering the monastery's gates, Amvrosy led them into the Church of the Dormition of the Mother of God. A service was finishing in the church at that same time and Elder Innokenty walked through the royal doors of the iconostasis carrying the Communion chalice. A ray of morning sun broke away from a grated window. The ray of sun was still weak. It slowly fought its way through the thick smoke of incense. It devoured barely perceptible dust motes one by one: once inside, they began swirling in a pensive Brownian dance. The ray of sun brightened the church as it played on the silver of the chalice. That light was so brilliant that those who entered squinted. Amvrosy pointed to the chalice and said:

The elixir of immortality is in there and there is enough for everyone.

At one time, the abbot transferred Amvrosy from the kitchen to the scriptorium because there were not enough scribes at the monastery. Three other people sat there along with Amvrosy. Elder Innokenty brought manuscripts for copying. His bold notations of *hence* and *hither* were all over the manuscripts' pages. Ambrosius followed those instructions meticulously.

Amvrosy's work days began with sharpening quills and marking paper. He would place a wooden block near the edge of the page of the manuscript being copied so it would not close. A thin strip of paper slid down the manuscript page, allowing him not to lose his place. He held the strip with his left hand and wrote with his right. The strip moved down, revealing line after line.

And another brother was deade, after being very ill. And one of his friends cleansed him with a sponge and went into the cave: he wished to see the place where his friend's body would be laid, so he asked the Venerable Marko about this. The blessed man answered him: Go, tell the brother to wait until tomorrow while I dig his grave, and then he can pass from this life into repose. The brother said to him: O Father Marko, I have already even used a sponge to cleanse his body, which is dead. Who do you bid me to speak with? And Marko said again: as you can see, his place is not ready. I enjoin you to go and tell the departed: the sinful Marko is telling you, brother, live this day, too, then tomorrow you will pass on to our beloved Lord. So I will send for you when I have prepared a place to put you. The brother who had come listened to the venerable man. When he arrived at the monastery, he found the brethren in song over the departed, as was the custom. And he stood alongside the deceased and said: Marko tells you that your place is not ready, O brother, wait until tomorrow. And everyone was surprised by these words. And as soon as the brother uttered them in the syghte of everyone, the departed saw the light immediately and his soul returned to him. And he dwelled that day and all night with open eyes but said nothing to anyone.

After Confession, a certain warrior happened to lapse into fornication with a farmer's wife. He died after committing adultery. And the monks of a nearby monastery had mercy and buried him in the monastery church, and they held the third hour of the prayer service. As they were singing the ninth hour of prayer, they heard a wail from the grave: have mercy on me, servants of God. After unearthing the coffin, they discovered the sitting warrior inside. Once they had extracted him, they began questioning him about what had happened. But he, choking on his tears, could tell them nothing and asked only that they bring him to Bishop Gelasy. And only on the fourth day was he able to tell the bishop what happened. As he was dying in sin, the warrior saw certain monsters, figures more terrifying than any torments, and his soul began thrashing at the sight of them. He also saw two fine young men in white robes and his soul flew into their arms. And they raised his soul into the air and led him through a series of ordeals, carrying with them a small chest containing this warrior's good deeds. And for each wicked deed there was, in the chest, a good deed and it would be taken from the chest, to cover the cost of the wicked deed. But the warrior lacked enough good deeds for the last ordeal, which was related to fornication. When the demons brought out all the carnal and debauched sins he had committed since the days of his adolescence, the angels said: God has forgiven him everything he committed before he confessed. To which their formidable adversaries replied: that is so but it was after Confession that he committed adultery with the farmer's wife and then died immediately. The angels were saddened after hearing those words, and they left, for they had no more good deeds with which to cover that sin. And then the demons grabbed him and the earth parted and they threw him into a narrow, dark place. He dwelled there, weeping, from the third hour until the ninth, when he suddenly saw two angels coming down toward him. And he began praying to them that they would take him out of the dungeon and rid him of this frightful trouble. So they answered him: you are summoning us in vain, for nobody who turns up here can leave here until the actual resurrection of the world. But the warrior continued to weep and pray to them, saying he would serve to benefit the living after returning to earth. And then one of the angels asked his friend: will you vouch for this person? And the second angel answered: I will vouch for him. They then brought the warrior's soul to the coffin and ordered it to enter the body. And the soul glowed like a bead, though the dead body reeked and was black as mire. And the warrior's soul exclaimed that it did not want to enter the body, for the body was so darkened. The angels then told the warrior: you must redeem from within a body that has trespassed. And the soul entered the body through its lips and resurrected it. After hearing what was told, Bishop Gelasy ordered that food be given to the warrior. He kissed the food and immediately refused to eat it. And he lived forty days, fasting and keeping vigil, and he told of what he saw and appealed for redemption and learned his own death would come in three days. Reliable fathers related this for our spiritual benefit.

Emperor Theophilos was an iconoclast, and this brought great sorrow to Empress Theodora. It happened that Theophilos got sick with a fierce illness, through God's rage. His jaws came apart so his mouth would not close, making his appearance ridiculous and frightening. And so the empress took the icon of the All-Pure Mother of God, placed it to his mouth, and his mouth closed again. But in a short time Theophilos vanished from this lyfe and became deade from that illness. The empress was horribly saddened for she knew her husband would be taken for torture with heretics, and so she thought unceasingly about how she could help him. She freed those banished and in dungeons and implored the patriarch that all bishops and the priestly and monastic rank pray for the Lord to rid Theophilos the emperor of his torment. At first the patriarch would not yield but, touched by the empress's pleas, he said: the Lord's will shall be. He ordered that all the bishops and the priestly and monastic ranks pray for Emperor Theophilos. The patriarch himself wrote down the names of all the heretic emperors and placed that writing on the table of the altar of Hagia Sophia. And they prayed for Theophilos during the first week of Great Lent. When the patriarch came on Friday to take his writing, all the names on it were intact but God's judgment had blotted out Theophilos's name. And an angel sayde to him: your prayer was herde, O bishop, and Emperor Theophilos received mercy, so do not trouble the Divine one about this more. We will behold, O brethren, the benevolence of our Lord God and we acknowledge how much the prayers of his bishops can do. We marvel at the blest empress Theodora's faith and love for God: it has been spake of such wives, since she will save her husband in death. Nevertheless we remember that since the soul is one, there is but one time for lyfe, and we do not trust in the offerings of others to save us.

Amvrosy's manuscripts are currently kept in the Kirillo-Belozersk collection of the National Library of Russia (St. Petersburg). Researchers who study them unanimously note that the writer's hand is firm and the script round. In their opinion, this attests to the strength and inner harmony Amvrosy acquired, and the tall height of the letter known as *er* indicates that he had left the kitchen for good by this time and questions related to food for his earthly body were of little interest.

At Confession, Amvrosy told Elder Innokenty:

At worship services I am not always attentive and at times I ponder unrelated things. Yesterday, for example, I was remembering one of the unforgettable Ambrogio's visions.

What was it about, in brief? asked the elder.

Here is what Amvrosy told the elder.

August 30, 1907, the village of Magnano. Francesca Flecchia, a young girl of twelve years whose origins trace back to Alberto Flecchia, Ambrogio's brother, wakes up due to a vague feeling of fear. The fear is rising from somewhere in her belly. She feels a roiling deep inside, jumps out of bed, and runs to the privy that stands in the yard. She begins to feel better there. Francesca cracks the privy door open and watches what is happening in the yard. Her grandmother is standing in a flickering ray of morning sun. It is coming through the branches of a stone pine: it is the branches that make the ray flicker. Her grandmother is pale and wrinkled. Her grandmother is pensive. Francesca notices, with sadness, that she has never seen her grandmother like this. Maybe it is also because of the stone pine. Or maybe her grandmother is just relaxed because she does not know someone is observing her. Francesca has already seen how a person can look young when out and about but then age immediately upon walking around a corner. Certain things depend on willpower but it is impossible to bend one's will constantly. Francesca sees that her grandmother truly is old. She understands where her grandmother's old age will lead her. The girl's stomach is seized by a spasm once again and tears flow from her eyes. Her grandmother disappears into the summer kitchen.

Francesca's sister Margherita comes out into the yard. Margherita sees the privy is occupied and goes back into the house. Francesca's mother appears. She has Margherita's bridal gown in her arms: Margherita is getting married today. Her mother blows invisible dust from the dress and goes back into the house. Their father goes inside carrying an enormous bouquet of white roses in his extended arms. The roses stand in a bucket of water; they are wrapped in gauze. Their father's face is not visible at all behind the gauze. Margherita comes out of the house and asks Francesca to hurry up. Their father takes a mouthful of water from a mug and noisily sprays it over the flowers. Francesca remembers that today she dreamt of a severed head.

Margherita has only just turned eighteen. She is marrying Leonardo Antonio. Francesca has loved Leonardo for several months now. He is as supple as a leopard and his name constantly reminds Francesca of his suppleness. And of how shrewd he is, especially of soul and intelligence. Sometimes she catches Leonardo's sad glances and it seems he is only wooing Margherita to distract attention. Just so he can be near Francesca. And if that is how things are, it is incomprehensible that he is wedding Margherita. Francesca is weeping again.

Margherita thinks Francesca is sitting in the privy for a long time on purpose, to not let Margherita in. She complains to their mother. Francesca vaguely hopes Margherita will go to the altar all soiled. Their mother drags Francesca out of the privy. She does this in a kindly way because she knows travel awaits Francesca tomorrow. Their mother wants to give her at least a little warmth for future use. Francesca was accepted at a Catholic boarding school for girls and is leaving for Florence. The parish school in Magnano is not enough if one wants to achieve something in life. Francesca is scared.

The wedding party, unhurried, comes down from the mountain. From Magnano, it goes into a valley where the Church of San Secondo stands, all alone. It is a beautiful Romanesque church from the twelfth century. There are no regular services but they open it for the weddings of Magnano's residents. Carriages wound with garlands of flowers ride ahead, carrying the bride, groom, their parents, and the witnesses. They ride slowly, very slowly. Numerous guests surround them. The road is wide, allowing them to walk alongside a carriage. The procession moves toward a photographer who is hidden under a black cloth hung over a tripod.

Coachmen in top hats hold the horses back on the steep slope. A wind that has come up catches the bridal veil and it straightens, floating over the walkers like a spectral white banner. Trees sway and rustle over the road. Ripe chestnuts fall from the trees onto the procession. One chestnut sonorously bounces off the coachman's top hat. Everyone laughs, including the coachman. The carriages' wheels ride over the fallen chestnuts, crunching.

It is cold inside the Church of San Secondo. This is the coldness of the ages, which is a little frightening to those present. Of course the bride looks the most vulnerable. She looks like a butterfly that has flown into a gloomy crypt. The padre smiles. The fat man Silvio stands behind Francesca. He is breathing on her back. Breathing and snuffling. She senses the warmth of his breathing on her back and that is pleasant. It is a breath of life, despite originating from the nostrils of a fat man like him.

The crowd of attendees seems incongruous to Francesca, set against the antiquity of the church. Like a gathering of ghosts that will evanesce in a moment, leaving the church (it has seen so much!) all alone with eternity. Francesca tries to imagine everyone looking like skeletons. A church full of skeletons, one wearing a bridal veil.

Everyone squints as they go outside. The young couple is showered with small change and grain. The wedding returns to Magnano. On the way back, Francesca has time to tell the padre her dream. About blood bubbling on a headless neck. How it came pulsing out of the chopped-off aorta.

I think this concerns Ambrogio Flecchia, says the padre. It is not surprising it was you who dreamt about him, since you are, after all, relatives. If you dream anything more about him, be ever so kind as to write it down. For all intents and purposes, we still have very little factual material about Ambrogio Flecchia.

Tables with refreshments have been set up on the village square. Around the tables stand stools with boards on them. On the boards are bedspreads. Everyone is in an elated mood at seeing the bountiful table. Everyone is happy for the young couple. Grandfather Luigi rolls a cigarette, takes it between his two fingers, and inhales. Hardened calluses prevent his fingers from bending. His face looks like pumice. He says he has never seen such a sumptuous wedding. His words come out with the smoke and seem steeped in antiquity.

In the evening, they put candles on the tables. Their shadows dance on ocher-colored facades. People blow out the candles at some tables. The smoke floats for a long time in the still air. Couples keep getting up from the table and disappearing in the darkness. They do not, in reality, go far away. They stand, leaning against the buildings' warm walls. Sometimes they return to drink a glass of wine.

Francesca gets up from the table. She knows she no longer belongs to this world and she feels unhappy. She does not know what world she belongs to. They are celebrating but she is no longer here. They are feasting but she could not swallow even a small bite. Francesca goes to stand in an alcove by a door and now nobody can see her. Darkness engulfs her. This is soothing.

Someone draws a hand along her face. Someone's finger moves from her forehead to her nose, from her nose to her chin. Francesca is motionless. Someone strokes her hair. She feels the cold of a door handle at her back and finds it with her hand. She grasps it with all her strength. His lips touch her lips. He turns around as he leaves the darkness of the alcove. It is Leonardo.

Francesca left for Florence the next morning and never returned to Magnano again, not once. She married Lieutenant Massimo Totti when she was twenty years of age, after graduating from the Catholic school for girls. They moved to Rome. In 1915, Lieutenant Totti set off for the front and was killed in his very first combat. Francesca gave birth to Marcello, the now-deceased lieutenant's son. Francesca studied at the university's physics department and worked in a shoe store as she raised her son. Sometimes she felt like chucking everything and leaving for Magnano. She graduated from the university with a degree as a physics teacher. After much effort, Francesca found herself a part-time job at a school in Naples. She was disastrously short of money. To keep herself afloat, Francesca returned to Rome and went to work at a morgue. The pay was not bad at the morgue. She read Joyce in rare free moments during her shifts. Sometimes she wrote down her dreams about Ambrogio, finally publishing them under the title *Ambrogio Flecchia and His Time*. Among other things, Francesca developed Einstein's theory of the relativity of time in the book, based on material from the dreams she had written down. Unlike works by the genius physicist, her book was written in simple, straightforward language and was wildly successful. Francesca became rich and famous. She left the morgue. After buying a mansion on the Ostia coast, she lived there for twenty-eight years, right up until her death. In one of her last interviews, Francesca was asked what day in her life was most memorable. After thinking, Francesca answered:

It was very likely my sister Margherita's wedding day.

One day, people representing the Moscow boyar Frol came to the monastery. Frol and his wife Agafya had been in marriage for fifteen years but had no children. Agafya's womb was closed, though they had visited many monasteries and called for the most skilled doctors. Their hope had begun to ebb, little by little, and the very desire to have a child had ebbed, too, thanks to the approach of the seven thousandth year since the Creation of the world: in light of the possible end of the world, the child's life could be assumed to be brief and joyless. This is why boyar Frol did not rejoice when he heard tell of the amazing healer from the Kirillov monastery.

Why give birth for death? boyar Frol said to the servants of his house.

But everyone is born for death, the servants objected. We have yet to see other types.

I can inform you that Enoch and Elijah were taken to the heavens alive, answered the boyar, but you truly have not seen them.

You know, life should not be stopped until it is stopped by the Almighty, advised the servants of his house.

Boyar Frol thought a bit and agreed. He said:

Go then to the Kirillov monastery and ask the monk Amvrosy for some prayers to grant me the fruit of childmaking.

Boyar Frol's emissaries set off on their journey and rode for twenty days. Amvrosy greeted them when they entered the monastery's gates on the morning of the twenty-first day. Without asking his visitors anything, he said:

I believe your journey is not in vain and, through the prayers of The

Most Holy Lady the Mother of God, the Lord will grant boyar Frol and his boyar wife the fruit of childmaking.

With those words, Amvrosy held out two prosphora, for the boyar and his boyar wife. The visitors went to a service after kissing the giver's hand. They genuflected for half a day and then rested after their journey for the next half-day and night. Boyar Frol's representatives set off on their return journey at dawn and it was half the length because the scent of the prosphora satisfied their hunger and the sight of them relieved fatigue. When they returned to Moscow, the boyar asked, first thing, about the prosphora. And they handed him the prosphora and two children were born to him within the next two years: first a boy, then a girl.

How did you know about the prosphora? asked the representatives of his house.

And the boyar told them that on the night when his emissaries were resting at the monastery after their distant journey, he and his boyar wife had dreamt of a holy elder with two prosphora. The elder spoke without moving his lips but his speech was distinct:

You will be comforted with a son and daughter. We will pray here that nothing happens this year before Easter. For only on Easter Day will it be possible to hope the world has held fast.

All the bells of the Kirillov monastery sounded on the Great Day of Easter in the seven thousandth year. That ringing poured out over the Belozersk land, proclaiming that the Lord had shown His boundless mercy to all mankinde and given more time for redemption. It was decided to reset the calculations in the computus: up until this day, nobody had even known if Easter would come in the seven thousandth year.

Tears of gratitude flowed from the eyes of many people. Those with loved ones were comforted because their parting had been delayed, those who had not settled their affairs calmed because they had received time to settle them, and only those craving the end were not joyful, since their expectations had deceived them.

On Easter Day of the seven thousandth year, Amvrosy said to Elder Innokenty:

I seek seclusion, O elder.

I know, replied Elder Innokenty. There is a time for interaction and there is a time for seclusion.

I have been cognizing the world for a long time and have amassed so much of it inside me that from now on I can come to know it within myself.

The time for seclusion has come now that we are more or less calm regarding the end of the world. Prepare, O Amvrosy, to accepte the schema in this yeare.

Treating the ill became Amvrosy's preparation. The flow of patients increased tenfold when it became clear once and for all that life would go on in the foreseeable future. Those who had recently taken ill were united in that flow with those who had preferred to wait out all those last years but then changed their minds in light of the favorable outlook that was unfolding.

The large quantity of visitors disconcerted the brethren and impeded concentration on prayer. Several of them complained about this to the abbot.

What, you mean to say you could concentrate on prayer before? the abbot asked the complainers.

We could not, answered the complainers, and the abbot thanked them for their honesty.

Amvrosy himself, however, was having doubts about the propriety of what was happening. Sometimes he remembered the words of the father steward, about how many of those who came to see him thought only about health, without giving a thought to prayer and redemption. Those words had sown a grain of doubt within Amvrosy. He began feeling disquiet, but Elder Innokenty was no longer alongside him. By this time, Elder Innokenty had moved to a secluded cell a day's journey from the monastery. Knowing the distance was not a limitation for the elder, Amvrosy told him from the monastery:

I fear that my cures are becoming a customary matter for them. They receive the cures automatically, which does not prompt these people's souls to stir.

What do you know about automatism, O Amvrosy? replied Elder Innokenty from his secluded cell. If you have the gift of healing, use it because that is why it was granted to you. Their automatism will pass quickly, when you are no longer with them. Believe me, though: they will remember the miracle of the cure forever.

On August 18 of the seven thousandth year since the Creation of the World, Amvrosy took the schema in the Church of the Dormition of the Mother of God. The rite for taking the schema was reminiscent of the rite in which his head was covered by the mantle several years before. This time, though, everything was more ceremonial and austere.

Arseny entered into the church, as was befitting, during the "little entrance" in the liturgy, the procession to the altar with the Book of the Gospels. As he entered, he took the mantle from his head and the sandals from his feet. He bowed thrice to the ground. His eyes became accustomed to the church's semidarkness and the dark mass of those in attendance took on faces. A man who looked like Christofer stood in the choir. Perhaps it even was Christofer.

To the Creator of all and the Doctor of the sicke, O Lord, save me even before I die, Amvrosy whispered after the choir.

A late summer wind blew through the open doors. The flames over the candles began fluttering a little but then stood still, all stretching in the same direction. The fire behaved exactly the same way in his childhood when he had stood in this church with Christofer. And that was all that linked Amvrosy to that time because he had become someone else long ago, and Christofer was lying in his grave. Or at least he had been laid there. It occurred to Amvrosy that he no longer had an exact memory of what Christofer looked like. How could Christofer be here? No, this was not Christofer.

Do you renounce the world and what is in the world, according to the Lord's commaundemente? the abbot asked Amvrosy.

I do renounce it, answered Amvrosy.

He heard someone slam a door in the back, and the candles' fire evened out. There was no agitation in the flame now. The soul should become thus, thought Amvrosy. Impassive, placid. But my soul will not come to peace because it aches about Ustina.

The abbot said:

Take the scissors and offere them to me.

And Amvrosy gave him the scissors and kissed his hand. The abbot then slackened his hand and the scissors fell to the floor.

And Amvrosy picked up the scissors and handed them to the abbot and the abbot dropped them again.

And then Amvrosy again gave him the scissors and the abbot dropped them a third time.

When Amvrosy picked up the scissors this time, too, everyone in attendance was assured Amvrosy was being shorn voluntarily.

The abbot set to the shearing. He sheared two locks from Amvrosy's head to form a cross so that he would leave behind his hair, along with the weighte of the thoughtes that drew him to erthe. As he looked at his gray locks on the floor, Amvrosy heard his new name:

Our brother Laurus is shearing the haires from his heade in the name of the Father and the Son and the Holy Ghost. We shall say for him: O Lord, have mercy!

O Lord, have mercy, answered the brethren.

August 18, when Amvrosy took the Great Schema, was the day of the martyr saints Florus and Laurus. Amvrosy was Laurus from that day on.

Elder Innokenty said from his secluded cell:

Laurus is a good name, for the plants that carry this name, *laurus*, are medicinal. Being evergreen, they signify eternal life.

I no longer sense unity in my life, said Laurus. I was Arseny, Ustin, Amvrosy, and I have just now become Laurus. My life was lived by four people who do not resemble one another and they have various bodies and various names. What do I have in common with the light-haired little boy from Rukina Quarter? A memory? But the longer I live, the more my reminiscences seem like an invention. I am ceasing to believe them and they thus lack the power to link me to those people who were me at various times. Life resembles a mosaic that scatters into pieces.

Being a mosaic does not necessarily mean scattering into pieces, answered Elder Innokenty. It is only up close that each separate little stone seems not to be connected to the others. There is something more important in each of them, O Laurus: striving for the one who looks from afar. For the one who is capable of seizing all the small stones at once. It is he who gathers them with his gaze. That, O Laurus, is how it is in your life, too. You have dissolved yourself in God. You disrupted the unity of your life, renouncing your name and your very identity. But in the mosaic of your life there is also something that joins all those separate parts: it is an aspiration for Him. They will gather together again in Him.

ЯІ

Three weeks after taking the schema, Laurus left the monastery and went to find a secluded cell for himself. This was Laurus's inner intention for himself, but it raised no objection from the abbot and brethren.

Strange though it was, they felt a certain relief after Laurus's departure, since the flow of people longing for healing had disrupted the monastery's established way of life. They had only opened the gates for visitors with special permission, but the crowds of people waiting at the monastery walls could not help but trouble the brethren.

Both the brethren and the abbot tried to regard those who sought Laurus with understanding. They remembered the Lord's words about how a city that is set on a hill cannot be hid, neither do men light a lamp, and put it under a bushel, but on a lamp stand; and it gives light unto all that are in the house. It is something else altogether that, in a cenobitic monastery, this light could feel too bright for those who thought a monastery's particular power lies, above all, in collective prayer. That, apparently, was how the light felt.

Laurus left the monastery, taking only a chunk of bread. They attempted to compel him to take more since it was unclear what was waiting for him in his new place but Laurus said:

If God and His Most Blessed Mother forget about me in that place, then why would I be needed?

And so Laurus set off in search of a place where his soul would feel at peace. He walked through the damp autumnal forest, not memorizing the path he had taken. This was something he did not need because he did not foresee returning. He understood that his movement was the beginning of another, more important, departure.

Laurus stepped on half-rotten branches that broke under his feet without a crack. Frost shone white on yellow leaves in the mornings. Toward noon the frost turned to tiny drops that shone coldly in the sun. Laurus drank water from black woodland lakes. And each time he bent over the water, the figure of a timeworn elder in a monastic hood, with white crosses on his shoulders, rose toward him out of the depths. Laurus lifted his eyes to a sky lined with branches and pointed out the elder in the lake to Ustina:

One would think that is me, since there is no one else here to be reflected. I still continue to live through you and see you: you remain the same but you, my love, would no longer recognize me.

Sometimes Laurus thought he had already seen this reflection many years ago, but he simply could not remember when or under what circumstances. Perhaps, he thought, it was in a dream, for when dreams present images, they do not go to the trouble of observing relative things, one of which is time.

Each day, Laurus broke off a piece of the chunk of bread he had taken but it did not shrink. That circumstance surprised him so he asked Elder Innokenty:

Listen, O elder, maybe I just think I am eating?

You are a grown man and a doctor besides, but you are reasoning like a child, said the angry elder. So you tell me, how is it that a body can survive without nourishment? By what biological laws? Obviously you are eating in a most natural way. It is another matter entirely that the chunk of bread increases in weight every day, otherwise you wouldn't have gotten off so easily.

Calmed by Elder Innokenty's explanation, Laurus continued moving. He saw many worthy places along the way but had no preferences for any of them. He understood each time, with an inner sense, that this was not yet the final point of his wanderings. Some places were too narrow. Trees would be clustered there, standing almost right up against one another, and could, in Laurus's opinion, crowd out any soul who settled in that place. By contrast, other places were too broad and their open spaces demanded considerable effort to adapt, for his soul to make them his own. It had been stated in one of Christofer's manuscripts that many expanses submit to the Russian people but that these Russians will not be able to make those expanses fully their own. Being a Russian person, Laurus was wary of events taking that turn.

He wandered for many days, so many that he recognized his own notches on trees in some parts of the forest. One night, he dreamt of a place on a rise. It was a glade surrounded by tall pine trees. Bushes grew along the edge of the glade and a stone cave was visible through a thicket. The sun's rays shone freely through the pines' trunks, making the place bright and peaceful.

Laurus headed toward that place after waking up in the morning. He walked with the brisk pace of a person who knows his way, walking without inner doubts. Toward the end of the day, Laurus reached the place he wanted. It proved to be exactly the same place he had seen in his dream. After saying a prayer of thanks, Laurus kissed the ground he had discovered and said:

This shalbe my rest, here wil I dwell.

He said:

Take me, O wilderness, as a mother her child.

He gathered some brush and pulled up some grass, and laid them in the cave. And then he lay down to sleep there and his sleep was as serene as in a real home. And he was happy in his sleep for he knew this was his final home.

31

For several days, Laurus worked on fixing up his new residence. The cave where he had settled amounted to two huge boulders capped by a stone block that was even larger. One side of the block touched the ground, forming a third, sloping, wall. Laurus got to work building the fourth wall himself. The only tool he had was a knife he had taken from the monastery.

Laurus noticed some fallen tree trunks nearby and attempted to drag them to the cave. He did not even go near the fattest of the trunks. But when he wrapped his arms around one of the medium-sized trunks and tried to move it from its place, he could not even do that. Once his heartbeat was back to normal, Laurus pondered the underlying reason—the weight of the tree or his old age—and decided it was old age after all.

And then he got to work on thin young tree trunks that had been knocked down by large fallen trees. He dragged those saplings to the boulders and drove their lower parts into the ground, nestling the tops against the uneven surface of the rock. He tied the trunks together with thick cords woven from vines. He filled the crevices between the trunks with grass and moss. Laurus even managed to make a door by tying together branches. The door leaned in place rather than hanging from hinges but it sheltered him from the cold no worse than a genuine door.

After constructing the wall, Laurus realized the thin trunks were most appropriate here anyway because thick trunks would not have fit together as firmly. He told Ustina:

What a person is able to do using his strength is the very best. But what is beyond his strength, my love, is not useful.

Laurus made a hearth by piling up rocks that were lying around here and there. He understood that old age had arrived, so he no longer counted on his body's strength. To preserve the life within his body, Laurus began building fires in the hearth on the coldest days. Later, after he had settled into his new place, he began burning fires once a week. On Saturdays he started fires using a steel and tinder that he always kept dry in a hollow place he had found under the ceiling. Laurus burned the fire from morning until evening, watching how the damp smoke from the branches he had gathered slowly stretched through the doorway. In one day of burning, the cave's stones absorbed enough heat to hold him until the next Saturday. Almost always enough to hold him. If the cave cooled down earlier, Laurus endured, not changing the set day.

Laurus came to love his home. It sheltered him from cold north winds and turned out to be unexpectedly spacious. He could stand at full height in the part nearest the door. He had to bend, though, where the granite slab sloped down. Sometimes Laurus forgot about the hanging block of stone and hit his head hard against it. After wiping away the tears that had come, he blamed himself for his pride and unwillingness to bow his head. Smiling, he was glad the lessons in humility he had been given were so easy.

Laurus understood he was being treated like a child. This was the first time since his childhood that he had been so calm. This is my repose for all time, he repeated to himself, surprised at the depth of his repose. He thought he could hear springs of water under the ground. Clouds breathing in the sky. Lots of things had happened to him in his former life but, somehow or other, everything had happened in the presence of others. And now he was completely alone.

He was not lonely because he did not feel that people had abandoned him. He sensed everyone he had ever met as if they were present. They continued a quiet life in his soul, regardless of whether they had gone off to another world or were still alive. He remembered all their words, intonations, and movements. Their old words gave rise to new words and integrated with more recent events and Laurus's own words. Life continued on, in all manner of variety.

It moved along chaotically, as should a life composed of millions of particles. At the same time, though, it also had some sort of discernible overall focus within. It began to seem to Laurus that life was moving toward its origin, though not toward the origin of all of life—what the Lord had created—but toward his, Laurus's, own origin, where all of life had also opened up for him.

Laurus's thoughts, which used to be taken up with events of recent years, now began turning back to the first years of his life. As he walked through the autumnal forest, sometimes he would feel Christofer's hand in his. It was scratchy and warm. Looking up at Christofer from below, Laurus finally remembered where he had seen the face reflected in the lake. It was Christofer's face. From grandfather to grandson, for the days when he had grown old.

Christofer led him along animals' trails, stopping from time to time to catch his breath. He told of herbs that went to sleep at this time of year and of the characteristics of roots touched by light frost. He told of the journeys of birds who rushed south from the cold, about their difficult life in foreign lands, and about their surprising ability to return.

To return, O Laurus, is characteristic of people as well as birds, Christofer had once said. There should be some sort of finality in life.

Why are you calling me Laurus? asked Laurus. You knew me as Arseny.

What's the difference? said Christofer. Remember how you wanted to be a bird, too?

I remember. I did not fly long then...

When the boy was exhausted, his grandfather sat him in a bag on his back. He carried him home and the little boy's eyes would close from Christofer's even stride. He dreamt he had become a caladrius bird. After taking the sores of others upon himself, he ascends into the firmament and disperses them above the earth. He awakened at night, on his own sleeping ledge. He listened to water evenly dripping in the corner of the cave.

Ⓗ

Toward November, the chunk of bread Laurus had taken from the monastery had begun to dwindle perceptibly. Laurus noticed it dwindling but that did not cause him concern. He understood: if his existence on earth still had any point, then daily bread would be given to him in good time. And that is what happened.

One morning Laurus heard cautious steps by the cave. He went outside and saw a person with a loaf of bread in his hands.

I am miller Tikhon and I brought you some bread, said the person.

His clothing was covered in flour, and he was around thirty years old. Miller Tikhon bowed and gave Laurus the loaf. Laurus silently took it and bowed, too. The miller left.

He returned the next day, leading his wife by the hand; she walked with a heavy limp.

A grindstone fell on my foot and I have not been able to put weight on it since, said the miller's wife. My health is worsening with every passing day.

How did you get here with a foot like that, unless your husband carried you in his arms? asked Laurus. Not even every healthy person makes it to my forestland.

It was not that difficult, said miller Tikhon. Your forestland, O Laurus, is only an hour and a half on foot from Rukina Quarter. People walking in the woods saw you and now everyone in the quarter knows you live here.

Laurus looked intently at the visitors. He realized that his many-day journey had, in fact, turned out not to be so very long. And that he had gotten lost during his journey but had, as a result, come to the place he needed to come.

Helpe us, O Laurus, pleaded miller Tikhon, for what kind of helper is she at the mill with a hurt foot?

Tears streamed down the miller's wife's cheeks because she knew this matter concerned her life, not her foot. Laurus signaled to her to remove the headscarf wound around her hurt foot. After she had done so, Laurus crouched by her feet. Her foot was swollen and had begun to fester. He began slowly probing the foot. Miller Tikhon turned away. Laurus pressed on the foot with both hands and the miller's wife began sobbing. He again wound the headscarf on the hurt spot.

Do not cry, woman, said Laurus. Your foot will heal and you will return to work at the mill and you will be a helper to your husband.

Will everything be like before? asked the miller's wife.

No, not everything will be as it was before, answered Laurus, since nothing in the world recurs. I do not think you want that anyway.

And they bowed to Laurus and left.

From that day on, people began coming to him from Rukina Quarter. After seeing that the ascetic monk Laurus had helped the miller's hurt wife, they understood he would not refuse them, either. After hearing the miller's story of how Laurus had accepted his bread and how he had thanked him with a low bow, they began bringing him food. And each time they brought food, Laurus asked them not to. But they brought it anyway, maybe bread, maybe boiled turnip, maybe pots of oatmeal porridge. Based on the miller's story, it followed that these sorts of offerings did no harm. Besides, people in Rukina Quarter had long believed that only paid work brought results. Even if it was the work of healing.

Realizing that it was impossible to refuse, Laurus began sharing the food with birds and animals. He broke the bread in two, flung his arms wide open, and birds landed on his arms. They pecked the bread and rested on his warm shoulders. A bear usually ate up the porridge and turnip. The bear just could not find a suitable den to sleep in, and that made his life miserable.

When he came to see Laurus, the bear complained about the cold, an absence of proper nutrition, and his generally unsettled life. Laurus let him into the cave to warm up on the coldest days, appealing to his guest not to snore or distract him from his prayer. Laurus suggested the bear see their rooming together as a temporary measure. Laurus breathed a sigh of relief when the bear finally found himself a den at the very end of December.

Beginning that winter, Laurus lost track of forward-moving time. Laurus now sensed only cyclical time, which was a closed loop: the time of a day, of a week, or of a year. He knew all the Sundays in the year but counting the years themselves was, for him, hopelessly lost. Sometimes people told him what year was coming up but he immediately forgot because it had been so long since he had believed that information held value.

The events in his memory no longer correlated with time. They quietly spread through his life, falling into a distinct order unconnected with time. Some events surfaced from the depths of what had been lived, some had submerged into those depths forever because the experiences had led nowhere. What had been lived gradually lost its definition, turning more and more into general ideas of good and evil that were devoid of detail and color.

Among temporal indicators, the words *one day* came to mind ever more frequently. Laurus liked those words because they overcame the curse of time. They also confirmed the singularity and lack of repeatability of everything that had occurred: one day. One day he realized this indicator was quite enough.

(One day) Elizaveta, a Novgorod boyar woman, was brought to Laurus's cave. She had slipped and hit her head on a rock many years before. Her vision had been dimming ever since; a while after the accident she could see only the outlines of objects. Not long before coming to see Laurus, the boyar woman Elizaveta had ceased seeing even those.

When Laurus came out of his cave she said:

Anoint my eyes with that water you take from the spring, so I may see the light again.

Laurus marveled at his visitor's belief and did as she asked. Right then and there she saw the outlines of Laurus's face and, behind his back, the movement of those who had accompanied her. The boyar woman Elizaveta began pointing at them and calling them by their names. She also gave the names of the herbs and flowers growing around Laurus's cave. Sometimes she made mistakes because there was still a murkiness in her eyes, but she could already see the main thing: light. She kept lifting her head up and looking at the bright summer sun without squinting: her eyes did not hurt and simply could not get enough sun. The boyar woman Elizaveta's vision had completely returned by the beginning of autumn.

(One day) they led God's servant Nikolai, bound in chains, to Laurus. Ten men led him because a lesser number would not have been capable of restraining him and controlling his movement. Nikolai was not tall but the demons who had settled inside him gave him a frenzied energy. His appearance was frightening. Nikolai snarled and howled, and gnawed at his chains, revealing teeth broken on the iron. A bloody foam frothed on his lips. He wildly rolled his eyes so only the whites were visible. Dark blue veins bulged on his temples and on his neck. There was barely any clothing on him since he tore to shreds anything he was dressed in. And he was not cold, despite the frosty weather: the alien forces sitting within warmed him.

Let him go, Laurus said to those holding Nikolai.

Those restraining Nikolai exchanged looks. After some hesitation, they tossed away the chains and stepped away from Nikolai. Quiet set in. Nikolai no longer howled and flailed. Half-bent, he stood and looked straight into Laurus's eyes. His mouth was half-open. Saliva stretched from his mouth, dangling. Laurus took a step toward Nikolai and laid a hand on his head. They stood like that for a time. Laurus's eyes were closed but his lips were moving. The two men's heads slowly moved closer together, until Laurus's forehead touched Nikolai's forehead.

In the name of our Savior Jesus Christ, I order you to leave God's servant Nikolai, Laurus said loudly.

At those words, Nikolai extended his arms toward Laurus, as if he wanted to embrace him. His body slackened. Nikolai slowly slid to the ground, his chains clanking. He lay on the snow at Laurus's feet and nobody dared approach him. Nikolai's eyes were open, as if he were dead, but he was not dead.

They have abandoned him and his spirit is on the road to recovery, said Laurus. Let him rest until the end of night, he can go take Communion in the morning.

And so they carried Nikolai off to Rukina Quarter and he lay unconscious at the end of that day and through the night. When he opened his eyes early in the morning, there shone in them the light of reason, as befits a person bearing God's image. Nikolai was still very weak because all the pitch-black energy he had possessed departed with the demons.

With prayers—his own and from people around him—Nikolai found within himself the strength to make it to the church and take Communion. He felt better after taking Communion because a new firmness had entered him along with Christ's blood and flesh. Accompanied by the public, Nikolai headed for Laurus's cave straight from the church.

Laurus came out to greet them and wordlessly blessed them. And they all fell to their knees before Laurus because they saw this person's strength was firmer than demonic strength. After that, they all asked Nikolai why he had resisted so much when they brought him to Laurus's cave, screaming at the top of his lungs, louder than humanly possible. And then Nikolai answered them:

You beat me, forcing me to come here, and the demons beat me, too, disallowing me to do it, and I did not know which of you to heed. And after being beaten by one and the other, I screamed a double scream.

And everyone was surprised at what had happened and they praised God in heaven and His earthly oil lamp, Laurus.

К̃

In a year of great hunger, the young woman Anastasia came to Laurus after losing her virginity. She prostrated herself before Laurus, weeping, and said:

I feel that I am carrying a baby in my womb but I cannot bear the baby without a husband. For when the child is born, it will be called the fruit of my sin.

What do you want, woman? Laurus asked.

You know yourself, O Laurus, what I want, but I am afraid to say it to you.

I do know, woman. Just as you know how I will answer you. So do tell me, why did you come to me?

Because if I go to the wise woman in Rukina Quarter, everyone will find out about my sin. But you can simply pray and then the fruit of my sin will leave me the same way it entered.

Laurus's gaze rose along the tops of the pine trees and got lost in the leaden skies. Snowflakes froze on his eyelashes. The first snow had covered the glade.

I cannot pray for that. Prayer should carry the force of conviction, otherwise it is not effective. And you are asking me to pray for murder.

Anastasia slowly rose from her knees. She sat on a fallen tree and held up her cheeks with her fists.

I am an orphan and now is a time of hunger and I cannot feed the child enough. How can you not understand?

Keep the child and everything will turn out fine. Simply believe me, I know this.

You are killing both me and the baby.

Laurus sat on the tree alongside Anastasia. He stroked her head.

I beseech you.

Anastasia turned away. Laurus sank to his knees and pressed his head against Anastasia's feet.

I will pray for you and the baby every hour. May he become a child born in my old age.

Are you refusing me because you are afraid of destroying your soul? asked Anastasia.

I am afraid I have already destroyed it, Laurus said quietly.

Anastasia looked back at Laurus as she left, and he was weeping. And she felt pity for him.

Winter turned out to be very cold. It was dust that fell from the skies, not snowflakes. A white sparkling dust that settled on trees and bushes. It was actually as if there were no longer any bushes. First they became drifts and then the drifts disappeared in the endless snowy coverlet that had been thrown over the forest. Even at the beginning of winter, Laurus said to Ustina:

It seems, my love, as if this is the coldest winter of all those I have had occasion to experience. Or perhaps the trouble is simply that my body is no longer capable of standing up to hardship. I will try to make fires twice a week so my body and soul do not part ways before their time.

But Laurus did not end up heating the cave twice a week. The supply of branches he had readied quickly dwindled and it was challenging to find branches under the deep snow. Up to his chest in snow, Laurus would get to the closest trees and break off their limbs but that required great effort. After bringing a branch or two into the cave, he could not catch his breath for a long time. Worn out, Laurus would fall on his sleeping ledge; it was difficult to restore his breathing, which was constricted by a chesty cough. To economize on firewood, he began heating often but only a little. The stones did not warm from this sort of heating so it was always cold in the cave.

The food that people had brought from Rukina Quarter from time to time, before the large snowfalls, was also coming to an end. Laurus had previously refused what people brought, saying he had many of his own supplies. In the summer and autumn, he truly did have numerous plants and roots, enough to satiate him, but they were now inaccessible under the piled-up snow. Patients had stopped coming to Laurus because of the deep snow and, consequently, also stopped bringing him food. They forgot about him during this difficult time, not with the harsh oblivion of the ill-intentioned but with the forced oblivion of the afflicted. Snow had joined with hunger, and it was not easy for anyone.

Toward the middle of winter, Laurus was already seldom leaving the cave. He was saving what warmth and strength remained. One day he found, in a far corner of the cave, the remains of the chunk of bread he had brought from the monastery at an earlier time.

This bread may not be in its first freshness, Laurus told Ustina, and there may not be very much left but, you know, it will be enough for a while if I do not give in to gluttony. In situations like mine, my love, the main thing is not to be finicky.

After resolving his difficulties regarding proper nutrition, Laurus found the means to warm up, too. He began thinking about Jerusalem.

Laurus wandered the city's sun-filled streets from morning till night and sensed the scent of the cooling stones even as he was falling asleep. He stroked their rough surfaces. The stones lent their warmth to Laurus's freezing hands and he was no longer cold. On the third day of February, he met Elder Innokenty on the Mount of Olives. The elder's face was tanned so it was obvious he had not just arrived in Jerusalem. Instead of a greeting, the elder pointed to the Temple Mount and quietly began singing.

Now lettest thou thy servant departe in peace, O Lorde, acordinge to thy promesse...

Elder Innokenty sang, his head bared, and a warm February breeze ruffling his gray hair. Insects of the Holy Land and dry blades of grasses plucked from familiar old haunts floated through the air, mixing with Jerusalem's ancient dust and blowing into their eyes. Tears glistened on Elder Innokenty's eyelashes. He had already closed his mouth but his song was still spreading over the Kidron Valley. As Laurus looked at him, he thought the righteous Simeon must have looked like that in the 361st year of his life.

And it is today that there is a commemoration of the righteous Simeon, smiled Elder Innokenty, did you forget about that or something? And how could we not sing in praise of the liberation whose daye is approaching for me?

I knew that from how you have been drawing nearer, Laurus told him. You have been doing that with a sense of liberation, like a person who has seen everything he should see. Truth be told, I did not expect to meet you here, though where else would we part, if not here?

Elder Innokenty embraced Laurus.

Grieve not, O Laurus, for you will not remain locked up in time much longer.

They were standing atop a mountain. Laurus watched as a cloud, from which not a single drop of rain would fall, drifted out from behind the elder's shoulder.

$$\overline{\mathrm{KB}}$$

In the spring it became clear that the hunger would not end in this newly arrived year, either. A very hard frost struck at the end of May, when grasses and grains had come out from under the soil and fruit trees had just finished blooming. It came amid warm days and raged for only one night. Everything that was capable of sprouting and blooming died that night.

All sorts of misfortunes occurred in Rukina Quarter, but nobody could remember a frost like that in May. The quarter's miller likened it to the Devil's breath, which ices up everything it touches. That comparison opened many people's eyes to the true nature of events and provided direction for the drawing of inferences. It was clear that things like this did not happen by chance.

The search for causes was brief. Despite her baggy medieval clothing, by spring it was no secret to anyone that the orphan Anastasia was with child. When the trouble occurred, they asked her who the father of her child was but she refused to answer. And they asked no more because the answer was already obvious to everyone in Rukina Quarter. The father of the child was the one whose icy breath had destroyed all the grasses and grains and the fruits of every tree. And there was only one way out and nobody uttered what that way out was, for everyone already knew what had to be done.

One bright June night, Anastasia's decrepit cottage burnt on all four sides. Nobody extinguished the fire, though nobody from Rukina Quarter was sleeping. Many wept and prayed because they felt sorry for Anastasia despite her relations with the forces of evil. To many people, it seemed that if this girl living without parents had become easy prey for the Devil, then fault lay not just with her but also with the circumstances. And all that bound these people together in their characteristic kindliness was their concern for saving Rukina Quarter from hunger. They surrounded Anastasia's cottage so she could not escape and covered their ears with their palms so as not to hear her dying screams. They did not hear them through the noise of the flames anyway.

When the cottage had burned down, the bravest ventured to rummage in the ashes, to pierce what was left of Anastasia with an aspen pole. After finding no traces whatsoever of the burned girl, the quarter's residents were even more certain of her guilt since at least something should be left of a nonguilty person. And they were all convinced Anastasia had disappeared, like as the smoke vanisheth, and died, as wax melteth before the fire, from those who love God, and those who mark themselves with the sign of the cross.

But Anastasia had not disappeared. She understood where this was all going, so had secretly fled Rukina Quarter the night of the fire. Nausea and dizziness complicated her flight but the main thing was her heavy belly, where her child tossed and turned. The main complication, however, consisted of having nowhere to flee. The only person she had on earth was the elder Laurus, who had predicted a happy outcome of events. And his prediction (Anastasia smeared the tears on her cheeks as she walked) seemed not to be coming true.

With branches snapping back and scratching at her face and hands, Anastasia cursed the elder for his refusal to help her and nearly called him the perpetrator of her troubles. When she neared Laurus's cave shortly after midnight, wrath had left her heart and strength had left her body. She no longer had either reproach or even tears. Breathing heavily, Anastasia sank to the ground and called Laurus. She vomited.

Laurus came out of the cave with a saucer of water in his hands. He cleansed Anastasia's face and hands.

They tried to burn me, whispered Anastasia. They think what is in my womb is of the Devil.

Laurus silently looked at Anastasia. His eyes were filled with tears.

Why are you silent? Anastasia shouted.

Laurus placed a hand on her forehead and Anastasia felt its coolness.

К̄Г̄

Laurus divides his cave in half. He and Anastasia collect branches and construct an inner wall in the cave by tying the branches together using cords made of vines. They cut an entrance in the outer wall for Anastasia to use. Against the entrance they lean a door made of branches, with ferns woven in. They try to make the second entrance to the cave unnoticeable.

On sunny days, Anastasia goes for walks behind the cave and Laurus stands on the path that people take from Rukina Quarter to come see him. He receives patients in the glade in front of the cave and signals to Anastasia when they have gone.

It is better for them not to see her, Laurus tells Ustina. You never know what is on those people's minds: there is still so much ignorance in their heads, my love.

Talk with me, Anastasia asks of Laurus. I cannot take it when people are quiet all the time.

Fine, I will talk with you, Laurus responds.

Patients are again bringing Laurus food but far less now than before because there is hunger in the surrounding villages. Moreover, they are used to Laurus refusing compensation. But now Laurus is not refusing. He treats patients and gratefully accepts what they bring. Patients are surprised. They say that in the previous years of plenty, Laurus did not take anything from them but now, in a time of hunger, he takes anything and everything, including meat. Patients sadly note that hardship does not even change ascetics for the better. They are slightly annoyed but do not let it show. Laurus returns their health and life, and food is useless without those.

Laurus does not explain anything to them. He knows Anastasia needs to eat well and he takes care that she does.

I have never eaten so well, says Anastasia.

It is not only you eating now, but your little boy, too, Laurus answers.

How do you know it is a boy?

Laurus takes a long look at Anastasia.

That is how it seems to me.

One day, Laurus says to Ustina:

Perhaps, my love, I will teach her reading and writing as I once—remember?—taught you. Maybe later she will happen to read what they would never teach her in Rukina Quarter.

Laurus begins teaching Anastasia to read and write. Surprisingly enough, reading and writing comes easily for Anastasia. Laurus has no books but he has birch bark, on which he writes what Anastasia reads. Most often, though, he writes on the ground with a stick. To write something new, he brushes away the old. Sometimes he does not.

The people who come to Laurus see these writings but do not guess who they were made for. They simply try not to step on them. They do not know what, exactly, is written on the ground but they are aware that Slavonic letters are sacred, for they are able to represent sacred notions. They have not seen non-Slavonic letters. They move around the inscriptions on tiptoe and make exaggeratedly large strides. This was inquired of Aristides the righteous: how many yeares is it good for a man to live? And Aristides answerd: untill he does understonde death is better than lyfe. People leave without reading the conversations with Aristides. They bow to Laurus and wish him many more yeares.

God forbid, Laurus answers them soundlessly.

Before bed, Anastasia asks him to tell her a story. Laurus wants to tell about his journey to Jerusalem but cannot remember it. He thinks for a long time and recalls the *Alexander Romance*. Evening after evening,

Laurus tells Anastasia of the Macedonian king's wanderings, of the savage people he saw, and of his battle with the Persian king Darius. Anastasia regards the events of Alexander's life sympathetically. They push aside the events of Anastasia's own life; she can calmly fall asleep. And Alexander is lying on the iron earth under a sky of ivory. He is miserable. He does not understand the purpose of all his wanderings. Or the purpose of all the conquering. And he does not yet know that his empire will crumble in an instant.

Opening her eyes without waking up, Anastasia utters:

What a strange life Alexander had. What was the historical goal of his life?

Laurus looks steadily into Anastasia's eyes and reads his own questions in them. Bending over the sleeping girl's ear, Laurus whispers:

Life has no historical goal. Or that is not the main goal. I think Alexander only grasped that right before his death.

The clamor of voices awakens them early in the morning. Laurus goes outside the cave and sees men from Rukina Quarter. They have pitchforks and stakes in their hands. Laurus silently looks at them. They are silent for a time, too. Their faces are covered with large beads of sweat and their hair clings to their foreheads. They have hurried here. They are still breathing heavily.

The blacksmith Averky says:

You know, O elder, that there was hunger last year. And the reason for that was the wench Anastasia's relations with the Devil.

Laurus is looking straight ahead but it is unclear if he sees anyone.

We burned Anastasia, continues blacksmith Averky, but the hunger has not lessened. What does that speak of, O elder?

Laurus shifts his eyes to the blacksmith.

It speaks of there being ignorance in your heads.

You, O elder, are incorrect. It speaks of our not having burned her.

We did not even find her bones, sighs the miller Tikhon.

Laurus takes a few steps in Tikhon's direction.

Is your wife healthy, O Tikhon?

With God's blessing, yes, answers the miller.

He notices traces of flour on the hem of his shirt and begins brushing them off.

People have seen Anastasia here, says blacksmith Averky. They have seen her go inside your cell... We know, O elder, that she is here.

The visitors are looking at blacksmith Averky and are not looking at Laurus.

I forbid you to go inside my cell, resounds Laurus's voice.

Forgive me, O elder, but our families stand behind us, blacksmith Averky says quietly. And we will go inside your cell.

He walks slowly toward the cave and disappears inside. A shriek resounds from the cave. Blacksmith Averky comes outside a moment later. He is holding Anastasia by the hair: it is wound around his red fist like strands of flax. Anastasia shrieks and tries to bite Averky on the thigh. Averky smashes her face against his knee. Anastasia quietens and hangs on Averky's arm. Her large belly sways. To those standing there, it seems as if that belly will separate from Anastasia any minute and out will come the one who should not be looked at.

The Devil has possessed her, shriek those standing there.

They liven themselves up a bit with those shrieks because they cannot resolve themselves to approach Anastasia. They are stunned by the courage of the blacksmith who is holding her.

The Devil possessed you, says Laurus, gasping, for it is you who are committing a mortal sin.

Anastasia opens her eyes. They are filled with horror. They are so frightful on her upside-down face that everyone involuntarily steps back. Fear grips blacksmith Averky for a brief moment, too. He flings Anastasia away from himself. She is lying on the ground between him and Laurus. Averky pulls himself together and abruptly turns to Laurus:

She has not named the father of her child because he is not here, among those born of this earth!

Anastasia raises herself up on her elbow. She is not shrieking, she is wheezing. That wheeze takes an entire eternity to float to the ears of those standing there.

That is the father of my child!

Her free hand points to Laurus.

Everyone goes silent. The morning breeze slackens and the trees are no longer rustling.

Is that true? asks someone in the crowd. Tell us, O elder, that she is lying.

Laurus raises his head and looks around at everyone with a lingering weathered glance.

No. It is true.

Everyone exhales. The crowns of the pine trees begin swaying again and clouds set sail. A smile flickers on blacksmith Averky's lips.

Ah, so that's what's going on...

Averky's smile is barely noticeable, lending it a particular indecency.

These things happen to everyone, miller Tikhon whispers into someone's ear. Absolutely to everyone. This is a realm where, as they say, there are no guarantees.

The callers dissolve unnoticeably into the woods. Their pitchforks and stakes turn into branches on bushes. Their voices fade, no longer distinguishable from the birds' sharp shrieks. Or from tree trunks rubbing against one another. Laurus absently takes heed of this disappearance. He is sitting, his cheek pressed against the trunk of an old pine. Its bark consists of separate tiles that seem almost glued on. The tiles are crinkled and rough; some are covered in moss. Ants run up and down them. Swarm in the moss. In Laurus's beard. The ants are not inclined to distinguish him from the pine tree and he understands them. He himself feels the degree of his woodenness, too. It has already begun and it is difficult to counter. A little more and he will not return, ever. Anastasia's animated voice drags him from the province of the wooden.

You were forced to tell them an untruth.

Sounds form into words. Untruth. Forced to tell them.

Did I really tell them an untruth?

During the next days, numerous loiterers appear in the vicinity of Laurus's cell. News about him and Anastasia has spread instantly and now the neighboring residents are coming to have a look at them. Even the dire circumstances of their life do not stop the curious: for many people, the attraction of seeing someone else's fall with one's own eyes is stronger than hunger. There were few sensational stories in the Middle Ages but what happened with Laurus is, without a doubt, one of them because it concerns the fall of a righteous man.

The residents of close and distant villages are not exactly glad about what happened, it is simply that their ridiculous life, mired in betrayals and squabbles, now seems a bit better. Against this backdrop, they understand that what is demanded of them is not so great. In their conversations, many of them even sympathize with Laurus, noting as they do that a high flight unavoidably carries the threat of falls this profound. It is thus not surprising that they themselves have no intentions of soaring very high in the future.

A week later, the flow of callers is diminishing sharply. There are now far fewer callers than in the previous times, which were not spoiled by all the gloom. It is obvious that this period of hunger plays a role: people think less about their health at times like this.

There is another reason for this, which is likely the most important. After everything that happened, many are losing faith in Laurus's healing capacities. After all, it had always been obvious that, unlike regular doctors, his capabilities rested on more than just knowledge of the human body. Laurus did not treat: he healed, and healing is not tied to experience. Higher powers encouraged Laurus's gift, and he was driven by renunciation and a love, of unprecedented strength, for those near and dear. Nobody could have expected that this love (those speaking are laughing behind his back) could take on such forms. The right-mindedness of the rumor mill lies in recognizing that the right to heal attaches itself only to a worthy person. And Laurus is no longer that sort of person.

People still come to him out of old habit but they do so somewhat uncertainly and generally for small things. Laurus has to deal with toothaches and wart removal ever more often. There are more serious cases, too, but their carriers do not themselves know if it is worth entrusting those illnesses to unreliable hands.

The very worst thing happens during those days: Laurus understands that now he cannot handle even the simplest of illnesses. He senses that the healing power no longer emanates from his hands.

Any healing arises first and foremost from belief in it, Laurus tells Ustina. They no longer trust me and that, my love, breaks my bond with them. Now I cannot help them.

And tears wash his cheeks.

Laurus gives Anastasia the small scraps people continue to bring them. To Laurus's joy, the chunk of bread he took from the monastery has still not all been eaten. He partakes of it with gratitude and trembling.

Nobody has come to see Laurus since the beginning of August. This does not surprise him. Everyone understands the healing has run out, so they consider visits to Laurus needless. Some might still have come to him but the general mood has spread to them, too. After what they have heard about Laurus in Rukina Quarter, it is somehow awkward to go see him. People fear appearing naive or—even more disagreeable—like they connive at sin.

Laurus is lonely. He did not experience loneliness when he escaped from the world because there had been no feeling of abandonment then. Now the world is escaping from him, which is something entirely different. Laurus is unsettled. He sees that the time is nearing when Anastasia will be delivered of her burden. And he does not know how he ought to proceed.

Anastasia is unsettled, too. She feels Laurus's agitation and does not understand its cause. It surprises her that the great doctor Laurus is so worked up about delivering the baby, a crucial matter but, really, a common one. Laurus has suggested several times that she go to Rukina Quarter to give birth so a midwife can deliver the baby, but Anastasia flat-out refuses. She does not know what to expect from Rukina Quarter. She is afraid to return there.

There are also days when she is afraid to stay with Laurus. Sometimes Anastasia thinks he has lost his mind. Laurus calls her Ustina at times. He tells her she should not refuse a midwife's help. That if she is afraid to go to the quarter, they should summon the woman here. Laurus is covered with sweat and shaking. She has never seen him like this.

Anastasia listens to the words addressed to Ustina and says "yes" on a lovely August morning. She will not go to Rukina Quarter to give birth but agrees to have a midwife come to her from there. Laurus presses her hand to his chest. Anastasia senses his heart's desperate beating. She feels that the hour when she will be delivered of her burden is nearing.

Laurus leaves his place of seclusion for the first time in long years. He walks along the path worn by those who have come to him for help. Now he is the one who needs help. And he has nobody to send for it because nobody comes here anymore. Laurus walks, wondering how Anastasia will feel in his absence. He tries to hurry but his breathing is uneven. Laurus stops for a minute and breathes deeply before entering Rukina Quarter. He closes his eyes and breathes. He feels better already. He enters the quarter, keeping his heartbeat in check.

People appear in the doorways of their homes. They soundlessly surround Laurus. Do not take their eyes off him. Even after everything that has happened, the residents of Rukina Quarter cannot believe he has come. Had the Kirillov Monastery itself come to them, the effect would have been the very same. Laurus indicates the forest as he addresses the residents. They cannot hear him because a gust of wind swoops down. He is asking for help. His lips are moving. The quarter's residents know he is asking for help but there is no help. The midwife is away now. She has never in her life gone anywhere but now she has gone away, that's just how it is. And nobody can take her place. Absolutely nobody. This has nothing to do with their unwillingness.

Laurus looks around at the crowd and sinks to his knees before them. He says nothing. Everything he said has already entered ears that he treated. Been absorbed by eyes he also treated. He asks for the kindness he showed them for so many years. Many weep, for their hearts are not made of stone. And so, somehow, nothing is working out in a normal human way, but what can they do? Turning aside, they wipe away their tears. They look down at the visitor. Laurus's figure is wavering in their eyes, its form and contours changing. Rising. Withdrawing.

Laurus does not immediately understand he is going to the hamlet. His feet still remember this path. He and Christofer walked it so many times. Does he hope to catch him there? Christofer apparently died long ago. So long ago that it is impossible to be certain about anything. No, of course, he died and is lying in the cemetery: it was Laurus, after all, who covered his grave with a sheepskin. Then why is he going to see him?

Christofer is in place, in his grave. He spent all the years that have passed here. His grave can still be seen in the thick greenery by the fence. If, of course, this is his grave. But Christofer's home is not here. Just as Christofer foresaw, a church stands in his home's place. A church is more important than a home at a cemetery because a cemetery is a home in and of itself.

The church's door is open. Laurus breathes in the scent of August before entering. He looks at dry autumn birch leaves that are touched by the first yellowing, a little tired of summer. Splotches of sun on the railings. A spider's thoughtful gliding. This is a return, but his home has become Home.

Candles are burning in the church. Alipy, abbot of the Kirillov Monastery, comes out through the royal doors of the iconostasis. There is a Communion chalice in his hands.

Thou hast come, O Laurus?

I have come.

Elder Innokenty died and could not meet you today. (Alipy is slowly moving in Laurus's direction.) That is why he made this request of me.

There is a murmur of a warm breeze behind Laurus's back. The candle flame wavers and the icons come to life. After taking Communion, Laurus says:

You know, I have a favor to ask, too. When I leave my body, do not be very ceremonious with it, for I have, after all, synned with it. Tie a rope to the legs and drag it into the swampy wilds for the animals and vipers to tear to pieces. That's basically it.

As he stands in the doorway of the church, Laurus contemplates Alipy's doleful face.

That is my last will, says Laurus. And it should be carried out.

Laurus returns to his cave in the evening. The expectant mother's labor pains have already begun. He settles her in on the sleeping ledge in the cave and prepares water to bathe the newborn. He prepares a knife to cut the newborn's umbilical cord. He starts a fire in the glade in front of the cave. Laurus is calm. And he once again feels the power in his hands.

Anastasia (Anastasia?) does not feel like lying in the dark cave and she asks to have bedding arranged for her in the glade. Laurus looks at the sky. There are no rain clouds in the sky. Only bright clouds tinted by the sunset—there will not be rain. He arranges bedding for her in the glade. She lies down facing the cave. The two entrances to the cave remind her of a pair of enormous eyes, open and full of darkness. The cave is like a head. She asks him to help her turn toward the other side. Now she is looking at the forest. The forest is tall and kind. Cozy. Quiet.

Do not leave me, she asks of Laurus.

I am here, my love, Laurus replies. And we are together.

He takes her palm into his hands and coolness flows into it. He takes her pain into his hands. Absorbs drop after drop. Occasionally stands to toss a branch on the fire. In the darkness that has fallen, she can see only his face. The flame from the fire lights it. The terrain of his wrinkles is animated. The fire crackles, spraying sparks. The sparks fly up to the very crowns of the pine trees. Some go out. Others fly higher, to mix with the first stars. Her eyes are directed at the sky, she sees everything. Her eyes reflect the fire's blaze.

Laurus's hand is on her belly.

Is that better?

Better.

She shrieks. The whole forest shrieks with her.

Be patient a little longer, my love. Only a little longer.

She is patient. And shrieks anyway.

Laurus's hands feel the child's head. It is as if it has stuck to his hands and is gently coming outside. Shoulders. Belly. Knees. Heels. Laurus cuts the umbilical cord. He bathes the baby with warm water.

Here he is, my love.

He shows her the child and tears glisten on the folds of his cheeks. The little boy is improbably pink in the fire's reflection. Or maybe he is still not completely bathed of her blood. The little boy fills his lungs with air and shrieks. She inhales that shriek into herself, all of it, leaving nothing. She lays the baby to her breast to feed. Her eyes are half-closed. She is calm for the first time in many days. She falls asleep. On the soft, warm grass of the glade, Laurus swaddles the newborn in a clean kerchief. He takes the baby in his arms. Laurus is also calm.

Anastasia wakes up early in the morning from the cool air. The fire has burned down. Laurus is half-sitting, his back leaning against a pine tree. He is holding the baby in his arms. The baby is breathing evenly. He is warm in Laurus's embrace. After taking the baby from Laurus's arms, Anastasia gives him her breast. The child wakes and hungrily smacks his lips.

Laurus's eyes are closed. The sun's first rays lie on his eyelids. The rays slide through morning's vapors. Pine needles shine. The shadows are long. The air is thick, for it has not yet lost the scent of the awakening forest. The moss is moist. It is filled with creatures for whom home is a leaf and life is a day. Anastasia sinks to her knees before Laurus and looks at him for a long time. She touches his hand with her lips. The hand is cool but not yet cold. Anastasia sits alongside Laurus. Presses against him. Anastasia knows Laurus is dead. She knew this even in her sleep.

I slept through your death, Anastasia says to Laurus, but my child saw you off.

Ionah, archbishop of Rostov, Yaroslavl, and Belozersk, is walking along the shore of Lake Nero. He always takes a walk there before the morning service. This is the deepest lake on earth but the water is only clean at the surface. What is deeper is silty: it does not release anyone who ends up there. Ionah knows this. He admires the lake's depth, even as he is aware of its danger. In keeping with his given name, he is not afraid of depths, but he does not recommend that his spiritual children leave firm ground. Ionah is surprised when he sees a person gliding along the surface of the lake.

Who are you who walks on water? asks Archbishop Ionah.

I am God's servant Innokenty. I report to you of the death of God's servant Laurus.

Just you be careful in the depths, says Ionah, shaking his head.

Based on Innokenty's smile, Ionah understands his advice is redundant. With that same smile, Innokenty visits Pitirim, bishop of Perm and Vologda, in a divine dream. He announces Laurus's death to Pitirim.

Ask that they not bury him yet, Bishop Pitirim tells Innokenty.

No need to worry, O bishop, answers Innokenty, because he will not be buried.

Anastasia takes the child and goes to Rukina Quarter. The residents gather around her. Anastasia tells them of Laurus's death. She declares that the real father of her child is miller Tikhon, who forbade her to tell of this, under threat of death.

If this information corresponds to the facts, the residents tell Tikhon, you had better confess because this would cast a shadow on a righteous man and Final Judgment will not be easy for you.

For some time, Tikhon does not confess. He keeps his silence, choosing between earthly and heavenly judgment. After weighing everything, the miller says:

I confess in the syghte of all that, after offering flour in a time of hunger, I deflowered the aforesaid Anastasia, and also that, fearing disclosure, I threatened her with death, though if I think things through, I wonder who would have believed her. I see this girl's youth and freshness as the reason for my fall along with, however, the withered condition of my own spouse, who was under the care of the deceased Laurus.

Abbot Alipy arrives in Rukina Quarter. He is gloomy. Alipy has ordered Laurus's body not be touched before the arrival of the bishops. After delivering the liturgy, he does not allow any residents older than seven years to Communion. The residents are anxious. Alipy leaves.

The news of Laurus's departure spreads with lightning speed. People sense this most of all in Rukina Quarter, where soon there is no room in any of the houses. There is no room in any of the nearby villages, either. Those who arrive build shelters in the surrounding areas. Some, in light of it being summertime, spend the night under the open sky. Everyone knows miracles can occur at the interment of a righteous man.

There assemble the maimed, blind, lame, leprous, deaf, mute, and those with impediments of their speech. They carry those sick of the palsie from various places, some distant. They lead the possessed, who are tied in ropes or shackled in chains. There arrive impotent husbands, infertile wives, the husbandless, widows, and orphans. There come the black and white clergy, brethren of the Kirillov Monastery, princes of princedoms large and small, boyars, mayors, and colonels. There gather those who were once treated by Laurus, those who had heard a lot about him but never seen him, those who want to see where and how Laurus lived, and also those who love a large convergence of the people. It seems to those witnessing the proceedings that the entire Russian land has gathered.

Laurus's body continues to lie under the pine tree by the entrance to the cave. It contains no traces of decomposition but those guarding it are on the alert. They approach the body every hour and inhale the smell that comes from it. Their nostrils quiver with diligence but they detect only the aroma of grass and pinecones. The guards proclaim this in the glade, with cries of astonishment, but at the bottom of their souls they themselves firmly know this is exactly how everything should be.

On August 18, in the year 7028 since the Creation of the world and the year 1520 since Christ's Birth, when the number of people who have come reaches 183,000, they raise Laurus's body from the earth and carefully carry it through the forest. This transfer is accompanied by funereal birdsong. The deceased's body is light. One-hundred eighty-three thousand people are waiting at the forest's edge.

As Laurus's body comes out of a thicket and into sight, everyone drops to their knees: first those who have seen him and then, row by row, those behind them. The bishops and monastic clergy accept his body. They carry it on their heads and the crowd before them parts, like the sea. Their path leads to the church built where Christofer's house stood. The funeral service takes place there. Tens of thousands wordlessly wait outside.

The service inside the church is not audible to the crowd. At first even the words Abbot Alipy utters just outside the church are not audible, either: he is proclaiming Laurus's last will. But Alipy did utter these words. They spread through the crowd like rings from a stone cast in water. A minute later, this human sea goes silent, for something unprecedented lies ahead

In full silence, they carry Laurus's body through the crowd. They place it in the grass on the edge of the green meadow. The grass gently envelops Laurus, expressing its willingness to accept him in his entirety, since they are not alien to one another. It was on this meadow that Christofer showed the deceased where the earthly firmament and the heavenly firmament meet.

Laurus's feet are tied with a rope, with the rope's two ends extending outward. Screams are heard in the crowd. Someone rushes to tear away the rope but he is brought down immediately and pulled off into the crowd. If viewed from above, those standing appear to be an unprecedented accumulation of dots and only Laurus has length.

Ionah, Archbishop of Rostov, Yaroslavl, and Belozersk, approaches one end of the rope. Pitirim, bishop of Perm and Vologda, approaches the other end of the rope. They kneel and soundlessly pray. They take the ends of the rope in their hands, kiss them, and stand up straight. Cross themselves in unison. The hems of their robes and the ends of their beards flap in unity. The proportions of their shapes are uniformly deformed by the wind, for both are flaring out to the right. The two of them work as one. Their gazes are addressed above.

Archbishop Ionah nods ever so slightly and they take their first step. The endless crowd behind them repeats that step. The crowd's endless sigh overpowers the sound of the wind. The arms on Laurus's chest shudder and burst apart as if in an embrace. They drag behind the body. Fingering the grass just as rosary beads are fingered. The eyelids quiver, making everyone think Laurus is ready to wake up.

Constrained sobbing is heard behind the bishop. The sobbing becomes louder with every moment. It turns into a solid wail that spreads over the entire inhabited expanse. Ionah and Pitirim silently continue their movement. The wind carries their tears to the opposite end of the meadow.

Laurus gently glides along the grass. Following him first is Gavriil, the Pskov mayor. He is gray and infirm and he is led by the arms. They are nearly dragging him but he is still alive. Behind Gavriil walks the Novgorod boyar Frol with his wife Agafya and their children. They are greater in number with each passing year. Further back are the boyar woman Elizabeth, who receaved her syght, and also God's servant Nikolai, of sound mind and sober memory. And behind them are numerous others who have seen the light and become wiser. At the very end of the procession are the merchant Zygfryd from Danzig, who found himself here on trading matters, and the blacksmith Averky, who is ashamed of his conduct.

What kind of people are you? says the merchant Zygfryd. A person heals you, dedicates his whole life to you, and you torture him his whole life. And when he dies, you tie a rope to his feet, drag him, and tears stream down your faces.

You have already been in our land for a year and eight months, answers blacksmith Averky, but have not understood a thing about it.

And do you yourselves understand it? asks Zygfryd.

Do we? The blacksmith mulls that over and looks at Zygfryd. Of course we, too, do not understand.

GLOSSARY

adamant (n.)   A legendary rock or mineral to which many properties, particularly hardness, were attributed; traditionally associated with diamonds.

bast   Bast fibre is collected from the bark or bast of certain plants, such as flax or stinging nettle, or trees such as linden or lime. It can be woven into matting and coarse cloth, and made into shoes, yarn, or rope. Bast fibre is still in use today.

cenobitic monastery   Cenobitic monasticism is a monastic tradition that stresses community life, where members live together, rather than in solitude.

computus   This is the calculation used to determine the calendar date of the Christian Easter; varying methods are used in Eastern and Western Christian traditions.

honor board   Honor boards, usually wooden, are used to recognize achievements or awards in schools, universities and work places. Soviet-era honor boards were sometimes permanent outdoor structures with slots that held large photographs and were placed in locations that greeted visitors to a city region, government building, or factory.

immortelle

Immortelle is another name for the plant everlasting, belonging to the sunflower family. It symbolizes eternity and immortality, and has been used for centuries as a digestive remedy, in skincare, and for its essential oils.

Kathisma

A Kathisma is a section of the Psalter. Eastern Orthodox Christians, who follow the Byzantine Rite, divide the Psalter's psalms into 20 Kathismata to facilitate recital of all 150 psalms, which are the foundation of the Canonical Hours, during the course of a week.

kremlin

A kremlin is a fortress, a highly fortified complex found in medieval Russian cities, the most famous being the Moscow Kremlin.

kvass

A drink often made from fermented rye bread, kvass has a very low alcohol content. Cold soups are sometimes made with kvass in summer.

prosphora

A prospheron is a small loaf of leavened bread used in the Orthodox Christian liturgy.

sazhen

The *sazhen* is an obsolete Russian unit of measurement, slightly longer than the old English fathom, measuring roughly seven feet or a little over two meters.

Schema

The Schema is the highest degree of asceticism in Eastern Christianity; it assumes observing the strictest ascetic rules. There are two levels: the Little Schema and the Great Schema.

sleeping bench

Many old Russian houses had wide, built-in benches on which to sleep and sit.

splinter lamp Splinter lamps were thin strips of dry wood specially cut to be burned as light sources. They were usually placed in metal bases with a vessel of water underneath, both to reflect light and help protect from fire.

stadia A stadion is an ancient Greek and Roman unit of measurement, equivalent to 600 *podes* (feet) or 202 yds/184.9m, an eighth of a Roman mile.

vershok Like *sazhen*, the *vershok* is an obsolete Russian unit of measurement, measuring roughly 1¾" or 4.445cm. A *vershok* is the length from an index finger's tip to its second knuckle.

verst A verst is equivalent to 500 sazhens, or roughly 3,500 feet or 1.0668km/0.6629 miles.

well sweep A well sweep is a device used for raising and lowering buckets to draw water from a well. It consists of a long pole with a bucket tied by a rope to one end, pivoted in the middle on another pole, acting as a fulcrum.